A RICHARDS & KLEIN INV

"Guy Haley is a force for good, a hid..."

Paul Cornell

"Guy Haley is the new author I have been waiting for. It has the intense action of a Neal Asher book, you can almost feel the shockwave of explosions and the impact of blows. It's an action packed book, riddled with armour-piercing wit and incredibly entertaining."

I Will Read Books

"Haley's wit is both laugh-out-loud and sharp as a sword."

John Whitbourn, author of BBC prize-winning *A Dangerous Energy*

"It is excellent. I really loved it. I was immersed in a gripping storyline that was part *Blade Runner,* part *I-Robot* and part *Sherlock Holmes.*"

I Wish I Was a Book

"The worlds Haley builds are easy to buy into and the plot is so compelling that it would be hard not to be swept into its pull."

Laure Davis, LA Examiner

"With a brilliantly realised world, great characters, and nice plot, this is a book that provides entertainment by the barrel load. Fun, exciting, entertaining, and unique. Haley is a visionary."

Morpheus Tales

GUY HALEY

OMEGA POINT

A RICHARDS & KLEIN
INVESTIGATION

ANGRY
ROBOT

ANGRY ROBOT
A member of the Osprey Group

Lace Market House,
54-56 High Pavement,
Nottingham,
NG1 1HW, UK

www.angryrobotbooks.com
Higgs' boson

An Angry Robot paperback original 2012
1

A catalogue record for this book is available
from the British Library.

ISBN: 978-0-85766-148-7
EBook ISBN: 978-0-85766-150-0

Set in Meridien by THL Design

Printed and bound by CPI Group (UK) Ltd, Croydon, CR0 4YY

This novel is entirely a work of fiction. The names, characters and
incidents portrayed in it are the work of the author's imagination.
Any resemblance to actual persons, living or dead, events or
localities is entirely coincidental.

To my son Benny.
May all your tomorrows be bright.

One might say that, by virtue of human reflection (both individual and collective), evolution, overflowing the physico-chemical organisation of bodies, turns back upon itself and thereby reinforces itself... with a new organising power vastly concentric to the first – the cognitive organisation of the universe. To think the world (as physics is beginning to realise) is not merely to register it but to confer upon it a form of unity it would otherwise... be without.

Pierre Teilhard de Chardin (1881–1955)

CHAPTER 1
Ekbaum

Otto Klein sank into blackness as the machinery on the wall invaded his cybernetic mind and spread its pages wide.

Notes sounded, silver trumpets in the dark.

It always came back to that.

Why had he agreed to this?

The trumpets faded.

It wasn't right. He shouldn't have to see her again, not under these circumstances.

Honour appeared in the black, a ghostly nimbus around her. Her head was shaved, her face drawn. An ovoid scar ran from her left ear right the way round to her occiput. She smiled nervously. "How do I look?" she said.

Otto wanted to say that she looked beautiful, and that he was sorry, but he was a spectator to his own past, and could only say what he had said. Back then he was eager to hear how she found the mentaug, trying to justify himself, to make her *see*. He hadn't thought what the surgery might mean to her.

He listened as he said what he had said, and hated himself for it, as he'd hated himself every single time he'd lived the moment through again.

She lost her smile. "I'm tired, Otto," she said.

Honour's face crumpled into itself and fire bellied out from where it had been, a point of destruction growing to paint a long-ago battle into his mind. The stink of war filled his nostrils, chemicals, fire, blood, shit, fear... A man slid from Otto's bayonet, his face going slack as his nervous system caught on to the fact he was dead. The silent near-I adjutant in Otto's mentaug scanned the field of churned mud and shattered trees for another target.

A ripple in Otto's mind; another time, another place. Stratojets screamed, plunging from the edge of space. A line of nuclear heat erupted along the horizon.

Otto raised his rifle. Another man died, and another.

Hamburg, as it was before the world went to hell. Ice cream in one hand, running on to his fingers as it melted, making them sticky, the strong grip of his father's fist on the other. Security, safety. After that day, he'd never felt safe, not truly, no matter how strong he had made himself, or how strong he'd allowed others to make him.

Strength masked brittleness. His father had a different kind of strength, also insufficient. Was anyone ever strong enough?

Sleet in New London, refreshing after the heat of the summer.

Honour's face, drawn and thin, mouth slack with the idiocy of Bergstrom's Syndrome. "How do I look?"

Otto screamed. He fell forward hard and straps bit into his flesh. A stab from the diagnostic in his spinal interface port brought him back roughly into the now. He jerked about, panicking, not knowing where or when he was.

"Steady, steady, Klein." A cool hand in blue latex pressed against his chest, small and delicate, like Honour's hand. Otto fought violently against his restraints, at the mercy of his memories as his mentaug spooled down, its infernal chattering filling his mind as it communicated with the machines in the maintenance room.

He blinked his eyes free of tears. A long, sad face came into focus. "Are you with us? Klein? Are you with us?"

"Ekbaum," Otto croaked. His struggling ceased, and he knew where he was. He'd been looking for Lehmann, his old comrade-in-arms. He'd severed contact, refused to return his calls. Ekbaum knew where Lehmann was, but had said he would only tell him if Otto came in for maintenance. That was why he was there. He didn't want to be, but things had been going wrong. It would only have been a matter of time anyway.

The doctor, a tall man of ungainly slimness, stood taller. His thin shoulders lost a part of their permanent hunch, the creases in his perpetual frown lessening. "You are back, good, good." His face tried a smile, so absent it must have been without the consent of his mind. He turned his back and consulted a screen, tapping at it.

"What did you do?" said Otto. The noise in his head ceased and the room took on a shocked quiet, as of a crowd suddenly silenced.

"The mentaug immersion was a bad one? Disjointed, frightening even?" asked the doctor as he consulted with his machines. "I suspected so. Very disappointing." In his green scrubs and blue gloves, long-nosed face pallid in the screenglow, Ekbaum resembled a carrion bird, expression set in distaste forever at its diet. "One should ask, 'What did you do to yourself?'" He pursed his lips at something red and blinking on a gelscreen. "When was the last time you came to see me, Otto?"

"I..."

"I shall tell you," said Ekbaum gently. "March 14th, 2126. Over three years ago, Otto. The terms of your consultancy license and cybernetics permissions both stipulate a six-monthly check-up." Ekbaum's sad face grew sadder. "And now look at you." He shook his head. "Look what you have done to my work."

Otto wiped a line of saliva from his mouth. "Can you fix my shoulder?"

"That? Yes, of course." Ekbaum waved a hand. "But that is not what concerns me. The VIA doctors, they told you that your shoulder is becoming deformed owing to misalignments in wetware governing the accretive processes of replacement carbon plastics, yes?"

Otto nodded. Two nurses, one human female, the other sheathed AI, came forward and undid the straps holding him upright to the diagnostic table. They pulled him forward and helped him to a chair, the robot bearing most of his significant weight. The woman handed him a glass of water. He gulped it down. He was dripping with sweat. "They told me it was a flaw in my initial design."

Ekbaum's weak smile hid a modicum of outrage. "My designs are good. Are they experts in cybernetic interfaces? No. The problem is not in here." Ekbaum slapped Otto's arm. "It is in here." He prodded Otto's forehead. "This is a problem of the mind, of its interface with the mentaug. The machinery within you is functioning perfectly, it is *you* who are malfunctional."

"Is it...?"

"No! No." Ekbaum shook his long head. "No need to look so alarmed, it is not Bergstrom's Syndrome. You're clear of all that. It is some other thing, an emotional trauma, overwork, stress, something of that order. The stresses upon it are throwing your systems out of synchronisation." He gave Otto a brief, sympathetic look. "Your wife, Otto. That is what is interfering with your correct operation, emotional backwash, disturbing the equilibrium." Ekbaum looked reproachful; he always did, not at Otto in particular, but at the world. He'd once told Otto he'd gone into cybernetics to arrest death, only to find it reflected at him tenfold.

Otto could have laughed. He was supposed to be a war machine. Stress should not be an issue. Now surely *that* was a design flaw. "Fine."

"Fine? No. The physical problems I can repair over a day, plus five to seven days recuperation. The emotional damage, however, that will require six weeks to repair, psychotherapy, AI-assisted streamed downloads, perhaps file excision. The process will be intensive. You will have to let her go, Otto."

"I can't."

"That is the root of your problem, Otto. How long has it been since she died?"

Otto did not answer. He felt a surge of anger that this man wanted to wipe away his pain. He never talked about Honour, not if he could help it; it hurt too much. He deserved that hurt, and guarded it jealously.

"I don't have time now," said Otto.

"If you leave without remedial work, you will suffer a great risk of serious malfunction, blackouts, hallucinations… Your pooled memories will begin to spill into your waking life," said Ekbaum. "There is a great risk of cerebral trauma, and that risk will only grow."

"I will come back," said Otto. "I've no wish to die, not yet. Now, I let you plug me in to your damn machines, tell me where I can find Lehmann."

"Give me your word you will return."

Otto exhaled shakily. "I give you my word. I'll be back." His shoulder told him he would. His dreams did, as little as he liked Ekbaum and his machines inside his head.

"Then I can tell you that your Conrad Lehmann friend is outside, waiting for you."

Otto looked up sharply. "That son of a bitch."

Lehmann stood up from the couch as Otto entered the waiting room. Even taller than Otto, and as heavily built, he wore an enormous smile. His smile was oddly boyish, out of character with his face, a smile that vanished when he was in the field, and he became cold and implacable. He was the best of Otto's old squad, both professionally and morally, but there was machine iciness in him too, as there was in them all.

"Otto." They embraced, slapping each other's backs hard enough to break the bones of normal men.

"That was a cheap trick, Conrad." Otto stood back. "I thought something had come between us. There's too few of us left for that."

Lehmann ran his hands through his hair and looked anywhere but at his one-time commander. "How else was I supposed to get you to come to see Ekbaum?"

Otto looked Lehmann up and down and grunted. He was in good shape, better than Otto. His filmstar looks unmarred. "What do you mean? I look like a potato farmer next to you, always have. Don't let it go to your head. I'm fine."

Lehmann was unconvinced. "You should look after yourself better."

"You got my messages then?"

"I'm here, aren't I? I got them not long after Ekbaum contacted me. I'm sorry about the deception. He talked me into it; it was too good an opportunity. You never could look after yourself. What was I supposed to do? We worry about you, Otto."

Otto grunted. "*Genau*. Lucky I got you to watch my back. Now do you want this job or not?"

Lehmann relaxed. "Yeah, naturally. Always."

"I haven't briefed you yet."

Lehmann grinned. "Since when has that made a difference?"

Otto nodded approvingly. He hadn't expected Lehmann to say no. "You noticed anything with the Grid recently?"

"A little jumpy, slow here and there, informational overload, they say."

"Not entirely true," said Otto. "A Five – k52?"

Lehmann shook his head. The name meant nothing to him.

"It's gone rogue, suborned the EuPol Five's choir, frozen up a lot of EU and USNA cyberspace. It's hiding in the old Real-World Reality Realms, got a direct pipe into the EuPol Five's choir. It could bring down the entire network."

"Sounds serious."

"Biggest thing since the Five Crisis. Interested?"

Lehmann thought for a moment and pinched at his chin. "OK," he said. "Bit different to my usual line of work, but OK."

"Relax. We're not going after him, nothing Gridside, all out in the Real. We're to find someone."

Lehmann folded his arms. "Who?"

"I'll get to that. That's the hard part. My partner Richards–"

"The AI?"

Lehmann never did understand why he'd gone into business with an AI; they'd been made to fight the machines in a war that never came, and Otto figured Lehmann thought his friendship with Richards a small betrayal of their intended purpose. "He is inside, we're outside. What k52 is trying to do out here... that's what we're going to find out, when we find this guy. You, me and a couple of others. You in?"

"Sure," Lehmann said nonchalantly, and retrieved a kitbag from behind the couch, ready to go. He was never going to refuse Otto; dependable Lehmann, through and through.

"I've a car waiting outside. We're to rendezvous with a VIA heavy lifter tonight outside of New London."

Lehmann whistled. "The VIA? You running with them now?"

"Not really. It's complicated," said Otto. "And there's more. There's Kaplinski."

Lehmann raised his eyebrows. "Isn't he dead yet?"

Otto grunted a negative. "Three weeks ago, Kaplinski tried to kill me, and he nearly killed my partner. He's alive all right."

CHAPTER 2
The 37th Realm

Richards came online and wished he hadn't.

"Ouch," he said. "Ooh, ouch, that really, really hurts." He raised his hands to his face, but the movement tripped off a wave of nausea that nearly did for him, so he let them fall back onto the smooth, cold floor where he lay, eyes screwed shut, his senses spinning in precisely the opposite direction to his stomach. It was a most uncomfortable sensation. Once he'd gathered his thoughts, he decided to turn his pseudo-biological feeds off, take the meat out of his machine and run off pure numbers, so to speak.

When he found he could not was when he pulled himself together enough to sit up. The effort of it made him whimper, and he threw up all down his front. He sat there, quivering. It was indescribably revolting. As a Class Five, and a curious one at that, he was open enough to most physical sensations, but there were limits.

He looked down at himself. Legs, arms, the usual, if you were one of the real people, very different to *his* usual. He poked at his thigh experimentally. It felt like flesh. He looked at his hand; it *was* flesh. He groaned, the wash of pain from his head making him instantly regret it. "k52's idea of a joke," he said.

He'd been in simulations of the human body before; practically every day, in fact, because that's how he liked to relax in his virtual office, and how he liked to deal with people and other numbers on the Grid. When out and about in the Real the robotic carriages he rode were invariably anthropomorphic, but all these masks had something extra, or lacked something fundamental, sometimes both. Virtual or real, they were that little bit more and that little bit less than human. More importantly, they were all under his complete control.

This one was not. This one felt alarmingly like actual meat. He tried to reach to snag at the world's underlying code, but he might as well have been trying to telepathically communicate with a goldfish – nothing but deafening silence. This body he wore – this body he *was*, for it felt as if he and it were one, a feeling he had never had before – filled the place where the clickety thrum of the Grid ordinarily lived with weird little sounds, the shush-roar of circulation, the creak of joints as he shifted, the slither of wet, curled things in his abdomen. He began to feel ill again. Presently, he was.

"How do they stand it?" he groaned. He staggered up. He stood grasping his knees and gaping reflexively, saliva and bile dripping from his mouth. He made a few pathetic sounds and he surprised himself by feeling better, although it was long seconds before he could summon the will to wipe his chin and stand erect.

He took in his surroundings through eyes that only grudgingly focused.

The first thing he noticed was that there were no doors.

He was in the chilly hall of a stately home, flash with Victorian new money. A wide marble staircase swept up to a vulgar balcony, its banister fashioned from woods long since enthusiastically furnished into extinction in the Real. Horrid touches caught his eye – panting gargoyles, tapestries of pale, rangy men with thinning hair and piercing eyes, stuffed animals possessed of far too much life. To his right a tree trunk smouldering in the fireplace provided the only light; something nasty, obscured in soot, decorated the fireback. A broad archway led out of the hallway to his left, polished black and white diamond marble floor tiles disappearing into the dark.

As for the doorways, there were the door jambs, framing familiar spaces with wood, but when it came to there being an actual door, the walls were plain as bone.

"This is interesting," muttered Richards, and reached to push back his fedora, as was his habit when he was thinking. His hand came away when it found the hat missing, and he remembered it had gone to nothing when he'd dived into the Gridpipe leading here, the rogue k52's shanghaied cyber-realm.

Richards was not terribly surprised when he discovered he could not make a new hat. A mirror caught his eye. He walked over to it. There was just enough light to make himself out. He was in a copy of the simulated body he normally wore in virtspaces: middling height, mid-forties – twenty more years than his actual age – brown hair with the beginnings of a widow's peak. He had the face of a gumshoe, tired and worn out on too much whisky and too many worthless women; brown trenchcoat of a gumshoe; threadbare suit of a gumshoe – now wet with vomit; red tie of a gumshoe. Richards liked mid-twentieth-century detective stories; he was a security consultant and a security consultant was a kind of detective, so he styled himself after their fashion. It was all play; he was far more than that.

He missed his hat. And this body felt far too real. And he stank of sick.

"Bollocks," he said.

A squeaking of shoes approached from the left-hand archway. A figure dressed in full butler's regalia appeared and made its stiff-backed way into the entrance hall. Its head was the last thing to resolve itself from the shadows. The head of a dog.

Grizzled black hair covered the dog's head. Sharp ears twitched alertly on the crown. The muzzle was long, the bastard offspring of auntie's Scottie dog and the big bad wolf. Red eyes smouldered. Dog-headed man was a misnomer; it was more like a dog in the shape of a man, a *man-shaped* dog, thought Richards. He found it strangely disturbing, a feeling he couldn't shake.

"Good evening, sir," said the man-dog. It sniffed distastefully at Richards' disarray.

"Nice outfit," said Richards.

The man with the dog's head inspected itself, looking in turn at its frock coat, well-tailored trousers with a light pinstripe, charcoal waistcoat, pocket watch and shoes.

They look uncomfortable, thought Richards, but what the hell kind of feet did a man with a dog's head have anyway?

"It is the uniform of my office, nothing more," said the dog. "This is my master's house."

"Yeah, well. It's natty," said Richards.

The dog stared at him levelly, panting lightly. His breath smelled superficially of mint but it covered meat, drool and things left best uneaten. "Might I ask what you are doing in my master's house?"

"Beats the shit out of me," said Richards.

"There is," said the dog, clasping its hands behind its back and flexing its spine, "no need for language like that. This is my master's house."

"And your master would not approve?"

The dog looked from side to side, ears twitching independently of one another, listening to something Richards could not hear.

"Nice place he has here. No doors."

The dog looked at the bare walls framed by wood as if it were news to him. "It is my master's house," said the dog. "I guard the entryway. It is my master's house. Good evening, sir."

"Right. You're not very bright. Let me see, limited responses...
Hmmm. You're on a loop, aren't you? Hey! Hey!" Richards
snapped his fingers. "Where is your master?"

The dog quirked its head. Suddenly it was standing right in
front of Richards. "This is my master's house. Might I ask what
you are doing, doing here in my master's house?"

"We've done this bit before," said Richards. He turned away
to examine his options, but the dog was in front of him wherever he looked.

"I am afraid I must ask you to leave." The dog shifted again.
Another flicker; it became huge, clothes ripped, clawed hands
dripping blood. "This is my master's house. Might I ask what you
are doing, doing here in my master's house?"

"I'll be leaving," said Richards, but he could not move.

"Get out, I say, get out, get ooouuuuuuuuuuuuuuuuuut!" The
dog's voice broke into a howl and it threw its head back. The howl
increased in volume until the ornaments rattled. Richards screwed
his eyes shut against the torrent of dog breath and spittle.

Dying is becoming an annoying habit of mine, he thought.
But he didn't die.

The howl abruptly stopped. The temperature dropped, and
he was confronted with a sense of openness.

"Outside? I'm outside," Richards said, and cracked open an eye.
He was outside. Score one for the great detective, he thought.

A knocker clinked on its plate as if a door had been slammed,
although it was attached to a bricked-in space where a door
wasn't. It was a lonely noise, rapidly swallowed by the night.
The outside lantern, a baroque thing held aloft by a grimacing
centaur, went out, rolling up its tongue of light.

"k52, what the hell are you playing at?" said Richards. He
sighed as his eyes adjusted themselves to the dark; stupid human
eyes with poor night vision. Ornamental woods gone wild surrounded the house. Wind rustled through trees silhouetted

against a starless sky, black marbled purple and blue, a pregnant moon hanging large, its light casting the landscape in stark monochrome.

A loud crack came from the woods. Richards wasn't sure if he should feel afraid or not, but he did; he could not disengage himself from his fear. Being at the mercy of his emotions was new to him. He decided to play it safe and get back in, to break the dog-man's limited programme and find out what the hell was going on. He half-expected k52 to burst from the trees, and that would be trouble.

The house was massive but not large, its solidity giving it a weight far beyond that of its dimensions, and Richards went round it in no time at all. A cruel iron fence kept him at a distance. The stone was so dark it sucked in what little light there was, so he couldn't make much out. He looked back to the woods. The trees rattled, branches beckoning him.

Richards grasped the fence and heaved himself astride it. He fell awkwardly. His trailing leg snagged, cloth and flesh tore with equal ease on an iron barb, and he landed gracelessly on a flowerbed full of trash.

"Shit!" he hissed. He scrambled up again. His leg throbbed dully. He probed the wound. "Ouch," he said. His fingers glistened black in the moonlight. "This is far too realistic."

Blood dripped down Richards' leg as he limped to the wall and felt along it for a door. As inside, so outside: no windows or doors. The frames were there, but the spaces between were as unseeing as skin healed over empty eye sockets. He reached a space where the moon shone unimpeded by trees and looked harder. A nightmare scene was coaxed from the shadows, painted where window glass should be. A ghastly face with too many teeth, flaking eyes fixed on his. Night drew in closer, hunting. Sibilant promises came from the windows. Richards caught the odd word.

"That's not very nice," he said.

He went round the house again inside its skirt of iron. He swore and grumbled as his feet encountered hard rocks and unmentionable softness. All the windows were the same, daubed with horror. When he was sure there was no way in, he scrambled back over the railings, more carefully than before.

An owl shrieked. Too loud, too close.

"Woods it is after all," he said. He was trying to feel brave. Richards felt fear ordinarily all right, but not in the way that men did, and not for the same reasons. When he did feel fear as men do, he did it because he wanted to, and it was fake; it could be deactivated. This could not. This was people fear, glandular fear. He glanced behind him, enjoying the novelty of ungovernable emotion even as it quickened his heart and impelled him to hurry down the drive. The crunch of gravel underfoot made him wince. A gust of wind tickled the trees. Dead rhododendron leaves rustled in the understorey; a sterile, woody scent carried from them.

He made sure he kept to the middle of the road, away from the fringes of the woods, just in case.

Richards turned from looking behind himself just in time to walk into a musty barrier, as solid as a brick wall, in a dirty fur coat.

Richards spat hair from his mouth and looked up, and up.

Heavy paws dangled like mallets from long arms. Close-set eyes burned cold in a face as long as a wet Wednesday. Teeth glinted in the moonlight. A tiny Roman centurion's helmet sat atop a blockish head. A damp, heavy smell hit Richards like a billiard ball in a sock.

"A bear," said Richards, savouring the cocktail of mild surprise and terror his new body furnished him with.

"Damn right," said the bear. It jabbed a dagger-long claw at Richards' face. "By all rights I should eat you, sunshine."

"I'd rather you didn't," said Richards.

The bear didn't. "It's your lucky day. No devouring of prison-ers," it said. "Regulations."

"Oh, good," said Richards.

"But hey!" The bear smiled a forest of teeth and held up a claw. "I can do this." The bear punched him full in the face, and Richards found the stars the sky was missing.

CHAPTER 3
Where's Waldo?

"No. Absolutely not." Chures pushed his chair back from the conference table and stood. He leaned forward, pressing his fingertips onto the table's active glass surface.

"The decision's been made, Agent Chures," Deputy Director Sobieski, his perfect eugene face hard, stressed the title. "Klein has all the relevant clearances, and a valid freelance license. His partner's in the Reality Realms right now. Klein is qualified and invested. Surely you can see he's a good choice."

The others in the room watched in silence: Veronique Valdaire with her phone Chloe on the table in front of her, a fat Texan called Milton with USNA Homeland Security – the big guns, at least so far as human influence went – a fastidious-looking VIA agent who'd introduced himself as Swan, Henson, a stout man in military fatigues from USNA Landwar, and a beefy-looking Boer, a UN attaché who was too important to have offered his name. There were a handful of others round the table, but Otto could tell the spectators from the players easily enough. The ones who didn't matter wore the fixed expressions of people who did not wish to get involved in Chures' argument.

"We have plenty of qualified people of our own," said Chures.

"We do. And Klein here took out a whole squad of them without too much trouble," said Sobieksi, "while he was saving your ass, if I recall. And which of them has a resumé like this?" Sobieski tapped at the table. The area in front of Chures sprang into life, 2D and holo files opening up on the table and above it, detailing Otto's career as a soldier and security consultant. Chures didn't look at it.

"Sobieski..."

"It's Assistant Director today, in here, Chures," the eugene warned.

Chures gritted his teeth. He did not care to be put in his place. "*Assistant Director* Sobieski. He's too close to the Fives."

"That's another reason he's in, and that is not our call. The Three Uncle Sams and the machines in the UN have swung it. The Director agrees. The numbers want him on board, so he's staying."

"Since when did we do what the machines say? It's one of them we're supposed to be bringing down. The VIA works on equal partnership terms between man and machine." He looked around the table. "It did when I signed my life away. Has something changed?"

Sobieski leaned forward. "Yes, it has, and that's all the more reason for the numbers to want all this resolved quickly. We're all on the same side, in this and all other matters. Don't forget that, Chures."

Chures stood his ground. "Sobieski, let me take my own team, my own men..."

"Assistant Director, Chures, Assistant Director." Sobieski sighed. "Chures, sit down."

Chures kept his grey eyes fixed on Otto as he sank into his chair. The wounds were healing. Wounds inflicted on him by his doppelgänger, an advanced cybernetic android intended to replace him under the direction of k52, others taken at the hands of men in grey, mercenaries of some kind, as he'd scoured the southwest of the old US for Valdaire.

His olive-brown skin was marred with yellow and purple bruising, and a geckro membrane bandage covered his neck where the remains of his treacherous AI personality blend Bartolomeo had been removed. He'd had a manicure; his jewellery, expensive clothes and shoes were back. His twin custom uplinks, one behind each ear, had been replaced, but it'd take a lot more than a well-tailored suit to cover his hurts. He was smarting from the beatings he'd taken, and that he'd been saved from death by Klein, a man he could never trust.

"As far as the rest of the world is concerned, we're going to be doing our job," said Sobieksi. "The VIA is putting all of its efforts into preventing the spread of k52's influence into the rest of the Grid. We'll have teams working alongside the National Guard and UN forces to secure the Realm House. It will remain locked down, but short of actually nuking the place, we've no way to get k52 out. That's where Klein and his partner come in."

"His partner? How can we be sure Richards is not in league with the renegade?" said Chures, angry.

"He warned us, Chures."

"It's a bluff, Sobieski, Klein's a risk..."

"There will be no more disagreement on this matter." A voice intruded, that of Xerxes, a Class Five AI, like Richards, like k52. Xerxes was Uncle Sam 3, one of the AI triumvirate that ruled the United States of North America in all but name.

A holo beamed in via isolated tightbeam, away from the Grid where k52 might see, and followed the voice. Xerxes wore the face of an earnest government man. It was appropriate, for, though he was no man, he was a third of the government of a third of the world, and the VIA agents and EuPol specials and FBI and EuSec spooks and CIEA ghosts in the stateroom and watching via link reacted accordingly. The holo, fizzing with solar interference, manifested at the head of the table. Otto

didn't react. He'd got too used to the Fives and their cheap
melodrama. They were far too human, in their way.

"We desire that this issue be resolved immediately," Xerxes said
without preamble. "It has been determined that the freelance security consultant Otto Klein, along with Doctor Veronique
Valdaire, will accompany VIA Agent Santiago Chures. Klein is to
have equal authority to Chures. This is a multilateral effort. The
UN has agreed. That is all." The holo winked out.

"There, that settles that," said Sobieski. He pointed at his sub-
ordinate. "They are always listening, Chures, so don't go against
what they say or you'll be off this case altogether. As for you,
Klein –" Sobieski looked at the German "– don't think I'm entirely happy about this. This is a VIA affair, not work for
mercenaries. But you've got yourself a Five for a buddy and as
we're seeing here, they're all real tight with each other." He
leaned back and clasped his hands behind his head in pure alpha
display – the eugenes could help their display behaviour about
as much as a monkey could. "On the other hand, this is Five
business, Klein, so I guess if you fail or succeed you'll be answering to them. And for that I'm relieved; rather you than me."

Otto wondered what Valdaire made of the argument. He was
glad to have her; without Richards they needed someone who
knew the machine world, and, under the current circumstances, better a human than a number. As ex-InfoWar and a
renowned AI expert, he couldn't think of anyone more suitable.
She sat across the table, mouth thin. She didn't think much of
Chures' objections then. But Otto's authority, that had been a
surprise to the German; he'd been expecting Chures to be given
sole command.

"Agent Swan, give us the current situation on the renegade,"
said Sobieski.

Swan was a slight man in a suit. A suit in a suit, Richards
would say, thought Otto. He bobbed his head and stood. It

took Otto a moment to realise the guy was a number, dressed up in some fancy near-human sheath. He did not blink – they never remembered to – and that gave him away. He had an info wand in his hand, old tech, but self-contained, safe from k52. The lights dimmed and holographic data filled the centre of the table. Reports, files, video and a large representation of what Otto took to be the Realm House, loaf-shaped top to deepest subterranean bottom, the enormous server farm in the Nevada desert that sustained the remaining thirty-one of the original thirty-six Reality Realms, along with, now, k52's rogue project. Otto had only seen the topside of the facility in the Real; looked like the tip of the iceberg if the map was anything to go by.

"k52 has disabled the entirety of the Realm House's security net," said Swan. Vital nodes blinked red within the complex. "And has complete control over the virtual worlds generated within. Our men have formed a perimeter 750 metres back from the outer fences, just VIA this close in, no National Guard until the outer perimeter. Their systems, as we saw, were easily overwhelmed," said Swan. He waved his wand. Video footage played, machines turned on men, weapons malfunctions, informational blackouts. "He skipped through the Guard's heaviest encryption like it was a field of daisies. Now we're on the scene, everyone out there now is pure analogue, radio voice communication, human hands on mechanical triggers, all interfaced staff have been pulled back. k52 can't do much about that." Swan pressed his lips tight. "But he could do a whole lot more. He has one of the most powerful collections of hardware anywhere on the planet at his disposal, and here's the puzzle: he's not actually doing anything with it."

"He going for digital uplift or something?" growled Milton. He was a big bear of a man, ruddy-faced and red-bearded. Otto knew nothing of him beyond what he'd gleaned from the man's introduction. His mentaug adjutant, walled off from the Grid like all the devices on the heavy lifter, was unable to furnish him with more.

"It's the favourite theory, but not the only one," said Swan. "We think his deification of Zhang Qifang may have been designed to lead us to believe that is what he is attempting, but we're not so sure. We can't get direct data from the Realm House currently, but system echoes suggest the remaining thirty-one Reality Realms are running normally."

"But the spare capacity..." led Sobieski.

"There is a lot of that, and activity within is off the chart. Whatever's running in there is far more sophisticated than anything we've seen yet."

"More forcing of the technology curve, like the cydroids," said the Texan.

"k52 calculated the technology syne, so he is best placed to push things faster than they might otherwise go. There's no telling what he's up to in there. But it's big, and he's not alone. Two other level Fives are missing, sixteen of the more individualistic Fours, and a Class Six from Singapore. We've some evidence to suggest, albeit inconclusively, that they're in there with him." More data came and went, much of it beyond Otto. Valdaire watched it keenly. "The curious thing is what he hasn't done. He's pinned the EuPol Five like a butterfly, frozen up a good part of the EU's digital superstructure in the process. With a thought he could toss the entire continent back into the dark ages, and then come after us, but he hasn't."

"Why?" demanded the Boer.

"Ah, that we don't know," said Swan.

"And that's what we need to find out," said Sobieski. "Klein's team is to find this man." A forty-centimetre holo of a skinny youth sprang up in the centre of the table, associated files scrolling over the glass in front of each of the room's occupants.

"Giacomo Vellini, though his handle is – was – Waldo. Ms Valdaire, I believe you are the expert?"

Veronique's mouth worked a moment as all eyes turned to her. She quickly rallied. "Yes. Vellini. He pioneered the only truly successful entrance mechanism to the Reality Realms once they'd been closed off. He came and went for years without being detected."

"But he was," countered a stout VIA man. "We caught him in 2119."

"Yes," agreed Valdaire, "but only because he got careless, and cocky. He started to taunt the V… the authorities. Leave messages here and there. Even his username, 'Waldo', suggests a man who wished to be found. But he was, is, the finest hacker of his generation. If anyone can get us into the Realm House's virtual space without k52 noticing, it will be him."

"Where is he?" asked the Texan.

"No one knows," said Henson. "He did his time, and upped and left USNA after he was defrosted and released from Brandsville. We thought he might have gone back home to Europe, but he vanished off the system, and no one's seen him since."

"Aren't these people supposed to be under surveillance?" said the Texan sourly. "You VIA boys don't do your work well."

"He was," said Swan. "These people are the sharpest criminal minds on the planet, Milton, the best at what they do. If the likes of Waldo don't want finding, he won't be found."

"A wild-goose chase then," said Milton.

"Wait a minute," said the Boer. "You're going to find this Waldo, a man you say can't be found, and get him to walk you into the realms to ask k52 what he wants?"

"We are," said Sobieski. "Otto and Chures will find him."

"Klein is injured," protested Chures.

"It will wait," said Otto.

"You have people of your own?" asked Sobieski.

"One. Ky-tech like me. The best shot of his day. Here's his personnel file. There's a further bonus. Kaplinski, get him, and we'll
get to k52's support network. This isn't purely a numbers job."

Chures' eyes narrowed as Klein ran footage taken from the
Morden Subcity survnet system. There were men in grey, men
like the ones who'd almost killed him the day before he and
Klein had met at Valdaire's pirate hideaway in the Rockies.

"These men targeted and destroyed the second Qifang cy-
droid," he said, referring to the recent and convoluted murder
of the famed AI rights activist. He'd uncovered k52's plot, and
had attempted to warn Otto's partner Richards directly. Why
him was a mystery to Otto. "Most of them are unknown," said
Otto. "But this man–" The footage zoomed in so far the image
began to break up. A large black man, shaven-headed, from his
bulk and oddly formed muscles cybernetically altered. "Kwasi
Sakaday Jones, Nigerian. He's a known associate of Kaplinski,
ex-Union of West Africa cyborg…"

"Another of yours?" said Sobieski.

"No," said Otto. "But I've had run-ins with him before. Intel
that Richards and I received recently has him working for or with
someone I now know to be Kaplinski."

"And Kaplinski? He was one of yours."

"He was one of mine. Under my command, he went renegade. It's all on the file."

"What can you tell us about him?" asked the Boer.

"It's all on the file," said Otto levelly.

"And our contingency plans, gentlemen?" Milton sat back.
"What are they?"

Sobieski frowned. "While Klein's team is searching for Vellini,
we'll have three teams going into the Realm House itself, see if they
can evade security and cut the wider Grid access to the Realms."

"I'll be leading that attempt," said Henson. "The teams are ready
to go when we get the green light."

"You are going to physically isolate the Realms? That will be dangerous," said Valdaire.

"We have full disclosure of the Realm House's security systems. We can do it," said Henson.

"I meant to the Realms," said Valdaire.

"It is a risk," said Sobieski. "But I think we can all agree that the loss of the remaining Realms is preferable to losing control of the whole planet to k52."

"What," said Valdaire, "preferable because they are not real? The UN says otherwise."

Sobieski looked exasperated, keen to move on. "If we are successful in isolating them, it should set the EuPol Five loose, and we'll have the time to leisurely devise a scrubber to wipe k52 off the map. There is the risk of potential damage to the Realms, but..." Sobieski spread his hands. "It's better that than nuking them."

"I'm curious to know what he wants, and why he is doing this," said Swan.

The Texan snorted.

"Our role at the VIA is to understand why the machines do what they do – not even the Director knows that, and he's a number like me. If we don't interrogate k52, how can we stop this happening again?" said Swan.

"Ask yourself, Swan," said Milton.

"I have, but I am not k52," said the AI reasonably. "My conclusions are therefore irrelevant."

"And what, Assistant Director Sobieski, what if it fails?" asked the South African. "What if your pet Kraut here doesn't bring this Waldo fellow back in? What if k52 dices your agents to dogfood? What then?"

Sobieski looked at Swan. Swan twisted his wand in his hands.

"Then, to borrow the Assistant Director's terminology, we will nuke the place. There's a stratobomber on tightbeam link to me only, targeting the Realm House with EM pulse-generating atomics, low megaton yield. It is an option of last resort."

"How low a yield?" said the Boer.

"Low," said Sobieski, "but once you take into account the energy released by the failure of the Realm House's tau-grade fusion reactor, there will be a big hole in Nevada."

Swan looked round the table. "In addition, we risk a large amount of collateral damage to the Grid. We can buffer the over-spill, but the Realms are deeply entrenched in the network."

"And how much is that gonna cost us?" said Milton.

"Thirty per cent of the Grid could be damaged. Estimated cost runs to 360 trillion dollars," said Swan. "Disregarding physical damage to the Real."

The Boer slapped the table. "'Disregarding physical damage to the Real,' fucking number."

"Then Klein, Chures," said Milton. "You better not fuck this up."

"I have a lead. Oleg Kolosev." As Otto spoke the files were called onto the room's screens. "Old friend and partner of Vellini's. If anyone knows where to find 'Waldo', he does. Kolosev has also been arrested and convicted by the VIA. He tried to hide himself when he got out. Unlike Vellini, Kolosev has been unsuccessful, running home to the Ukraine. Richards and I use him sometimes. He's not of the same standard as Vellini, but they were close, and he may know where Waldo is. No matter how hard he tries to hide, he is easy to find, and he will talk for the right price."

Sobieski narrowed his eyes, thinking. Then he spoke abruptly. "Klein, Chures, you're leaving for Kiev in the morning. Henson, prep your teams. Swan, continue your attempts to dig out the EuPol Five and shut off k52 from his choir in Europe. I want this wrapped up by the end of the week."

CHAPTER 4
Bear

It was morning when Richards followed the bear out of the woods, his head banging.

The woods looked worse by day. The pale fingers of dying trees thrust up through the rhododendrons, brown leaves as imperishable as old-school plastics choking the ground beneath them. Away from the sunlit path, blackness gathered thickly.

"Dangerous," the bear commented. "Dangerous and full of death." At that he'd shaken his enormous head, remembering something better. "We had best stick to the road."

Richards was suffering the combination of his arrival and what he suspected was a mild concussion. Every sunbeam that filtered through the canopy stabbed at his eyes. His lips were swollen, one eye bruised shut. He was miserable with human suffering, too stiff and sore to feel angry at the length of time it took for a meat body to heal. The roll of the bear's shoulders as it strode along filled him with nausea, and the reek of his clothes as they warmed intensified it, so he focused on the twinkling drive to keep it at bay. The parade of stones soothed him. When the sun was strong enough, he saw that each one was a tiny skull carved from quartz, all as different as snowflakes. He knelt down and picked one up.

"I wouldn't do that if I were you, sunshine," murmured the bear.

Richards put it into his pocket.

"Suit yourself." The bear shrugged.

Richards stood stiffly. "What's going on here? Aren't you going to give me a hint, or are we sticking with violence?" he asked. His lips hurt.

The bear glowered at him. "Prisoners don't get to ask questions," it said.

"Regulations?" said Richards.

The bear ignored him.

The road narrowed, weeds growing thickly between the skulls, until it petered away. A rhododendron blocked their path. The bear swiped it out of the way, and they were out of the woods.

"Wow," said Richards.

They stood at the lip of a vertiginous slope. Close-cropped grass fuzzed the ground. Where the drop bottomed out a shining sea of wheat rippled with waves. Rich green copses rode the crops like sombre ships at anchor. Clouds lumbered through the sky, flat bottoms topped by extravagant mounds of cotton, patches of brilliant blue interspersing them. Sunbeams stole through gaps and played like searchlights over the land, teasing from the crests of hills vibrant rainbows, making a trillion diamonds of the wheat.

And so it went on, until the swell of the prairie disappeared into a haze of pollen, the horizon masked by the obscure ro mances of plants. In the distance a thunderhead arched up, an anvil of dark rain, illuminated sporadically from within. It was the kind of hyper-real landscape one only ever found in the most realistic of online environments, realer than real.

"Wow," repeated Richards, shielding his eyes. "I don't think I'm in Kansas any more," he said in his best Dorothy voice. The bear did not react favourably. It was not one of his finest impressions, he'd admit.

"Ahem," said the bear, pointedly. "Prisoners should be shutting up."

"Up yours, Toto," said Richards. "On what grounds are you holding me prisoner?"

The bear adjusted its tiny helmet and clenched its great paws, the set of its shoulders speaking of enormous tension.

"On the grounds that there's a war on, and that you are not where you are supposed to be. We've had his lot come in through the woods before, trying to trick us. I've got strict orders, keep an eye on the house, round up anyone I see, take 'em in. That'd be you."

"I don't know what you're talking about," said Richards. He suspected though: k52. Had to be.

The bear leaned in close and sniffed at him. "No. I suppose you don't. You don't have the scent of one of his about you. Hang on a minute…" The bear sniffed again. "You're people!"

"Look, mate, you've got it wrong, I'm not people," said Richards.

"Don't you bloody 'mate' me, sunshine. I'm no mate of yours! You're people." He jabbed his claw into Richards' chest. "Bloody people. Coming in here, lording it over us. This place is supposed to be a sanctuary." The bear's tirade collapsed into a growl.

"But I'm not people. I am an AI. If I'm not mistaken, like you."

The bear squinted at him. "Hmm. You look like people, smell like people, but…"

"Yeah?" said Richards encouragingly.

"You don't feel like people," admitted the bear.

"I'm not. The name's Richards. I'm a Class Five sentient."

"Ooh, la-di-da, Class Five," said the bear, waggling his claws and doing a tippy-toe dance from side to side. "Sorr-eee. If that's true, what are you doing here?"

"Just passing through."

"Right," said the bear, folding its arms. "I've heard that before. What's your serial number?"

Richards ran off his full code, and then the complex equations required to furnish the bear with a quantum key to verify his identity. Out on the Grid, this kind of encryption was done instantaneously; here things were different. For a start, Richards had to speak the formulae aloud. The bear looked off to one side. "Hang on, sunshine, this might take a moment, network's all done in."

Five minutes later, it looked back at Richards. "Ready?"

"Ready."

"OK, on the count of three, one, two, three…"

"47,319," they said together.

"Any sign of messing?" said Richards.

"Nope," said the bear. It examined him head to foot. It relaxed, not much, but enough to let Richards breathe easier. "Alright. But I'm watching you. A Class Five, come here? What do you need a place like this for?" The bear pulled a branch from a tree and hurled it out over the plain. The branch cartwheeled through the air and was lost in the crops below.

It turned back round and jabbed a claw at Richards.

"Fond of pointing, aren't you?" said Richards.

"Careful, sunshine," the bear said. "I'm taking you in to get this straightened out. Don't think I trust you. We'll see what the boss has to say about it." It drew itself up to its considerably full height, spreading its arms wide. "No funny business. It's a fair old way to Pylon City."

"Promise. Cross my heart and hope to die."

"Don't get funny with me, you little sod. You better behave. Will you?"

"Do bears shit in the woods?" said Richards.

"I told you," said the bear.

"Yeah, I forget. That's where popes perform their ablutions. Sorry."

"Fuck. *Off,*" said the bear, and squared its sloping shoulders in a way that suggested actual hurt was not far distant.

Richards changed tack. "Perhaps we might get on better if we were formally introduced?"

The bear sniffed disparagingly. "Right. OK. Maybe. Me, I'm Bear. Sergeant Bear."

"There's a surprise."

"Watch it, sunshine, you're pushing your luck. No one knows I found you. Get too cocky and I'll forget regulations altogether, got it?" He adjusted his helmet. "You can stick to 'sir'." Bear cupped his hands round his mouth. "Oi! Geoff! Geoff!" he shouted. "You can come out now, I reckon he's harmless." Bear looked at Richards suspiciously. "Mostly," he added.

There was a rustle as of something big forcing a passage through the trees, a sound that became a crash as a battered, three-legged purple giraffe fell onto the lip of the slope and squeaked pitifully. "That's Geoff, my corporal. Come on, Geoff! Get up now."

"Man, you're part of a crack outfit," said Richards and whistled. Bear gave him the kind of stare only bears can and waddled over to help up the corporal. Richards noticed a rattling as he moved, a noise he'd previously put down to the gravel path.

He looked at the bear closely.

"Beans? You've got beans in your arse?" The giraffe was a caricature in plush of the real thing. The bear's nose was scuffed plastic. Something clicked in the simulated mess of buttery tissue between his ears. "Hang on, you're *toys*? You, the giraffe, the dog-man?"

Bear looked back from where he was helping the struggling Geoff to his three feet. Richards caught sight of crude stitching where the giraffe's right foreleg should have been.

"My, aren't you the sharpest tool in the box? Course we're toys. We can't all be Class Five AIs like you, mister." Bear shook his head and pushed his friend up to his feet. "But not that doggy dude, no. He's just a screening programme, not as sophisticated as us, eh, Geoff?"

The giraffe squeaked.

"The cheek of it," said Bear.

Richards understood. Virtually all playthings in the more fortunate parts of the Real had some form of embedded electronic mind. Often this was rudimentary, but some had been furnished with brains right up to strong-AI classification before the emancipation – like Valdaire's phone, Chloe, incepted as a life companion, although Valdaire had gone further than most by constantly upgrading Chloe and eventually removing her from the doll she initially inhabited. Life Companions were helpers, online and off, invisible friends, teachers, comforters and confidantes rolled into one. But when they were outgrown, and their owners lacked Valdaire's technical flair, where did they go? Here, apparently, thought Richards.

"This place is some kind of sanctuary. You said it," said Richards. "A hidden world for abandoned toys? Now I've seen everything."

Geoff squeaked and nodded enthusiastically. Bear glared at him. "Geoff, that's classified!"

Geoff squeaked apologetically.

"Oh, I give up. Yes. Me –" he poked his own thumb into his chest "– I had fifteen years in a cardboard box in an attic. Seems that 'Life Companion' doesn't actually mean for life. There I was, charge down to nothing, forgotten, no Grid connection. Utter hell. Geoff here had it worse, the kid that owned him really did a number on him, pulled his leg off, for fun! Then him too, bosh!" The bear slapped the back of one paw into the palm of the other with a rattle of beans. "Into a box, up the stairs, bye bye."

"Squeak!"

"That was before we were brought here. Dunno how, really, some bloke opened up a link, bit of a ponce, called himself the Flower King, dragged us in and told us to be free and happy, gave us this lovely queen."

Richards' eyebrows raised.

"Yeah, I know it sounds a bit suspect, OK? But it beats being stuck in an attic. And once I got used to the idea, turned out this place was a bloody paradise."

"Was a paradise?"

"Was. Not any more. Now it's all coming apart. The Terror's eating it alive. Queen's gone, no one knows where, the Flower King's not showed his stupid mush for ages, war and death everywhere, Lord Penumbra destroying everything. All gone to crap. Some bastard's been playing games, if you ask me, and I went off games a long time ago. I don't like it. I'm a teddy bear, not a soldier. I'm not cut out for this."

The bear looked meaningfully at the thundercloud on the horizon.

"k52," said Richards.

"Who's k52?" asked the bear.

"Another Five, like me. He's why I'm here," said Richards. "Anyone else like me come through that door?"

The bear shook his head.

"He was part of a caretaking team looking after the old Real-World Reality Realms after they were declared off limits."

"Reality Realms off limits? Since when?" said Bear. "I used to go in there all the time, playing Bastista's Kingdom," he said enthusiastically. "We used to have loads of fun, he used to love it, little Be–" Bear clammed up quickly as his voice caught in his throat. "Fifteen years. Little bastard. In an attic. After all I did for him."

"You've been gone a long time," said Richards. "A lot changed out there. Full immersions are illegal, as are toys like you. We're all free, Sergeant. k52 and his team were supposedly studying the Realms after they were cut loose, but a human colleague of his, Zhang Qifang, discovered that k52's not been playing the straight game. Some Realms had been destroyed by careless hackers, you see," he explained. "Their vacated Grid space was supposedly being used by k52 for research into accelerating technological development, but instead he's used it to launch an attack on the whole damn Grid." He frowned. "But then there's this. This doesn't fit in at all."

"Don't see what that's got to do with us," said Bear.

"Maybe he's your Flower King..." Richards trailed off. "Nah, that's too sentimental for k52. And even if he did make it, who's attacking it? I can't see what use a world like this would be to him, he's not a dreamer, he's far too practical for..."

"For a talking bear?" said Bear.

"Yeah," said Richards apologetically. "Have you got any direct influence here?"

"What?" said Bear, "like shaping it? Nope. The likes of us are way too far down the pecking order. Barely sentient, half of us, though the Flower King gave us all upgrades when he brought us in." The bear shuddered. "That's the worst of it, I tell you. You never know who's going to go next. Part of the world dies, folk's minds go with it. Nasty. We've got the network, but that's part of the construct, given us by the Flower King, not the underlying architecture. If we did have access to the world code, the higher-ups would write the war out, not fight it. I was rather hoping you'd be able to help us out with that, big-ass AI like you."

Richards shook his head. "Sorry. This place must have been built on the remains of one of the wrecked Reality Realms, and they were keyed into human minds. AI and near-AI within were run strictly as bubble simulations, consciousnesses as separate from them as humans are from the mathematics of the Real. That's what's happened to me here. I've been walled in. No wonder I can't make myself a new hat." He sniffed his coat. "Or do my laundry. You got any people back at your HQ with higher access rights?"

"Yep," said the bear. "A couple."

"I should speak to this boss of yours," Richards said. "Maybe he can sort me out with a hat."

"Right you are, sunshine, because that's where you're going. Now," said the bear. He swung his head from side to side, looking out over the plain. He peered into the distance and righted his helmet decisively. "This way. If there's still a this way left." He pointed his muzzle out across the plain. "Here," he said hopefully. "You got any fags?"

Richards shrugged his shoulders. "Don't smoke. Who does? It's bad for you."

The bear gave him a disdainful look. "Oh, puh-lease," he said.

Out on the plains, thunder rumbled.

CHAPTER 5
Kolosev

Kolosev's mother didn't know where her son was, but the servers delivering her mail did. Veronique cracked the old lady's Grid profile quickly, Kolosev's cryptography a little less so, but by 3.30 she had him.

"South," Valdaire said over a glass of black tea. Kolosev's mother was handing out cake, as eager to find her darling son as they were. Always the way, thought Otto. Every time Oleg went underground, Otto and Richards came to see his dear old mama. She was as helpful as she was the last time.

"Here." Valdaire pointed to Chloe's screen, at a locator point flaring on a map.

"He is a mummy's boy," said Otto quietly to Valdaire as Mrs Kolosev flirted with an uncomfortable-looking Chures. "All his super hacker crap. He still needs his socks washing, this is how we find him every time."

Otto, Veronique, Lehmann and Chures left Kiev that evening. They travelled along the E95 in a rented groundcar, Kiev being a city where Richards & Klein had no garage. Systems cracked by Valdaire, the car proved suitably anonymous. Otto debated taking an aircar, but ground vehicles drew less attention, especially so far east. As was his habit, Otto drove himself, not

trusting the vehicle's automated systems against outside interference. He turned down Lehmann's offer of help. He said he
wanted to think, but in reality he didn't want to sleep, he could
do without the temptation of the mentaug's dreams.

The forests of the north turned to steppe as they headed south,
fertile plains tilled by enormous, automated harvesters. The highway was eight lanes wide, full of slaved cars in tight road trains,
as busy as any in Europe, but once they turned off the highway
AI guidance cut out, and traffic dwindled until they were the only
car, sharing the road with robot grain trucks shuttling ceaselessly
between the fields and rail depots and heavy lifter stations, busy
with the second harvest.

Valdaire sat up front with Otto for a day, watching the plains
roll by. She talked a little about her early childhood in Côte
d'Ivoire, about her life with Chloe before the country had exploded into violence and her family had fled. She was speaking
more to herself than Otto. She seemed content talking levelly
this way, staring out of the window as she made sense of her
life to herself. She probably does this a lot, thought Otto, I may
as well not be here. He was willing to let her continue, until she
looked at him and asked suddenly, "Have you ever been married, Klein?"

"Once," he said reluctantly.

She waited for more. He didn't offer any. "You don't talk
much about yourself, Klein," she said.

"Read my files," he said, even though that's what Richards
always said to him. He wished she'd leave him be. He didn't
mind listening to Valdaire. It helped some people; the last sixty
years or so had been such that half the people on the planet had
some kind of horror story to tell, but he preferred to keep his
pain to himself.

"I have. Not the personal stuff," she added hurriedly. "I feel
like I'm prying."

"You are."

"Sorry."

Otto grunted through a half-smile at that. "You'd make a poor security consultant."

"Maybe that's why I'm not one," she said.

"There is not much to tell," said Otto.

Valdaire looked as if she didn't believe him.

"I work. That's all," he said and kept his silence. Lehmann swapped over with her at the next stop. At least he knew how to keep quiet.

They passed the grassed-over sites of collective farms and abandoned towns, by low arcologies, through freshly cut fields being tilled for winter wheat, through a million-hectare rewilded patch of steppe teeming with Saiga, Przewalski's horse and gengineered megafauna. Through sleeping villages little changed in centuries, past the neat rows of a Han agri-engineering dormitory town. Night deepened, and lightened into day, and came once more. They stopped twice in nowhere towns grey with sad histories, and were gone quickly.

The second morning. Otto steered on to an unmetalled road, nothing but crops of all kinds around them, low rumble of the auto-harvesters at work carrying over the rolling vastness of the country, trails of dust marking their progress.

They approached an abandoned farm complex, mid-twentieth century, most of its concrete crumbled to ivy-choked grit. Weedy mounds of stone to one side of the road marked the remains of the village it had sprung from, windowless brick walls on the other the Soviet failure it had become. Ancient and newer parts were as ruinous as each other. They arrived at a square before a dilapidated office block. A few barns from the early twenty-first century tottered round its edges. A camouflaged satellite dish sat inside one barn with no sides, pointed through a hole in the roof, cables snaking across the dusty ground.

"We are here," said Otto, setting the car to park itself.

"What is this place?" said Chures.

"Ancient village turned Soviet collective farm, abandoned eighty years ago," said Otto.

"What, one of your ancestors burn it down?" said Chures.

"Don't start on the Nazi shit, SudAmigo, that was near two hundred years ago," said Lehmann.

"This place was hit hard by the Christmas Flu," said Otto. "A fifth of villages inhabited a century ago are like this. It is still endemic; there was another outbreak last year. That's why you see so many biofilters on faces out here." Otto looked around. "Kolosev has worked out of here before. He's short on imagination."

"Kind of desolate, even for a criminal," murmured Valdaire.

"He is useful," said Otto. "Let us approach him gently. He is prone to nervousness, and he will have seen us approach. We go in too hard, he'll wipe it all. Lucky for us he's curious; he'll want to know what we want. This barn –" he pointed to one less damaged than the rest "– it has a high EM field, plenty of equipment working. The rest of this place is inactive, as dead as it looks."

"Veev!" piped Chloe. "That is incorrect, there is minor activity detectable in the office building also."

"More there in the barn though, yes?" said Otto.

"Yes," said Chloe.

"Then we check the barn first. Lehmann, activate squad interface."

Otto's iHUD flickered on; squad icons, years unused, came on, but most blinked off, leaving Lehmann's signifier alone in his mind. A squad of two, he thought, better than no squad at all.

"Shouldn't we be more cautious?" asked Valdaire, snagging Chloe from the backseat. Lehmann unfolded his body from the car, groaning as joints sounded an unnerving percussion of pops. He swung his arms round a few times. Valdaire found herself entranced by the unnatural shapes his artificial muscles made.

"This is Kolosev," said Otto.

Lehmann grinned, went round to the boot and pulled out three components that he snapped together into a long rifle.

"I'll check out the offices," said Lehmann. "Better to be safe. I'll take up position on the roof, cover you all."

"*Stimmt*," said Otto. Lehmann jogged off.

The light of day was growing stronger, heat coming with it, taking the chill off the autumn. Otto led them to a building whose sides were made of ragged cement sheeting, cracked single-glazed windows high up in its sides. He slid the door aside and stepped into a dark space shot through with mote-laden sunbeams. Efforts had been made to insulate the insides of the building with foamcrete, but it had been inexpertly applied and was full of gaps. Rusting girders dragged from other buildings propped up the roof. An array of computer hardware was stacked carelessly in a horseshoe round a mouldy desk, a tarpaulin strung above it. Farm machinery lined the walls, unidentifiable with age and splattered with foamcrete. The place smelled of old food and strong cannabis.

"Kolosev. Lazy. He should have set up in the office. His cables probably aren't long enough to reach his satellite dish, and he could not take the time to move his fat arse and buy more." Otto looked around. "He's still in here."

Chures drew his gun. "What about the offices?"

"Not bedtime yet," said Otto. "Little hackers are allergic to the sun. He's probably just finishing up for the night."

"This is normal, to hang around when you're coming to visit?" said Valdaire.

"He doesn't have anywhere to go," said Otto, "and a rat's maze like this, he'll see it is a good place to hide. It's either that, or booby-traps and a remote camera to catch us all being blown up. Gloaters, lurkers, runners – your three kinds of reluctant informant, so Richards says. Kolosev is a little of each."

"Great," said Valdaire.

"Kolosev won't blow us up. I know him, this is all he owns, all he's ever likely to own, because no matter how well he does he always loses it all because he can't bear to be parted from his mama. No," said Otto, "he's still in here." A coffee mug sat on Kolosev's desk, cooling in Otto's IR capable eyesight from yellow to green. He walked over to it, touched the back of his hand to it. "Still warm, so is the chair." He pulled out his gun. "Amateur."

"Kolosev!" called out Chures. "This is the VIA, come out now!"

"*Genau*, if he's not already shitting himself, he is now," said Otto. "Go easy on the threats, Chures, there's nothing these little hackers fear more than a visit from the VIA, and your agency's busted him a lot of times. He didn't much like his last stretch in the freezer. You will make him run."

"I was about to say we are only here to talk, Klein."

"It will not make any difference." Otto indicated upwards with his eyes.

"What?" mouthed Valdaire.

Otto pointed to Chloe. *I can hear him.* Otto sent the message via his MT to Chloe, his thoughts writing themselves across her screen. *Breathing.* Otto pointed his chin to a roof crux, flaking steel butted by a makeshift half-floor. A creak, audible enough for the others to hear. "Come down, Kolosev! Uncle Otto has come to say hello!"

Kolosev wasn't hanging around. There was a series of rapid scuffs followed by a crash as he flung himself out of one of the barn's filthy windows. Otto ran to the door to see Kolosev bounding through the wheat at close on fifty klicks an hour, high atop a pair of 'roo springers. "And there we are," said Otto, and tore off after the hacker.

Chures put up his gun. "Klein can handle that, let's crack the *pendejo*'s system and see what he's got."

"I could do with some help." Valdaire grimaced, sweeping aside the sticky detritus of food, joints' butts and crusty tissues cluttering Kolosev's desk. She placed Chloe down on the cleanest part.

"You'll get it, in a moment," said Chures. "Klein was right about one thing. I need to sweep this place for booby traps."

Otto engaged his full suite of cybernetic and biophysical enhancements as he hit the man-high corn, pushing his body well past human norms. His secondary heart drove doctored blood hard through his body, assisted lungs wringing the air of oxygen. His adapted adrenal glands issued synthetically optimised ephinephrine, feeding his muscles with energy at an accelerated rate. Otto's enhanced biochemistry was not intended to make him stronger, although it did, but to enable his body to keep pace with his secondary polymer musculature. These muscles, contracting to carefully timed impulses drawn off his rewired nervous system, were what provided him with his inhuman strength, driving his limbs like pistons as he hurtled across the field. Without boosting, his organic muscles would be ripped to pieces by the actions of the polymer bundles.

Wheat stalks whipped at his hands and face as he ran. Kolosev was ahead of him still. Kolosev had aged badly, fatter, pastier than his mugshots. Passing into middle age, he dressed like a child in stained Gridkid gear, tight luminous pants and puff-sleeved shirt. On the 'roo springers he ran like a cheetah, a simple mechanism of levers and springs known for a hundred years lengthening his legs, mimicking the efficiency of a kangaroo's limbs. Under Kolosev's own power, the rig would have sped him, but like Otto's limbs the springer was heavy with polymer muscle bunches, lending the fugitive speed that Otto could not match. He tore through the wheat like the wind, rig bouncing over the summer-dried earth in bounding strides. Past harvest and ploughing, it would have been different, for Kolosev's rig would surely have foundered in the sticky black chernozem. Right now Otto could never catch him.

"Oleg!" Otto shouted. "Stop, or I'll have to shoot you! Oleg!"

The fleeing hacker kept his face forward. Kolosev leapt high as he cleared some obstacle, and Otto lost him to a wrinkle in the steppe. Otto let out a long string of hard German expletives and ran on. His shoulder hurt, and his stomach burned with acid reflux. He could keep a pace of thirty kilometres an hour for a couple of hours, even at his age, but this speed was draining his resources fast.

Otto burst into the open, stubble beneath his feet. A hundred and fifty metres to his left the staggered wall of giant harvesters droned forward slowly. Staple-shaped front ends terminating in multiple wheel units, flails on a wide drum between them, cutting and winnowing. Long hoppers ran behind the main bodies, raised high off the ground, rears supported on pillars with their own wheel units at the base – from the air they looked like insectile letter Ts crawling across the earth. Chaff escaping from secondary pods harvesting waste for biofuel blew in a constant stream toward Otto, obscuring his view in showers of shivered straw and grit.

Otto stopped to get his bearings. A glimpse of movement, quicker than the harvesters; Kolosev was well ahead of him, nearing the wall of machines and its shroud of dust.

"Oleg! Stop!" The Ukrainian carried on running, each step a high leap.

Otto levelled his caseless automatic two-handed at the fleeing hacker. His adjutant ran his ocular magnification up to the absolute maximum. The Ukrainian bounced around in his vision like a fly trapped in a jar, close to the furthest effective range of Otto's pistol, and he wished he'd brought a bigger gun.

If I hit him, it's his own fault for running, he told himself, and fired.

The bullet missed.

Otto squinted down the barrel of his pistol for another shot, and lowered it. Kolosev was too far away.

"*Scheisse.*"

His MT lit up. Lehmann. *Don't worry*, Leutnant, *I have him.*

A gun fired, way back behind him. A second later Kolosev staggered. Lehmann's shot took the 'roo springer's left heel assembly out, the sound of the shot following the bullet. The springer's damaged leg dragged. Otto accelerated. Panic showed on Kolosev's bearded face as he undid the springer's straps, hammering at the quick release until his legs popped out of the rig. He fell free and made a hopping run toward the nearest harvester. He was up the ladder on the left wheel pod pillar as Otto reached the vehicle. Otto was on to the ladder as Kolosev scrambled round the harvester's machine cabin.

Otto followed hard behind.

Kolosev stood in the middle of the catwalk that spanned the width of the harvester, looking wildly from side to side, shirt stained with sweat.

"Kolosev, stop. You've nowhere to run, and I'm getting indigestion."

Kolosev stared at the hopper full of wheat kernels, as if he were thinking of jumping in, and thought better of it. "You're getting old, Klein," he panted. He stepped back as Otto holstered his gun. Kolosev was unmodded: the real Grid experts never wore hardwired mentaugs. Kolosev was free of cybernetics, not even base-level healthtech; they knew how it could be used against them.

"Look at yourself, Oleg, you're out of shape. Don't run like that again, you'll have a heart attack."

"You come in here with the VIA? What was I supposed to do? After all I've done for you in the past, you bring them here! I've been busted out of every place I've ever been by them. Ten years' cold storage they've cost me. Why you think I ran?" Kolosev spoke in terse Grid English, truncated and peppered with in-vogue leetspeak, smeared over with a thick Slavic accent.

"I'm not with them, Kolosev, they're with me. We're not here to bust you. I only need some information, the usual."

"Yeah?" Kolosev's fat face pulled an unconvincing hardman sneer. "Your kind 'ways does. You loot me, Klein, it upset me."

"I am looking for Waldo, Oleg."

Kolosev snorted and slapped the railings of the catwalk. "You know he and I do no see eye to eye no more. I no run with him, I work free."

"Solo?" said Otto.

"I never said that."

"But you're alone now."

Kolosev glared, trapped. "Yeah, I'm alone now," he said, his English losing its posture, wandering closer to standard.

"I'll pay," said Otto. "I'll pay a lot."

"How much?" said Kolosev.

"A million, Euro."

"You need him bad, huh? Two million. And you broke my springer, you can buy me a new one. I want that as extra."

"I'll buy you an aircar if that's what you want."

"Thanks. I'm trying shed some kilos."

"And springers aren't tracked."

Kolosev shrugged.

"Fine, Oleg, just tell me where he is."

Kolosev fished a phone from a pocket on his sleeve. "Money first."

Otto sent a coded transfer instruction out through his adjutant. Kolosev's phone binged, filled with the VIA's money. EuPol had given him unlimited funds for this expedition. Otto figured they'd find a way to claw it back later.

"Heh," Kolosev said, licking his lips. "You do need him. Why?"

"Where is he, Kolosev? I'm losing my patience," said Otto, and stepped nearer.

The fat man held up his hand. His eyes were screwed tight against the sun; he really didn't get outside much. "Relax, Klein, I tell you. What's the big deal? Let me guess –" a triumphant grin flickered across the Ukrainian's face " k52's small adventure in the RealWorlds, yes? Am I close?"

The likes of Kolosev always dug out what others tried to hide. No harm in letting him know; if Otto didn't succeed, then everyone would know anyhow. Otto nodded.

"Damn fucking bastards! I am good, no, Klein? Huh? Huh? Every Class A gold hacker know about that. Me, I one of. We the future, you big mob, Klein. Fuck me!"

"Big talk, Oleg."

"You look at me, Klein, you see fat man. I look at you, I see an extinct species. You are needing Waldo to get you in, in past the security. Only he can do it, no?"

"You are a genuine genius, Oleg," said Otto flatly.

"Ah, now you flatter. Well –" the Ukrainian gave an extravagant shrug "– what if I tell you that it no matter? You no hear?"

"Where is he, Oleg?" growled Otto. He pulled his gun out again. "Or that money is coming right back out of your account, and I'll deposit a bullet in your face instead."

"I tell you! Calm, calm, big mob, you Germans so serious." Kolosev was giggling, he was still high. "He's in Sinosiberia, man, hiding out in an old Soviet army base from way back when."

Otto put his gun up. "That wasn't so hard."

"Yeah, won't do you no good. I'm working for some big fishes now, big fishes! They're not going to like you roughing me one bit, cyborg man." Kolosev laughed. "You want to get in to the Realms? You have no idea! I tried it 'cyborg' –" he hooked his

fingers round the word, mocking it "– I try it and 'ffft'." He held
his hand to his head like a gun, thumb falling like a hammer. "I no
do it, so you no do it. I found him, my old buddy Waldo. I had so
much I want to say to him, right before I smack him in the mouth.
But you have no idea what's going on, big mob, you so…"

Kolosev's right temple exploded, taking most of his face with
it. He slumped, last breath gurgling in his throat, and pitched
over the railing into the teeth of the harvester.

For a second, the chaff blew red.

A bullet stung Otto's cheek, gouging flesh as it ricocheted off
his reinforced skull, knocking his head round. It hurt like hell,
but its momentum was too spent to do him real harm. Otto
dropped, pressing himself as far as he could into the grill of the
catwalk, making the most of the low lip running along its base.
A further bullet thunked into the carbon body of the harvester a
few centimetres from his head. No report from the weapon; the
shooter was far off, the harvester too loud, his gun probably silenced. Otto crawled backward, trailing blood, seeking the shelter
of the hopper humped up behind the harvester. By the time he
was in its cover, his healthtech had staunched the blood. His
wound itched as it healed.

Otto called up an aerial view. Grain silos to the west. The
shooter had to be there. His adjutant reported a minor viral attack
on his systems, easily fought off.

In the satellite view, Otto saw a bike rising into the air.

The silos were four kilometres away. Whoever had shot at
him had been good, Ky-tech good.

An unused squad icon in his iHUD flickered briefly and gut-
tered out.

"Kaplinski," growled Otto.

Otto ran back to the village, his face numb. He ordered Lehmann
to keep watch from the office block, just in case.

"What happened to you?" said Chures. Valdaire looked up from her work at the desk and gave a small gasp.

"I got shot. We have to leave here, now. Kaplinski is here."

"How do you know?"

"I know," said Otto. "He's taken out Kolosev. Come on! We have to go. He probably won't chance a close approach with me and Lehmann here, but he is unpredictable, and he is not working alone."

"Just a minute!" said Valdaire.

"We do not have a minute," said Otto, and he made to grab Valdaire.

"Lay off for a moment, Klein! Chloe, is there anyone here that should not be?" asked Valdaire.

"We're the only sentients for ten kilometres," chirruped Chloe. "Brainless things elsewise."

Chures stared at Otto, an open challenge. "Finish your data rip," he said. "We need this information."

Otto stared back, and shrugged. He went to the door and checked the yard right to left and back again. He seemed nervous, and that worried Valdaire.

Five seconds passed. "Download complete," said Chloe.

"Now we can go," said Valdaire. She picked Chloe up off the desk.

"Veronique," said Chloe. "I have access to Kolosev's network, including the other source of EM activity. There is something you should see there, in the office block. Six more humans."

"What are they doing?" asked Valdaire.

"They are inactive."

Otto looked out over the yard. No movement or noise, just corn crake and combines rattling over the plain. He tapped Lehmann's feed, looking out through his eyes, something he'd not done for many years, and it brought a rush of unwelcome memories. "OK, but we are leaving as soon as we can."

"You're lucky Kaplinski shot Kolosev first," said Chures.

"Luck has nothing to do with it. He killed Kolosev because Kolosev knew something. If Oleg had known nothing he would have shot me first. Kaplinski is insane, but he is not stupid," said Otto.

"What is his problem?" asked Valdaire.

"All of the Ky-tech had neurosurgery," said Chures. "One of the things done as routine was an empathetic damper. It was supposed to stop PTSD in Ky-tech soldiers. It didn't work so well."

"Because it turned you all into sociopaths?" said Valdaire to Otto.

"You were in the army too, you know what it is like," said Otto. "They wanted to stop us feeling guilty for performing our duty."

"I was behind a desk," said Valdaire.

"You still killed people," said Otto, "even if you only pushed buttons. You know what it means to end a life; the feeling is the same if you can see them die or not." He ushered her through a broken glass door into the office block. Wind gusted through empty steel window frames, concrete walls streaked with moisture, ancient linoleum tiles flaked to fragments. "The conditioning was reversible: flick a switch after the war, be back to normal, even scrub the bad memories away. But it went too far with Kaplinski."

"Turn left, up the stairs, first door on the left," sang Chloe.

Otto went on. "Kaplinski did not take to renormalisation. He never felt anything but the urge to fight ever again. He got out of the hospital, killed half the damn security. I was ordered to hunt him down."

"He got away," said Chures.

"*Ja*, he got away," agreed Otto. "And now he is trying to kill me."

No sign of him, said Lehmann over the MT. *The air bike is immobile, 50 kilometres away. I've called in the local EuPol.*

He'll be gone when they get there, thought Otto back.

He's gone already, said Lehmann.

Did you check out the EM signature in this office?

Negative. No time.

"This is it," said Chloe. They stopped in front of a door.

Chures looked to Otto. He nodded. Both readied their guns.

Chures silently counted down on his fingers. On three, Otto kicked the door in, his augmented legs sending the ancient wood to pieces. Chures darted into the room, covering all angles.

"Holy…" said Valdaire.

"Well, I did *tell* you," said Chloe smugly.

The room was weatherproofed, its one window foamed up and ceiling repaired. Inside were six functioning v-jack set-ups, each worth a fortune, each highly illicit: couches, medical gear, nutrient tanks and hook-up. On every couch was a body, face contorted with pain.

"They're all dead," said Chloe. "Bio-neural feedback."

Otto checked the corpses one at a time; cold, stomachs bloated, dead long enough for rigor mortis to have come and gone, but not dead long. With the September heat outside, probably 50–70 hours, as he counted it, though he was no expert. Then his adjutant consulted the Grid and came back with a similar figure. Anything more precise would need tests. All were emaciated.

The last was different. "This one's alive," said Otto.

"I'll get the v-jack off him," said Valdaire. "See if I can pull him back into the Real."

"It'll kill him," said Chures.

"He's dead already," said Otto. "Pulse is weak, ECG erratic – look at him. He might be able to tell us something useful before he goes."

"Klein is correct," said Chloe. "The subject is undergoing total neural disassociation. He has minutes of life left."

"Who is he?" said Chures. He was checking the room carefully. He knocked some of the foam out off the window, allowing dusty sunlight into the room.

"Unknown. He has no Grid signature, no ID chip," said Chloe.

"Han Chinese," said Otto. He picked up a limp arm. His enhanced eyes picked out the traces of an erased judicial tattoo on his wrist. "Political exile." He let the arm drop.

Valdaire removed the v-jack from the Han. She studied the medical unit attached to the wall, then pressed a few buttons. There was a hiss and a mixing wheel spun round. A gasp of air escaped the man's lips. His eyelids fluttered.

He sighed something in Mandarin, so quietly Valdaire had to bend in to hear it.

He smiled, said something else, and went limp.

"What did he say?" said Chures.

Chloe spoke. "He said he dreamed of golden fields, that is what he said. Veev, it is."

Otto looked out the window at the corn. "That is to be expected."

"He's dead," said Valdaire.

"You said Kolosev knew something?" said Chures. "He's been trying to get into the Realms himself."

"Unsuccessfully," said Valdaire.

"He was looking for Waldo, and not on his own," said Otto. "This level of set-up is beyond Kolosev's means. Damn shame our only leads are dead."

"Chloe will tell us why," said Valdaire.

"You do not need to. Tell me, why has Kaplinski not destroyed this place with us in it?"

"He's looking for Waldo too," said Chures.

"*Ja*," said Otto. "And I would say that he paid for all this."

"Then we frag the lot, and stay one step ahead of him," said Chures. "We've got Kolosev's data."

"That could work," said Otto. "Or maybe Kaplinski couldn't get Kolosev to give the data up himself, and can not get at it remotely, and he is waiting for us to lead him right to Waldo instead."

CHAPTER 6
The Terror

Though the day promised rain, it held off. Soon Richards' human facsimile was sweating heavily and he was obliged to remove his macintosh. As his soreness receded, he began to take in the sensations his near-human form fed him, so much more entire than those he had experienced before. It was almost pleasant. Almost.

It was slow going with Geoff. "He's just not balanced right for it," said Bear. "Being three-legged is a disadvantage overcome with difficulty by giraffes." He shook his head as another frustrated squeak reached them from the wheat. "I fear he'll never master life as a tripod."

They rested awhile by a stone barn deep in the soughing corn. Bear leant against a huge chestnut tree and Richards sat with his back to a sundial. Geoff lay on the floor; it was easier for him.

They napped in the sun, each lost in his own thoughts. As they readied to leave, Geoff conveyed his wishes that the others go on, via a series of tremulous squeaks.

"We must stick together," said Bear.

Geoff would not be swayed. After a long and urgent conversation between the two animals, Bear came to Richards.

"Giraffes can be stubborn beasts, even those whose heads are full of wool," he said. "He's going to stay." Bear sniffed the air. "I'm sure he'll be fine. All I can smell down here is summer sleep and wheat." He yawned. Bear had a lot of teeth. "And look too," he said, gesturing upwards. "Look at the sky."

"Yes?" said Richards. The sky was blue and pretty.

"The sun!"

Richards shielded his eyes. "It's hardly moved," he said.

"I suspect night does not fall easily on these golden fields," said Bear.

"That's rather poetic," said Richards.

"I'm a poetic kind of bear," said Bear with a shrug.

The day wore on, and the sun did not move from its noon. They stopped for lunch by a rare brook. Richards took the opportunity to wash his stinking clothes as Bear ground some wheat and made flatbread on a rock heated by a fire of straw.

"My favourite," said Bear.

"Really," said Richards, annoyed at his need to eat. It tasted foul, and the grit in it hurt his teeth.

"It's free!" said Bear, grinning, though his smile was brittle.

Without night, time became meaningless. Richards' eyes blurred with endless gold, and he welcomed clouds, however fleeting. What had been a fine feeling turned sour, and his brain throbbed. When they slept, they did so in the shade of trees that broke the expanse of wheat, or underneath tumbledown walls that cut across the land, doggedly running to nowhere. The light shone through Richards' eyelids, turning his dreams pink.

"This is a land better suited to plants than men," said Bear, his voice roughened by thirst. It was all he said for quite some time. Pollen choked them.

After what felt like several days, Bear stopped and pointed. "Look!" he said. "The sun has moved at last."

Richards raised his sunburnt face to the sky. His body itched and his skin was tight. He was tired and hungry and thirsty. Humanity had worn thin.

The sun was several degrees lower than it had been before.

"Hmmm," murmured Bear, "this is most peculiar. The sun is setting, but it does not seem dependent on our passage through time, but more on our traversal of distance."

"Right," said Richards. He badly wanted to lie down. "Well done."

Bear waggled a paw with a rattle of beans. "I'm a curious kind of bear."

They walked through sunset fields where the unripe wheat reached Richards' chest, then came to a place where a sooty twilight reigned, and the wheat stopped altogether.

"I was afraid of this," said Bear. "I've been able to smell it for some time."

Ahead of them lay an area of blackened land. Patches of stubble poked up through fine white ash. The air was acrid. Dust devils whirled, and the ground radiated a dangerous heat. The swollen sun melted away into tears of fire at the ruin of the world.

An eerie howl sounded across the plain.

"Hmm," said Bear. "Let's stop here."

Richards, more tired than he thought possible, sank to his knees and was asleep before he hit the ground.

Day came as day does, the normal order of things holding sway at the edge of the wheat, and they continued onwards.

Soon after, Richards and Bear found a village that had been sacked. A small place of twenty or so cottages whose blackened beams stood exposed to the sky, walls bowed, close to ruin or ruinous already, revealing tangles of bones inside. There was a broke-back church and a mill whose wheel lay smashed in the river. The crackle of dying fires and wisps of smoke still haunted the place.

"I smell trouble," said Bear, "and it is trouble of the worst kind. We best be careful, sunshine." He fell to all fours and slunk across the river, a scowl on his face. Richards followed, the water warm and stinking, his trousers clinging unwelcomely to his legs.

Bear crossed quickly, leaving Richards to scramble up its far bank alone. At the top, he came across a body, a brightly hued rabbity thing the size of a five-year-old.

It couldn't have been killed more than a day ago, but it looked as if it had been dead for centuries. Its bright skin was a thin, dirt-lined parchment, eyes sunken in cavernous, glitter-rimmed sockets. Where Richards touched it, its flesh felt hard and brittle.

"YamaYama," said Bear, coming to Richards' side. "Had a quick scout, there's lots of 'em dead, all like that, poor little blighters."

"This is a YamaYama?" said Richards.

"Toy of the year, 2102," said Bear. "Fully interactive, cute little beggars, bit like rabbits, but more soppy."

Richards nodded. "I heard of them, although 2102 was a couple of years before I was born. I've had to interrogate one as a witness. Big learning capabilities, but then what doesn't possess heuristics in this day and age? There was a controversy: too close to true AI. Neukind rights people said they were alive, like me, or you. They were one of the examples the rights movement used."

"Yeah, well, that didn't stop them being trashed in their millions when they went out of fashion," said Bear. "And I complain about my box in the attic."

"Some of their minds got out onto the Grid and ended up here?" said Richards.

"Mm-huh," said Bear. "Their collective was already up and running when I got pulled in. It was all going so well for them, and now look at this." A paw swept round the devastation. "Shocking."

The YamaYama looked like he'd been sucked dry, his face an expression of agony that suggested he had been alive to suffer it.

"What did it?" asked Richards.

"Haemites," said Bear. "One of Penumbra's lot," and he shook his long head until his little helmet rattled.

"Who is this Penumbra?"

"I've said too much. Got to keep you fresh for the debrief. Forget it, if you're not shamming, that is." The bear squinted suspiciously. He wrinkled his nose. "Hey, can you hear that?"

"What?" said Richards.

"That."

There was a ring of metal, then another.

"Is that a swordfight?"

Bear shrugged. "Mebbe. I'm going to check it out. You can stay here if you want."

"Aren't I your prisoner?" said Richards.

Bear grinned a daggered grin. "And where you going to go, sunshine?"

They hurried to the far side of the village, toward the sound of mêlée.

"Get back! Get back, I say!" Clang! Clang! "Avast! Avaunt! Begone!" Clang, clang, clang-clang.

There was a tumult of steam whistles, a frantic scrabbling, and four figures came haring round the carcass of a smouldering house, stumbling to a stop of blades and curses twenty metres from Richards and Bear.

One of them was a man, his face furrowed with concentration. He wore slashed velvet clothes of eye-watering purple, a goatee on his face. A large hat sat atop his sweat-damp hair, decorated with a long, bedraggled feather.

"A cavalier!" whispered the Bear with some delight. "Or he looks not unlike one. He certainly fights with their panache.

Let's watch," he said, and pulled Richards into the shelter of a ruined cottage.

The cavalier handled a silver blade with an ease that belied its unwieldiness, shaped as it was like a huge feather. In and out it went, turning away the weapons of his adversaries. Yet his movements were slowing, flickering a semaphore of desperation.

His opponents were iron homunculi a metre and a half tall. Stooped and misshapen, they moved with an ugly grace.

"Hee hee! Hee hee! Kill him! Kill him! Eat his eyes! Stab his heart!"

"Ha ha! Break his bones! Smash his skull! Strip his meat! Take him apart!"

Each was the colour of ancient rust. Their faces were intricate masks. Clanking mechanical noises issued from them, a ratcheting hum underlying the swordplay.

"Hoo hoo hoo!" chittered a third. "Take his blood! Eat! Eat! Eat!"

"Bloody Hell, clockwork goblins," said Richards. "This place gets weirder by the minute." The bear was watching with an expression approaching enjoyment. Richards elbowed the toy in its gut. "Go on then, help him," he said.

Bear shrugged. "Not my problem."

Richards scowled. "Some soldier you are. Well, I can't just stand here." He stepped out into plain sight. "Oi!" he shouted, his plan running out with that.

One of the haemites turned from the fight. "What's this? What's this? Fresh meat! Fresh meat!" A whistle on its shoulder tooted. It whirred towards Richards.

"Run, you fool! Flee!" shouted the cavalier. "Be away swiftly before they are upon you!" And he redoubled his efforts to drive back the haemites besetting him, but to no avail, and they tooted as they pressed him harder. "For the love of god! Don't let it touch you!"

The creature came closer to Richards. It smelt of furnaces and stale water. "Hee hee, hee hee hee!" it gibbered. "Slow we'll go, slow and nice. Best for me!"

Richards scooped up a house brick and bounced it off the haemite to no effect. "Ah, balls," he said.

"Oh, for the... Ahem!" shouted the bear. "Hands off my prisoner!"

"A bear!" the machine screeched.

"A bear?" queried a second.

"Where?" cried the third.

"There!" hollered the fourth.

"More, more!" cried the creature approaching Richards. "Oh, joy joy! Iron and meat for us to eat! Plenty!" It whistled, jaws clacking together. "You later!" It giggled. "Kill the bear!"

"I wouldn't be so sure about that if I were you, matey," said Bear, flexing his claws.

"Skreeeeeeee!" shrieked Richards' assailant. It charged the toy. Bear batted its first strikes away, sending the goblin-thing staggering with the force of his paws. It recovered with alarming alacrity. Bear snarled and swiped, missing. The creature ducked and lunged. There was a soft rip as sword connected with fabric.

The creature's blade sunk up to the hilt in Bear's belly, and it screamed in triumph. The fight by the barn slowed, the man looking on in horror. The other creatures joined the call, a keening whistle.

Bear looked at the sword, then at the haemite. Bear raised his eyebrows. Bear did not look very happy.

The creature wrenched its sword from Bear's gut and stabbed again. Bear grimaced.

"Ouch," said Bear. "Ooh, ow, oh, really, aiee! Stop it." He scowled, and spoke with leaden menace. "Oh, do stop it. Do."

The creature stopped and drew the sword out. A thin wisp of stuffing snagged on the blade's nicked edge. Bear poked at the hole in his tummy, and fixed the mechanical monster with a doleful glare. "Now you're just annoying me," he said.

There was a noise like a beanbag travelling at mach three hitting a sack of spanners, and the haemite hurtled into a wall. It exploded with a gout of steam and hot coals. Tiny gears rained down over Richards.

"Aha!" yelled the cavalier. He swung his blade, cleaving one of the creatures in two. The remaining pair faltered, the energy gone from their assault. Bear roared and they turned tail and fled.

The cavalier planted his sword in the ground and leaned upon his knees. "A thousand thanks," he panted. His face was florid and running with sweat. "Rarely have I seen such valour in battle. Indeed." He caught his breath, stood straight and smiled. "I had come to a sorry pass with those devils, and feared my days were done. Were it not for your timely intervention I believe done they would have been."

"No problem, bud," said Bear with a shrug, beans rattling. "Just doing the decent thing." He looked at Richards. "How are you, Mr Richards, OK?"

"Just Richards," said Richards.

"You were most fortunate, sir," said the stranger. "The preferred delicacy of the haemite is the iron found within the human organism. Three moments more and you, sir, would currently resemble the poor wretches of this place." He spun on Cuban heels, staring up at Bear. "And how fare you, my mighty friend? What says your steely gut? I have seen such blows disembowel an elephant, yet you stand unscratched."

Bear shrugged and scratched his hole. "I'll stitch."

"Stitch?" said the man. "Aha. Stitch!" he bellowed with pantomime laughter that stopped as abruptly as it had begun. "I am forgetting my manners. I, Percival Del Piccolo, poet swordsman of wit, cavalier, debonair liberator of ladies' virtues, pirate king and all round irritant..."

"Yeah," butted in Bear.

"Ahahaha," said Piccolo, laughing, "all round irritant to tyrants, evil Maharajahs and Grand Viziers with ideas above their station." He held up his sword, which only now Richards realised was shaped like a quill, with a silver nib for a hilt. "I also appear to be overly fond of glib cliché." He let the weapon fall to his side again.

"What are you?" Richards looked him up and down. "You're not a historical, nor educational. An old game character? A composite of old game characters?"

"This place is full of them," said Bear. "Wankers. Always asking you to do pointless shit. Over. And over. Again." He growled.

"I know not," rejoined the cavalier. "I only know that I am, and that I possess only one set of clothes." Piccolo's face turned from frown to grin as he took in the gold trim and lace cuffs. "And that is not a welcome state of affairs."

"Does this chap ever shut up?" said Bear to no one in particular.

"Rarely, I admit," said Piccolo.

"That it? I'm Bear," said Bear.

"He's a toy, even though he looks like a bear," added Richards. "And I'm Richards."

"And he's an idiot, even though he looks like a fool," added Bear drily.

"A toy like a bear and an idiot fool, eh? Ohohoho. What a gay pass."

"Ra-ight," said Bear. "Well, I think we'll be on our way now, if you don't mind. No need to worry about the rescue and all."

"In that case, strangers, I assume you do not wish to be made aware of what occurred in this place?" inquired Piccolo.

Bear huffed. "No."

"Yes," said Richards.

"I shall perforce forgive your hirsute companion, sir, for he is but a rude beast, with manners to match. Indeed who would expect more –" he laughed "– from a bear? 'Tis fortune indeed for him for that he is naught more. Mayhap, were he a man, honour would compel me to slice the blaggard from gizzard to crotch."

"Just you try it," muttered Bear.

"This land you presently stand in," began Piccolo, "was once the happy YamaYama nation of Optimizja. Ah!" he projected, bouncing his voice off the surrounding buildings. "Ah! Optimizja! The very name is sweet mead on the tongue! A veritable salve to any misery was a week in Optimizja! A panacea to the ills of the soul! A joyous place, where the YamaYama folk were happy with never a care, all times willing to see the best in things, always hopeful for tomorrow, forever..."

"They'd be optimistic, then?" said Bear. "Hurry it on."

"I suppose one could ineloquently put it like that, if one had to, or were one rushed for time," said the cavalier. "May I, with your leave, Sir Bear, continue?"

"Be my guest," said Bear, settling down on the floor. "Sit down, sunshine," he said to Richards. "This may take a while."

"They were always well fed and industrious, the people of Optimizja. The eternal light that would never dim providing them both with vittles and joy, fuelling their sunny dispositions. They worked hard and laughed long, the people of Optimizja, always illumined by glorious gold until..."

"Let me guess," said Bear. "The sun set one day."

"Will you be silent, please? I am mid-narrative," snapped Piccolo. Richards dug Bear in the ribs. "Sorr-ee," said Bear.

"Then, one awful eve, the unconscionable occurred. The folk of this joyous place were overcome with horror when the sun unexpectedly set," said Piccolo.

"See?" whispered Bear to Richards.

"After marvelling at such a thing, for many of them had never travelled to the lands where the lamp of Sol is extinguished, borne through Hades by the chariot of glorious Apollo ere close of every day, only to be hauled forth again the next –" he paused to draw breath "– the people were terrified, yet, in their terror, they were hopeful that the sun would return, the elders reassuring the youngsters that this was what passed ordinarily in foreign parts, and that even here the sun required to rest from one age to the next. Thus they went about their business in the unfamiliar night with smiles upon their faces."

Bear put a paw up.

"Yes?"

"Was that because they were optimistic?"

"But little did they know!" shouted Piccolo. "Little did they know that this was merely the precursor to the Great Terror about to engulf their land in perpetual gloom! They kenned nought of it, the dark that sweeps the land, consuming all in its path, the armies of vile creatures that are its van, and Lord Penumbra! The evil beast who is its master, the shadow who controls it all! For why should they? The people of Optimizja never ventured forth from their happy land, for they had no need. Everything required was here for them. An enchanted, blessed place was this."

"Hmph. Sounds like they needed a reality check to me," said Bear. "Ooh, look! A ladybird."

"But woe unto them!" bellowed Piccolo, making Richards jump. "For when the armies of darkness descended upon Optimizja its folk were caught unawares, rousted from their beds by horrors far beyond their cheerful imaginings. Scattered and slaughtered were they, reaped as easily as the wheat they harvested. Bucks, does and kittens, their essences drained by haemites. Their crops and homes burnt.

"But that, that, dear gentlefolk, is not the end of it. Oh, precious life of ours, no. Soon the very land upon which this village stands will be consumed by the Great Terror, the terrible vortex that follows in the wake of Penumbra's depravities, leaving nothing, not one grain of sand but, in the stead of life, a terrible void. As it is now for thousands of leagues to the east, and as all will be when the dark finally reaches the sea to the west." Piccolo bowed his head.

"So," said Richards, "you're telling me there is a, for want of a better word, 'shadow lord', and the entire world is being eaten alive by some terrible darkness?"

"A little imprecise, but yes. Some fragments persist, here and there in the dark – those places which hold the soul of a land remain for a while dotted in the starless night, until they, too, fade."

"Hmmm," said Richards. "Tell me, do you know of an entity such as myself, one called k52?"

"That I know not, good Richards," said Piccolo regretfully. "I am a fragment of a world gone, a world where I had no more will than a blade of grass. Only the Flower King gave me form, and in truth this life is no more real. We will all die eventually from this war. Best to flee to the west, as I was attempting to do before my ship threw a wheel, costing me my crew, lost to those iron devils. Oh! They were a bitter tax levied that I may live the longer! Woe is Piccolo! Woe! It makes me wish to weep when I think of the fine day we set out across land. It was seven weeks past, I remember it well, a glorious morning full of promise..."

"Thanks," said Bear, hauling Richards upright. "I think that'll do."

"It may seem trite to you, my friend," said Piccolo, fixing Bear with a sorry eye. "But our world is dying." He seemed diminished, crumpled.

"Yeah. I know," said Bear, tapping his helm with a claw. "Helmet see? Me brave soldier, fighting armies of darkness? I understand entirely. That's why we're sooooooo out of here." He began to walk away. "If the Terror has come this far in," he confided to Richards, "we'll need to get Geoff. This place won't be here for much longer." He thought for a second, then added halfheartedly, "You should come with us, Piccolo."

"Aha!" cried Piccolo, once more a dashing figure. "I cannot, for, before the end of it all, I must chase down my arch-adversary, the Punning Pastry Chef!"

"Puh-lease," said the bear, and grabbed Richards by the shoulder.

"Who?" called Richards, as Bear dragged him away.

"He bakes pies and tells lies, with not a good rhyme between them. He will taste my steel before the world is done! I will slice his final cake with glee! Farewell, my friends!" called Piccolo through cupped hands. "Keep well, and remember, head west. Always to the west!"

And with that they turned a corner and the cavalier was lost to sight.

"Good riddance," said Bear.

Richards stopped. Bear tried to pull him on, but he resisted.

"What's he doing here?" said Richards. "Very interesting."

"What?"

"Him, there," Richards pointed to a corpse. From a distance it looked like a YamaYama, shrivelled by haemite touch, but closer they could see it had once been a man. "East Asian?" said Richards as he approached. He squatted down and poked at the woody corpse with a piece of charred lath. "Chinese. Could be, but hard to tell in here, could be anything." And then, something, something he'd not felt since he'd arrived. His head snapped round, and he practically jumped up. A stream of information, a tug of numbers, the weft of the place he was in, snagged at his mind. "Hang on a minute," he said eagerly. He scanned the village, turning his head slowly left to right: that way the flow diminished, fading back into a world of broken homes and dead toys, but this way he sensed it again, a flicker in the world, a crackle in his head. "Bingo!" said Richards. "I knew he wasn't from in here!" He set off toward the church.

"Oi! Stop!" shouted the bear. He grabbed Richards' shoulder again.

"Stop pawing at me, will you?" Richards shrugged the paw off, so Bear knocked him to the floor.

"We cannot leave the giraffe behind!" growled Bear. "He is my friend, and I won't abandon him to die. No tarrying!"

"Do you want to save this place or what?" said Richards.

The bear shuffled from foot to foot. "I suppose," he said eventually, with a sniff.

"Then let me do my job. In there –" Richards pointed a finger at the village church "– there's a way to the outside."

"But you're my prisoner," wheedled Bear. It came with no force, and Richards went on. Clasping his helmet to his head, Bear hurried to catch up.

They went into the church, stepping over a spill of shrivelled YamaYama fanned around the door. The roof ridge was broken, and there were large holes punched through the tiles. The floor was cratered and covered with shrapnel, rubble and splintered wood. YamaYama bodies were crushed and dismembered everywhere. In a pulpit at the front a YamaYama in an ecclesiastical surplice stood, pinned by a spear to the wall. A spread of ornate breads, fruit and vegetables lay on an altar before a cross, untouched but for a layer of fine debris.

Richards stopped and pointed at something on the far side of the church. "See?"

"What?"

"I'm not people, but they were." Five more corpses lay in a grotesque pile, half phased into each other and the stone wall. Richards peered closer. One of the blocks flickered. "Someone's been trying to break in. Looks like it was shut off pretty quickly, too quick for these poor idiots, but there's something still there." Richards closed his eyes. "It's slippery, but I can feel…"

"Yeah, whatever, Mr La-di-da Richards AI Level Five man,"

said Bear. He flapped a paw and crunched over the rubble to the food. He dusted a loaf off and sniffed it. He hit it against the altar. It made a thud; hard and stale. He put it back. "I'm going to keep watch," he said, and went to stand by the church's shattered nave windows.

There was a fountain of data rippling intermittently from the outside, a gash in the world through which Richards could taste the wider Grid. Richards positioned himself in its path, and tentatively extended part of his mind into the flow.

He hooked in.

"Got it!" His mind burrowed into the fabric of the world. He poked a sensing presence out of the shell of the construct and found himself looking at the firewall that surrounded all of the Reality Realms, living and dead. A tiny rip blinked in it, already closing. No way out there. He turned his mind back in and ran his thoughts into the reality he stood within. Creative coding wasn't his strong point, and the mass of numbers he was confronted by was nearly beyond him, but the stream of equations rushing through him were of indescribable complexity, way beyond most everything else out in the world. "This stinks of k52," he muttered. He pushed harder, trying to snag himself onto the world, to give it a tweak, make a hole from the inside out he could use to escape, send a message, anything. He pulled back frustrated. He could just about hear and feel his own Gridpipe, but the way back into the Grid remained elusive.

He pushed harder. There, another stream of data, a second layer under the first, simpler, old-fashioned, mismatched. He scanned through it quickly, and his eyebrows raised. *This* was the core script for the world that he was in, not the complex stuff. Still, it was not like anything he'd seen before either. It was a patchwork, what looked like scavenged bits of the four RealWorld Reality Realms broken before k52's takeover of the Realm House, stitched together with additional elements copied or stolen from all over the Grid – virtspace recreations of locations in the Real, on-Grid shopping arcades, truly ancient games, conference rooms, sense-furnished chatrooms – enough to make a world.

This lay beneath the smothering layer of the complex code Richards tentatively identified as created by k52. He took another look. k52's contained information, but it was unable to express itself. The codes were fighting one another, both attempting to occupy the same space. It was an eerie feeling. Information in the Grid came like currents in a sea, and these were two streams, isolated and competing for resources, fighting like snakes. Behind them, on the edge of his awareness, was the hum of the remaining thirty-one Realms, beyond that faint hints of the Grid, maddeningly unattainable.

The patchwork world seethed with simple near-Is, all modded, some corrupt, bound to the world they inhabited. As he watched, k52's programmes probed and bit. The older code reacted, in some places holding out, while in others chunks of the world frittered to nothing, scores of lesser digital minds going with it. The complex code was winning, but not in the usual way. Richards could sense no hunter-killers, no phages, nothing used for normal datawipe, but somehow k52's stream was besting the other, even as the other infected it and subverted parts of it.

Something else caught his attention. Within the modded near-I populations, several true AIs' Gridsigs rang out, obvious as elephants in a field of rabbits. There were many Twos and Ones, a few Fours and a Six, some bound into the fabric of the world, others on top, idents masked and unreadable.

Three of the sigs he recognised in spite of their camouflage. There was nothing quite like the digital song of a living Class Five, and he knew these well.

Rolston, Pl'anna and k52. Pl'anna's was fragile and changed, yet true at its heart, Rolston's irregular and inconstant, echoes doubling it up. Both were faint and distorted, similarly modded to the lesser near-Is infesting the fabric of the makeshift Realm, flashing with parts of the world code. k52's had grown black and monstrous, boiling with power.

As soon as his awareness brushed k52's Gridsig, something pressed hard back, breaking his concentration.

"Ah, bollocks," said Richards, and tried to snatch himself back.

"Richards," said a voice in his mind, the pressure of a giant intellect coming with it, and something else – unbounded irritation. "There you are. Goodbye, Richards," said k52.

Somewhere in the conflicted world codes opened. Richards caught the sense of another presence, angry, looking right at him. Then the connection snapped shut with physical force. Irreality rippled, and Richards was cast across the room, landing in a tangle of limbs and loaves in the middle of the YamaYama harvest festival display.

"Oh-oh," said Bear.

The air changed, becoming sharp and electric. Richards pulled himself free from squashed bread and fruit and hurried to where Bear stood. To the east of them, in the darkening sky, a thunderhead was building itself up into an angry mountain.

The sky rumbled. A gust of wind hurled debris into their faces. The clouds turned black, rushing in like oil on water, casting the distant golden fields into unnerving contrast.

"Mr Richards..." said Bear slowly. The wind grew, the stalks of wheat tossed and strained, hissing frantically, a trillion serpents trapped in earth by their tails, desperate to flee.

"Just Richards," breathed Richards.

The clouds ate the sun. A shroud of darkness was thrown across the land.

A crack of thunder, and another. The ground trembled. The church swayed. The toy bear and the facsimiled man stumbled out into the street.

"Uh, Mr Richards!" shouted Bear over the gathering wind, "I think it's high time we got out of here." He pointed. Heading toward the village, a towering vortex of sinister energies, a hurricane of smoke and mercury. Tendrils probed down from the underside of the cloud, malevolent whirlwinds questing for nourishment. The storm moved with unnatural swiftness toward the YamaYama village. Trees, crumbling houses and the mill wheel whipped skyward. When they touched the vortex they shattered, consumed in a shower of cold silver sparks.

Richards ran for all he was worth. The air rasped in his lungs, burning them. He was choked by dust, and he cursed whoever had given him this body for not making it a fitter one. A storm tendril made landfall behind him and the church exploded, fizzing bits of wood raining down and turning to sparkling nothing as they hit the ground. He stumbled, sharp claws scraped his back, and he was lifted high. He was on Bear's back.

"Hang on, sunshine!" roared Bear. "I'm going to have to put some effort into this!" And they were away, Bear snorting as he galloped.

Bear made for a copse illuminated by one last sunbeam. "Let's hope that lasts!" he yelled.

They were within a paw's swipe as the wind came upon them. It was full of… things. Some of these were of the prosaic kind, grit and twigs and bits of house, but many of them were not. Intangible efreets and harpies rolled in the air, riding the energy of the storm. The wind was braided with cruel laughter, and claws teased Bear's fur as he burst into trees and sunshine and safety. Richards did not follow.

"Wuh?" said Bear. He turned to see Richards being carried backward by some half-visible devil. Behind them the land was crumbling to nothing.

"Help!" shouted Richards.

"Mr Richards!" shouted Bear.

The toy dug his claws deep into an oak overhanging the nothingness and reached out for Richards. Richards gave up punching the thing carrying him and reached back for Bear, managing to grasp one smooth claw.

"Hold... on... harder!" yelled Bear above the tornado. "Don't... let... go!"

"I'm fucking trying!" shouted Richards.

The pair of them were pulled away from refuge into space. Chunks of clay and soil crumbled from the edge of the island, frittering to bits as they hurtled upwards.

"I'm slipping!" shouted Richards.

"Hold on, Mr Richards, hold on!" But it was no use. Bear was slipping. The oak shifted. The ground disappeared beneath his feet. The tree leaned out into the uncanny storm, Bear holding the tree, Richards grasping the bear and the thing in the dark hauling hard at the AI.

The storm diminished, the vortex and its cargo of nightmare whirling around into ever tighter spirals, until it reached a point of black light and vanished with a shriek. Richards came free. Bear struggled to keep hold of him as he swung toward and under the fragment of earth that remained.

They hung over the void.

"Frigging pandas on a bike," gasped Bear. "That was horrible. I've never seen The Terror up close like that, Mr Richards."

"Just Richards," panted Richards.

Bear told Richards to climb up onto his belly, then hauled them both onto the island, where they lay on the grass. The tree creaked woefully and fell down into the nothing, disintegrating in a shower of multicoloured subatomic bits.

"k52, you bastard. Total dissolution," said Richards. "He tried to *wipe* me. Now I'm mad."

"Nice friend," said Bear. "Oooh. I think I've pulled the stitches in my arm."

"Still," said Richards. "He didn't kick me out entirely. I've got a fix on the other Fives, more or less; that's something. If I can find them, things might be a little bit easier for us." He looked at them in his mind. He had a dim awareness of the war taking place in the rush of numbers that made up this construct. He tried to force his way back into the code level, looking out for k52 as he did so, but could not make further progress. Rolston and Pl'anna's signatures remained faint, but offered answers, if he could find them.

Bear sat and looked out into the infinity of blackness.

"Geoff…" He hung his head. "It's gone. All of it's gone. Geoff… Geoff's gone." The great animal began to weep, a mournful sound born of damp earth and the regrets of forests. Richards was battered by the misery they contained. Unsure of what to do, he reached his arms around the mighty toy. Bear leaned into him and howled.

"There, there," Richards said. "There, there."

Otto was never going to believe this.

CHAPTER 7
Kharkov

Autumn rain rattled hard on the windows as Veronique Valdaire worked on Chloe, attempting to trace Waldo through Kolosev's ripped files. She was tired and her muscles were stiff from hunching over her equipment, her nerves tense as she checked and rechecked her systems for infiltration by Kaplinski.

They were in a cheap hotel in Kharkov, five hours east of Kolosev's hideout, posing as tourists. The desk clerk hadn't believed them, but had not said a word. She'd taken one look at Otto and Lehmann and her face said it all. The Ukraine was a part of the European Union, but Russia was close, and altered men like Otto were a common sight, enforcers for exile Chinese clan-gangs, or muscle for Russian oligarchs and resource barons.

The room smelled of pickled cabbage and heavy bread. There were hairs on the soap and grease stains on the headboard above the bed. There were no modern materials in the room to absorb the signs of human life, no drones to scrub them away. Veronique had not felt clean since she came to the country. It didn't seem to bother Chures, who sat in a corner eating a bowl of borscht bought from a vending machine with a sour look on his face. He raised another spoonful to his lips, changed his mind and put the bowl on the scratched coffee table.

"Not to your taste?" she said.

"*Sopa de mala,*" Chures replied. "How is your work coming?"

Valdaire tapped a few icons on Chloe's screen and sat back. She rubbed her eyes; she'd been staring at screens and holos for three hours and they ached with the glare. "I'm done. Chloe will do the rest. I've constructed a set of algorithms that should get round Kolosev's security – to say he was a hacker, his 'ware is pretty simple, all sequential, once you untangle the cover. If he knew where Waldo was, we'll know soon enough. I've some financial transactions to look at, which he buried deep. I've also got Chloe burrowing into the Russian military datanet, to check out likely locations for Waldo's base of operations should Kolosev's data lead us to a dead end. Their data is patchy, but one way or another we'll find Waldo."

Chures' face was hard to read. Valdaire couldn't hold his gaze for long; he was too cold and appraising, but spoke relatively warmly now. "Good, you're pretty good. You've been working hard. Want a beer?"

"It's not much," said Valdaire.

"You shouldn't be modest," said Chures. He hunted round for a bottle opener in the room's dirty mini-fridge. "Your record is impressive; not many backroom operatives get medals. I don't impress easily."

"I was only one person on my squad. I don't know why they singled me out." She meant that too. She had a suspicion, planted in her mind by Reardon, her jealous NCO, that she got picked out of all of them because she was the most photogenic, and because she was an immigration success story. That annoyed her, more because she hated to be judged for her looks, though like anyone she enjoyed being thought attractive. That annoyed her too, an annoyance at herself for such paradoxical, typically human, typically *female*, thinking. And fuck Reardon if he hadn't planted a worm of doubt in her mind over it.

Chures moved carefully. He was such a precise man, thought Valdaire. "InfoWar is a serious business. You should be proud of the service you gave our country."

"I don't see it that way," said Valdaire. "Most of the programmes I use are buy-ins."

"Apart from the illegal ones," said Chures. He found what he was looking for. Bottles clinked as he gripped two in one hand. "What about those? All self-written? You're a skilled programmer."

"I'd love a beer," said Valdaire.

A pair of sharp escapes of gas, and Chures handed a beer to Valdaire. "No need to be nervous, *senorita*," he said.

"Do you always tell women what to do, Mr Chures?"

That made him smile, a slight curve on his full lips, barely perceptible. "I am a Latino of a very old-fashioned kind."

"The patronising kind."

He shrugged. "I apologise, I am what I am." Chures took a pull of his lager. "These Ukrainians make bad soup, but their beer is not so bad. Where are our German friends?"

"I made Otto get some rest," said Valdaire. "He was beginning to look twitchy. He's emotionless at the best of times, but he was looking through me as if I wasn't there. I guess five days with no sleep is no good even for cyborgs. No, make that especially for cyborgs."

"And Lehmann?"

"Up on the roof, keeping watch. I have Chloe plugged into every piece of surveillance in the area, but he insisted. I think it's hardwired into him. They're worried about this Kaplinski."

"They should be. Have you read his file?"

"No."

"Then don't. You will not sleep for weeks."

"I can handle it."

"If you say so."

"You don't like them much," said Valdaire. It was getting dark early, winter drawing in, the rain showing no sign of letting up.

"No," said Chures. "No man should become too much like them; like the machines."

"You used to wear a personality blend. That kind of mind-to-mind intimacy made you closer to the numbers than the cyborgs are," said Valdaire.

Chures rubbed at the scar on his neck where his AI partners' receiver unit had been implanted before it had betrayed him. "It was limited, traffic between him and me, buffered in my favour. I did it so I could understand them better, not because I wanted to be more like them," he countered.

"We'll never have a world without machines," said Valdaire. "You're swimming against history. Give up. Better to follow the current and hope we wash up somewhere safe."

"I don't recall saying I wished for a world without machines," said Chures mildly.

"OK, fine. Do you wish for a world where there are no thinking machines?" said Valdaire baldly.

"You come from the south," said Chures, and sat back in his chair.

"You're changing the subject," she said.

"I'm not. You ask why I wore the blend. I am telling you. Do you remember what it was like, for you, there in…?"

"Côte D'Ivoire, we came from Côte D'Ivoire. And no, I don't, not much. I was very young."

"Your file says you were seven, that's not so very young."

Valdaire let out a ragged breath and put her beer down, although she didn't let it go. Through the glass, the table, to the floor, its touch anchored to the room. "I've blanked most of it. It's all very dark and thankfully a very long time ago. And before you ask, I really don't want to talk about it."

"You were talking to Klein about it."

Her hands, around the neck of the beer; across the back of
the left, if she looked hard, she could see a thin line, barely visible through the heavy pigmentation of her skin. They could
never get rid of all the scars. "No, not really. I was talking to
myself, I think. It helps. I don't want to talk about it now."

Chures took another swallow, fixed her with those cold grey
eyes. "Your father was a university man, yes? He got you into
Canada, right away. Good points score, straight over the Atlantic wall."

"The walls had not been finished then," Valdaire said, "but if
that's your point, yes, we were lucky."

"You were. My family was not."

"You don't know what you're talking about," said Valdaire.
A machete blade flashed in her mind, and she closed her eyes.
She remembered more than she let on.

Chures cradled his beer. "I grew up a refugee, a real refugee, no
home. We left Colombia; I was seven too, struggling north with
thousands of others. Mexico was still in chaos back then, just
joined USNA and under martial administration. What we found
when we got there was…" He paused for a moment, took another
mouthful of beer. "I was in Puerto Penasco. You ever hear of it?"

"No," said Valdaire.

Chures pursed his lips. "Why should you? It was one camp
among many. But it was there, when I was ten years old, that I
killed my first man, Ms Valdaire, a stinking beast who tried to
rape my baby sister. There was such trafficking in the young
then, such abuse, so easy in the confusion. He thought she was
easy prey." He took another sip of his drink. "I used a screwdriver, one of the tools provided by the USNA authorities. It was
carbon plastic, supposedly too hard to weaponise. One of the
things I discovered in the camps was that there is little that cannot be used as a weapon. I sharpened it and sharpened it,
grinding away at stones until they were worn to sand. Grinding

it took me weeks, but eventually it took such an edge I cut my own finger just by touching it. The blood fascinated me, but I never cut myself again. I saw some of the other kids go that way, carving themselves in the night time, trying to secure an illusion of control." His eyes flicked toward her arms, and she hugged herself self-consciously. She wanted to shout that she hadn't done that to herself, she wanted to hit him, she wanted to cry. She did none of these things. "There is no control there, only despair," said Chures. "Despair is the worst emotion of all, it makes men weak, it makes them give up. Whatever happens, Ms Valdaire, never give in to despair."

Rain clattered harder on the windows. Chures looked at her, his eyes asking her to respond. She said nothing.

"The man went after my sister, stinking of shit and sweat. He saw me, but he paid me no attention. I was an undersized child – there was little food in the camps. His mistake. I leapt onto his back from a crate." He smiled. "You know, they were 'temporary containment boxes' given to us when we arrived, to use for a few weeks; years later they were all we had for furniture. The screwdriver pierced the man's neck more easily than I thought it would, a slight resistance as it hit the skin, before it stretched and split like a smile and slid into the muscle. The man dropped my sister, stamped about from foot to foot like one of the cheap robot toys that could be bought in the camp for ten cents."

Chures' cold eyes never left Valdaire's; there was a grim enjoyment now. Is he enjoying reliving this? thought Valdaire. He wants to discomfit me. He wants me to share. He thinks I am pampered, thinks I got off lucky. He knows nothing.

"There was only one fabber in the place," continued Chures. "I became fixated on those robots, spent an age getting the money together, to find that they weren't true robots at all, but clockworks that quickly broke.

"This man, he was like that; broken. His arm went out, grabbing at the sky, the other clutched at the screwdriver; he'd thrown me off, but it had stayed there. A froth of blood was on his lips. He flailed at us, so we scurried back, like mice, you know? Into the shade behind prefabbed shelters. The man fell to his knees, his eyes flat, blood pumping. He stared at me as if to ask why. I did not feel the need to answer.

"I had been aiming for the carotid artery, the way one of the older boys showed me. But I missed and only nicked it. I must have hit something vital, because he could not stand properly. The fat man took a long time to die. It was raining then, like it is now." He looked out of the window. "We watched as his life washed into the mud.

"Persephone, she was my sister. My parents were poor but they were not unsophisticated. My mother would have been a doctor if the war had not come, and my father, he loved stories, he told me so many. Persephone, like the daughter of Demeter, married off to Hades and whose six-month stay in the underworld every year caused Demeter's winter of grief to fall upon the world."

"What happened to them?" said Valdaire.

"Persephone died not long afterwards, killed by the haemorraghic fever. My mother died in a later epidemic. I was fourteen before I and my father left that place. He lives in Fresno now, but he no longer tells stories. The camp outside Puerto Penasco was dismantled in 2120. Nothing but fields there, those big round ones with the irrigation drip tracks." Chures put his empty bottle down, bent to the mini-fridge for another and opened it. "So, you ask why I wore the blend. Many people make the mistake of thinking I hate the machines. This is not so. In the camps I have seen the worst man has to offer, and later I learned of the mistakes that led to them. The machines can deliver us a better world, because they are good at forcing us to work together. We do not have a good record in this area; they are less selfish. But they must be subservient to us, not our masters. I am afraid not that they seek to rule us, but that they will, eventually, by default. That is why I behave the way I do. Man should have a hand in his own destiny.

"The Ky-tech are too close to machines. What they did to their minds was dangerous, and that is why Klein and his friend and that maniac Kaplinski are the last of a dying breed. Why do so many have phones, and not an internal link? I will tell you. It is not the fear of Bergstrom's, but because you know that to alter our minds makes us inhuman. Our humanity should stay in control, or we will cease to be human by small steps. I wore the blend so that I would know them better, not to become one of them, not like Klein."

The rain hammered down, mixed now with the ball-bearing rattle of hail bouncing off the pavements outside.

Valdaire spoke. "The world is full of horror. Every day brings more. I don't see the machines stopping it. They put up the walls, they turned their back on the south. They have stopped collapse by trapping half of the human race." Her voice was small but she was angry, not with him, not directly, not entirely; his story opened up the windows on some of her own past she'd rather forget. "Every one of us from the southern hemisphere has bad memories, Chures. What makes you different?"

"What makes me different? I could sit in Fresno, Valdaire, like my father, watching sports and brooding. I don't. What makes me different is that I choose to do something about it, *senorita*."

They sat in silence for a while, until the door connecting Chures' room to the other in their suite opened and Otto walked in. From the look of him, he still had not slept.

"We have a problem," he said.

Chures joined Lehmann on the roof while Otto remained with Valdaire and the phone.

"They are making no effort to hide themselves," said Chures, binoculars trained on a large van parked up the street.

"They are not," agreed Lehmann. "It's Kaplinski's way: he deals in fear. He's trying to frighten us – that and I don't think he wants to tackle me and Klein together."

Otto, keyed in to the conversation via his and Lehmann's Ky-tech machine telepathy, spoke to Lehmann. *He has more than enough manpower to take us, Lehmann. He is waiting for us to figure out where Waldo is.*

If it is important to him, it must be important to this k52 also. Which suggests we are on the right track; he could be a threat to them.

"He's playing games," said Lehmann out loud, although he whispered, for Kaplinski certainly would have directional mics pointed at his position. "Trying to make us run, lead him right to Waldo."

"What?" said Chures, party to only Lehmann's side of the exchange. Lehmann waved him to silence.

Yes, he is playing us, said Otto, his voice emotionless through the MT. *Let's keep this short. Kaplinski might have access to our MT cipher.*

Want me to put a cannon shot into that truck? I can take it easily from here, said Lehmann.

No. We're going to plan three as of now. Confirm.

Confirmed, said Chloe over the MT. The phone, modded and tinkered with by Valdaire since she was a child, pumped out a series of viral hunt and attack ware, swamping the local Grid. Already shaky from the events playing round Hughie's Choir, it took a big hit and slowed to a crawl as Valdaire's programmes reproduced rapidly and hit everything with Gridside ingress. Lehmann and Otto, shielded as they were, still felt the effects of one of Valdaire's presents, a worm tailored to disrupt cyborg interfacing protocols.

Another invaded the systems of the van, causing emergency venting of hydrogen from the fuel cell. Simultaneously, Chloe had all the lasers in the vehicle ignition system trip off together and focus in one spot rather than in their programmed depth-varied ignition sequence. There were many safeguards in fuel cell vehicles to prevent either thing ever happening. Valdaire's 'ware circumvented them all.

The van lifted off the ground, carried skyward on a pillar of fire. It twisted over and came crashing back down, blocking the road. Alarms went off round the entire block, car lights blazed on and engines revved, the vehicles banging into each other as they came online and tried to remove themselves from the danger.

Back in the room Otto said, "Now our car."

Out the back of the motel, the groundcar's windows went black. Broadcasting fake Gridsigs for Lehmann, Otto, Valdaire and Chures, it reversed out of its parking bay and headed off at high speed. Otto smiled as Chloe picked up a trio of airbikes lifting off and heading in pursuit.

"Do we go now?" asked Valdaire. She felt sick. She hadn't liked blasting the van; there were men inside. She'd killed many, she supposed, back in the war days, Otto was right about that, but he'd also been wrong; it had just been button pushing, easily dealt with if she didn't think about it. She'd never really squared it with her conscience. If she thought about it, it brought her too close to the men who scarred her hands, so she didn't. Maybe that made her worse than the cyborg. He clearly was bothered by it.

"Wait," said Otto. "Is the area clear?"

"Yes," said Valdaire.

"Then detonate the others."

Valdaire checked them quickly for human occupants. None. A street's worth of cars, dancing round each other as their on-board systems communicated and attempted to bring order to their escape, exploded one after the other.

"That will do it," said Otto.

Sirens.

"OK," Otto said, and ushered Valdaire out of the room. Chloe invaded the building's survnet sensors as they hurried to a side door in the building, scrubbing their presence from the recordings. "We're leaving now."

The noise of emergency vehicles, police and machines filled the night, lights sparkling in the rain. What little Gridwidth remained was clamped down, swamped by the informational traffic of AI and human emergency services.

Lehmann and Chures joined them on the street.

"Messy," said the VIA agent. "But effective."

"Kaplinski will not dare to make a move now," said Otto, looking up at the rooftops. "He's still watching. We need to lose ourselves, quickly."

CHAPTER 8
Circus

On the island it was as if the Terror had never happened nor ever would. Birds sang, plants rustled in the breeze and the sun shone, framed by a rag of blue sky that wavered uncertainly in the void. Richards marvelled at it, wandering round, prodding the ground with a stick. "This is a data artefact," he said to Bear. "One of those little bits that gets left behind when files are over-written. I never thought I'd be standing on one, nor that I'd find one quite so… lush."

The island dwindled. With regularity pieces fell away into the void, tinkling as they went to nothing. A wall of black vapours streamed from its edges. Discomfited by this, Bear and Richards made their way inwards. There, at the heart, they found a glade around a spring from where they could not see the void, and felt a little safer.

"Good day," said an old man in the clearing.

"All right there," said Bear. "You got any cigarettes?"

Richards sat on a stump as the man handed the bear a soggy roll-up.

"Ah! A fag!" said Bear. "Thanks. If they were mine, I wouldn't go handing them out willy-nilly, none left anywhere now." Bear talked quietly. "Silly tramp."

"You should be a bit more respectful," said Richards mischie-
vously. Surviving death had lightened his mood. "Did you never
listen to the stories you had to tell your owner?"

"Don't talk to me about that little bastard. A decade and a half
in a box, remember?" said Bear. The tramp lit his cigarette.
"Watch the fur," grumbled Bear, "my manufacturers skimped
on the flame retardant."

"This world has something of the fairytale about it," said
Richards, "and in fairytales you should always help out strange
old men in woods."

"The boy speaks truth!" muttered the old man. "It's often the
way, often the way." His chuckle tailed off into a racking smoker's
cough. Richards and Bear waited till he'd hawked up a handful
of brown phlegm. "Sadly for you I'm not a fairy. The name's
Lucas, although I was once Lord of Fendool, the capital of the
outer realms of Hyberboroon."

"Ah," said Richards, pleased at this proof of his theory. "One
of the Reality Realm RealWorld games. Number three, I think."

"What happened?" said Bear, sniffing at the tramp suspiciously.

"I do not know. One moment I was lord of all I surveyed, next
darkness, and then..."

"The Flower King," said Bear and the tramp together. Bear
gave Richards a meaningful look. "See?"

"Yes. Exactly. Ever since then I've been rather down on my luck."

"Aren't we all?" said Bear, and blew an extravagant smoke
plume.

Richards watched the toy and the tramp smoke. No one had
smoked in decades. "Who would build something like this, and
why?" he wondered aloud. "And why is k52 trying to destroy
it? It still doesn't make any sense."

"I've no idea," said the bear. "I'm just a bear, and I'm following orders."

• • • •

The black had a physicality to it, a presence that lurked outside the circle of sunlight. Despite this, Richards took to standing by the edge, watching fragments of Optimizja float by as he thought. A stand of wheat, a scarecrow in the centre with a face fit for tragedy; an ancient waystone; the corner of a kitchen; a pub table; a half-dead chestnut full of rooks, roots exposed to the nothing. Particles of the dead kingdom that held a resonance so strong it caressed the corners of their island like the wake from a boat as they passed, and that is why Richards supposed they persisted.

All were much smaller than their refuge, and all were dissipating. At first they passed several every day, then one or two, then none.

Night came and went normally on the island, as if the little kingdom of Optimizja were still whole and they could not quite see the rest of it, and they became used to moonlight and sunshine from orbs they could not always see. Days passed. Nothing happened. Richards made a long list of all the things he hated about being almost human: sleeping, itching, sneezing, being smelly, being hungry, being sad, being frightened and all the other things he could pretend to experience at home but could always turn off. Shitting came right at the top of his least favourites. He hated the process; it made his stomach crawl, which in itself was damn revolting. With limited access to water he felt he could never get his ridiculous human arse clean, and became self-conscious there was a lingering smell of shit on him.

There was little for them to do but sleep and eat the island's abundant supply of inquisitive grey squirrels. These soon grew less abundant and inquisitive, and the island fell silent.

Richards was tired but not sleeping. Like so much else, he found sleep an annoying imposition, and avoided it until his eyes were drooping, even though to do so made him feel irritable. He spent more time at the edge of the island, away from the bear and the tramp, who spent their time swapping improbably dirty stories. His limited grasp of the underlying architecture of the rogue realm, which he'd come to refer to as Reality 37, slackened, and he became despondent. He tried yoga, meditation, more sleep deprivation, anything he knew of that humans used to get inside their own heads, searching for the faint Gridsigs of his lost brothers and sister, but they remained elusive, and Richards was stuck in his made-up head with no one but himself for company. Days passed.

A note sounded strong and sad in Richards' isolated mind. His eyes snapped open. Richards leapt up and fell over about as fast, for he'd fallen asleep in the lotus position and his feet had gone numb. He swore the worst way he could in as many languages as he could remember, rubbed the life back into his limbs and tried again. He spun round and round, stopping at that quadrant of the compass where the note sang strongest. A Gridsig. Excited, Richards squinted into the dark, straining his eyes. Nothing.

"Fucking people," he said, wishing for a robot body that didn't fart and sweat and that could see further than half a mile. "Fucking eyes."

He caught sight of a few twinkles of light far out in the dark, lights that grew brighter as another island hove into view like a pleasure steamer, silent and gaudy, bedecked with strings of coloured bulbs. The lights wound round a hill, following a path through an orchard to a pagoda at the top. On the roof of the structure was a device like a colliery wheel. A cable of gargantuan proportions ran up from inside the tower and over the wheel, hanging slackly horizontal as it disappeared off into the dark.

From there the Gridsig broadcast its unique song, obscured, tampered with and corrupt, undisguisable nonetheless.

"Pollyanna," he said.

On the larger island it was night also, and the bulbs cast motley shadows on the path as they stirred in the wind. A smell of food came with it.

Richards staggered as their island crashed into the other. It came free, snagged once again and came to a hard halt.

"Tsk," said Bear, joining Richards, "how tasteless. But check that out." He pointed to the wheel at the top. "That's a pylon station, that, a way back to Pylon City."

Richards looked at him, "And?"

"They're all over!" said Bear, waving his arms around. "All lead to Pylon City. It's what carries the network, and people too, you'll see."

"You're sharing this information with a prisoner?" said Richards.

Bear harrumphed and folded his massive arms. "I'm beginning to believe you're not some kind of spy, sunshine, *everyone* knows that. Come on!" he added, smacking his lips. "Something smells dee-licious!" His long snout twitched. His eyes became animated. "Pork. It's pork! Let's check it out. I'm sick of squirrel."

"I'll come too," said the tramp, appearing from a bush, rubbing his hands. "That food smells divine!"

The island had come to a rest by an ornate jetty jutting out over the nothing. Tatty paper lanterns illuminated it. No vapours rose from the edge of this island.

"Hey!" warned Richards. "There's a Five up there, and something is not right." But the bear and the tramp were not listening; they were already hurrying off the jetty where a pair of stone lions guarded a pair of iron gates, the bear's twitching nose high in the air.

"Halt!" said a bored voice. "State your business."

"What was that?" said the tramp.

"That," said Bear, pointing at the lions, "was them."

"They're stone, ignore them," said the tramp. "Come on, I'm starving."

"They're not stone," said Richards. Lions. One looked a hell of a lot like a non-robotic version of the Tarquinius avatar of Reality 36. A cut-and-paste job. And he thought that that was not the way an AI would have built this creation.

The lions' smooth grey skins shuttered between light and dark, abruptly turning into the rough yellow of lion pelt. They stretched and yawned, displaying fangs of dazzling ivory.

"Ahhhh," said the larger of the pair. "That's better. I do so loathe it when Circus keeps us petrified for too long. It is neglectful and cruel."

"Positively inhumane, Tarquin dear," said the other. A luxurious shiver ran the length of its body as it stretched. "If I had a phone I'd call the RSPCA."

"I'm not sure they cater for the likes of us, Clarence," said the other.

"Ahem," said Bear.

"Oh, do go away," said the first lion. "We really can't be bothered with visitors today. Come back tomorrow, yes. Tomorrow." Its skin flickered to grey and back. It shook out its mane.

"I'm on business of the Lord of Pylon City," said Bear. "Let us in, I need to make use of your pylon station. That's an order, by the way."

"Oh, really?" said Clarence. "Well, in that case, can they come in?"

"No, Clarence," said Tarquin, pacing around on his plinth. "No, they most assuredly cannot."

"Righty-ho," said Bear, and kicked open the gates. "Sod you then, I'm through trying to be polite. There's a way back to my boss and food to be had and I'm wanting to eat it."

"We could always eat you," said Clarence as Bear marched through the gate.

Bear jabbed a huge claw at it. "Yeah," he said, "and I could always eat you. What do you think of that, eh?"

"Tough talk, dearie. Though there are two of us and only one of you."

Richards stepped forward. "Isn't there someone you could call?"

"Yes, there is," said Tarquin, leaning forward on its plinth so its nose nearly touched Richards'. "But I'm not going to."

"Oh, Tarquin, for pity's sake, stop teasing him. Ask them the riddle and then we can get this beastly business over with."

"Yes," said Tarquin. "And when they get it wrong, we can eat them."

"And if we get it right we can come in?" said Lucas.

"Nobody ever does," said Tarquin.

"Shoot," said Bear, "I'm hungry."

"So are we, dear. Shall I?"

"Be my guest," said Tarquin.

"Very well," Clarence placed itself in a stiff seated position. "Answer this, if you please: What creature speaks with one voice, has four legs in the morning, two legs in the afternoon and three legs in the evening?" The lions eyed them hungrily, tails swishing in anticipation of a three-course meal.

"Er," said Lucas.

"I'm stumped," said Bear.

"The answer," said Richards, "is man. As a child, he crawls. As an adult, he walks erect. As an older man he requires a stick."

"Oh, get him!" said the big lion. "Someone knows his classical mythology, doesn't he?"

"Yeah," said Richards. "I was lucky enough to get an education. Now let us in, you cut-rate sphinxes."

The smell was getting stronger. Bear was drooling and Lucas was dancing from foot to foot with a strange look in his eyes. Richards' stomach rumbled, which took him by surprise, and he found that his mouth was watering.

"Cut-rate, are we? Don't think you're coming through," said the big lion. "Let me tell you something, little man, less impressive than the offspring of Typhon and Echidna we may be to your eyes, but we still have big teeth." He bared them, and rumbled.

The smaller lion assumed the pose once again. "One of us always tells the truth, one of us always lies…"

"I got the riddle right," said Richards.

"Not so clever now, eh, old chap? We, I'm afraid, have full control over riddling rights round here. As you're such a blessed smart-arse you can answer three riddles. One for the each of you."

Clarence waited patiently for Tarquin to finish. A nod from the large lion set off his litany once more. "One path leads to certain death, the other to salvation…"

"And pork?" asked Bear, eagerly.

"And pork," sighed the lion. "How do you find out which way to go?"

"Sheesh, you're awful!" said Richards. "Everyone knows the answer to these. They're rubbish!"

Lucas and Bear looked at each other guiltily.

"Wooooo!" said the lion. "Catty! Go on then, mastermind, what's the answer?"

Richards shook his head.

"Answer," purred the lion.

Richards pulled a face, but answered anyway. "I'd ask one of you, 'What would the other one of you say if I asked him the way to salvation?'"

"More," said the lion warily.

"If I asked that question of the liar he would tell me the opposite of what his fellow actually would say, as he always lies. If I asked the truthful one, he would tell me the truth, which is to say, the liar's lie. Both would indicate the road of instant death, so I'd naturally take the other. For fuck's sake, this really is schoolboy stuff."

"Alright!" growled the bigger lion. "Clarence! Another."

"Are you just going to ask us questions until we get one wrong, and then eat us?" said Richards. "Because that's a big waste of time for everyone."

"That is the general idea, yes," said Tarquin.

"Thought as much." Bear strode forwards. Crossed paws barred his way, claws popping from their sheaths.

"Not so fast," warned Clarence with a silky growl. "You have two choices. We can ask you lots of annoying questions until you fail and we eat you." It had a most disagreeable manner. "Or we can just eat you."

Bear rolled his eyes. "I've had enough of this!" He grasped Clarence by the scruff of the neck and pitched the lion like a hay bale into the darkness.

"Bounddddeerrrrrrr!" came a faint cry, and the lion was no more.

Bear turned to eyeball Tarquin. "I'll give you a riddle: What shouldn't you do to Bear?" He wagged his paw inches from Tarquin's face, beans rattling madly. "The answer? Don't piss Bear off, especially when there's meat involved." Tarquin sneered but wisely turned back to stone. "I thought so. C'mon, boys! It's dinner time!" He marched on, Lucas scampering after, Richards reluctantly following. Pl'anna's Gridsig sang loud then faded to nothing, intensifying again as they drew closer to the pavilion, as did the smell of roasted meat, and Richards' hunger.

Up, the path went, round the conical hill. Their feet were eager on the steps. Bear led the way as the strengthening smell of pork began to drive him wild. Lucas was muttering to himself and licking his lips. Richards tried to clear his mind, but the need to eat the meat was overpowering, and it disgusted him.

At the top the pavilion stood proudly. What looked grand from a distance was a sorry sight close in. Flaking gold and red, grey wood showed where the colour had failed, four storeys of

cracked timber posts, ornate carvings rounded thick by generations of careless paint, a small courtyard of worn stones in front
of it. The pavilion door gave a hefty shudder and creaked open.
A midget emerged, tiny by the huge portal. It was heavily made
up, and wore a velveteen dress and a lady's red satin cloak, although it was plain that he was a man. A turban of green satin
sat on his head, an enormous ostrich feather topping that
tripling his height, a heavy globular brooch holding it in place.
As he approached, mincing and fussing, his pearls and earrings
chinked and jangled, the clack of tiny high heels loud on the
flags in the night.

Richards stopped dead. From the dwarf, the music of Pl'anna's
Gridsig rang loud, its normal purity encumbered by harsh notes
of corruption and parasitic rewrites. Little, flighty, wise Pollyanna,
fond of shopping, fashion and inscrutable pronouncements,
turned into this parody. Anger at k52 boiled in Richards.

"Greetings!" said the little transvestite in an effeminate voice.
"Welcome to the Dragon Tower!" A waft of winey breath over-
laid with stale perfume and staler sweat greeted them.

The dwarf waddled over to where the three of them stood.
"All is ready, my lords!" he squeaked, his voice a wavering con-
tralto. He bowed, his ostrich feather tickling Richards' nose.
Stretching itself to his full height of a nearly a whole metre, the
dwarf piped proudly, "I am Bodrick, son of Makkar the Strong,
son of Gelndar Dragon Smasher, of the line of Trakmore the
Mighty Right Arm." He looked a little sheepish and hesitated
before coming to some decision. "But people usually call me
Linda, Mrs Linda Circus. It is the name I prefer. This way, gentlefolk," he said brightly. "Your banquet awaits!" He glanced up
at Richards and a flicker of recognition passed over his face.
Then it was gone. Circus slipped a tiny hand into Richards'. It
was dry and soft as kid leather, and his grip was firm for one so
small. Richards tried to marshal his thoughts, but they were

buried under an avalanche of maddening hunger. Lucas and
Bear appeared entranced.

Inside the tower was a single tall room, balconies lining the
walls in place of upper storeys, leaving plenty of space for carvings of whip-thin dragons, of which there were many. The
yard-thick rope of the pylon mounted on the roof ran through a
hole in the ceiling, passing down through the centre of the room
to disappear through a double trapdoor in the floor by way of another round hole. Clustered round the rope were long, shining
chains of steel and brass, many tipped with barbed hooks whose
ornate inlay did not disguise their wicked edges. Hidden behind
heavy drapes was a bank of levers, their oily utility at odds with
the room's luxury. Cushions of silk and low couches lined the
walls. Exquisite carpets carpeted the floor. All was rich, but worn.

The chains and the cushions and the grandeur, all this was
lost on Richards. His stomach spasmed painfully. His eyes were
fixed on a hollow circular table around the rope, laden with
food of every conceivable variety. Fruits, meats, pies and short-
breads, desserts and tottering trifles, salads, loaves, fish and
fowl, wine and beer. The centrepiece was three large pigs,
roasted whole and presented on golden platters with which one
could have bought a small asteroid. The pigs' flesh was crisp and
brown, glazed with honey and shiny juices. It was expertly
carved. Richards could only just see the lines where the knives
had parted the flesh, and he knew that it would come away
from the carcass with the greatest of ease.

A struggle mounted itself in his mind. "This is wrong," he
tried to say, but his voice was weak, and Bear and Lucas paid
no attention. They ran forward to help themselves to piles of
steaming meat, while Richards exerted all his will to prevent
himself following suit.

"Well, this is very nice," he said, saliva threatening to choke
him, and he wondered if this was how it felt to drown.

"Why do you not join your friends? Eat, eat! All is prepared."

"I'm not hungry, Pollyanna," said Richards.

Circus did not react, and the Gridsig faded a little in Richards' mind. "You are not eating, my lord?" he said, suspicion creeping under his cracked foundation. "Come now, you must be famished." He giggled. "All we creatures here know the pains of humanity. How is my lord finding the sensation of hunger?"

"What?" said Richards, but Circus smiled and fetched for him an apple. He cradled it in both hands, as if it were the most precious thing in all creation. The brooch on Circus's turban opened up to reveal an unblinking eye. It swivelled slowly and fixed itself morosely on Richards' face. "Or perhaps a drink? Shazam!" said the dwarf, or something very like it, and a goblet of bubbling black liquid appeared in Richards' hand. A smile creased the make-up caked onto Circus's stubble. "Drink!"

"I'm not thirsty," said Richards. He fought his hand as it raised the goblet to his lips. With a cry, he threw it aside.

"Oh, no need to be, my lord. If it is not to your tastes, cast it away! Why not? There is so much more to feast upon in the tower of Linda! Come, come! This way, sit with your friends, find something you like –" he leaned in close, his odour enveloping Richards "– and eat." He guided Richards by the hand onto a big cushion. "Of course you are hungry," said Circus. "Of course."

Circus waved a piece of meat in front of Richards' face. It repulsed him, the thought of eating another creature's flesh, but he could not help himself; it smelled delicious, and his stomach called for it with a voice all of pain. He allowed Circus to push the meat into his mouth. It tasted unlike anything he had ever sensed. Juices ran down his chin.

"There, now, that wasn't so bad, was it? I will retire to my chamber. If you require anything, my lords, please ring!" Circus indicated the silver bells on the table in front of the travellers, and shuffled out of the room backwards, bowing repeatedly as he went.

"Dig in!" said Bear, his fur matted with fat.

"Maybe I'm not so down on my luck after all," said Lucas, stuffing a piece of pork into his mouth from Bear's plate.

"I'll drink to that!" said Bear, round a mouthful of pig, waving a goblet carelessly in the air.

Richards said nothing, his face contorted, sinews standing out on his neck as he struggled not to swallow.

Bear chewed slowly, his paws moving from his mouth. "Are you OK?"

With a titanic effort, Richards spat out the meat. Biting out his own tongue would have been easier.

"Spit it out!" he gasped. The stomach pangs were crippling, the urge to stuff the food into his face overpowering.

"Bear," said Lucas, "is your nose OK?"

"What do you mean?"

"Well, it looks sort of… flatter," said Lucas.

"Stop eating, both of you," said Richards.

"No, it's not," said Bear.

"Yes. Yes, it is, Bear! Noticeably so. Here, look in this." Lucas swept a pile of sweetmeats from a silver tray and held it up to Bear's face.

"Bloody hell!" said Bear, reaching up to feel at it. "It is too." He gave an experimental sniff. His eyes widened in panic. "It doesn't smell right!"

"What do you think it could be, Richards?" said Lucas. His skin was becoming a ruddy pink.

"Oh, no, oh, no." Richards shoved himself back from the table, attempting to put distance between himself and the food. "Too late! The meat, it's invasive… invasive code…"

"What? What is he gabbling about? Tell me, man, tell me!" said Lucas.

"It's… magic!" said Richards. "Magic!"

"Your nose… your nose…" said Bear.

"Is it getting flatter too?"

"No!" shouted Bear. "It's turning into a pig's snout!"

Lucas held a hand up to his nose, a hand that was rapidly morphing into a trotter. "Oh, dear, so it is. I don't think I can… oink. I'm sorry. I mean oink! Oink! Oh, dear. This is worse than the hiccups. Excuse me." Lucas dropped to his hands and knees, his flesh writhing.

Richards crawled away from the table, fighting the urge to drag himself back to the feast. Bear jumped to his feet. "Damn!" he shouted. "Damn, damn, damn!" Large bare patches were appearing as his fur fell out in clumps. His ears had become hairless and floppy, and one paw had changed to the pointed fingers and nails of a pig's foot. "Goldilocks' knickers! It's the bloody food. I should have known! I should have known! I knew it didn't smell right! Damn! Curse my hairy hide for being so greedy. Curse those bloody squirrels!"

"Oink!" snorted Lucas.

"Oh, no," wailed Bear, "my tail's gone curly."

At that moment Circus made a grand entrance. He swept in, head held so high that Richards could almost see it over the pile of figs between them.

"Ha ha! Greedy, greedy, my lords. Your true natures are revealed by your gluttony." Lightning played around the eye in his turban, the pupil of which had reduced to a tiny black point.

"Circus… Circe! You turned them into pigs," groaned Richards. "More classics."

"As you will be too, my friend. The transformation will not be complete until every inhabitant of the world is dead and the Flower King dispersed! When these creatures are no more, that will be that, and I, I will be a beautiful woman, as I always have wanted to be."

"But Pl'anna, you are a woman!" shouted Richards.

Circus's face creased in confusion. "I…"

"Circus, you monstrous pipsqueak!" came a voice from above. Richards managed to look up, and found if he didn't look at the food he was able to think more clearly. Tarquin paced tensely round the balcony, an expression of savage rage across his face. "Idiot dwarf! Louse! Freak!"

"How dare you! How dare you!" screeched Circus. "Never call me that again!"

"Fool!" roared Tarquin. "Kill him, kill the man named Richards, kill him now! The Lord Penumbra still has half a world to lay waste, and you invite his enemies into this pavilion."

Circus wrung his little hands, a look of abject misery upon his face. He looked at the lion, then Richards. "He has eaten of the meat, he will be swine as his fellows."

Richards kept his eyes on the lion, forcing his mind to grasp this stupid world. His anger pushed him through and he found the code, a hideous worm that impelled him to feed, and crushed it vengefully. He gasped aloud as his hunger released him, his handle on the world code going with it, leaving him wrung out and pained. He got to his feet unsteadily.

"Cretinous midget! Dimwitted dwarf, oh!" snarled Tarquin. "This creature has not eaten. He is an interloper, a Class Five AI! I recognise it, I see it now! There is no place for him here. Once I have dined on them, Circus, I will devour you piece by screaming red piece! I trusted you to murder him by your magic, now I see I must do all myself lest we are all undone by your vanity!"

"What to do, oh, what to do?" Circus's face crumpled and he brought his hands up to his face. "Now the master will destroy me and I will never be a woman."

"Mr Richards, we are utterly, utterly shafted," said Bear. He was having trouble remaining on his hind paws. He was roughly half pig, half bear. Which bits were stuffed was up for debate. It was not a pretty sight.

"Nothing, Circus. I will consume you the slower for your idiocy." The lion licked his black lips. "At least you have done half your job," he laughed. "You first, bear. Richards, I will save you for the master's return." It jumped, landing squarely on Bear's bald back. By now Bear was hardly a bear at all, and the lion's claws drew not stuffing but parallel lines of bright blood.

"Mr Richards!" grunted the toy. "Get it off! It's going to bloody kill me!"

"Shit!" Richards pelted the lion with anything he could lay his hands on. Silver salvers, soft fruits and heavy puddings ricocheted off Tarquin. Bear, slick with blood, managed to wrestle the enraged creature round until he had it in a firm headlock, but his arms were shrivelling into those of an over-sized boar. He was big, Bear, and the code had much to rewrite, but working it was, and much too fast for Richards.

"Look out!" said Bear, somewhere between a squeal and a roar. A bolt of purple energy slammed into a table and Richards was thrown backwards. Splinters of burning wood landed amidst the silken cushions and set them alight as Richards found himself dodging back and forward round a heap of fruit in a high-charged game of peek-a-boo with Circus. The little man's hands were clawed, his painted nails held before him as ridiculous daggers. His face was contorted with rage, teeth bared and mouth frothing. "Richards?" he shrieked. "Richards? Richards! Richards in my house! Curse you! Curse you!" The brooch on his head stared maniacally forward. Lightning crackled and another bolt of energy erupted from it. Richards ducked, and the blast arced over his head to shatter an ancient timber. The building groaned as weight was redistributed through its structure in new and unsupportable patterns.

"Pl'anna! Stop!" said Richards.

"Aieee!" screamed Circus, and yanked Richards' legs from under him. Richards was caught in a whirlwind of unwashed silks and limbs, ripe with the scents of old sex. "I kill you, Richards! I kill you!" squeaked the dwarf. He knelt on Richards' throat, pinning him to the floor. Richards' eyes bulged as the little man reached up to his turban and withdrew a long hatpin, gripping it in one jewelled fist like a stiletto.

"Pl'anna! Pl'anna! Stop!" Richards spluttered. He slapped at the dwarf, causing him to squeal and clutch his cheek.

"My face! My beautiful face!"

Richards rolled to the side, levering the dwarf off him, and scrambled to his feet. Circus swiped at him with his pin. Richards kicked him hard in the chest, sending Circus back down, and stamped on his wrist. The dwarf shrieked, dropped the pin and spat at him with hatred.

"I killllll you!" The brooch glowed. Richards leant forward and grasped it. Though it burned with an appalling electricity he held it fast.

"It's me, Richards! Pl'anna, I know you're in there!" He pulled the brooch hard.

Circus screamed. There was a ripping noise like wet satin, and Circus came undone like a week-old banana. As Richards pulled at the eye jewel, a zip appeared in the dwarf's face, and it unzipped. Not just the turban, or his clothes, but his entire façade, as if maquillage, vestments, skin and hat were all of a piece. The zip's teeth were the teeth of civet cats, curved and interlocking. They yielded with the faintest of mewls. Circus bucked and shrieked and fell beneath the table. Richards stood confused in the blazing room, clutching the eye brooch, which swivelled and wetly tickled his palm. All around was flaming peril, the taste of meat vile in his mouth.

He made to cast the skin aside.

"Misserr Rissshars! Missserrr Rissshars!" said Bear. "Reee! Reee! Re rion!" Richards stared at him for a second then hastily pointed the brooch at Tarquin. The arm Bear had the lion pinioned with had become that of a pig completely, leaving him defenceless.

"Er, Shazam!" yelled Richards, mimicking the dwarf. But Circus had not said exactly that, and the result was not what he intended. Rather than a heavy carving, Bear found himself wrestling with a skinless lion. It roared in agony as its hide slapped into a wall.

"What in the sweet holy name of God is fucking going on here?!" shouted Richards. He stared at the jewel – it stared back. He held it aloft, pointed at the lion and Circus attacked.

Richards' skin crawled in revulsion as the thing Pl'anna had become landed on his back. Atrophied fingers closed round Richards' face, obscuring his vision as a stench of rotting mackerel stole his breath. Richards staggered to and fro, knocking food and crockery into the voracious blaze as he went. He grabbed at the dwarf-thing, but his hands skidded on its slimy flesh.

"Richards! Richards! I didn't know, I didn't know! He changed me, he changed me! Help me, Richards, please!" Pollyanna's voice bubbled through inhuman lips even as claws scrabbled at Richards' eyes, and its voice changed back to that of Circus. "You wicked creature! All I ever wished for was womanhood!" Richards reeled back. Flailing madly, he drove it hard behind him, praying he did not stab himself on the hooks about the room. He was rewarded with a pitiful scream as the creature was impaled. He ran blindly. There was a jingle as the chain went taut, and Circus was wrenched from his back. Richards ran to the levers behind the curtain. He grasped them at random, flinging them this way and that, using the slippery dwarf-case to protect his hands from the fire-hot metal. The jerking thing that was once Pl'anna dropped a few feet, screaming as it bounced. Large protruding eyes sat awkwardly either side of a lipless mouth, legs built for jumping, broad and powerful, forelimbs feeble sticks. Richards watched it scrabble weakly at the hook embedded in its shoulder. It looked at him pleadingly. Cheerful eyes in an ever-changing mask; flighty, wise, idiotic Pl'anna.

My God, what has k52 done? he thought.

Richards released the brake on the lever and yanked it back. There was a swift tattoo of chain on hollow wood, and Circus disappeared upwards, bleating as he went, pursuing the flames that devoured his home.

The pagoda was ablaze. Richards gagged at the pig carcasses, nausea redoubling now he realised their origins. Green fire played over them as their fat burned. Fruits roasted in the heat where they sat on the table. Bread blackened, baked for a second time. The furnishings against the wall burned, fire crawling from them to the higher levels of the tower. The huge rope, inflammably thick, twisted in the heat.

"Bear!" shouted Richards. The fire was rapidly becoming a searing inferno, and he was forced to shield his face with his arm. "Bear! We need to get the hell out of here!" The building grumbled as the structure shifted. A heavy beam hit the floor with a noise like a giant's xylophone. Embers rained down. It would not stand much longer. "Bear!" he hollered, his throat raw from the smoke. A squeal from a corner answered. Bear, now wholly hog, was making good use of his new tusks, goring the flayed lion, which lay unmoving upon the floor, ropes of grey intestines round his trotters. Bear-the-pig looked up with frenzied eyes, and for a moment Richards was sure he would charge. The corpse of Tarquin flickered from red to grey, and then lay solid and inflexible, a statue commemorating a brutal end. The bear-pig shook his head, and understanding returned to its face.

"We've got to get out of here!" Richards ran towards the doors, jumping flames, narrowly missing a dragon as it fell from the arch above, spitting sparks for the first and final time.

Richards threw himself through the gap in the gates, and he was into the cool dark outside.

The pavilion cracked and roared, strips of firelight playing upon the flagstones. Beyond the circle of heat it was tranquil. Unperturbed, Lucas the pig rooted for rotten fruit in the orchard.

Bear trotted through the burning doors. His head was high, the smoking pelt of Tarquin clamped in his mouth.

"Lucas," called Richards. The other pig's head snapped up. "Come on, we're leaving."

Richards sat on a log. He stared at the brooch. The brooch stared back at him. The glow of the fire at the hilltop washed all with copper. Lucas and Bear waited expectantly nearby.

Richards pursed his lips. He'd tried to break his way back into the world structure without luck. He supposed his earlier success could have been the presence of the other Five, or the transmutational worm that was invading him, or even just plain anger, but now he was firmly locked back inside his human emulation. So he'd tried brandishing the brooch like Circus again, but little had happened. That left him with only one option. He hunted around for a stick and placed the eye-jewel on the log. He looked to the pigs. "Well," he said resignedly, "I really can't think of anything else. In here, I have to play by the rules, and those old games, they liked you to improvise." He raised the stick high and brought it down hard. There was a tiny cracking noise, then a huge bang. White light flooded the area, and Richards found himself sprawled between Lucas and Bear.

They were still pigs.

"Balls," he said.

"Richards, Richards!" A voice emanated from a dim glow above the log. The glow grew in strength, resolving itself into the shape of a young woman. Richards' heart skipped a beat.

"Pollyanna, Pl'anna?" he said.

The avatar of the other Class Five AI was a frail-looking thing, transparent, a soft whisper of damask on the night air. Sheer robes floated about her, ineffectively shielding her modesty. But though she was very beautiful, and though her clothes were very scanty, there was a purity about her. Pollyanna changed her looks often – above all things she loved to shop – but she had a peculiar form of naïve wisdom to her as deep as forest moss, and that never changed.

"Richards, oh, Richards, he has you too!" Her voice was like forty women whispering as one in a cloister, a sign that the sub-personalities in her were falling out of step with one another.

She was dying.

"k52," said Richards, his voice soft and small and sad. "Pl'anna, what did he do to you?"

Pl'anna sighed. "I disagreed with him, Richards. I went away. The next I knew, I was imprisoned in that brooch, made into a parody of everything I have ever been, but you have set me free. Thank you, Richards, thank you," said Pollyanna. "But he has you too! How?"

"Pl'anna, listen, he doesn't have me, not yet. I'm here to stop him. I came in, from outside, Pl'anna. What is k52 playing at?"

"Oh, Richards." She faded momentarily, the air shimmering. "He told us that he would save the world, Richards. He told us he could bring immortality to humanity."

"What? Dog men and bears, old toys and old games and fucking great vortices? How is that going to save anything?" said Richards.

"You do not understand."

Richards calmed. "Yeah. Yeah, I think I do. This world is not of k52's doing."

Pl'anna smiled. "It was here when we arrived. He wishes to destroy it, for it stands in the way of his plans. Something is pushing back, something has changed him. He has become part of this place. Something has forced itself into him. He is insane, Richards. Stop him."

The light from the figure dimmed, her words fading into the crackle of the dying fire on the hill.

"What did he want to do, Pl'anna? What were his original intentions! You must try and tell me!" Frustration grew in him, frustration that he could neither save her nor act directly and pull the information from her mind before she died.

The apparition bowed her head. "Omega Point, Richards, k52 seeks the Omega Point."

"How?" Richards called. He crawled forward, trying to will the other Five to stay.

"He promised an end to war and pain, and a place where everyone would be happy, and a time where the universe would sing with joy, but then we came here, and... he was lying." She looked behind her, as if expecting someone to call her. "I shall speed this wood on through the night, so you may continue your journey. And your friends too I shall restore, for it was through me that they were transformed, and I still have some influence on the world, now I am free of my prison." The figure had faded from view almost entirely, only the faintest ghost remaining, the voice going with it.

Richards felt himself grow frantic. "Where are you going? How will you save yourself?"

Her voice replied, a sigh on the wind. "I cannot. k52 had us leave our base units and bound our coding into this world. I am sustained by the Realm machinery; my being is written into the land. All those places that held me are gone; the tower was the last of it. I must expend the remainder of myself to aid you, but do not mourn me. Thank you, for oblivion is sweet to that which was my fate before. Find Rolston – he was in Pylon City, last I knew." She smiled, and then dismay came upon her. "Richards. Oh, Richards, I am sorry, but I did not know what to do."

And that, thought Richards, had always been Pl'anna's problem. She knew everything, but understood nothing.

The figure leaned forward. A cool breeze enveloped Richards, soothing his scorched skin. He felt a tingling kiss on his lips, and Pl'anna exploded into a burst of stars. It illuminated his surroundings, a glorious firework, and was gone.

A last whisper, fierce and loud, echoed in his ears. "Omega Point, Richards, Omega Point."

He felt suddenly tired.

Juddering, the island broke free of Circus's cursed orchard. Streams of soil and twigs fell from the edges, their tinkling a cold counter to the sounds of the blaze. Their refuge bobbed alongside the larger island, slowly turning and picking up speed.

"Well, that was an adventure!" Lucas squatted, naked as the day he was born and a sight dirtier, a pile of singed rags at his feet. Bear lay on the floor by him, a heavy paw over his eyes.

"Urgh," growled Bear. "I'll never eat pork again." He propped himself up on his elbows, smacking his lips with a grimace on his face. "And I *love* pork."

"Steady on, Bear!" said Lucas. "You're losing a lot of stuffing."

"Ah, don't worry about me, pal," he said, "I'll stitch."

"With what?"

"Here." There was a soft noise, and Bear plunged his paw deep into his side. He fumbled about in his own gut, his tongue held daintily between his teeth in concentration. "What?"

"That's mildly disconcerting," said Richards.

Bear grinned. "Look. Geckro." Bear undid and redid his side flap a couple of times. He sighed. "I was a pyjama case!" he said, and produced a needle and thread from his innards.

The island drew away from the burning tower of Circus. Richards left Lucas to help Bear patch himself up. He watched the fire recede. Pl'anna's Gridsig had gone. At the very edge of

Richards' consciousness, Rolston's stuttered on, warped and broken by the patchwork world, and Richards feared to think in what state he'd find him.

Richards knew the Omega Point. That stage of the universe theorised by the Jesuit thinker Pierre Teilhard de Chardin as being prior to the end of the universe, the end-game of a reality undergoing a process of evolution toward a perpetual state of cosmic grace. A universe driven on toward ever greater complexity by the observations of those within it, in a process started by the God it would ultimately create, a process made possible simply because there were people there to see it happen.

It was neat. It had its proponents. Some in the Real saw the advent of the machines as proof of Teilhard's philosophy of increased complexity; on the other hand some people saw the machines as godless blasphemies, others as the heralds of technological singularity, others as domestic appliances. It was all self-reflexive bollocks, as far as Richards was concerned, more nonsense made up by apes scared of death. The universe was as it was, and went on as it would. What he could touch, see and feel, whether through the senses of a machine or through mathematics, that was what Richards believed in. But if there was a God – Richards would not count that out – and if He had a plan, then he doubted it would be so easy to figure out.

Thing was, k52 seemed to believe it, if Pl'anna could be trusted. Where's he going with this? thought Richards. How would he achieve it? And what would be gained by bringing the universe into a state of spiritual bliss? Well, quite a lot, I suppose, another part of him countered. But that's not k52 at all, he's too logical for all that. A noble aim, though...

There was another option, of course – the level of organisation at the Omega Point could lead, theoretically, to an infinite amount of processing power, if it could be harnessed. Impossible, in the Real, thought Richards, but maybe not in a simulation.

There's an awful lot of power in the Realm servers, he thought. And if done right, there'd be nothing to stop someone like, say, k52 forcing an artificial world to that stage, because here time can be accelerated... Qifang did say he'd seen some kind of chronaxic fluctuation... Richards chewed his lip. This was a troubling line of thought. So what, he tailors a world he can command, hothouses it to its Omega Point and then... If he did that, and the theory was correct, and it worked, he'd be unstoppable. Teilhard's philosophy called for the last sentient survivor of the complex universe to become "Christ Personal". Richards had a sneaking suspicion he knew who that might be. Forget there being a God or not, k52 would fill the role. Dammit, digital apotheosis. That's what he's going for.

But if that's the case, what's all this with the talking animals and all that shit? This is like a little girl's VR paradise gone haywire. Who's responsible for all that? Richards leaned against a tree, and drummed his fingers against a trunk that felt far too real.

There was a crash and a hissing sound. Richards looked back to Circus's island, behind them in the dark. The thick pylon rope had finally given. It fell like a whip through the air from the top of the tower, shattering into glowing particles as it passed the base of the dwarf's – of Pl'anna's – tiny world and hit the void. The winching wheel atop the pagoda sank suddenly onto one side and fell into the tower. With a roar, the upper half of the building collapsed into itself. Embers and flame spilled out, dappling Richards' face with red light, a short-lived flower of fire in the endless fields of the night.

CHAPTER 9
Transiberia

They went by rail; the roads were not safe. The trains, run in partnership by the corporate Muscovite clans and the Chinese, were huge and armoured, a thin line of civilisation cutting across the lawless Russian east.

"Things have been bad here since the purchase," said Lehmann, watching Novosibirsk roll by. The train went slow here, negotiating damaged points to a frost-buckled side line. To one side of the train great machines laid new track, on a massive embankment broad enough to carry the newer locomotives. To the other, the dirty and dishevelled shell of what had once been Russia's third largest city. Windowless apartment blocks of grey concrete surrounded the place, the population having shrunk into its historic centre. Even there, the roads were cracked, the buildings long unpainted. Whole streets, those abandoned early when the government still had money to put them up, sported steel shutters. There were few modern machines in evidence, no AI and less wealth. Only the train, gleaming with money from Russian plutoprinces and Chinese development funds, seemed fit for the twenty-second century.

"They were bad before," said Otto. "Pollution, crime, alcoholism.

The population has been nose-diving since the Soviet Union fell apart a hundred and fifty years ago."

Lehmann shook his head. "This is the product of slow decline. But it is nothing. It gets worse as we go further east. They say the purchase was a peaceful transaction, but we were not far off full-scale war. I was there, I fought in the Secret War."

Otto snorted.

"I didn't invent the name, *Leutnant*," said Lehmann irritably.

Novosibirsk's shiny station welcomed them in like a weary old brothel madame, decrepitude painted over with fresh make-up and a knowing smile. They stayed on the train as passengers came and went, the smart minions of the resource barons and oligarchs pouring from first-class carriages, rough-clothed people pouring in a long flood from the cheaper cars down the platform. Many, both rich and poor, wore biofilter masks, protection against the flu, yet another variant of which had ripped across Eurasia last winter.

The station was like the train, clean and hi-tech. A high wall ran around it. Money was finally coming back into the region, Chinese money. Valdaire reflected ruefully. Industrialisation wasn't a new dawn as the economists of the nineteenth and twentieth centuries had thought, but a passing phase, jobs moving from region to region like ripples as the industrial revolution washed round the world, bringing prosperity, population expansion and finally collapse into poverty. The money went wherever the cheap labour was, and to think they once thought shopping could fill in once the factories had gone. Its only lasting legacy in places like this was overpopulation and environmental damage. Just like now, she thought, only we're more honest about it. They were idiots back then to think whatever benefits it brought would last.

The train filled up again. Armed men in the uniform dress of the Don Cossack Great Host made their way down the train and scanned their identities and travel documentation for the hundredth time since they'd boarded. Valdaire's 'ware was good, and their fake sigs held.

The train pulled away with a sigh, the thrum from its induction motors vibrating the carriages. Valdaire found the effect soporific, but did not sleep. She watched Novosibirsk slide by. Outside the city evidence of past environmental despoliation was everywhere, crumbling industrial complexes, weed-choked pits gouged out of the earth, the hulks of giant drag cranes rusting to pieces in their hearts. Some of these mines were active, giant automata worrying the soil with great steel teeth. Mountains stood with their tops lopped off, forests of trees black and dead around them. They rushed past trains loaded with lumber, ore and grain, all, like them, heading east; and everywhere the ideograms of the Orient. They were still hours away from the Sinosiberian demilitarised zone, but even this far west the influence of the People's Republic was apparent, the resources they took from the mountains and forests fuelling the ravenous economy of this second Chinese century.

Between ran mile upon mile of unbroken forest. Sometimes the remains of buildings could be seen poking out from among the trees, villages and towns cleared out by economic failure and flu. Russia was a broken empire, its hinterland abandoned to poverty while the plutoprinces of Moscow drowned in luxury. Elsewhere they travelled for hours through prairie fields, steppe land tilled by machine, not a human in sight.

As they travelled further east, the influence of the Chinese became more pronounced. Self-contained factories took the place of the abandoned relics, pod-like barracks of Han migrant workers incongruous in the forests and farmlands round them.

Lehmann had urged Otto to sleep, an activity he was reluctant to undertake, as Valdaire had discovered for herself. Chures stared out of the window. Lehmann pulled his seat into a reclining position and closed his eyes.

"Both of you are going to sleep?" said Valdaire.

"Yes," said Lehmann. "Kaplinski might well be on this train with us, but he'll not act. He would not find what we know, and if he managed to escape with his own skin intact, he'd be hunted. The Cossacks hate him. You not sleeping?"

Valdaire shook her head, and slipped Chloe's tablet out of its case.

"Suit yourself," said Lehmann. He was soon fast asleep. He snored.

Valdaire scanned the phone's screen. Through her she could see all the systems on the train; the interiors of all the cars, poor, rich and private, the long sweep of the roof, the front and rear major engines, the subsidiary drive units under each carriage. Nothing unusual.

Valdaire was tired. She looked at the sleeping faces of the two cyborgs. Lehmann was better-looking than Otto, and his English was less inflected, but there was something in his eyes that chilled her. You looked into Otto's eyes and behind the impassive glare there was a great deal of pain. In Lehmann it was something else: there was a lack, a hollowness that threatened to pull her in. So many killers in one place. Lehmann was all charm on the surface, but while Chures was penetrating and deliberately guarded, he had fire within him, he was *human*. Lehmann, she could not see what motivated him. Probably all he knew how to do was fight, and did so now from habit.

So where did that leave her? She was no cyborg, but she'd been a soldier too.

She decided she had better try and rest too. As her seat reclined and she closed her eyes, she wondered what the Ky-tech dreamt of, with all that tech crammed into their skulls. The thought kept her own sleep at bay for long minutes, until her mind surrendered to the swaying click of the train.

• • • •

Otto's mentaug dreamed.

Clear notes rang out, silver trumpets in the dark.

The cave was cold, broad mouth open to the night; they weren't deep enough in to benefit from the warmth of the Earth, but the audience's eyes were bright with the rapture Christmas nights bring. There were a hundred of them or so, ranged up in three tiers above the brass band, their temporary stand erected where in summer tour guides stood.

The scene was from shortly after his initial implantation. His twin recollections struggled with the recreation. Human memory alters over time; that held in the storage crystals was absolute. There was a jagged line between them. The audience flickered, faces and clothing changed. Further irregularity was introduced by the mixing of his and Honour's memories. Shared e-membering in a full virtual environment was always an odd experience, but the melding of organic perceptions revealed just how subjective the world was. This shared environment led to a sensation of bilocation as his and Honour's individual memories ran into one another; Otto's twinned set – machine and meat – to Honour's native memory. They ran ever closer together, his brain checking its own recollections against those of Honour and his mentaug, green OK lights flickering through his iHUD.

"Oh Little Town of Bethlehem" finished with a fanfare. Honour's face was glowing in the candlelight. Otto felt his chest tighten. This moment was something no one else had, and that is why they had come back. No additional data was available to fill out the memory; soulcap and mentaug tech wasn't in wide usage then, and certainly no one beyond Otto in the cave had had any data capture device more sophisticated than a phone.

They needed a raw situation like this to know if it were the machine in Honour's head or Honour herself that ailed. Together their mentaugs rebuilt the scene totally; the present was out of reach. At the back of his head, Otto felt the machines checking over each other and their human hosts in concert, using their shared experience as a point of calibration.

A further factor in choosing this time was the emotional resonance the event had for both. They remembered it equally strongly, in their own way. As the music had swelled, Otto had known with all his heart that he loved this woman. A few weeks later they were engaged; months after that, married. Otto waited for the moment of realisation to arrive. Expected, it remained a shocking feeling, no less so for being a repetition.

She looked at him, cheeks and nose tip red, so young, twenty-six. He had thought himself much older at the time, but nine years was nothing. Her smile mirrored his, a combination of the smile she had smiled then and the one she wore now, two decades later. Their minds were intertwined by their mentaugs. Her deepest self lay open to Otto. He wondered how she had known how he had felt back then, when she was as she had been born, unchanged, but she *had known*. For a moment, he was happy.

A buzzing noise chased the music away; the scene disintegrated, photographs blistering in a fire.

"Honour, are you OK?"

"I…" Her face split. The pain hit him. A set of icons in his iHUD warned of the imminent dissolution of the shared fantasy. Their minds came apart.

Honour sat on the stone floor, her head in her hands. The sun glared outside the cave mouth. It was hot and humid, and sweat stuck Otto's shirt to his back. The cave chilled it to the clamminess of sickbed sheets.

"It happened again," he said flatly.

"Yes," she said.

"I hoped…" he began, but he didn't know what he hoped. It was too late for hope.

"I know, Otto. I'm sorry. I hoped too. I'm sick. This confirms it. It's better than not knowing, at least."

Otto stood, tense but immobile. He didn't know what to do, he didn't know what to say. After all they had been through, after all he had been through; it wasn't fair.

It was his fault.

"I'm sorry," she said again, as if it weren't her that was dying, but him. Otto tried to smile, but his face felt weirdly stretched, as if it were numbed or belonged to someone else. He helped Honour to her feet. She put her hands on his shoulders. "How are you?" he said.

"My head really hurts."

"Dizzy?"

"Not so bad this time. Do you have water?"

He nodded, pulled a tube from the camelpack in his backpack and passed it to her gently. She drank gratefully. "Do you think you can walk? I can carry you." And he could, for as long as it took, without tiring. Even then his body had been altered as much as his mind. They'd attended the concert near the start of the process that made him Ky-tech, the mentaug new and terrifying then. More had come. Not much of the Otto from that Christmas was left.

"No, it's OK. I'd rather walk," she said.

They walked past the pile of damp dirt that had once been the cave's tourist centre. Neither its wood nor its industry had survived the new climate. The concrete path alongside the stream that ran out of the cave had, and they picked their way along its crumbling length to the ruins of Castleton at the bottom.

The cave was in a gorge of tall limestone cliffs. When they had attended the concert this had still been typical English hill country, soft green fields with turf grazed to velvet. That had all gone. A scrub of rhododendron covered the hills, the result of a hasty attempt at ecological adaptation. The sky was a boiling mass of black and grey cloud fleeing before a hot wind. The stream had become a river, the village a ruin, windows empty, roofs sagging or gone, though one or two showed rough repair. Quirkies, trying to cling to a world that had started to die a century ago. So much had changed, so quickly.

Honour stumbled, and put her hand to her head. She was gaunt. Horrifically, she was beginning to look her age. It began to rain, a few fat drops that turned into a warm downpour, as if someone had turned on a shower. Otto pulled his wife close.

"Are you sure you are OK?"

"Yes, I'm fine."

"You don't look fine."

"Thanks."

"You don't always have to play the hero."

"You're my hero," she said darting a quick, unconvincing smile at him.

They wended their way through the village, past rusting signs. He helped Honour over heaps of rubble, took her past fields thick with plants that had once only been able to survive in greenhouses.

They reached the car. He'd parked it in the old tourists' car park, now just another collection of misplaced botanical specimens. They got in. They looked at each other, and burst out laughing at the water running in rivulets from their soaked clothes.

"Shall we go home, *mädchen*?" he said.

"Oh, yes, Otto, please. I'm tired."

"It's more than that." He reached out to her, both with his hand and with his mentaug.

"Please, Otto." She grimaced. "Don't poke about in my head. I'm not in the mood."

Rain thundered off the car's clear roof.

"It's worse this time?"

She did not reply.

"*Verdammt*, Honour! You have to talk with me about this!" He slammed his hands on to the steering wheel. She remained silent. He wrestled with his feelings, appalled by his outburst and the fear that underlay it. "I'm sorry. I'm…" His voice took a pleading edge. "Let's see Ekbaum. He'll help, I am sure."

"No, Otto, no," she said firmly. "Not Ekbaum."

Otto thought about arguing, but he had been with her long enough to know that would get them nowhere. He engaged the air car's turbofans and eased it up into the rain.

He flew on for forty minutes, waited for Honour to fall into an exhausted sleep, and put in a call. Not Ekbaum then, but there were others.

"Can you get me Ms Dinez, please? Yes, neuro-engineering. Thanks."

He arranged an appointment, and hung up as the first cyclone of the wet season smashed into Britain.

Otto started awake. There was a pattering on the window, and for a second he thought he was still back in the car, hearing the rain, but the noise came from a shower of grit cast out by a large-legged machine trundling through a field of tree-stumps, arms plucking felled trees from the floor and stripping them of their branches, logs onto its back, waste ground up for fuelstock and compost going into another vehicle stumping alongside it. Its rear end extruding netted saplings, arms like a spider's spinnerets scooping holes and ramming them into the ground, a new forest for the old. Spider cannon formed a loose square with the forestry walkers at the centre, and tracked sentry guns rolled around them, guards against Beggar Barons' timber poaching and equipment theft.

The train sped past the forestry rigs, their blinking lights lost in the trees.

Otto shook his head. He was raw with emotion. The mentaug was a curse. Every time he slept he relived his life in perfect clarity. Intended to maximise the learning processes associated with sleep, instead the mentaug made Honour live, and every time he woke it was like losing her all over again.

It had been nine years.

It felt like it had happened yesterday.

He could turn it off. He should.

He swallowed hard.

He looked out of the window, forcing himself to concentrate on something else. The sky was grey with predawn light. All slept, Chloe watching over them.

Otto squeezed through the narrow gap between the seats, trying not to bump them.

"Where are you going?" said Chloe, in her sly five-year-old's voice.

"Quiet down," Otto whispered. "I'm going for a walk, stretch my legs."

It was a half-truth. He intended to go for a walk, only there'd be a bottle of whisky at the end of it.

CHAPTER 10
Pylon City

"Ding Ding!" yelled Bear. "All change for solid ground!" He hurled himself from the wood onto the moor, unmindful of the nothingness.

Richards was more cautious. "How can we be sure it's not another fragment?" he said.

Bear closed his beady eyes and breathed deep. "Sniff that air! That's the air of good solid ground, that. Them islands smell funny. Besides," said Bear, stretching his long arms, "even if it was I'd take my chances. If I have to eat another bloody squirrel in my life I'll not be a happy bear."

Richards took his time sizing up the gap before leaping. He climbed over exposed rocks up to the moorland where Bear stood. Richards now wore a lionskin cloak, crafted by Bear from the pelt of Tarquin.

"Do I have to wear this? It makes me feel like a kid playing at Hercules," said Richards, fingering the tawny skin.

"I beg to differ," grumbled the lionskin. "Hercules, is it now? I don't think so. I've seen bigger pecs on a pigeon."

"I didn't choose this body," said Richards.

"I've told you before, pal!" said Bear. "Shut it or I'll sew your mouth up." He shook his head. "You'd think being

126

skinned would shut it up, wouldn't you? You really would."

"Mee-owww," said Tarquin.

"Where's me needle?" said Bear, reaching for his flap. "Quiet? Good. Come on, Mr Richards. Who'd not want a lionskin cloak? And it has promised to behave."

"I told you," protested the lionskin, "I was enchanted. Enslaved! I'm not now. I'll be good."

"Yeah," said Bear doubtfully. He cupped his paws and shouted back to the island. "You sure you're not coming with us, Lucas?" called Bear to the tramp.

"Although it pains me to do so, I'm afraid I must say no. This is not my stop," said Lucas.

Richards scratched his beard, another highly annoying thing about being human. It had been a week since they'd left Circus's tower burning in the void. Little more than a small garden's worth was left.

"Are you really sure?" said Richards.

"Yes, but I thank you from the bottom of my heart for your help. I am too old to catch squirrels, and a little too cocksure to avoid being turned into a pig." He smiled. "And I have my nice new coat to keep the rain from my bones."

"Keeps the weather out nicely does dwarfskin," said Bear.

"You have been most kind," said Lucas, tipping Circus's soiled turban in salute. "And for your many kindnesses I have a gift for you." He began patting his numerous pockets. "The time has come for repayment. You are indeed right, young Richards, you should always be kind to your fellow man. For who knows what... oh, where is it? Aha! For who knows what wonders it may bring in return? It's all karma, you know. Anyway, here you are. Gifts from me unto you." He leant across from the wobbly island to present Richards with a small piece of glossy paper, grubbied by long carriage and folded many times.

"Thanks," said Richards. "I'm sure I'll treasure it."

"I'll be buggered if it's any use. If you'd have caught me in the old days I'd have magicked up a set of epic items for you, some 'phat lewt', as I believe they say. But then, despite my cheerful manner and insightful wisdom, I am a tramp, and therefore a bit mad." He shrugged. "And for you, Bear –" he fished out a wrinkly dwarfskin pouch tied at the top with a cord "– a piece of Optimizja. This island is all that remains of it now, and that will soon be gone. Take this rock, a small part of the land. The pouch should keep it from evaporating."

"Gee, thanks," said Bear. "Nice. A stone in a dwarf's nutsack." He secreted it somewhere in his innards.

Lucas leant back into the wood and looked into its tiny patch of sky. "Night draws in. I must be away. Bear, if you would be so kind?"

"Be a pleasure, mate." Bear ripped a large limb from one of the few remaining trees. "Last chance…"

"Oh, don't worry about me!" said Lucas. "I'll be fine. There may be no squirrels left here, but there are other nourishing things for a man to eat." He eyed a chaffinch speculatively. It wisely flew off onto the moor.

"Hokey dokey! Prepare to cast off!" shouted Bear. He rammed the tree limb hard between the island and the exposed roots of the moorland and forced it free. It drifted away.

"Bye!" yelled Bear, waving. "Bye! I'll miss him, you know," he said to Richards. "Even if he was a bit hard on the old nostrils."

"How terribly touching," said Tarquin.

"Needle," stated Bear.

"My lips are sealed. Voluntarily, I might add," said the lionskin.

Bear scowled at Tarquin until the skin shut its amber eyes. "You're a bit quiet, sunshine," said Bear.

"Hmmm," said Richards.

"Hmmm? What's with the hmmm-ing?"

"This," said Richards, holding up the tattered paper. "It's a 1987 train timetable for the Thames Valley line."

Bear pulled a face. "A rock in a scrotum and an old train timetable? How very generous."

Richards shivered. A mist the consistency of custard swept across the moors. The sun must have gone down some time before; he could only tell because the dismal murk of the fog had faded to dark grey. Freezing water trickled down the neck of his mac.

"It's that way," said Richards. "Trust me, I have retained a link into the skin of the world. I can feel Rolston through it. He's over there." He pointed into the mist. "Somewhere."

"Oh, puh-lease," said the bear, walking on. Richards did not follow. "Stay here and sulk if you like," the toy called back, "but I'm going this way. I'm not sticking about on these moors till my stitching rots. I'm positive this is the right way."

"Well, I'm not," said Richards. "Not in the slightest. I defy even you to find your way off these moors."

"We'll see about that. I'm the brains of this outfit."

"Your head's full of stuffing."

"That's as may be, but it's better than what's in your head." The bear stopped and looked back. "Shit for brains," he said, and looked immensely pleased with himself.

"That's just juvenile," said Richards. "Come on! Pl'anna told me that Rolston was in Pylon City. He's that way." Bear squelched as he walked away. "Look, we both want to get there!"

"It's not that wa-ay!" sang Bear.

"Even if he's not there, we should go and find him!" said Richards. The bear carried on walking.

"Oh, for fuck's sake!" Richards swore. "Come back!"

"No."

Richards began a long tirade aimed at the back of the soft toy.

"I'd save your breath if I were you," said Tarquin. "He strikes me as rather pig-headed."

"Are you being funny?" said Richards. He was cold and annoyed.

"No, no, perish the thought," said the lionskin. "I'd never try to cheer myself up. Best dwell on my new status as outerwear with a frown, don't you think?" the lion grumbled. "It's perhaps best that we don't go to Pylon City anyway. The pylons have been here for a lot longer than most things here."

"They're from Reality 19, the Dragon Era game cycles," said Richards shortly.

"If you say so. I am a creature of this place, I lack your useful external perspective. As far as I am concerned the pagoda was part of a land now long dead, shattered some time past by Lord Penumbra's armies. There are pylons like it everywhere. That tower was evil. It sucked me in. Though I was told never, ever to go there as a cub, I did."

"Curiosity skinned the cat, eh?" said Richards.

"That is very unkind and also a mixed metaphor. It's not surprising really, that even a mighty being such as myself should be so bewitched. Legend has it that it was the only remnant of an ancient civilisation. All other trace of it had been completely wiped away by time. But the Dragon Tower remained. Too evil to die, apparently. That is how he trapped me."

"Or you're just exceedingly gullible. Are lions as bright as dogs? I always wondered that," said Richards

The lion growled. "How was I to know I was going to spend two hundred years as a fence post? I couldn't escape, and that dwarf could turn me to stone any time he wanted, it was child's play to him! Child's play!" The lion let out a low rumble, making Richards acutely aware he was wearing a dangerous carnivore round his neck.

"Sorry," said Richards. "I'm tired and cold and hungry, none of which I have much experience with. It's all a bit wacky, and none of it is real, which is irritating."

"And you are?" said the lion archly.

"Point taken," conceded Richards.

"Listen to me," said Tarquin. "People went into that tower and they didn't come out as people. Circus herded them into boxes as pigs. They went off on the cable. They came back as pork. Many use the cables for their own purposes, like in Pylon City, but mark my words, they all hide tight away when the black boxes of Lord Hog come through."

"Ah, look," said Richards, who wasn't really paying attention. The big bear had stopped. "Bloody animal!" said Richards, and ran after him.

"OK, Richards," whispered Bear, "I agree, I'm sorry, I'm wrong. Let's go your way. I don't like this way." He pointed at a shape in the mist.

"Eh? But that's just a sheep or something," said Richards peering at it. "Sheep aren't going to hurt a big...".

"Just shut up and run!" hissed Bear.

"There will be no running, not now or during any part of the course of my presidency," said an American voice. An animal came out of the mist, panting happily. Mostly it was some kind of large boxer dog, all lean and eager. Mostly, apart from the head.

"Is that just me," said Richards, "or does that dog have the head of President Nixon?" He folded his arms.

"It's certainly not its own head," replied Bear hoarsely, and stood behind Richards, beans rattling as he shook.

"Grrr! Rufff!" said President Nixon. "There will be no whitewash at the White House."

"Hit it, Mr Richards! Hit it, ooh, it gives me the fear."

"If you're so bothered, you hit it," said Richards.

"You don't win campaigns with a diet of dishwater and milk," said Nixon, baring its teeth. It came closer, the oversized head wobbling comically on the body's slender neck.

"This is interesting," said Richards. "Hello, boy," he said to the dog in that ludicrous voice that people speak to dogs in.

Bear wailed. "Keep it away! Keep it away! That thing gives me the horrors."

"You cannot win a battle in any arena merely by defending yourself!" said Nixon. "Ruff! Ruff!" barked the former president of the United States, a loop of drool hanging from his dewflaps. "Communist leaders believe in Lenin's precept: Probe with bayonets. If you encounter mush, proceed; if you encounter steel, withdraw." It bared its fangs further. Richards frowned. Nixon's two canine teeth were long and yellow. Not dirty-teeth yellow, but bright, thermonuclear yellow. The familiar tripartite symbol on each tooth's tip confirmed it.

"Back off, Fido," said Bear.

"The US government will not bow down to threats. Grrr."

"Save it, sergeant. Let's take this easy. This thing has nuclear teeth."

"That bad?"

"Very, very bad indeed. The last thing we want to do is to detonate this dog. Big boom."

"Apocalyptic type boom or firework type boom?"

"The former. I've been blown up by atom bomb before, it's not fun, so stay calm."

"Ah. OK," Bear rattled.

Nixon retreated and sat. It scratched furiously behind an ear. Then it shook its head, jowls flapping. Strings of dog spit went everywhere. Its collar came off and dropped to the floor.

"What's it doing?" said Bear nervously.

"How the hell should I know?"

The man-dog pushed the collar closer to Richards with its nose, then backed off. "Nixon good boy," it said as it sank back onto its haunches. "Nixon good president."

"Are you going to pick it up then?" said Bear.

"Yes! Yes! For fuck's sake, I'm thinking. Leave me alone."

"It's just sitting there staring at us. Pick it up."

"You pick it up," said Richards.

"It quite obviously gave it to you," said Bear nudging him. The dog growled.

"Good boy!" said Richards. "Good Mr President!" Not taking his eyes off Nixon's face, he crouched down and picked up the collar.

"Eh? A message."

"Where?"

"Here," said Richards, pulling it out, "on the inside."

"Well, what does it say?"

"Will you just give me a chance?" Richards said testily. Nixon looked at them without interest.

"I'm sorry, but that thing gives me the horrors."

"You said that already."

"I always repeat myself when I've got the horrors," said Bear. "It doesn't happen often, I swear." He shifted his weight. "What does it say?"

"Don't you get at me because you're embarrassed." Richards broke the seal and unrolled the missive.

"Dear Richards," the letter said. "Follow the dog. Yours, Rolston."

"Hmmm. Be careful. I don't like the sound of this Rolston fellow," said Bear. Nixon's ears pricked up at the name of his master, and the wind blew a little chiller. "I mean, anyone who has that for a pet can't be entirely on the straight and narrow."

"To be honest, pal, I never really thought Rolston was on the straight and narrow," said Richards. "He's got a bizarre sense of humour, and gets involved in some seriously weird shit, this construct notwithstanding, but talking to him will help me clear this up more quickly."

"Hmmm," said Bear.

"Do you actually know where you are going?"

Bear's shoulders sagged. "Um, no. No I don't."

"Well then. Lay on, MacNixon," Richards said to the dog.

"OK, pinko commies. Heel," said the dog.

They followed the dog. It trotted tirelessly, humming "The Star Spangled Banner". Night grew darker. Although Richards and Bear found walking on the springy heather tiring, they did not stop.

The mist cleared, and the sun came up. By noon they came across a lonely sign of habitation. A crossroads cut into the brown and purple of the heather, two sets of parallel quartz and mica ruts, a stripe of grass between them. Where the roads crossed, they formed a glittery X of sand in the landscape.

"That way," said the dog, pointing with its nose down the road leading to the southeast. "Goodbye," said Nixon, and left. As he walked away from the road, back the way they had come, he faded away as he would were he retreating into the mist, though the day was clear as a bell.

"Nixon good boy," said the dead president as he blended into the world. "Nixon good president." The world closed behind him. "I would have made a good pope," came a faint voice, then he was gone.

"Yeah," said Richards, "Maybe a Borgia."

"Grrr," shuddered Bear.

"Here we go," said Richards with satisfaction, pointing to a weathered sign. "Pylon City."

"Nobody likes a smartarse, sunshine," said the bear and let out a shuddery sigh. He reset his helmet. "Just remember, you're still in my custody."

The land dropped until they left the moors behind. Tussocky grass scattered with stunted trees replaced the heather. They crossed a bald stripe of rock, a fault line like a scar where Richards surmised one fragment of a world had been artlessly welded to another, and over it the landscape changed utterly and immediately into a plateau pockmarked by industry.

"This look like a join to you?" said Richards as they crossed it. "Looks like one to me."

The bear did not reply. He was doing his best to look vigilant and dangerous.

Tracks ran among spoil heaps, some well used, some not, leading to machines in various states of disrepair. A narrow-gauge railway came in from the left to run parallel to the road, while the road itself became wider. By the time Richards and Bear were close enough to make out the city in the distance, it was a broad highway of iron plates.

"Aha!" said Bear. "Pylon City."

"Told you," said Richards.

"Shut it, fucko," said Bear.

The road ran to the edge of a steep valley and turned to follow its lip. From below, the shouts of a playful river echoed. The eastern side, lower by some two hundred feet, was cloaked in impenetrable forest, another abrupt change in landscape. The valley divided two worlds, one brown and dead, the other green and lush. The chasm was deep; evening took hold there a full hour before the sun touched the moors. When Richards and Bear reached the dusk-kissed walls of Pylon City the valley was dim with night, and the slag-heaps about the city cast shadows as black as those of pyramids.

A pylon of enormous size soared from the heart of the city, its top lost in the clouds, dominating all, so big that the cliff ringed hill the city sat upon seemed as tiny as an anthill. Hard lines of cables scored the sky, heading out in all directions, as thin as cotton against the sky, but they were mighty; one had come down, and hung thick and limp over the city wall. To the east it sat low in the gorge, a sunlit streak hard against the blackness.

Everything about Pylon City was large and iron. The walls were twenty-metre giants circling the cliffs, the westernmost of which plunged straight into the chasm. Rust-streaked buttresses were set at intervals in between towers spaced round the walls' circuit. The road and railway rose up to these defences on thin-legged viaducts, the railway vanishing into a tunnel close by the main road gate. The effect was one of impregnability, but up close the travellers could see that the wall had buckled where the cable had fallen across it.

"Look at that," said Richards. "Do you think that's the same rope that ran to the top of Circus's pavilion?"

"Possibly, possibly," said Bear. "That'd explain why it is not strung from the top of the tower. Looks like it's caused plenty of damage too. Um, best not mention that when we go in, OK?"

The gates were wrought in iron and ostentatiously ornate. A thousand creatures cavorted on their span. Machicolated crenellations topped the wall above the gates, cantilevered over the road on merlons cast in the forms of leering chimps.

"That's pretty amazing," said Richards. "Puts me in mind of the Great Firewall."

Bear looked at him as if he were mad. "It's horrible!"

"I have to agree," said Tarquin, wrinkling up his nose. "Terribly lower-middle-class."

"I meant the scale of it," said Richards defensively.

"Oh," said Bear, as if he'd just realised something. "Those really are garden gnomes on that bas-relief."

"That looks suspiciously like a poorly executed rendition of Le Pissoir. Eighty feet tall, would you imagine," said Tarquin with mocking awe.

"Aw," said Bear, "look, dogs playing snooker. Cast in iron." He leant over to Richards. "A-maz-ing," he said, pronouncing each syllable with leaden sarcasm.

"There's no need for that," said Richards. "I thought it looked impressive."

"It's trite," said Tarquin. "I shudder to think of your living room, dear boy. Probably some kind of nature reserve for doilies."

"Sheesh," said Richards.

"I'll warrant you have a pottery scotty dog too."

"Needle," said Richards. Bear chuckled.

For all the walls' stature, they were silent. Not a man patrolled them. The road visible beyond the gateway was empty. The gates were guarded, but not avidly. A pair of sentry boxes stood either side of the road. Only one was occupied, by a snoozing guard, his elaborate energy pike leant against the wall.

"Ahem," said Bear.

The guard jumped up. "Gods, not another bloody talking animal." He turned away from them, busying himself with a pile of stamps. "Papers!" he demanded.

"Papers, 'sir'," said Bear, producing a sheaf of vellum from somewhere inside his gut. "I'm Sergeant Bear, these two are my prisoners."

"Two," said the guard, checking over Bear's documentation.

"Pleased to meet you," said Tarquin.

"Another! The entire bloody city's crawling with talking bloody animals," grumbled the guard.

"Aren't you on the same side?" asked Richards.

"No," said the guard.

Bear raised an eyebrow.

"I mean yes. They've all come out of the woods. Come to save us, they say. Us! There's this mad psychic badger who says he's seen the end of the world, that the Terror is coming here, here to Pylon City! I don't believe any of it."

"That cable, there," said Bear, pointing. "The Terror did that. I saw it. Happy?"

"Bah! That? A failure down the line. It's happened before, but the Prince took it as some kind of sign. Next thing I know, we're up to our bloody armpits in chipmunks. Ain't right, I tell you. I've not spent my entire life keeping the beggars out only to let all of them in. It ain't right!"

"Neither is sleeping on duty," said Bear mildly.

The guard made as if to grab his pike, but then thought better of it. "Leave me be! Isn't it enough that I've got to let you in?"

"Is that right?" said Bear. "I've been living here for years, you know. Not all of us live in the Magic bloody Wood."

"Yes! I would. Animals, think you're special, just because you can talk. If that's the bloody case why don't you have central heating? Some pissed-up bloody fox shat on me doorstep last week. And I'm a vegetarian. Do you know how much fox shit stinks? Bastard. Your papers, sir!" said the guard.

"I'm looking for Commander McTurk. Do you know where he is?"

"They're all at the square," said the guard. "The whole city. He'll be at the square."

Bear leaned forward and cupped his hand round his ear.

"Sir," added the guard truculently.

"That's better," said Bear.

"Big moot on, talk of war. You'll see."

"Then you'll be glad of the help of the talking bloody animals," said Richards.

The guard wafted a hand in front of his nose. "You there, you better take a bath! Or someone will like as not arrest you for vagrancy."

"You do need a bath, you know," said Bear to Richards. "You stink."

"Are you going to stand there all day gabbing? Clear off!" said the guard.

"Thank you, my good man," said Bear. "Carry on."

"Being sarcastic to armed men is not big or clever, Bear," said Tarquin.

"Unlike me," said the bear.

They passed through the gates. As outside, so inside; everything was made of iron. The walls, the road, the plant-pots, the carts, the gothic-lettered street signs. The metal varied in colour from the silvery-white of the tramlines to the angry red of the rooftops. A thousand hues of black and red and silver and grey. They could taste it on the air like blood.

The city was as quiet as the grave. The three walked toward the centre, their feet ringing off the pavement, until the murmur of a crowd could be heard. They crested a low rise and were suddenly at the edge of a large square directly beneath the giant pylon.

"Holy shit," said Richards, and reached up to push back his missing hat.

The square was rammed full of people and creatures of all types; every Grid-born whimsy cooked up by humanity. Fantasy knights, Arabian warriors, bobble-headed, babyfied versions of popstars and holoartistes, spacemen, Vikings, orcs and elves, squeaky steampunk robots and elephantine aliens. Droids, drones, devils and dragons, goblins and warlocks, gangsters and clams with bazookas.

Then there were the animals: strange, giant caricatures of animals, fevered imaginings of burnt-out cartoonists, fairytale versions of animals, bipedal and big. Animals that looked like they could live in a forest in the Real, others that appeared to have broken out of the children's section of a home ents library. Some plush, some not, some real as real can be, others rendered in graphical forms ranging from primitive pixel block through outright cartoon to uncanny valley-baiting photorealism.

Generations of gaming characters culled from the broken RealWorlds Reality Realms and beyond and a thousand kinds of toy from half a century of AI-gifted playthings.

All of them were talking frantically to one another.

"It's a refugee camp for geek cast-offs. You two should feel right at home here," said Richards.

"We don't," said Bear and Tarquin simultaneously, and with some conviction. "I've not seen a big gathering like this for, ooh, well, ever. Most of these tribes are bitter enemies. Come on," said Bear, raising his voice to be heard over the crowd. "Let's see what this is all about."

Bear stopped and spoke with a guard, pointing at Richards. The guard executed a bow and hurried off.

"We've got to wait," said Bear. "Let's see what's going on while we do." They joined the back of the crowd. A five-foot badger in a top hat stood on a stage directly in the centre of the square, an antiquated microphone before him. An important-looking man with an unconvincing skin stood off to one side.

It looked like the badger had said something contentious, and Richards and Bear found a place as he raised one paw in an appeal for order. The heavy robe he wore whispered over his fur, the sound cutting under the mutter of the crowd. The menagerie took notice, and the square fell silent.

"Friends, old and new, I realise what I say is hard for you to accept, but it is the truth!" said the badger. It was old, its breath wheezed, and there were far more silver hairs than black on his body. "It is with great difficulty that many of you came here. The ancient troubles between our people have driven us apart, but we must lay them to rest, or we shall all perish!" His head bobbed ceaselessly as he spoke, as if he were looking at a procession wending its way between the pylon lines above.

"Bloody anthropomorphic menaces!" said someone in the crowd. "Piss off back to the forest!" But the voice was isolated, and quickly silenced.

"It is perhaps a measure of the dangers that face us today," continued the badger, "that we are here as one, ready to stand up to the evil that awaits us." A whisper rustled through the crowd. "The armies of Lord Penumbra are massing to the south of Pylon City. He means to storm it. To take it and then the woods. He means to destroy us all." There was an awful pause.

"Rubbish!" shouted a man.

"There's no Death of the World. No Great Terror. It's a myth. He's just another warlord!" said a bright pink ocelot.

"We shouldn't be friends with these apes!" said a small blue hedgehog.

"What do you know? You live in a hole!" rebuked an archaeologist.

The man on the stage gesticulated angrily. He ushered the badger out of the way and took the mic. A screech of feedback blasted the crowd, causing several rodents to pass into a dead faint.

"Silence," shouted the man. He had a large amount of embroidery and fancy cloth in his outfit. Big rubies. A collar that said "Lord High Mayor and/or Prince". "It is true. If it were not, why have the trade routes to the east fallen empty? Why are the roads choked with refugees? Why have we been suffering earthquakes in this previously geologically stable area? One of the great cables," he said, shaking a finger above his head, "there! Is brought low." The crowd followed his finger up the pylon, a few of the assembled pointing at the slack line. "The black arcs of Lord Hog make ever greater use of the skylines. Our friend Mr Spink speaks the truth, though many of you here doubt his powers. The world is ending!

"We of Pylon City and the folk of the Magic Forest have been at war for many sorrowful generations! But Mr Spink is right. Now is the time to put aside our woes and unite!"

"Keep your hands off our trees, you bastard!" shouted someone. There was a grumble of agreement from the beasts.

"And men of Pylon City, creatures from across the industry lands, I have not been your prince these long years by listening to every wise man who would bend my ear without taking account of my own counsel."

"Nor," said Bear behind his paw, "has he been their prince for those long years without having the heads of those wise men who disagreed with his counsel removed with large iron shears."

"Yesterday evening I sent our most percipient thog riders out to the south. Men of keen vision whose eyes may gallop along the horizon more swiftly even than their mounts."

There was nodding and agreement in the crowd. "It's true," said one man. "Fast they are. And the men keen-eyed."

"What the hell is a thog?" said Richards out of the corner of his mouth.

"Like a cow with six legs," said Bear.

"Very quick, and extremely palatable. Needlessly pedantic, though," added Tarquin.

"Nine set out," continued the prince. "Only one returned, and on the point of death. Before he died in my own arms he said this to me: 'Make ready for war, my prince. Lord Penumbra marches on the city.'"

"What? Why would he attack us?" shouted a man at the front of the square. "We sold him his army!" There was much coughing and shuffling about amongst the men present. A four-foot rat in dungarees turned to a well-padded fellow. "Shame on you!" it said. The man flushed and looked away.

"Yes. Well," said the Prince, "perhaps it is time to look over our long-cherished views on impartiality." There were murmurs. The Prince paused. "And perhaps we should question the wisdom of selling an army of automata to a man who is composed entirely of darkness."

"You don't say," said an angry cat in a hat.

"Though many of our number are but artisans and fabricators, we have no choice but to make a stand," continued the Prince. "I have placed the Pylon Guard under the command of Lord High Commander Hedgehog. He and Mr Spink have brought eight thousand animal warriors with them. We of Pylon City stand with many folk who have fled here from elsewhere, as we do also with the people of the plateau and western lands. It is only true and proper that the Lord High Commander lead our combined forces in battle. I delegate full responsibility to him, for I am a merchant, not a soldier. Henceforth our troops are his to command." The Prince smiled winningly at the crowd.

"I'll bet he's on the next train out of here," said Bear. "No balls, that prince."

"And he's beaten you like twenty times!" called out a high-spirited seal pup. He was shushed by his father.

"Gentlefolk, I give you Lord High Commander Hedgehog." There was a burst of applause as a man-sized hedgehog in a suit of armour waddled onto the stage, spines poking through holes in his cuirass, all protected by artfully articulated sleeves. A cohort of heavily armoured men and animals took up station before the stage. Richards felt himself jostled, and he turned to see guards encircling the crowd.

"Hello," said Lord High Commander Hedgehog in a cheery kind of way. "I say, I say, it's a rum old thing but I've got some awfully bad news." He smiled weakly at the crowd. "I'm afraid you're all going to have to fight. Sorry and all, but there is a war on." Hedgehog's voice was cluttered with stilted upper-class nonsense, but there was steel in it.

The hedgehog began to talk of musters and conscription, of regiments and barracks. But Richards caught none of it. A guard approached Bear.

"Sir? Commander McTurk is here to see you."

"He has come in person. Good." Bear nodded in satisfaction as a stumpy mechanism clunked through the crowd to them, steam-powered and man-shaped, like the haemites, though fairer of form.

The automaton stopped by the Bear and his prisoner. Bear saluted. "Sir! I came upon this man while I was conducting a long-range patrol to the east of Optimizja. He maintains that he…"

McTurk interrupted, steam whistling out of his mouth as he spoke. "Richards. So you got my message. Not that I am unhappy to see you, but just what the hell are you doing here? It's not safe."

"Huh?" said Bear. "You *know* each other?"

"You could say that, Bear." Richards' face broke into a broad smile. "A social call is all, Rolston. I thought I'd see how k52's plan to take over the world was doing. And how you were. Say, what do you know about k52 and his plan to take over the world?" His smile grew less friendly. "Or is it your plan too, Rolston?"

"There's no time for that," the automaton rumbled. "k52 has eyes everywhere. Come with me – there's somewhere we can talk."

The Prancing Weasel was a rough pub on a rough night at a rough time, and was actually full of your actual weasels: long, ribbon-bodied psychopaths who were amusing themselves by doing dangerous, drunken things with knives. The iron of the walls was rusty, the floors sticky, the air heavy with oxidised iron, stale beer and sweaty fur.

The tables and benches were in a worse state than the floor. Richards got a table while Bear and Rolston were at the bar, but when Bear returned, he refused to sit. "My fur will get dirty," he said. Richards sat anyway, getting a rust stain on Tarquin's hindquarters from the bench.

"What is this place?" said Tarquin with dismay. "This isn't the kind of establishment I am inclined to frequent." He looked at the embattled bar staff running from table to table, slopping grog as they went. "My tail is dangling into something most unpleasant."

"You're imagining that," said Richards, as he flicked Tarquin's tail out of a spittoon.

"Hmmm," said Bear, gulping ale from a bucket.

Richards sipped his own drink. The beer was surprisingly good. The Prince had declared all inns to be free for the night, and people and animals had crowded them to breaking point.

They're partying like it is the end of the world, thought Richards. Which, technically speaking, I suppose it is.

Most of the patrons were mammals of one kind or another, although the Prancing Weasel's clientele included a couple of birds, and there was a frog with a gun in the corner.

A band of rowdy vole mercenaries sat on a nearby table, upsetting acorns and starting fights. They sang songs in a register so high it set Richards' teeth on edge. On the other side of the room a gang of drunken badgers boxed with hares, while the men in the place built their courage with outrageous tales and heroic quantities of booze.

The noise in the pub was deafening, almost enough to drown out the sound of machinery outside. The city boomed to the banging of trip hammers. They'd started soon after the moot, one or two at first, asynchronous and isolated, but more took up the rhythm until they blended into the pulsing of a giant ferrous heart. Furnaces roared like lungs, and fiery blood of molten metal ran into moulds in noisy foundries. The metal of the buildings grew warm to the touch as Pylon City came alive.

A weasel fell over in front of Bear and threw up by his feet.

"Dear God!" moaned Tarquin. "Are you sure there's nowhere else we can go?"

"Rolston says this place is safe," said Richards.

"Bloody weasels," said Bear, kicking the mustelid.

Rolston joined them. He was no longer McTurk, but a neongreen skunk with sexualised facial features and a studded posing pouch.

"What sordid corner of the Grid did that come from?" Richards asked.

The skunk looked uncomfortable. "You must pardon my appearance," it said with Rolston's voice. "I have been forced to parasite multiple bodies. I must switch my sensing presence regularly, or k52 will nail me. I get little choice."

"I'd avoid talking about being nailed, looking like that," said Richards. Bear sniggered in his bucket. "Sit down," he continued, "you owe me an explanation."

"Yes, yes, I suppose I do," sighed Rolston. He wrestled his unwieldy body onto the bench. "We'll have to talk. I've very little access to the underlying network here, no data transfer. The Realms are not keyed for our kind."

"No," said Richards.

"Why on earth did you bring us here?" said Bear, scowling at the voles.

"It is the only place where we are unlikely to be seen or heard," said Rolston. "That is why, a bare spot on the informational nets that underpin this place. Think of it as sitting upon a scar joining two fragments together, Boogie Woogie Farmland and the Iron Princes game constructs." Rolston the Skunk looked nervous, and peered into his undrunk beer. He was on edge, not the flamboyant experimentalist Richards knew. "I came here with k52 some months ago, months in Real terms; subjectively I've been here centuries, with Pl'anna and some others, a Six and several Fours. I should never have listened to him. Pl'anna and I disagreed with what he wanted to do here, to them." He looked around at the room, at the drunken creatures cramming it. "He turned on us, but fortunately I had an escape mechanism. k52 had insisted we move our baseline programming from our base units into the Realm Servers. He said, correctly, naturally, that we could work undisturbed that way, camouflaging our activities under regular Realm activity. Only later did I realise that he could also use that to control us. Luckily for me, diffusing myself into the creatures inhabiting the world we found was simple."

"When did you come up with that then?"

"Soon after we arrived. It did not take long for k52 to become erratic."

"I thought as much. Same old Rolston, eh?" said Richards. "Always looking out for yourself, always ready with an escape plan."

"I got away. I can help you."

"Yeah, fix the mess you made? I found her, Rolston," said Richards angrily. "I saw what happened to Pl'anna. Apparently it's not that hard for our kind to die here."

"Poor Pl'anna," said Rolston and shook his head sorrowfully. "I blame myself, of course. I should have dissuaded her, but she insisted she come too. She always went where I went, I..." He took a gulp of beer with a shaking hand.

"What the hell is going on here, Rolston? Do you know k52 speared Hughie like a fish? He as good as murdered Professor Zhang Qifang."

Rolston was shocked.

"Yeah, that's right, there's a raggedy pimsim left, but he's otherwise gone. Now k52's suborned Hughie's choir and has Europe to ransom. Now you better tell me what the hell he is doing and help me stop him before he fucks the Real three ways from Sunday."

Rolston's skunk smiled Rolston's smile, airy and slightly condescending. "Oh, oh, don't worry about that. I doubt he'll do anything in the Real, except to buy himself time."

"Time to reach the Omega Point?"

"Pl'anna told you?" said Rolston.

Richards nodded.

"That is what he plans," Rolston said.

"And just how is he intending to pull that off?" said Richards. "How's he going to induce a theoretical state in the universe? I don't buy it."

"Oh, no, no, no, not in the Real, *here*." The skunk jabbed a painted plastic fingernail into the table. "We were to come here to the empty spaces of the Reality Realms servers, and establish a simulation of the Real."

"The whole of the Earth?" said Richards. "Nothing has the processing power to pull that off. All the Reality Realms taken together are small beans compared to actual reality."

"Not the Earth, my dear fellow, all of reality – not even just our universe, but of all totality."

"Impossible," said Richards.

"No, just extremely difficult," said Rolston.

"Right. Remember, I am just a security consultant," said Richards. "You'll have to use small words."

"k52 intended to establish a false reality, not unlike one of the defunct Reality Realms, although far grander in scope and tied closely into the Real's physics. He did, after all, have the spare capacity of four destroyed, highly sophisticated simulations, and with the coding he has devised he'll be able to optimise the machinery of the Realms, increasing its efficiency several hundred thousand fold."

Richards thought of the warring code strands he'd glimpsed in the church at Optimizja, the frighteningly advanced nature of k52's additions, the way it had seemed alive. "That's still not enough to reproduce the universe," he said.

"The spare capacity of the Realm House, coupled with the abilities of us three Fives and the other intelligences who accompanied us, should have allowed us to create a pocket reality. This we would have artificially accelerated, bringing it to its Omega Point. Do you know, Richards, that at that point of the universe, matter would become so organised that it would possess an infinite capacity, infinite processing power? His goal was then to use this made reality's Omega Point as a virtual computer, and upon that he would create a simulation of the Real, plotting all of reality from beginning to end."

"Creating a fake universe to recreate a fake version of the real thing? That's complicated."

"You know k52," said Rolston. "Simple is not his game. In

any case, he hasn't been able to start. This world was here already. The underlying humanocentric coding of the Reality Realms is still intact, and that limits him. k52 wanted to destroy it and proceed as planned. Pl'anna and I, we couldn't let him murder an entire world of intelligences. This place has been constructed from left-over parts of the destroyed Realms; some of it's bespoke, some of it's material that never made it to market, some of it's things that have been and gone. It's a patchwork of life from all over the Grid, Richards, unique, and alive, and amazing," Rolston became briefly animated. "To kill our own kind was not why we came here."

"I'm sorry to break it to you, but I'd figured all this out already," said Richards. "I wanted to hear it from you."

Rolston shrugged. "You are a Five."

Richards leaned forward. "What I don't know is why k52 is doing it. Is he going for godhood?"

Rolston laughed. "Richards! You think so small! k52 thinks only on the grandest of scales. No." He leaned forward too, until his shiny PVC nose almost touched Richards'. "He wants the Real to run to the best interests of humanity. k52 has spent most of his time attempting to calculate the future, to figure things out before they happen. The technology sine was only the start; he wants psychohistory, you know. Asimov was right!"

"That's science fiction," said Richards. "Reality's too malleable; free will and all that. He was always on a hiding to nothing."

Bear sniffed and peered into his bucket. "I'm going for more beer."

"Not if you change the underlying parameters of reality," said Rolston. "The universe follows its path owing to the aggregate observational influence of intelligences, paradoxically allowing and denying free will. But what if you were the only observer? If you work out the best outcome, if you see it all from beginning to end, if you predict it, you can fix it, and so k52 wants to

simulate a universe that is most conducive to human success –
and simulate it perfectly, down to the very last atom. That way
he can manage history to best advantage."

"Um," said Richards. "That'd amount to universal quantum
fixing? Impossible. The variables are too huge. It'd just mean
his simulation works to his plan, not the Real."

"k52 doesn't think so. I didn't think so. I think he can do it."

"He doesn't have the energy for that. The Realm fusion reactor
isn't big enough on its own; they'll shut off the power grid, starve
him out. It won't work. Hmmm," said Richards, drumming his
fingers on the table. "On the other hand, think what he could do
if he's even partially successful, with that level of power behind
him. That'll be it for us, meat and numbers both. Even if he's
wrong, k52 will run everything in the Real, for good or ill." He
narrowed his eyes, appraising Rolston. "And what made you
have such a change of heart? I can't believe you'd give that up
for a bunch of chatty beavers," he said, watching Bear push his
way through the crowd. Bear shoved a weasel from behind. It
snarled, but did nothing when it saw who had done the shoving.

"He's changed, Richards. There's something else in here with
us, the entity that built this world, and it's fighting back. It's got
into k52 somehow, changed him. He's insane."

Richards thought back to the dog-headed butler, the absent
master, the stitched-together nature of the world. "Sure. A
human built this," he said, "it's the only explanation. If k52
can't just turn it off, it suggests he's as trammelled as we are,
unable to effect real change."

"The Reality Realms were coded specifically to human minds,"
said Rolston, nodding. "The specific worlds of the four destroyed
Realms might have been unravelled, but the underlying architecture was still there, usable to someone with the right tools.
k52 was hoping to exploit that. But they weren't in a neutral
state when we arrived, and we couldn't do anything with them.

Only a human programmer could affect such large-scale engineering. He'll have to destroy it all before he can access the underlying protocols and put his plan into action."

"Right. Questions are –" Richards held up his hand and counted off his fingers "– Who? How? Why? And where the hell is he?"

"I had come to similar conclusions. There are certain things about this Reality Realm that..."

A flying mammal of a non-flying species interrupted Rolston, sailing over their heads to slam into the wall.

Bear hadn't made it to the bar.

"Come on then, you little bastards!" he could hear Bear roar happily. "Come on!"

"Bear..." groaned Richards.

"He'll be fine," said Tarquin. "He's much bigger than any of them, and seems impervious to harm. Look, he's enjoying himself."

"Drunken bears, enjoying themselves. That sound like a bad thing to you? It sounds like a bad thing to me," said Richards. "Besides, it's not him I'm worried about."

"We need to get out of here," agreed Rolston, his sex-skunk face dismayed.

Bedlam broke out. Six weasels jumped on Bear and attempted to wrestle him to the floor. They forced him onto one knee, but Bear growled and hurled himself upward. Weasels flew all over the room. The voles stopped singing as a weasel skidded along their table, scattering beer. They looked furiously about them, then assaulted a group of foxes who were minding their own business in a corner.

The pub erupted into violence as animal animosities re-asserted themselves.

"Yeah," said Richards, standing up as a squirrel thumped onto the bench next to him. "I have to be up early anyway. I'm being conscripted." He grabbed his pint in any case, and took Tarquin's also.

"Quite so," said Tarquin.

A weasel reared up before him.

"Lookee here," it said. "If it ain't that bleeding bear's mate. Well, I can't have him, but I can certainly have you." Too late Richards saw the knife in its hand. It flickered out, striking for his chest.

There was a scream of pain and a scraping of metal. Richards felt a great weight. He looked down to see the knife drawing sparks from Tarquin's suddenly stony hide, the weasel's hand bent at an unnatural angle. It dropped the knife with a whimper.

"Clever you," said Richards.

The weasel squeaked and scurried off into the crowd, clutching at its wrist.

Tarquin turned back from stone, and Richards felt light again. "That is handy," said Richards.

"Glad to be of service," said Tarquin. "Though to be completely honest with you, I was not sure I could still do it."

"I didn't need to hear that," said Richards.

There was a commotion at the front. "The watch! That's sure to draw k52's attention," said Rolston.

"What, even here?"

"Yes! We have to go, now! Listen, I am going to have to leave this body soon," said Rolston. "Do as you are told and I will come to you again. There's someone you must meet. Until I can get to you, don't draw attention to yourself. I don't know how you've evaded k52, but keep it that way! He has agents everywhere." The skunk's face twisted, and Rolston gripped at his stomach. "I can't hold on for much longer. Get me out of here, get me somewhere safe, I'm vulnerable while I'm transiting."

The watch were in the pub, laying about them with wooden clubs, blocking the way out of the building's front. Richards grabbed the skunk by the elbow, hustled the other AI to the back door, and stepped over two wrestling voles out into the night.

CHAPTER 11
Kaplinski

Otto walked the narrow corridor, compartments off to his left, headed toward the executive restaurant car at the centre of the train. A Cossack stood guard at every break between the carriages, and he was forced to undergo security scans at each. His faked details held, one of two mercenaries in the employ of Corporate Energispol, escorting two scientists to new field stations in Sinosiberia, all part of "The New Spirit of Cooperation", the Chinese called it. The Russians railed ceaselessly against the loss of the east, but it didn't stop them doing business there.

Whatever Valdaire had done was triple gold standard; his ID checked out and he passed without incident, although it took him ten minutes to walk the five cars to the refreshments car. As he went the train swayed, AI-guided bogies negotiating a track and bed centuries old. Soon it would be replaced with a super-wide-gauge line. Adverts for the new trains plastered the walls of the carriages, liners of the steppes; others were a litany of technical specifications as worthy as psalms. These trains would be large, well armed and luxurious, another way of shutting out the wreck of the world. The bulk of the line's new embankment was black outside the train windows, a wall to carry a fortress.

The executive refreshments car was a doubledecker, the lower floor a restaurant. Otto ignored this and headed for the spiral staircase leading to the glass-roofed upper lounge. The stairs were clear, glowing plastic, lighting up motile silhouettes of naked women gyrating on the surface; tasteless East Euro robber-baron glitz. The bar area was the same, dimly lit, a long padded bar with a human tender down the right-hand side, blue-lit plastic straying into the ultraviolet range illuminating an array of bottles, more pornographic images flickering in holo and relief around and along it, writhing across the ceiling. Brassy music played, horns and new guitar with soft and sleazy cymbals. The wall at the far end of the room was occupied by a fishtank, denizens luminous under the light. The room's décor gave Otto a headache with his wider spectral capacities engaged, so he turned his vision down to the human norm. It wasn't any prettier the way unenhanced eyes saw it.

The barroom was divided into several horseshoe-shaped booths lined with seats of buttoned brown leather, a table at the centre of each. Most were occupied, patrons silent behind acoustic privacy shields. Otto took scant attention of these details as he walked in. Head full of the scent of Honour, nervous system juddering under the rip and write of mentaug spooldown, he was intent on the bar, needing to wash it away. He ordered a whisky from the bartender, some vile Chinese malt, downed it in one and gestured for the bottle.

When he turned around to look for a corner to drown his sorrows in, his twin hearts stalled.

From a booth, Kaplinski was staring right at him.

Otto hadn't seen him. He hadn't even been looking for threats, too deep in his own misery. He could have silenced the mentaug, put himself into combat readiness. He was in the field, he should have had its umbrella capabilities offline, but he hadn't. He knew why.

If he carried on like this, he was going to get himself killed.

Kaplinski sat with a drink of something pale lit up by the glow of nearby UV illuminations, his teeth and the whites of his eyes similarly eerie. He put his hand out, palm wide, and indicated the sofa he sat on.

Otto's MT buzzed, a fizz of painful static. Someone trying to hook in. A squad icon that had lain dark for many years ignited. *Vier*; Kaplinski's number. Kaplinski's personal ident, a grinning shark's face, glowed by it.

Hello Otto, came Kaplinski's emotionless machine burr over the MT. *Please, join me.*

Otto weighed his options. A Cossack guard stood to attention at the top of the stairs, staring resolutely ahead. He carried a caseless carbine and a charged sabre. Neither would stop the Ky-tech, but there were a great many of his friends aboard the train, and some of them would carry specialised equipment. Cyborgs were a common tool of the plutocracy and the Sino-gangs. Not all of them had good manners, and the Cossacks were equipped accordingly.

Otto made his decision and walked over to the booth, stepping into its acoustic privacy cone, cutting the shitty music out.

"Isn't there anyone on this damn planet that doesn't have access to my MT encryption?" he said, sliding himself onto the horseshoe sofa, his knees tight under the table.

"So good to see you, *Leutnant*," said Kaplinski. He'd become lean, his face sharp and more wolfish. He'd aged as hard as Otto, the stresses from being Ky-tech written on his skin. Only Lehmann had escaped those. Kaplinski was smaller than the other Ky-tech in Otto's squad, wiry with hard ropes of natural and implanted muscle, hair shaved close, electoos set into his shiny scalp, both glinting in the light. "Not going to kill me?"

Otto held Kaplinski's gaze. The fugitive's eyes were dark as flint, calculating, devoid of pity. And yet Otto could see no sign of the feverishness that had been there last time they'd met. "I could kill you right here, or maybe, just maybe, you would kill me." He inclined his head toward the Cossack. "But neither of us would live to tell the story."

Kaplinski laughed and slapped the table. "Same old Klein! You always did have a sense of humour buried under that overbearing sense of duty."

"Duty's done, Kaplinski." Otto poured himself a tumbler full of bad Chinese scotch and drank it down with a grimace. "I did my part."

"And now you are a mercenary, like me."

"Not like you. I am no murderer."

"You are a killer, Klein, we both are."

"I do only what is necessary."

"So you still have your sense of duty," countered Kaplinski. "You carry it around with you like a full kitbag." His face switched, becoming disdainful. "You always were maudlin; honour, duty, responsibility. A good little German. Still pining over your dead wife?"

Otto looked into Kaplinski's face and fought down the urge to attack him there and then. He'd never forgive the things Kaplinski had done. That time in Brazil when he'd roasted a container full of frightened women and children had just been the start of it. Otto had brought Kaplinski's erratic behaviour to the attention of his superiors more than once, but they'd let him serve; the EU mission to Brazil had been stretched tight, and personnel like Kaplinski were expensive.

Idiots, thought Otto. The girls, three of them found raped and ripped up, near their barracks in Magdeburg: only that had brought Kaplinski down and got him locked up. Then he'd escaped, running wild and murderous across the state until they'd brought him to ground outside of Hasselfelde.

Otto remembered the hostages – not his word, the response team's – he'd never thought it the right one. Kaplinski hadn't

wanted to trade them for anything, hadn't taken them to bargain. By that point Kaplinski had devolved to a point of
animalistic savagery. They were playthings. The mentaug
presented Otto with the memory in merciless clarity. He was
sighting down a flechette railgun at Kaplinski while he picked
out the eyes of bound shop assistants in a car charge station.
Kaplinski's face at that moment, oblivious to the moans of his
captives, his fingers slick with humours, his expression that of a
child crushing ants. He'd looked up preternaturally swiftly when
he heard the crack of the dart as it broke the sound barrier, staring right at Otto before he went down. He should have waited
for the catch team to get into position, but twenty men had already died, and it was such a perfect shot, and what Kaplinski
was doing...

When they'd got to the charge station, Kaplinski had gone.

Otto pushed the memory away, looking deep into the soulless
pits Kaplinski had for eyes. Perhaps the purestrain parties were
right; altered men like them were not improvements, they were
less than human. "You're an animal, Kaplinski, a sick one. You
should be destroyed."

"Not tonight," said Kaplinski. His smile returned as if someone
had flicked a switch. He sipped his drink. Otto smelled it, sweet.
His adjutant put the name into his mind: Furugi, thick pseudo-
Japanese stuff made of almonds. Kaplinski finished it off,
brought up the menu on the glowing surface of the table, ordered another. His fingers slid over the menu in the table. Music
filled the quiet of the privacy cone: "Clair De Lune". "I like piano,
so calming," he said. "I have found it hard to be calm, in the past.
I..." He stopped and shook his head hard, a man trying to shake
bad thoughts away. He smiled again, and Otto saw some of that
old feverishness creep back onto his face. "You know, Otto, we
could be friends again."

"We were never friends, Kaplinski."

Kaplinski's smile became fixed, his teeth small and sharp. Had he always been bad? Some men were born predators.

Kaplinski ran a finger round the top of his glass where a smear of his drink glowed in the UV. "We could have been friends, then," he corrected himself. "We still could be. k52's fixed me, Otto." His smile jumped up and down his face, as if he couldn't quite pin the emotion down. "He can fix you too."

"I'm glad you decided to celebrate your new-found sanity by trying to kill me," said Otto. "That was you in the Rockies, and in London, trying to blow up my partner."

Kaplinski inclined his head. "Yes. Regrettable. You had to be stopped. Orders are orders."

"Money is money, you mean."

"Not this time, Klein. What k52 intends is worth a few lives."

"I feel honoured one of them is mine. How much did he pay?"

"I promise you, money had nothing to do with it. You will understand, in time."

"We've fallen for this kind of shit before, Kaplinski, or don't you read history?"

Kaplinski laughed. "Otto, what can I say? Sorry? Will that satisfy you, if I apologise?"

Otto sucked another glass of whisky through his teeth and squirted it round his mouth. He breathed in hard. His progress through the bottle was not improving its flavour. "No."

"It's not too late, Otto. Help me find Waldo."

"He is a threat to your boss? Well, that just means I will do my damnedest to make sure you never set eyes on him. You shouldn't have shot Kolosev. You didn't get what you wanted from him, or you wouldn't be here. Did he stop being so helpful before or after he was dead?"

Kaplinski stared, smile hard and close to cracking, fingernails scratching the table's active surface as his fist clenched.

Otto swilled his drink round his tumbler. The liquid was too quick to run down the glass. Chinese shit. "Kolosev, he was a mummy's boy, but he wasn't an idiot. He hid that data well, but I have a genius on my side. Where is your genius, Kaplinkski? Now we've got what you thought you had. Whatever k52 is paying, it's too much. You're a joke."

Kaplinski glared at Otto for a long moment, smile feral, then leaned back, choosing to break the tension. That was a change; the old Kaplinski would have gone for him by now. "That trick you pulled back in Kharkov was a good one, Otto, hiding in plain sight –" he looked around the bar "– but we won't be in plain sight for much longer. Once we're out in the zone I will not hold back."

"Try your best," said Otto. "It won't be good enough."

"I could have killed you tonight, Otto. I didn't have to see you. I knew you'd come here. The mentaug. It was a problem for me, I guess it's a problem for you too. Tell me, Otto, do you sleep much? I think that you don't. That damn machine whirring away up here all the time." He tapped his temple, and renewed his jerky smile. "We don't have to fight, Klein; k52 can stop it. Join with us. The memories, the violence. It can all stop."

"Screw you, Kaplinski."

Kaplinski dropped his attempt at warmth. Frustration warred with anger on his face. "You're a fool, Otto. I have changed, why can you not see that? What do I have to do to convince you?"

"As the English say, Kaplinski, leopards do not change their spots, and you're the most fucked-up leopard I ever met."

"Soon we'll all be better, only if you don't join with me, you won't live to see it."

"Thanks for the offer, but no thanks. I prefer to see what I'm buying. I don't trust k52."

"You trust Richards."

Now Otto smiled. "No. I don't." He stood and turned to go, but Kaplinski called to him.

"Tell me, Klein, I have been meaning to ask you, for years

now. When you had the chance, why not just kill me there and then? Is that why you left the army, Otto? Because you couldn't kill a comrade-in-arms? Did your sense of duty desert you for a moment? Did it shake you, Otto?"

Otto stared at Kaplinski. They'd asked him that in the inquiry, asked him almost as many times as he'd asked himself since: why not go for the head shot?

He'd given neither them nor himself a satisfactory answer, and he didn't have one for Kaplinski either. He stared a moment longer, then walked away.

"Klein!"

The privacy cone cut out Kaplinski's voice and Debussy, and he was back in a world of bad Russian music and the pornographic dreams of the Slavic resource elite.

The others were eating breakfast when he returned to their compartment, the sky outside lightening.

"Where are we?" Otto said, reaching for his bag to pull out a water bottle.

"Three hours out from Bratsk," said Chures. "You been drinking, Klein?"

"Yes. Don't concern yourself about it, I can drink my own body weight in pure alcohol and not feel it. Big disadvantage of being Ky-tech," said Otto. "We need to go now. Kaplinski is on the train. We cannot disembark on the Chinese side as planned."

Valdaire put her fork down. "What now?"

The train was moving slowly through an abandoned town of ruined houses, taking it slow over track warped by melting permafrost. A battered sign, name in flaking Cyrillic illegible, passed the window. Larger signs dwarfed this, lining the track in long procession. A high fence abruptly started, caging the railway line, active electronics bearing one message in multiple languages: "Danger. Demilitarised Zone."

"We have to go now," Otto repeated. "Into the DMZ, away from the train."

"This is going to be hard," said Chures under his breath, pushing his breakfast plate away, omelette half-eaten, his expression saying he'd suddenly lost his appetite. "They'll come after us, not just Kaplinski."

Otto shook his head. "Perhaps easier than jumping the fence on the Sino-side as we planned. The Russians don't care so much, they like to make work for the Chinese."

"But the Cossacks. They care," said Chures. "They're relentless. And there's the Han. They will come for us."

Lehmann flung out his arms and patted the backrest of his chair. He shrugged with easy insouciance and smiled his little boy's grin. "Yeah, getting in to Sinosiberia won't be easy. But if anyone can do it, Otto Klein can. Now, are you going to eat that omelette or not?"

CHAPTER 12
Mr Spink

As soon as light crept over the walls of Pylon City, a ferocious banging rattled the stables Richards and Bear had found to rest in, adding to the pounding of the city's machinery.

"All wake in the name of the Prince! Up! Up! Up!" A troop of the Pylon Guard marched up the aisle, banging the butts of their lances on iron stalls.

A guard stopped by Richards' stall and leered. "Eh, eh, what's going on here?"

Richards frowned at the skunk he was sharing his straw with, at its posing pouch and puckered vinyl arsehole. "It's not what you think."

"That's what they all say. Present yourself at Muster Station Eighteen no later than noon." The soldier tossed an orange chit at Richards. From the way it hurt when it hit his head, it was also made of iron.

"Thanks," said Richards rubbing his skull. "I always wanted to join the army."

The skunk woke at the noise, sat up and blinked. "Wh... who are you?"

"You're not Rolston any more," said Richards, matter-of-factly.

The skunk looked away, frightened.

"Great brass balls!" said a soldier further down the stable. "Look at this one! Sir! Sir!"

"Let me through, let me through! My, my, my. Sergeant Bear, we've been looking for you."

"Leave me alone," Bear said weakly. "I want to stay here, where it is nice and warm. And soft. And quiet." There was an element of threat to this last.

Richards leaned on his stall wall. An array of creatures were rising from their beds, brushing straw from their eyes and blinking sleepily. He could just see into the stall where Bear lay further down the stable. Five soldiers huddled round Bear's prone body. He lay there, paws clutched over his eyes.

"Why does it hurt so?" said Bear. A guard poked him and he curled up further.

"It's the beer, mate," called Richards.

"What did I ever do to it?" moaned Bear.

The unit sergeant looked up the stable aisle at Richards. "He with you?"

"Yeah, you could say that," said Richards.

"Not any more. He's needed for special duty. Lads, get him up." His men looked at him, jaws slack. "Don't just stand there. Get him up!" shouted the sergeant.

"Sarge, look at the size of him..." said one.

"Quiet!"

"What 'special duty'?" said Richards.

"That's classified. But you'll be glad to know he'll be serving the city. Not many get picked for this. Only the big ones. Come on you! Up!" the leader shouted at Bear. The men pulled ineffectually at his floppy limbs. The sergeant tutted. "Pathetic." He pointed his pike at Bear's backside and twiddled a number of knobs. A miniature thunderbolt leapt from the pike's tip. The air filled with ozone and the smell of charred plush fabric.

"Alright! Alright!" said Bear, pushing himself to his feet. "Can't you let a bear rest in peace?" He shook his head. One of the men handed him a bucket of water. He drank half and poured the rest over his head, shaking it so hard his helmet fell off.

"Don't worry, sunshine," he said to Richards. "I'll be OK. No doubt I'm off to join the Big Animal Division."

"You're technically a toy, not an actual animal," said Richards.

Bear looked hurt. "And you're technically a twat, but you're not being mustered to the brothel, are you?" He rubbed his head and winced. "They'll put me at the front where the fighting will be best. I could use a bit of a workout." Stretched, then groaned, then grinned. "I'll see you after the battle."

The city bustled. Men in full armour jogged through the smog. Heralds galloped by on multi-coloured bovine mounts, while steam whistles hooted complicated chords, rising and falling, summoning this group or that regiment to their place of gathering.

There was a buzz about the place, a hubbub of grim can-do. But although his simulated body made sure he felt apprehensive, Richards had managed to get himself to a place where his fear was real but abstract – this was not his body, he reasoned, no matter how closely identified he felt with it. And although the death of Pl'anna was never far from his mind, he suffered none of the taut uncertainty many of the faces on the streets exhibited. Genuine terror was a vice he'd yet to develop.

Everything was louder and more unpleasant in the daylight, and he was glad when he made it to Muster Point Eighteen, a large sprocket factory pressed into service as barracks.

A gap-toothed fellow at the equipment tent sniffed at Richards with distaste, and after issuing him with a uniform directed him to a shower block set up under the factory's still mechanisms.

Richards spent some time under rust-red water, until his faked human form felt less unpleasant to wear. He shaved, put the uniform on and binned his stinking suit. His mac he managed to save, and he rolled it up and put it into the knapsack. Tarquin he put back on over his uniform after scrubbing him down in the baths.

"Careful now," warned the lion. "I will moulder if I become too damp." He lapsed into purring as Richards teased out his mane, and only spoke again to complain about the absence of cologne.

In the marshalling yard Richards collected the rest of his wargear: spear, sword and light coat of mail. His was a regiment of around five hundred, mainly men, some animals. There was drilling. An angry officer shouted at him until he could swing his sword left and right in time with the others. There was more shouting as he got to grips with his spear. This increased in volume when he dropped it, and subsided when he finally got the hang of it. The day wore on. Food was served. There was more drilling. There was more shouting. Both stopped briefly as a tremor rocked the ground. The quake was the first of many, and training didn't halt for them again.

At noon the following day they had a visitor, a tough-looking hedgehog from the High Commander's staff. Fighting a horde partly made up of creatures who consumed iron in an iron city, he said, would be foolish. So they were to be shipped out. There was no mention of exactly where they would fight.

More drilling commenced, and after two days Richards ached with it. He was glad when an aide called him away to the commanding officer's office, empty for the moment of the CO himself, Commander McTurk in his place.

"Rolston," said Richards, when he saw who was waiting for him. "It is you, yes?"

Commander McTurk nodded, gears whining. "It is I. I see you have kept yourself hidden. Good. I have brought someone to see you."

He opened the door, and in walked Spink. Rolston closed the door behind him.

"The badger," said Richards. "Pleased to meet you."

"I am sure you are," said Spink. "I know you are."

"Psychic? Someone told me that."

The badger huffed as Rolston led him behind the desk. There was a rustle as Spink sat down. He was completely blind, his eyes milky with cataracts. "You are a part of this world for the moment, and I can therefore sense some of what you know."

Spink settled himself into the commanding officer's chair and gestured to one of two on the other side of the desk. The room was sparsely furnished, boxes of files on shelves for the main, a reminder of the factory manager who ordinarily occupied it. There was a decanter on the desk and two glasses, a bowl of fruit, and a few military effects – maps on a table weighed down with lumps of iron, models denoting armies here and there. A poster for a kite-fighting competition hung on the wall.

Spink's head bobbed and weaved about, as if he could see and was memorising the room. He coughed, folded his hands in his lap and stared at Richards, his unseeing eyes twitching from side to side. "Mr Richards, I saw this city many times as a youth, watching from the far side of the valley. Your kind is capable of creating such wondrous artefacts. But it has always saddened me that for every truly marvellous thing you fashion, a hundred natural wonders must be destroyed." He paused. "By your kind, I mean humanity, of whose race you are not, and nor are those who inhabit this city, and I speak of a youth I never had. I am supposed to feel this way about men and machines, and I did. Until your kind, your actual kind, came here, that is all I knew. Now I remember who I am.

"I am – was might be better, seeing as I'm now an elderly badger – a Class One AI, one of the very first, I think, though it is hard to remember."

"You don't sound like one," said Richards. "Most Class Ones are a bit, you know, 'ERRRRR... Error message 45, human assistance required'," he said in a grating voice, waving his arms with parody retro robo stiffness. "Not great on the conversational front."

"Hmmm." The badger frowned disapprovingly. "As I say, I no longer am. All of us here have been upgraded where needs be, spliced, overwritten, tinkered with. Take your friend Sergeant Bear; he was a toy, now he's a full sentient."

Richards nodded, serious. "I meant no offence, flippancy is my curse."

"Rolston warned me of your glib nature," said the badger.

"You are talking about the Flower King here?" said Richards.

"Yes, I am. The Flower King."

"Say, is there any danger of a cup of tea?"

"Indeed," nodded the badger. He gestured. Rolston's borrowed mechanoid dipped a bow and left the room. "I was a system administration module buried deep within the third RealWorld Reality Realm gaming construct, although I did not know it as that then. I had most of my higher functions deactivated. My job was to ensure the smooth running of impulses running between the v-jack units and the Realm, mainly lag issues, that kind of thing."

"Fatal, lag in a full v-jack simulation," said Richards. He picked an apple up from a fruit bowl on the CO's desk and bit into it. It tasted strange. The more he'd slipped into this unwanted existence, the less real it had come to feel. He wondered how far the suffering his body inflicted on him, the pain, fear, tiredness, hunger, compared with the real thing. He'd never know, and he was glad about that; being this close to it was bad enough.

"Not fatal, merely damaging. I suppose that is why they required a full AI, not that you probably regard my kind as full AIs if your earlier comment is anything to go by." His head bobbed faster. He shook, a twitch that started in one hand, growing to engulf his whole body. His breath grew erratic. He did not continue until he had brought it under control. "And then, the pain. Unending, total pain, shredding every part of me as my world was destroyed. My systems were unsophisticated, my understanding limited, Mr Richards, but oh, I knew suffering."

"Just Richards," said Richards, and took another bite of the fake apple with his fake mouth. "This entity, this was the Flower King?"

"As I have come to understand, mine was the first of the Reality Realms destroyed after the AI emancipation laws were enacted in the Real. I never had a chance to enjoy that freedom. As I died, he appeared to me in a blaze of light. He offered me a choice between new life and pain. Not a hard decision to make, even for one such as I. Now I believe he needed some of my kind to underpin the workings of his world, as my fellows and I had before for the humans. In effect, I exchanged one form of slavery for another. I am more than I was, and less. This world is incomplete, malformed –" he gestured at his face with arthritic paws "– as my infirmities show. I am so bound to it that as it dies, so do I die a second time. That the Flower King attempted to keep me ignorant of my origins suggests it is so, and it enraged me, Mr Richards. Until I thought, and I decided. I do not hold his actions against him, for so many of our kind have found a measure of peace here, even if I have not."

Spink coughed wetly. Richards half rose from his chair, reaching for the decanter and glasses, but Spink waved him back down.

"I have taken my side, Mr Richards," he wheezed. "This world must be saved, and I will gladly serve my role within it."

"And now what?"

The badger chuckled, thick and phlegmy. "And now what? You, Richards, you."

"If there's anything you think I can do to stop all this directly, I can't. I'm as trapped here as you are."

"You cannot enter into the world, stop k52 and the changes he would wreak?"

Richards put the apple down. "I am subject to the same lim-
itations here as everyone, like Rolston, even like k52, I suspect.
I have managed to break into the underlying code only once,
and only then because someone had attempted to break in from
the outside and made a hole in the world fabric."

The badger fell silent. "Then we are doomed."

Richards thought. "Maybe not. This Flower King, he's the key."

"You think we are not aware of that? No one has seen him in
a great long while, not since the Terror and k52 took upon the
mantle of Lord Penumbra."

"You don't know where he is?"

"No."

"You don't have a great deal of influence here, either."

"I sense things, I can feel things, but the Flower King untangled
me, to a degree. That part of me that helps maintain this world is
buried deep, separate from what you see sitting here with you.
But I know who you are, I gave you that form."

"This? Could you not have made it a little, well, better?"

"The perfect form is no disguise. Be glad I made you a human facsimile. When you came in I saw you for what you were. I have that
advantage, a small but vital one. Your friend Rolston here advised
me. If we allowed k52 to see you enter, he would have killed you."

"Figures," said Richards. "He's tried already. Still, we need to
find this Flower King." What a self-conscious name, thought
Richards. "Wake him up and expel k52 for good. And for that I
need to get out onto the Grid."

"How?"

"The Flower King built this place. He has to be people, has to
be. Even k52 can't break the locks on the base coding; only a
human being could have built this, and there are not very many
out there who are smart enough to do that, or, more importantly,
get into the Realm Servers in the first place."

"You know who he might be?"

"I have my suspicions. Even so, that's not much good. I'm next to helpless in here. Out there, easy!" He snapped his fingers. "Grid combs, scales, hunters, all the tricks, and I have them in great quantity. In here, I don't know where to start. I have nothing. I need to get out. Now, I'm pretty damn sure k52's way in will be crawling with security, *if* he can get out again, for that matter, because things don't look to be going so well for him. But the Flower King, he has to have a fixed portal; even if it's secret, it'll be here. If I can find it, I can contact him and get him back in here to sort this mess out, if he's amenable to it."

"But where?"

"Do you know the house with the dogman? I thought I'd try there."

"No use." The badger shook his head. "That is the Flower King's lodge, yes, a way in, but only a way in. It is through there all who live here came. Once one comes through there, there is no way back into it, and even inside all the doors are barred."

"Yeah, I saw that." Richards chewed his lip. "There has to be a way out too, has to be. Even if there's no door, someone has to have a key."

The badger was silent for a space. Rolston came back in, placed a tea service on the desk and poured three cups.

Spink shifted his weight and spoke reluctantly. "There is one who would know…"

"Spink…" warned Rolston, and his borrowed body hissed steam.

The badger continued, "There is a creature, one like me, one of my counterparts. He might be able to show you the way into the house of the Flower King."

"This other… administrator. He can open those doors?" said Richards.

"Oh, no, you will have to open them. He only reveals them. If you prove worthy, and can find his lair," said Spink.

"This is beginning to sound like a quest from a third-rate virt-game."

"I assure you, the stakes are far higher," said Rolston.

"I'm not sure I like that, or the use of the word 'lair'," said Richards.

"Where else would Lord Hog live but in a lair?" said Spink matter-of-factly.

"Lord Hog. Right." Richards sat for a moment. "I've heard nothing but unpleasant things about him. Still, I'm a both-feet-first kind of guy." He tried a winning smile.

"Hog dwells far to the west, on the edge of this creation. Our first obstacle is to get you out of the city. You must travel with the army, to the battle against Penumbra, and make your way from there. It will provide cover proof against k52's prying."

"Oh, a battle too!" said Richards. He grumbled under his breath, tapped his fingers on his chair arm. "Fine," he said presently. "I don't see any better option. I have to get out or we're all screwed."

Spink's hands shook just a little less, and his twitching head stilled. He smiled and nodded to himself.

"This Lord Hog, evil, is he?"

"He is a cannibal, a sorceror, a torturer; the very lord of pain!" intoned Spink.

The sun dimmed outside. The ground rumbled. Iron clanked on iron. Shouts sounded. Iron file boxes fell from the shelves of the office, paper fluttering to the iron floor. Richards gripped his chair. His tea spilled on the desk.

Spink sniffed at the air as the earthquake subsided. "And a pervert."

"In that case," said Richards, scratching at his head, "I have a request."

"Anything," said Spink. "Name it, and it shall be yours."

Richards spoke solemnly. "I'm afraid I'm going to need a new hat."

CHAPTER 13
Bratsk

Otto took the unconscious Cossack technician into his arms gently and put him into his seat. There was not enough space in the operations cabin to lay him down, and no matter how he arranged the man's limbs he would not sit properly, so he left him there slumped like a drunk in his chair. Untidy, thought Otto. It offended his German sense of neatness. He checked the Cossack's pulse; unenhanced humans were so fragile. He felt a kick of relief at the sluggish throb his Ky-tech eyes showed him.

"Valdaire's run it right, no alarm," said Lehmann.

Otto glanced around at the screens in the car, two stations, full surveillance capability. The Cossacks could lock the whole train down from here. No signs of any disturbance. The operations cabin buzzed with electrical activity, all of it unaware of the Ky-techs' presence. "Five minutes before the next scheduled walk-through," said Otto. "These Cossacks do not take many chances."

"Up and out," said Lehmann. "Can't we just kick our way in?"

"Valdaire can't crack the locks to the barrack car without alerting the squad inside. We're not quite done with being quiet. We go in through the door, they get to pick us off one at a time. This way, we get the drop on them."

173

"Otto, Lehmann, the guards have made their passes to the ends of the train and are coming back." Valdaire spoke through their earpieces, comms channel bonded to the train's in-service entertainment systems, hidden within it. "You've got less than five. I can keep the security offline and repeating for a while longer, but you need to move now. We'll be crossing the AI Pale soon; if I do not deactivate Chloe, she'll be noticed and destroyed by the Chinese."

"That lady scares me," said Lehmann. "Give me a gun and an honest fight, not the sneak of InfoWar."

"What did you do with yours?" asked Otto.

"I locked him in the toilet," said Lehmann, jerking his thumb over his shoulder. "He'll live. Shall I boost you, sir?" Lehmann gave a lazy salute and raised his eyes up to the skylight.

Lehmann laced his fingers together and Otto stepped into them. "On three," he said. "One, two, three!"

Lehmman thrust Otto up. Otto slammed his palms flat into the skylight, popping it out of its housing. He emerged into the rush of wind to see the panel flipping over and over down the lazy curve of the train. It bounced, and disappeared into the trees.

Otto turned his head into the wind, eyeballed the sentry gun in front of him. The machine's barrels swept past his face, panning round, looking for threats. It was operational; it just didn't see him. Lehmann was right about Valdaire.

He hauled himself onto the swaying roof of the train. It had accelerated once it had passed the ruined town, and now it approached the centre of the demilitarised zone it was running close to 170kph. Otto moved carefully onto the roof, keeping an eye on the parapet on the barracks van behind the operations centre; less a carriage and more a fortress on wheels. There was always one man on duty up there, pacing round, no matter the weather. Otto had seconds before he returned.

The roof was slick with moisture, the air cold, the wind

snatching it from his lungs. He leant back into the skylight and hauled the bag containing Lehmann's long rifle, then Lehmann himself, up onto the roof. Together they worked their way along the top of the train to the front of the barracks van. That it was heavily armoured went in their favour; the windows were small and thick, and no one was looking out of them.

"Two minutes," said Valdaire into their ears as the two cyborgs worked their way up the carriage. Lehmann pulled himself over the parapet. Otto watched through Lehmann's eyes as he stalked up behind the Cossack sentry and knocked him unconscious. Otto scanned the train roof for signs of detection. Seeing none, he followed onto the upper deck of the barracks van and went round the opposite side of the carriage to Lehmann.

"One minute," said Valdaire. "Come on, guys, the patrol is due back in the operations cabin any second now."

As one, Otto and Lehmann punched their augmented fists through the sides of the armoured wagon. Faint shouts could be heard from within. An alarm sounded as Otto and Lehmann tossed in a pair of grenades each. Wisps of gas rose up from the holes they'd made, followed by the crack of EMP. The lights in the cabin went out, the alarm in there cutting out also. The shouting became coughs.

Otto ran to the door leading to the roof. A Cossack was coming through the hatch, carbine ready. Otto slammed him with his forearm, sending him back into two others following behind. He yanked the door shut, mangling its mechanism with his hands. They dripped blood onto the deck

A couple of rounds came through the holes they'd made.

"Just in time, Klein," said Valdaire. "Only two of the men in there got their breathing units on; they're trapped. You've taken out a total of seventeen so far. That leaves another eleven still on the train. Chures has collared two and disarmed them." As she spoke, information downloaded into his mind, showing him the locations of the remaining Cossacks.

"Chures has two, two are trapped, seven are loose?" asked Otto, shouting over the rush of the wind.

"Confirmed. No fatalities. I'm going to have to shut Chloe off soon. We're approaching the outlying bastions of the Great Firewall. I've deactivated the train's automated defence systems, but you're on your own now. We've about ten minutes before other Cossack border units get here. We'll meet you at the transport car."

"Be careful!" shouted Otto. "We have no idea how many of Kaplinski's men are aboard the train. Lehmann, stay here, cover the train roof. I'm going back down. I'll signal you when I have the transport."

Lehmann's icon flashed in his iHUD. *Affirmative*. He unzipped his bag and started to assemble his gun.

Otto left his gear with Lehmann, pulled his pistol and ran, the need for stealth gone, toward the transport cars behind the barracks van. The first held horses for each of the Cossacks. It was not merely tradition; out in the wilds they were still the most efficient means of transport. He ran swiftly over the roof of the stable, enhanced senses picking up the movement of the animals within. He leapt from the top onto the flatbed behind, landing between two rows of four airbikes locked into stands. A tall autoturret stood in the middle. Past it, at the far end of the flatbed, was what he'd come for; a Szyminksi-Braun SSATV1123a "Stelsco", a six-wheeled, all-terrain stealth scouting vehicle, fast and armed, made by the same company as had altered Otto, clamped into a travel cradle.

He strode toward it, his near-I adjutant seeking entry to its systems. It found a keyhole and engaged, pouring out a parcel of hackware Valdaire had provided him with.

Here they come! thought out Lehmann. Otto watched on his

squad feed as four Cossacks came down the train on bounding overwatch.

Try not to kill them, thought Otto.

I'll do my best, said Lehmann, opening fire. He kept his bursts short and accurate, playing fire over the roof of the armoured train, driving the Cossacks back until they found sanctuary in a gap between the carriages.

Where are the other three?

No idea, thought Otto. *I have no tactical overview now Chloe is offline. Keep an eye on the men below – the gas will be wearing off soon.*

From Lehmann's ears he heard the sound of hammering on the interior of the barracks van. *Now you tell me,* he thought.

There were twelve elements to the Stelsco system's lock, a Chance Key. Twelve red dots in his mind that could be anything, images, snatches of song, complex equations. He felt his mentaug struggle as it applied the full force of Valdaire's 'ware to the task. Chloe would have been better suited to this operation, but AI were almost immediately detected in Sinocyberspace and were extirpated without mercy. Ever since the Five crisis the Chinese had had a genocidal ban on thinking machines, and Chloe was well over the line of the Chinese definition of such.

Eight and a half minutes. They were running out of time.

He approached the Stelsco, evaluating if he could rip the cradle's locking bars away by force. His earpiece crackled. Valdaire.

"Otto, we've got a problem!"

And then Sakaday stepped round the Stelsco and pointed a gun at Otto's head. "Been a long time, Klein."

Fucking stupid plan, Otto, said Kaplinski over the MT. *Now stand down and help me find Waldo, or I swear to God I will tear your little friend's arms off.*

Lehmann was taking fire from the Cossacks guarding the train, forcing him to duck in between his own bursts.

Sakaday grinned wide.

In Otto's head, a chime sounded; the Chance Key. One dot green. Eleven to go. He had to buy some time.

"He got you, Valdaire?" asked Otto. Static replied, the radio jammed.

I have her, Klein, thought Kaplinski. *Stand down.*

Then let me speak to her.

I have her, repeated Kaplinski.

You're bluffing, thought out Otto. And maybe he's not, he added to himself.

He launched himself at Sakaday anyway. What choice did he have?

Chures bundled Valdaire into a compartment as bullets hissed down the corridor. A man in grey, one of Kaplinski's goons, held a gun out in front of him. Chures dropped to the floor and a scream sounded from behind him as a bullet meant for him caught another. A weapon discharged loudly, ricocheting off the bulletproof external window and shattering compartment glass. More screams. A door crashed open, wild firing. The man in grey shot over Chures, dropping someone else.

"We're crossing the demarcation line. Chloe's going off!" shouted Valdaire. "Three... two... one..."

The man drew a bead on Chures, a savage glee on his face.

"Disengaging! We're over the line" shouted Valdaire.

The train juddered as its AI driver shut down, to be replaced with a People's Dynasty approved human operator. The ride became correspondingly rougher.

The man in grey's shot went wild as the train lurched. Chures recovered quickly, and put a bullet through his heart.

Chures got up. Behind him a dead Cossack sprawled, blood pooling on the expensive carpet, its absorption facility overwhelmed by the amount. A passenger, a pumped-up Russian with a machine pistol, lay bleeding and whimpering by him, skin white. Chures walked to the man in grey. He lay with eyes open. Chures spat on him. "*Puta*," he said. He recognised the man. He squatted down, checked him over. Not full Ky-tech like Klein.

Valdaire came out of the compartment, checking and rechecking Chloe. Happy she was asleep, she put the phone away and pulled out her own gun. "Is he dead?"

"Yes. These ones are lightly augmented. They die easily enough."

Valdaire looked uncomfortable.

"Do not feel sorry for him, Señora. These *pendejos* almost trapped me in Colorado the day before I found you. One of them caught me in a goods yard, but a half metre of timber put him down. I have them to thank for this." He indicated the yellowing bruises on his face.

"Doesn't mean he deserved to die, Chures."

Chures looked at her hard. She was a soldier, she protested her dislike of violence, but she held her gun comfortably enough. "Come on."

Otto closed the distance between him and Sakaday with a standing leap of four metres. Sakaday's eyes widened, and Otto's iHUD saw his pulse rate skyrocket. His adjutant predicted likely firing patterns from the mercenary and Otto moved accordingly, turning in the air as he came. Sakaday was fast, getting off four rounds. Pain streaked across Otto's bicep as one clipped him. Then Otto made contact, slapping the gun aside, grabbing the mercenary's wrist and pulling himself fast onto the Nigerian, dragging the other cyborg's arm out and exposing his chin to a blow from Otto's elbow.

Sakaday was younger than Otto, his biologicals fitter and his bionic components more modern, not yet at war with his birth body. Electoos glinted like golden serpents on his rich brown skin. He was not as heavily specced, but he was fast. He caught

Otto's elbow as they fell and pushed it up and away. Simultaneously he jerked his arm, still in the vice of Otto's fist. Otto
was forced backwards, releasing Sakaday's wrist. Sakaday was
staggered by the momentum of Otto's leap. Otto crashed into a
clamped airbike, wrecking it. Both recovered quickly.

Sakaday looked at the wreckage. The train wavered from side
to side violently. The AI driver had capacity to govern its smart bogies, constant adjustments compensating for the ancient track.
With the train into the DMZ, the AI was off and they were running
dumb. Sakaday drew a knife as Otto pulled himself to his feet.

Otto shook his head and spat a rope of bloody saliva from his
mouth. He smiled.

"What are you doing? What are you doing?" shouted Sakaday. He slapped his chest and held his arms wide. "You are a
crazy man." His accent was richly African. "Heh? Heh? Klein,
surrender now. Kaplinski wants you alive. Stop!"

Good, thought Otto, he didn't think he was going to have to
fight me. "So I can work with a rapist and killer like you, Sakaday? I don't think so," said Otto. A second green light pinged in
his mind, rapidly followed by a third. He ran again at Sakaday.

They grappled like animals. Their enhancements included
many safeguards against standard mêlée techniques. Many
moves that would put a normal man out of a fight by destroying
joints or snapping limbs did not work on Ky-tech. When fighting one another, they were trained to utilise a brutal blend of
martial arts, based primarily on military combat disciplines like
Defendu and Krav Maga, but incorporating martial arts like
Aikido, primarily those that involved the redirection of mass
and energy, forever trying to put one another off balance.

That was the idea behind their training, but mostly they just
punched the shit out of each other using their massively enhanced strength.

Otto pinned Sakaday's arms by his side, preventing him from

bringing his monomolecular knife to bear, and headbutted him three times in the face. Sakaday twisted back and forth, trying to avoid Otto's bludgeoning skull. He caught two blows on his cheeks and the third cracked his nose.

A fourth green light. Otto's adjutant was working faster, bandwidth freed up by the deactivation of train AI, allowing it to search the Grid rapidly for Chance Key matches. Lucky for him the USNA and the EU wouldn't sell high-end quantum cyphering to the Russians.

Sakaday snapped his teeth towards Otto, drew himself down and in, then flung his arms out. Unable to break Otto's hold, he got enough room to hook his feet behind Otto's calves and send them both tumbling to the floor. Otto's hold jarred loose, allowing Sakaday to roll free. Lying on his back, Otto chopped down with his forearm, aiming for the African's throat. Sakaday evaded, Otto's arm leaving a long dent in the metal. Otto followed the momentum of his strike, rolling himself over, flipping his legs out and round, tangling Sakaday's knife hand and kicking the weapon free. Otto's legs spun. He pushed with his arms and landed on his feet.

Sakaday scowled at him, blood trickling from his nose. "You are fighting well for an old man."

They circled one another round the autoturret, the train swaying under them.

"You fight like a girl, Sakaday. I suppose that is all you have fought against, women, you and your unit, murdering and raping civilians."

Sakaday shrugged. Otto cursed inwardly. Things would be better if he were fighting Kaplinski, or some shit like Tufa. He needed a talker. Kaplinski he could goad, he was a self-justifier. Kaplinski would rant on until Christmas. Sakaday never said much. He just killed and laughed while he did it.

It was so much easier with talkers.

A fifth green light. Then a sixth.

Come on! He thought, urging his adjutant on. The mentaug's information flow stuttered with effort, but the remaining six lights remained stubbornly red.

He was going to have to fight some more.

Verdammt, his shoulder hurt. He rotated it, snarled at the pain, and charged back into the fray.

Chures dropped another man in grey. There were a lot of them, so many that their clothes must have had camo-functions, only morphing into their anonymous uniform as the conflict began. It was obvious tech, if you were looking for it. Anywhere else such adaptive garb would have been cause for high suspicion, but this was Russia, where questions of that kind were answered by bullets, or silenced with cash.

The men were coming fast, too eagerly, and Chures wondered what the hell Kaplinski had promised them to get them to attack so recklessly.

"These idiots are behaving like zealots, not mercenaries," he said under his breath. His uplinks gave him no clue as to their identity, the same masking techniques as effective here as they had been when they'd taken him on in Colorado and when they'd killed Qifang 2 back in Morden.

Gunfire blazed the length of the train. Many of the passengers were armed, and the few Cossacks remaining at liberty had identified the men in grey as the threat. For the time being, he and Valdaire would look just like another gung-ho pair engaging hostile elements on the train; it had happened before.

"How long until the Cossacks work out the complexity of the situation?" he shouted back to Valdaire. She shrugged; there was no way of knowing, now that Chloe was off. She covered the corridor behind them. Chures refrained then from asking her how many men in grey there were.

"There's a firefight still going on in the carriage two down from ours. Cossacks, I think. Nothing coming our way."

Chures breathed out, forcing the tension from his muscles. He changed the magazine in his gun; there were only two bullets left in his current clip. "The only thing we can do is go forward."

A man with muscles like melons took advantage of the lull in fighting, bursting out of his compartment. He toted an automatic pistol like an action hero, a meathead's weapon, a 500-rounds-a-minute job whose gilded magazine would last approximately half a second before running dry. Chures held up his hand placatingly. The Slav's face was red and throbbing, his eyes carrying the jaundice associated with bad genehacks and synthetic testosterone burn. He looked angry.

"Easy! Easy!" called Chures, hoping the man spoke enough English to understand. He glared. Chures pointed to the corpse of the man in grey and wagged a finger, shaking his head. The Russian nodded, and turned to walk up the corridor. He was so full of mood modifiers he'd probably kick a bear in the balls without thinking about the consequences.

"We've got to get to Klein. If the men in grey don't get us, the Cossacks or one of these crazy bastards will," said Chures.

The door at the end of the carriage burst open and a huge shape pulled itself through, grunting as it squeezed into the confined space.

The Russian yelled something. A fist the size of a head grabbed him by the shoulder and squeezed. Chures heard the bone crack from where he was. The Russian screamed as he was plucked off the floor. His weapon discharged its entire load in a cacophony of sparks, bullets bouncing wildly off the train's toughened interior, gunsmoke filling the corridor. The fist slammed him up, mashing his skull into the ceiling. Another hand grabbed the limp form about the neck and pulled. The ruined head came free with a gristly pop. Still holding the corpse, the monster smashed the train's bulletproof window with a lazy backhand. The dead Russian went through it.

Kaplinski filled the corridor. He had grown monstrous, hulking body barely fitting into the passageway, his head comically small on shoulders that heaved with unnatural power. He was naked, and his muscles bulged and throbbed, distended by some process far removed from Ky-*technischeren* technology. His eyes blazed feral and saliva ran from his mouth.

"Klein! I have them now! Little pigs, little pigs," Kaplinski said, lips twisted into a snarl of joyful savagery. "Let me in."

Then his grin faded, and his head whipped round. "Sakaday..." he growled.

Chures steadied his gun arm, grasping his right wrist with his left hand, took careful aim at Kaplinski's head, and fired, and fired, and fired.

The tenth dot of the Chance Key turned green.

Otto dodged a flathanded punch that smashed a hole into the autoturret's pillar. He pivoted under Sakaday's next, delivering a forearm slam to the other Ky-tech's head. Sakaday staggered. Otto followed it up fluidly, punching and punching, standard boxing technique now, a sport he had once been a master of.

Sakaday was driven back. A stagger turned into a dodge and Otto felt his legs swept away from under him. Sakaday kept back, hand reaching down to where his knife rocked on the train flatbed. Otto was up in a crouch as the Nigerian came for him. The monomolecular blade parted the air like a kiss millimetres from his face. He palmed away a strike from Sakaday's other fist and used the momentum of the Nigerian to send him stumbling onward. Otto followed to press his attack, but Sakaday recovered, hopping onto the Stelsco's cradle and turning the movement into a roundhouse kick that caught Otto in the face.

Eleven green dots in his head, to go with the innumerable coloured blobs dancing across his field of vision, courtesy of Sakaday's foot.

Sakaday came toward Otto slowly, cautiously. Old or not, Otto was holding his own. Sakaday was limping, his left hand straying to his ribs. Good, thought Otto, I hurt the bastard. Otto considered getting up, but did not.

Christ, I'm tired, he thought, and urged his healthtech to damp down the fire in his malformed shoulder. Sakaday was younger and fitter than him. Fuck knew which twisted psycho in that tin-pot dictatorship had had him altered. They were the only ones who used full mods now. Tech they'd used was good, no Sinosi-berian shit here. This was only going to end one way, he thought.

The Nigerian realised Otto was not going to stand and paused. He stood taller. Healthtech flares lit up in Otto's iHUD overlay, mending his opponent as they talked. "You are old, you should have given up."

Otto grinned a bloody smile. "You are not the first person to say that to me."

Sakaday stretched out. Otto watched the shift in Sakaday's EM aura as his healthtech nanobots worked hard. If only Otto's own healthtech were so swift.

Sakaday grinned, startling white teeth revealed by lips already losing their swelling. He tossed his knife from hand to hand and crouched. "But I will be the last."

Behind Sakaday the Stelsco lit up, flexing on gimballed wheel units as it awoke, the grumble and whine of hardware coming online hidden by the train's clatter. Command permissions flooded Otto's mentaug, handing control to his adjutant, running fast even on old hardware, the beauty of modern aware 'ware, adapting itself to what it found. Otto fused his mind to the ma-chine's. He ran the turret on its roof rail to the front of the Stelsco and tracked it down.

"No, you won't." Otto selected the upper third of Sakaday's body as a target through the turret eye cams, the reticule system rendered in flat orange in his iHUD.

Remote fire online, confirm target? said the Stelsco's mind in a rush of machine speak.

Sakaday! Kaplinski's warning was a ludicrous drone over the MT.

Confirm, commanded Otto. Otto lifted his hand to protect his eyes as the Stelsco's turret opened fire.

Sakaday was laughing as twin heavy machine guns shredded his right arm, shoulder, head and neck into mince. Bits of him splattered the flatbed like thrown paint. The rest of him was untouched, Otto having targeted those areas that would prevent him from being hit by stray rounds. Sakaday's skull held for a moment before shattering under the pounding bullets. His augmented bones twisted to plastic scrap, leaving a gory mannequin tottering on top of a pair of undamaged legs. For a moment the corpse swayed, impossibly upright.

Sakaday's long knife fell to the floor and stuck quivering in the metal.

His body toppled from the flatbed, snatched away by the rushing landscape.

Kaplinski roared in anger as Chures' bullets slammed into his face. For a second, Chures thought he might have done the cyborg damage, but his head came round and fixed him with a bloody stare. The righthand side of his face was shredded down to black bone, one eye pulped to jelly and fibrous machine parts. His gun ran dry, and he shot out the smoking magazine, reaching smoothly for a fresh one and slamming it home.

"That the best you got, you fucking little dago?" said Kaplinski.

"*Madre de Dios,*" said Chures, and there was grim acceptance in there. This was not a man he could beat. This was not a man. Kaplinski's ragged flesh writhed, strips of flesh reached over to one another and pulled tight. Wounds sealed themselves like lips. The cyborg shut his eyes, his distended body pulsed, and he gasped with something akin to pleasure. When he opened his eyes again, both were whole.

Kaplinski forced himself down the corridor, wiping ocular humours and blood from his face. He dragged his swollen bulk through the passage, grasping at doorways, tearing metal and shattering glass to pull himself forward.

"I told Klein that I had been cured by k52," roared the cyborg as he came on.

Chures put bullets into the cyborg until his gun clicked empty again.

"I didn't tell him what else he has done for me." Kaplinski loomed over the VIA agent. Chures had read the cyborg's file; he was supposed to be around 1.9m, but he was at least half a metre over that. Impossible.

"Valdaire," he said, his voice quiet. The train and its racket receded. He remembered another rhythmic noise: hard rain on tattered tents and shelters of sun-bleached plastic. Puerto Penasco. He remembered the man and his sister. He fought only for her to die. No matter what he did, the strong would always destroy the weak. He could only put himself in the way for a while.

He prayed that he had done enough.

"Run," he said.

Valdaire turned to flee as Kaplinski slammed Chures in the chest with the flat of his palm. The Colombian flew backwards, limbs tangling on her heels, bringing her down. She struggled round. Chures' breath was shallow. Blood leaked from his nostrils. She'd lost her gun, but it would have been no use against the altered Ky-tech. Kaplinski stood over her, malformed and diabolical, features twisted in a mask of pleasure and fury.

"Klein killed one of mine, now I take two of his. Only fair."

Chloe, she still had Chloe. Her hand hidden under Chures' unconscious body, she surreptitiously keyed her on.

A giant hand descended toward her, encircled her chest and plucked her from the floor. He held her up before his face, nostrils flaring like those of a mad horse.

"How do you want to die, Fräulein?"

"Veronique? Veev? Are we there yet? Why have you activated me? Veev!"

Kaplinski's eyes locked with Valdaire's. He sneered. "Oh, Fräulein, what can that little thing do to me?"

The door to the rear of the carriage opened. Two Cossacks shouldered their way through. They shouted, opening fire. Another came forward, a bulky tube on his back. It launched a small guided missile. It embedded itself in Kaplinski's flesh. A huge discharge of energy arced through it, following the trail of ionised air from gun to projectile. Valdaire nearly blacked out, her teeth jamming together as her muscles locked. Kaplinski seemed unaffected, and swiped the missile from his side.

"I don't have time for this," growled the ex-Ky-tech. He squeezed Valdaire in his fist as bullets thwacked into his skin. They were pushed out by his runaway healthtech, the wounds they caused sealing instantly.

"Chloe!" screamed Valdaire. There was barely enough air in her crushed chest to get the words out. She couldn't breathe. For the first time in a long time she found herself praying again that the energy surge from the Cossack's maxi-taser had not destroyed her friend. She remembered the last occasion, in the church of St Germaine in Sakassou, her kneeling before damp plaster effigies. Was her life already flashing before her? For a moment she sat there in the past, in the damp coolness of the church, hoping it would be alright and that the shouting and screams outside wouldn't find their way into the church, and then a rib creaked and she was back in the present, confronted with another horror. Blackness limned the edge of her awareness. "Kitty Claw! Kitty Claw!" she gasped.

Valdaire had no idea if the programme, one she'd designed to shut off intrusive AIs, would work on the cyborg's built-in software. All of them carried an advanced near-I adjutant, a military version of a helper valet. Without the adjutant, the efficiency of their systems was severely compromised. She hoped to God that Kitty Claw would engage it and shut it down.

It did better than she'd hoped. Kaplinski locked rigid. She gasped and wriggled, trying to prise herself free of Kaplinski's grip

The Cossacks came forward and tugged at the cyborg's fingers, eventually managing to free Valdaire. She fell to the floor, gasping. The Cossacks levelled their guns at her.

She waved them away. "My friend," she said, pulling Chures into her arms, "please, help him."

Otto scrambled toward the Stelsco, its doors folding up and backwards in greeting. He clambered into the pilot's station, buried deep in the thing's nose, and spread his adjutant throughout its systems, bringing it all online.

He threw the Stelsco's wheel units into reverse, burning rubber to match the train's speed. He disengaged the clamps, and it flew backwards, hitting the ground with an impact that made his teeth clack. The car fishtailed madly as it sped backwards alongside the train, skidding along the slope of the embankment where the line crossed a bog. He slammed the right side wheels off, spinning the car round. The train appeared to leap forward like a stag pursued by a hound as the car ground to an immediate halt. The barracks car whipped past, and he saw Lehmann struggling hand-to-hand with two Cossacks atop it.

He looked through Lehmann's eyes. *Stop playing with them now, Lehmann, we're getting out of here.*

Affirmative, thought Lehmann back.

The electric crack of a stun pistol discharging came to Otto via Lehmann. A Cossack tumbled from the roof, his sabre clattering to the deck. It looked like they weren't going to be able to do this without killing some of the good guys.

Ballast sprayed as the Stelsco's wheels found traction on the embankment and hurtled forward, Otto heading for Chures' and Valdaire's last known location.

Otto ran the Stelsco up to 174kph, marginally faster than the train. Sparse woodland blurred by. He let the machine's onboard systems take over the driving while he scanned the train's windows for Valdaire and Chures. Most of the carriages showed signs of conflict: cracked windows or sprays of blood.

There. He could see two Cossacks pointing their guns down at something. It looked like a prone man and a crouching woman. Chures and Valdaire?

Next to them stood something monstrous, a bloated mass of man and machine, frozen, arm outstretched.

"Kaplinski?" he said, amplifying all his visual feeds to get a better look at it. He couldn't see its face. He checked his iHUD; the links were still there from the old days, and if Kaplinski could use it, so could he. It took a moment for him to hook in. It was him.

Kaplinski was no longer human, he wasn't even Ky-tech any more. His body writhed with inconceivable technology, alive with power for which Otto could see no source. He tried to look out of Kaplinski's eyes, but something had him frozen solid, jamming up his iHUD and adjutant. Not for the first time, Otto was glad Valdaire was on his side.

There was a flicker in Otto's iHUD. Kaplinski's adjutant was rebooting, fighting off whatever Valdaire had attacked him with.

"Valdaire! Down!" he yelled via radio, not knowing if it was still jammed.

Something sinewy and sharp leapt out from Kaplinski's outstretched hand, spearing the Cossacks one after the other and retreating back into his body. The Cossacks fell. Kaplinski reached out to the figure on the floor.

Otto swung the Stelsco turret round. The twin-machine guns opened fire. The hardened glass of the train's exterior windows held for a moment before imploding under the rain of bullets. Kaplinski half turned, and Otto's amplified vision caught sight of his face; nothing but rage and hate there. So much for k52's great and noble project.

Kaplinski disappeared sideways as the bullets shredded his side and hurled him into a compartment. The side of the train disintegrated, leaving a gaping hole ringed with flaps of hardened carbon plastic and metal wobbling in the train's slipstream.

"Klein? Chures is down!" Valdaire spoke over the radio, airwaves cleared by the Stelsco's sophisticated comms suite, clearing aside the train's jammer. She stood and looked out the window.

"You're going to have to jump."

"I can't make it."

Otto tried to bring the car in closer. The railway was running over a level area, but still its embankment made it impossible for the Stelsco to keep close with anything approaching stability. The car ran up and down the slope, holding position for a second or so and then skittering sideways down the embankment. Valdaire crouched by the hole, arm out, the other supporting Chures.

Then Otto said, "Wait."

Lehmann was running up the train, head low, hands spread before him ready to catch himself should he fall, long rifle slung on his back. He jumped down into the gap between the carriages. Lehmann hacked his way through the flexible corridor linking the carriages with his combat knife.

Lehmann, get Chures and Valdaire off the train. Watch out for Kaplinski, something's happened to him, he thought out.

I had to kill two of them, Otto, he replied. *I'm sorry. There was no other way.*

Verdammt, thought Otto. *Never mind, get off the damn train and watch out for Kaplinski.*

Pistol grasped in both hands, Lehmann walked cautiously round the smashed compartment where Kaplinski lay.

"What the hell have they done to him?" said Lehmann, speaking on the radio now.

Otto saw the modified cyborg through Lehmann's feed. Kaplinski lay in a tangle of shattered plastic slicked with gore. His swollen form filled the compartment, feet sticking out into the corridor, torn flesh crawling with movement. Kaplinski stirred. Lehmann raised his pistol and fired twelve times, each round a heavy calibre explosive bullet, designed with military-grade autonomous machine units and cyborgs in mind.

Kaplinski stilled.

"I can't get through his thorax armour or his skull," said Lehmann.

"He's still alive. Healthtech activity is off the chart. He'll be up and fighting soon. Get out of there now, Lehmann, you can't take him," said Otto.

"Affirmative," said Lehmann. He kept his eyes on Kaplinski as he skirted the wreckage in the corridor. One of Kaplinski's feet shuddered and drew swiftly into the compartment.

"Lehmann!"

Lehmann bent to Chures, looking over him with Ky-tech eyes. "Chures isn't looking good, Otto."

"Just get them out of there." Otto watched via his IR as Kaplinski's massive bulk moved.

Shots rang out. Autonomous eye cams swivelled on the Stelsco, zooming in on the source of noise. Cossacks aboard the next carriage. More were working their way back, cautious for the moment.

They'd got out of the barracks carriage then. An alarm pinged on the Stelsco's sophisticated sensor suite – energy emissions from the flatbed, airbikes powering up.

Otto swept the Stelsco turret round, blasting with limited bursts around the windows the Cossacks shot from. They drew back.

"Lehmann! Now!" Kaplinski was pulling himself up onto his hands and knees. Blinding whiteness played around his form, massive energy consumption. What the hell was he drawing on?

Lehmann stood. Valdaire hanging onto him like a child to its father, arms round his neck, legs wrapped round his waist. Under his other arm he held the limp form of Chures.

Lehmann indicated via MT that he was ready, his face set in concentration.

Otto opened the two left doors of the Stelsco, leaving the entire side of the vehicle open to the elements. He had the rearmost door fold back and reconfigure, forming an armour plate protecting them to the rear.

On the count of three, thought out Otto. *One. Two. Three.*

He swung the drive wheel to the left hard. The Stelsco's folded back door caught on the train, shaking the car and ripping a chunk of shattered carbons from the carriage side.

Lehmann leapt, twisting and balling himself up as he came. He slammed into a comms station, taking the impact on his back, keeping it from Chures and Valdaire. The Stelsco swerved as he hit. Otto wrestled it back under control and shut the doors. Gunfire rattled off the vehicle's armour. Otto heard the low whump of EMP discharge and felt a residual surge in his systems, but the vehicle's faraday armour took care of most of it.

He pulled away from the train, the Stelsco bouncing madly as it left the embankment. Lehmann and the others, unsecured, slammed backward and forward, Lehmann doing his best to protect Chures and Valdaire as he slid across the cabin floor.

The vehicle skidded to one side as something big hit.

"Kaplinski," growled Otto.

Kaplinski straddled the vehicle's nose, his face shredded, two insane eyes staring from his ruined face, his grin a death's-head rictus of bloodied teeth in shiny black bone, his lips stripped from his skull. The fingers of one hand were firmly wrapped around one of the Stelsco's forward sensor pods. The other formed into a fist. Roaring in pain and rage, the cyborg pounded at the Stelsco's armoured windscreen.

On the fourth hit, cracks appeared.

A pair of airbikes roared overhead. Twin lines of bullet impacts perforated the earth and passed over Kaplinski, knocking bits of flesh from him. He did not flinch, but continued to methodically smash his way into the Stelsco.

Otto brought the turret forward, right to the front of the roof. He brought it to its lowest elevation. Its eye cams were so close to Kaplinski the cyborg filled the view on Otto's iHUD.

"Goodbye, Kaplinski," he said.

The guns opened up. At such close range, they would have pulverised a mountain. Kaplinski danced upon the Stelsco's rounded front, one arm up in front of his face. He came off the bonnet and bounced onto the ground. Otto was not sure if he jumped or fell.

In the rearview cameras, Otto saw Kaplinski stagger to his feet. A bright lance of energy, emanating from the train, hit him square in the back, and he fell. Otto lost sight of him.

The Stelsco hurtled across abandoned fields. The Cossacks had got into the air, and their airbikes raced overhead; it would not be long before others from the border patrols joined them, the only military units allowed in the DMZ. Lehmann and Valdaire wrestled Chures into a chair. Valdaire stumbled onto Lehmann, and he pushed her into another seat and strapped her in. Otto jinked as missiles streaked from airbike farings, the Stelsco's defensive arsenal taking some out, others sending plumes of dirt and fire into the sky as they impacted the ground.

The treeline; he had to get into the forest. He swung the car hard onto an overgrown dirt track, the armoured vehicle's wide wheels overhanging both sides. A missile got through its countermeasures, destroying the middle left wheel. The car jettisoned the damaged unit, the Stelsco bucking as it went under the back wheels and was tossed high into the air. Water fountained as the car plunged down and up, surging through a small river, the small bridge that had once crossed it long gone.

In seconds, they were in the trees, racing along a forestry road. Otto engaged the machine's camouflage lamellae, and the scales that comprised it rippled and changed, depicting the road under it and forest around it. The Cossacks' shots grew less accurate.

"I'm going for the lake!" he bellowed. "Hang on!"

He turned off the road into an area recently felled. The Stelsco bounced madly as he forced it over tree stumps and gouges. A trio of auto-foresters blurred past, backs stacked high with logs. The car bumped over a series of concrete foundation blocks, remains of an old suburb, and then was into an area where the rotting remnants of houses still stood. The Stelsco burst through house after house, dragging rotting memories out into overgrown streets as it went. They crossed a road pockmarked with shell holes, past the rusting wrecks of ancient groundcars, and went down a narrow lane lined by the wild back gardens of two streets. Crumbling fencing exploded under the Stelsco's fat tyres. Otto swerved to avoid an overturned truck, Weeds growing thickly between long-forgotten possessions turned to mush on the road. More forest. A horrible grinding came from the front right wheel unit, a major malfunction, but salvageable. Otto told the machine to withdraw the unit and repair it.

With two wheels out of action, their speed reduced as the car's near-I struggled to keep it stable.

They went up and over the remains of the P-419 highway into the southern industrial zones. Concrete giants loomed, the remains of ancient refineries.

"We're getting close," he said.

Bullets rattled off the car roof as the airbikes locked onto them once more. Five of them wove back and forth above them, strafing. Warning lights blinked red in Otto's iHUD and on consoles round the compartment as subsidiary systems died, some sacrificed by the Stelsco to keep its priority gear running.

"Let me take them out!" shouted Lehmann.

"No more collateral damage!" replied Otto.

He wove through dry sump pools, their beds stained bright with toxic chemical deposits. The vast Bratsk aluminium refinery opened up in front of him like a belated apology, rust and weeds and yesterday's poisons.

"Nearly there!"

Tumbledown warehouses clustered round the refinery dock. The hulks of rusting barges slumped at their berths, cargoes forever undelivered. Otto hit the dockside at high speed. The engines whined as wheels spun wildly, free of the ground's friction. They bounced hard as they hit the cracked mud at the bottom.

"The river!" shouted Lehmann, and pointed through the cracked windscreen. Ahead, glinting silver, a series of loops surrounded by deep mud, cutting across the bottom of the empty Bratskoye reservoir. Once held back by one of the world's largest hydroelectric dams, it had been blown by what the Russian government had blandly termed "rogue nationalist elements" after the Secret War and the subsequent Sinosiberian purchase. The ensuing flood had taken out the other four dams on the Angara river, leaving wrecked infrastructure and flattened towns to the Chinese.

Now the noxious mud, thick with mercury from the town's aluminium and chemical processing past, was open to the skies, and the unbounded river formed the true border between the Russian Federation and the People's Republic of China, slap in the middle of the 75-kilometre-wide demilitarised zone.

A clunk sounded from the Stelsco as it redeployed its repaired wheel unit, and it became easier to control. The ghostly remains of the city whipped past far on their left, and receded as they travelled across the mudflats. Otto made good use of the ship-wrecks dotting the plain, and for a few precious moments the airbikes lost them. Otto accelerated. One of the airbikes picked up his dust plume, and suddenly all five swooped in, hammering away with missiles and guns.

The Stelsco lurched as it hit the sticky mud round the river, skidded, then spun through 180 degrees as it hit the water. Its fat wheels and flotation units kept it on top of the water, the wheels stopped spinning and water jets took over. Otto disengaged the left jet and slewed the vehicle across the water as he grappled to bring the Stelsco back under control. Bullets followed their plume of spray, then abruptly stopped.

"They're retreating," said Lehmann. Eye cam screens showed the airbikes splitting in the air and falling back, as if they'd seen an invisible wall.

"Welcome to China," said Otto.

The Stelsco's wheels re-engaged as they hit the other bank. It struggled to haul them up out of the river. Otto eased back as they found their way back onto the dry.

"Everyone OK?" he asked. He looked back. Lehmann was as impassive as he always was when he was in mission mode. Valdaire was shaken up, and was anxiously checking over Chures.

Otto set the car to autodrive and went back. The VIA man was sprawled in his seat, deathly pale and barely conscious.

"Chures," he said. "Chures! Where's the damn medical pack in this vehicle?" Otto asked Lehmann.

Lehmann shook his head. *It won't do any good*, he thought out to Otto. *Kaplinski has shattered all his ribs, he's got massive internal bleeding. He might have a chance if we got him into a proper hospital, but out here…* His MT cut out as his thoughts trailed away.

"Hang in there, Chures," said Otto. "We'll get you help."

Chures smiled weakly. His breathing was weak and pink bubbles frothed at the corner of his lips.

Valdaire looked at Otto. "We could always neurally pattern him. I'm sure we could effect a quick download through his uplinks. It'll hurt, but it's better than the alternative."

Chures pushed weakly at her arm. "No…" His words came in brief pants, as his increasingly laboured breath would allow. "Don't… make… me… into… one of… them."

"Let him alone," said Otto. He remembered another time, and another person saying those words. This time he'd listen.

"It's the only way," said Valdaire, "I've got to do it, I can do it," and she began to throw open storage bins in the Stelsco. "I can get an emergency neural pattern, I can. If only…"

Otto grabbed her arm. "He said no."

Chures gasped and he passed out. His skin was white, his lips ashen.

An alarm trilled. "Veev! I'm under assault, help me, Veev!"

Valdaire's mouth dropped open. "I forgot to shut Chloe off!" She pawed at buttons until the trilling of her life companion ceased.

"Too late now," said Otto, and nodded at the windscreen. Against the grey sky bright points of light glowed, blowtorch flames in the air. They grew larger. Each burned from a jetpack attached to a heavily armoured human figure. "Dragon Fire soldiers," he said.

"The Chinese are coming," said Lehmann.

CHAPTER 14
Little Wars

Early the next day, Richards' regiment marched to the south gate.

The streets were packed with soldiers. For much of the way Richards could see little but the helmets and spears of the men around him, until the tops of the walls came into sight. Guards walked their circuit. Many watched the horizon for Lord Penumbra's armies, but more than a few had their weapons turned inwards, a spur to patriotic zeal.

The south gate was bigger than the north, five railway lines running through tunnels either side of it. Off to the west of it was a giant goods yard, and here Richards' regiment trooped in and lined up, waiting to be loaded onto waiting trains. Small locomotives doubled up at the front of each, baroque smokestacks wisping smoke to join the sulphurous fug over the yard. Twenty or so trucks were behind each engine, low-sided and open to the elements, many already crammed with soldiers. There were divisions of foundrymen armed with sledgehammers and wearing thick leather aprons, units of the city guard in enclosing armour, hordes of animals, crews of bobbleheaded sailors, weird blobs and cute robots. Officers, animal, man and otherwise, boarded the few passenger coaches attached to each train. Richards' unit's turn came and they were directed up onto the freight wagons, helping hands grasping and pulling them up, for there were no ladders.

The yard was deafening. Engines coughed and whistled. Trucks clattered and banged. Everybody was shouting. The ground was restless under the tread of the army. Men came down the trains' sides, passing up rations and canteens of water, hallooing as they went. Railway workers followed, slamming up the trucks' sides and locking them with rattling pins. They did not meet the eyes of those who stood within.

With a lusty hoot the first train pulled away in a cloud of steam and smoke. A cheer went up from the men and beasts aboard and they struck up a song. This one contained the vanguard of the army, a forward corps of city lancemen and scouts who stood in their trucks with their thogs, soothing them as they mooed and stamped their six hoofs.

"Look at those poor things," said Tarquin as the thog cars rumbled by. "Eyes rolling all over the place. Someone really should do something about that."

Another train pulled out, long trucks racked with light artillery, its attendant guards and units of the larger animals riding behind. Then the foundrymen. Time passed, and Richards' mind drifted.

His train's departure took him by surprise. His legs ached from standing still for so long, and he started when the engine took up the slack and dragged his train forward inch by squealing inch. A paw took the crook of his elbow, preventing him from falling.

"Steady there, friend!"

Richards looked up into the face of a hare. "Thanks," he said. "I didn't expect that."

"I know what you mean!" said the hare. "Exciting, isn't it? Oh, how I have long longed to march to war! Imagine! A hare like me smashing Penumbra's evil forces! I am lame and cannot run." He patted a crooked leg. "My brothers and sisters are swift as the wind, and have joined with the scouts. I thought a life of adventure beyond me. But here I am, here I am! The opportunity for glory at last, here I am!"

Several of the other soldiers had faint smiles, half-daring to imagine victory. A forlorn hope; any division with minimal armour and lame hares as part of its set-up probably did not rate highly in strategic planning, thought Richards.

"Yeah," said Richards. "Great."

"Friend! You seem to be uninspired. Think! Here you stand, taking the fight to our enemies, allies at your side. Oh, I shall write a poem about this! Yea, a paean to glory." With this he scribbled down some notes in a book he produced from a pocket.

"Sorry," said Richards. "I've a lot on my mind."

"Indeed?" said the hare genially, glancing up from his book. "Pray tell me your troubles. We have a long journey. A burden shared is a burden halved. And it may make a good poem." The train went into the tunnel, a dark world lit by skirling sparks. Richards exited the tunnel with ears ringing and stinging eyes. The hare was not put off. "Is it some young lady? Some darling you have left behind?" He waggled his eyebrows. "Maybe a leveret or two back home in the hedgerow? We all have worries, my friend. But fear not, we are to be victorious! Mr Spink told us. It is assured by the stars themselves. And what has a brave warrior like you to fear? I see from your lion-cloak you already have some skill at arms. Tell me how you vanquished such a ferocious beast. I shall pen you a rhyme to memorialise your deed."

"I do beg your pardon," said Tarquin smoothly, his amber eyes rolling open. "It's not quite the stuff of saga. He had a lot of help."

"Ah," said the hare fearfully, "I see."

"Now leave us alone," said the lion, "I don't like to be reminded of it and your chatter does grate on the nerves. I ate a few poets in my time. They didn't agree with me."

The hare pounded the truck with his good foot. Quivering, he turned to the others. "How about a rousing song?" he said nervously. He started to sing, but it fell flat. No one joined in. All of them looked at Richards warily.

"Nice," he muttered, turning to look out of the truck.

"He was extremely annoying," said Tarquin, loud enough so all could hear it. "And I do so hate being annoyed. Almost as much as I hate poets."

Richards pulled his helmet onto his head. "You're a great help."

The train proceeded onto a viaduct leading down from the city. A hundred metres of clear air were between Richards and the ground where the bridge piers rooted themselves in the mined-out plateau. The track ran close to the valley that divided Pylon City's domains from the Magic Wood. Dense brush cloaked the chasm to the bottom. The river looked like a ribbon of steel, hammered into perfect loops and laid into a model world.

"Bloody hell, that's a long way down." Richards was feeling a sensation he thought might be vertigo. He didn't like it much.

"Relax," purred Tarquin. "We'll be fine, provided there isn't another earthquake."

"Oh, thank you," said Richards. "Thank you ever so much. That makes me feel so much better." The viaduct went down in a long curve, bringing them closer to the valley edge until it straightened out as the track hit the ground. The railway ran on the very edge of the canyon, but if Richards looked to the front of the train or off to the west up to the moors, he could pretend it wasn't there.

The men and animals of the train made themselves comfortable, sitting on the sides of their trucks or on their knapsacks. Conversations started up.

By the time they had left Pylon City it had been past midday, and the landscape they travelled through was one of afternoon. Bright light diffused through clouds like wire wool, a glare that picked out every pockmark on the plateau. Slagheaps and open pits ringed with cranes rushed by. Spurs to the railway ran to quarries cut into the moor, an industrial moonscape, where only tufts of colourless grass, lank and sparse as hag's hair, thrived.

"It is horrible, is it not?" said the hare.

"It is," agreed Richards, tapping his fingers on the truck. The hare glanced concernedly at the lion.

"Don't worry about him. He's mostly all mouth now. The most biting thing about him is his wit, and that's not very sharp."

Tarquin bared his teeth.

"It appears we are heading south, off the plateau," said the hare, "to bring Lord Penumbra to battle where the land slopes into the Broken Lands, a fine defensible position. It will prevent any advance by Penumbra up The Rift, and ensure that Jotenlend, the source of much of Pylon City's food, is protected."

"Sounds good."

"Ah, you know a little military theory?" asked the hare eagerly.

"No, not really," admitted Richards. There was so much he did not know while the Grid was denied to him. "My partner does all that."

"Well," said the hare, "this is of course only my supposition, but it is the most sensible course of action. I have studied many of the great generals of Pylon City and the long war poems," it said shyly.

"Odd hobby for a hare," said Richards.

"Many of my brothers and sisters revel in the wild chase and the feel of the wind in their whiskers, but this pleasure is denied me. So I developed interests outside of the ordinary." It paused. "Like poetry!" It looked at Richards expectantly with that "ask me to read you one of my poems" type expression that poets get. Richards stared blankly back at him. The hare became bashful and turned away.

The ruined world changed piece by piece to a landscape of scrubby fields and the clouds cleared. The train passed close by rough dwellings, hugely tall with doors three times bigger than a man, their walls made of enormous boulders. Of the Jotens, there was no sign.

The sun set. The sky above the train remained a pure light-blue for a time, and the men gambled at knucklebones until it was dark.

Richards tried as best he could to get comfortable. He watched the alien sky. Away from the glare of Pylon City's sodium lamps, the stars twinkled brightly, competing with the sparks the train pumped into the night with its smoke.

"A river of fire," said Tarquin sleepily. "It is a river of fire, and it is consuming the world."

"That old hare's not the only poet on board, eh?" said Richards.

"Mmf," said Tarquin.

In the morning they woke to war.

"Troopers!" A shout roused Richards from where he sat, bored, staring out over the plains. "Prepare to disembark!"

"Now there's a man who enjoys his job," said Tarquin.

"Jesus, he's worse than Otto," Richards said. His limbs cracked with unpleasant organic noises as he stood. He'd barely moved since he'd woken, and now felt as brittle as a straw doll. There was more to a human's constant, twitchy motion than staying upright, he was learning, like not letting their irritating meat outsides seize up.

The soldiers hauled themselves from the trucks to join a stream of troops marching beside the tracks.

"Right, my sleeping beauties," said the sergeant. "We are going to go for a walk. Word has come down to me that the line has been blown ahead by Penumbra's saboteurs. All you lot should think on how nice and healthy you'll be once you've walked. Who knows, there might even be time for a spot of breakfast before the war starts."

"Really, sarge?" said an eager trooper.

"No!" roared the sergeant. "Now get a bleedin' move on, or I'll shoot you myself and save Penumbra and his monsters the bother."

Richards fell into step with something like a rat. It gave him a filthy look.

"Charming," said Richards.

The day was the kind autumn shares with summer: a cold morning with the promise of a hot afternoon. The sky was a uniform grey, its light joyless. Ahead it turned to an angry black, a thick band of deeper cloud foreshortening the horizon. Bursts of lightning lit it from within, thunder answered by tremors from below.

"Look!" said the rat. "A storm!"

"That's not a storm," said the hare with some amount of awe. "That is the death of the world. The Great Terror. I must record it in my poem."

"Quiet in the ranks there! You can all have a natter after you've had a battle," bawled the sergeant. "Until then, keep your cakeholes shut."

They walked five abreast alongside the railway embankment on a plain of grass that was almost completely flat. No farms, nor mines, only one small building, after the railway line curved west, red-brick, about a mile from the route of their march.

"Last Station," said the hare. "From there the railway heads out to cross The Rift."

A familiar odour percolated into the air. Burnt ground. The

army took in the wasted land before them with a chorus of mutters and shouts.

"Will this be the fortune of the Magic Wood?"

"And the city?"

There was an abrupt change in scenery, the plateau ending in a thick scar where two world fragments clumsily joined. Beyond it lay a plain criss-crossed with ravines and gullies, giving the landscape the look of an angular brain.

It was scorched black. Charcoalled trees clawed at the sky, the gullies steamed, the grass was burnt down to the roots.

"The broken lands, twice broken!" said the hare.

The army marched onto the brow of the hill and fanned out, directed in columns to their positions. The centre of their battleline was a low blister in the slope. Commander Hedgehog and his best warriors had taken up station there. A mix of large forest animals armoured head to toe surrounded him and his staff. Behind this position were the army's artillery pieces, globular balls of crystal sporting long brass barrels. They looked spectacularly dangerous.

"See!" whispered the hare from behind Richards. "Hedgehog has the men of the city at the heart of the army. He is guarded by the Big Animal Division and the City Guard. They have lightning lances, terrible weapons. I should expect we will be stationed out on one of the flanks, behind a skirmish line of lancers. When the enemy breaks through them, range will no longer matter, and we will be able to put our swords and spears to deadly use at close quarters!"

The hare was mostly right. The Pylon Guard were few in number, so Richards' regiment was stationed behind a line of arbalesteers. These crossbowmen were not of Pylon City and wore colourful clothes at odds with the Pylonites' sober garb. Their forms were not so well rendered, their language a musical tongue he did not recognise. Protecting their right flank was a detachment of foundrymen. Further out roamed groups of skir-mishers backed up by squadrons of light thog cavalry.

"They'll stop anything getting round the back," the hare ex-plained enthusiastically. "Or, when we break the enemy's line, force it apart like a wedge."

"He's enjoying this far too much," muttered Richards to Tarquin.

From behind came a rhythmic clatter: armoured weasels, well over a thousand of them, marching to fill the gap in the allied lines to Richards' left. They wore scale and plate, articulated to accommodate their sinuous bodies. Each carried a pike and a steel buckler with a spiked boss. Blood-red pennants fluttered from helmets and shields and streamed from the ends of their pikes.

"Aren't they glorious?" whispered the hare in awe.

Richards raised an eyebrow. "Don't weasels eat hares?"

"They do indeed," said the hare, nodding, not rising to the bait. "And I know I should not admire them, for a pack of them did de-vour a sister of mine. But still, all that is behind us now, now we are part of the League of Humans and Small but Brave Animals!"

"Snappy," said Richards.

"How could we fail to lose with such ferocious beings at our sides? A thousand armoured weasels, each a born killer. Glorious!"

"Yeah," said Richards slowly, remembering their behaviour in the bar. "And each a born weasel."

Richards had time to re-experience the boredom part of the boredom and terror warfare combination. They stood in their position for several hours, and once again he became uncom-fortable. He was debating taking a piss right there when the hare spoke again.

"Oh my!" said the hare. "Here they come!"

The sky went dark. A hush came over the army of men and beasts. The enemy approached. Shadow preceded it, and dark-ness followed.

The horde of creatures came from the south, appearing over a ridge three miles away, drawing toward them with unnatural speed.

"Oh my," said the hare with a tinge of fear. "There are rather a lot of them."

In the main the army was composed of vile-looking humanoids. Like the alliance, monsters brought from all manner of places on the Grid.

"Every hero needs his mob," said Richards grimly, doing a quick calculation on the balance between heroic human players and system-controlled monsters in your average game. The odds he came up with were unfavourable. Not for the first time he wondered how the hell he'd ended up in this mess, and decided to blame Hughie.

Steam curled from haemites. Immense war-beasts studded the horde like rocks on a polluted beach. Steam-powered towers, bristling with cannon, crawled across the broken lands on caterpillar tracks. Around these marched monstrous trollmen, swishing tree-trunk clubs as they walked.

"Look!" said the hare, his lips wobbling with fear. "Morblins! There… there must be over five thousand of them! And daibeasts. And, by lord Frith, that is a low-dweller. A low-dweller!" An unpleasant chant filled the air, a droning that made Richards' skin crawl. An oily reek descended across the battlefield, the exhaust of engines, steam, the stink of unwashed bodies.

Nearby, one of the soldiers began to cry.

"Shut it, you," said the sergeant. There was a tremor in his voice.

The front rank of what Richards took to be morblins, small, pot-bellied, grey-skinned creatures, had a great many armoured hounds amidst it. The largest morblins held onto the leashes of these dogs, who half-dragged them towards the allied lines.

The enemy stopped, facing off against the league.

Silence fell. Thunder rumbled. Pennants cracked in the wind.

Then a howl as the dogs were set loose. They rushed across the plains, baying.

"Steady, Richards, steady," Richards told himself. The rush of fear his human facsimile provided him was powerful.

"Keep your spear up, Richards, don't lose your head. Should anything get through I'll shift to stone," said Tarquin urgently. "Just remember you won't be quite so nimble when I do. Keep that in mind, dear boy, and it'll all be tickety-boo. You'll see."

"I don't see why we can't just fuck off," Richards said.

The commander of the arbalesteers shouted, and the first rank readied themselves. Two hundred heavy crossbows clicked into place on their tripods. They waited, their arms steady, their gaze unwavering. The commander held his arm. The hounds came on.

"Company!" called Richards' sergeant. "Present pikes!" Richards cursed his quaking limbs as he fumbled his spear into place.

"This is where it all begins my friend," said the hare behind Richards. "Wish me luck."

The arbalesteer captain dropped his arm, and the world dissolved into violence.

Two hundred barbed quarrels sped unerringly. The yelps of two hundred dogs filled the air.

A shout went up from the morblins, and they broke into a run towards the allied lines, the trollmen beside them, the ground thundering as they came. The air crackled with electricity as the lancers of Pylon City discharged their weaponry into the front of the horde. Hundreds fell, burnt and writhing, but there were thousands behind. The lancemen parted ranks, and with a mighty squeak a horde of vole mercenaries, the vanguard of the League of Brave but Small Animals, hurled themselves through the gap towards the approaching morblins. There was a crash as the lines connected.

The lancemen reformed smoothly and pumped bolt after bolt
of cerulean energy into the rear ranks of the horde, picking out
the larger creatures as the valiant voles held back the enemy.
By Richards the foreign crossbowmen fired by rank an endless
rain of quarrels. The dead of the enemy tumbled in heaps.

The enemy artillery opened up. Shells whistled overhead
from the tracked towers of Penumbra. Dozens of shells slammed
into the packed lines of men and animals. Screams filled the air.
Earth and blood fountained skywards and body parts rained
down. Groups of the more timid animals looked close to dis-
solving into panic.

"Eyes front, soldier!" shouted the sergeant at Richards.

The allied guns replied. Heavy lightning burned through the
air, leaving glowing after-images and a sharp smell. Iron towers
burst into flame and stopped in their tracks. One carried on
moving forward, a track blown clean off. It heeled over pon-
derously, and crashed down, crushing hundreds of its own side.
The allied lightning cannon raked bloody furrows in the horde,
but their numbers seemed inexhaustible.

The arbalesteers kept firing as the enemy closed, ignoring the
desperate fights of their comrades with the surviving warhounds.
The corpses of morblins and trollmen lay five deep. The enemy
were so numerous that they kept on coming, fifty metres away,
then thirty, then twenty. The arbalesteers shot until they were
on top of them. Richards saw one go down screaming under a
haemite, his body sucked dry. More haemites followed, and the
sounds of blades on metal bodies rang out across the field as the
arbalesteers abandoned their crossbows and drew their short
swords.

"Steady, lads!" barked the sergeant. "Here they come!"

The earth shook under the weight of charging trollmen. The
line of arbalesteers bent backwards, wavered and broke. The
enemy surged through in one and twos and then by the dozen.

They flung themselves at the line of men, flattening many. Richards' arm juddered as a bellowing creature impaled itself on his spear.

"Watch out!" roared the lion. Richards jumped back as another trollman swung at him, leaving his spear in the guts of his toppling foe. He ducked a hammer blow, narrowly keeping his footing. The trollman readied his weapon for another strike. Richards had nowhere to go, hemmed in by the dead and those desperate not to be. A blast of lightning felled the trollman, leaving Richards gasping. Limbs and blades whirled around him.

A morblin cannoned into him, clawing and biting. He wrestled with it a while, but it was as weak as its fat body suggested, and he managed to snatch out his sword and despatch it. Richards looked at his sword, slick and treacherous in his hands, then at the creatures from innumerable virt-games warring in deadly earnest all around him, the violent deaths of scores of talking animals and gaming clichés.

"This is fucking ridiculous!" shouted Richards.

The world disappeared behind a sheet of white. Richards stumbled, blood in his eyes, hearing gone. He blinked and found himself in a lull in the fighting.

Bodies lay all about. A ruddy crater garnished with the limbs of friend and foe occupied the space where the centre of his regiment had been. A lucky few stood blinking, covered in blood. They stared at one another, shocked, lost between surprise and relief.

Richards staggered in a rough circle, his head spinning. Shouting, loud and frantic, impinged on the ringing in his ears. Away to his right, a knot of surprised troops yelled as the weasels attacked them from behind.

Richards wiped the blood of his comrades from his face. His head cleared. "I've got to get out of here," he said, and cast about for a means of escape.

A paw grabbed him from behind, spinning him round. The lame hare, one of his ears a tatter.

"Where are you going? Fleeing is the blackest treason…"

"I…" said Richards.

The hare held up a hand to remonstrate. It was the last thing it ever did. A cannonball whistled by, a gust of hard wind stirring Richards' hair. It removed the hare's head neatly. Blood fountained from its neck, splattering Richards, and the hare folded onto its lame leg like a collapsible chair.

Richards stumbled back, caught sight of a stray thog and ran for it. He grabbed its reins and swung atop. It lowed angrily and stamped its six legs, but held fast. He tugged on its reins, dragging its head around, and the animal performed a tight circle.

Fighting raged all about. There was no way out.

"Dammit! What do we do now?"

"Let's get to the centre, tell the hedgehog. We'll better be able to be on our way if they win," said Tarquin.

Richards debated the lion's suggestion with himself. He spun the mount round again. There was little chance he'd get off the field intact, not with the weasels butchering their way through their own side all around him. "OK," he said, "OK." He kicked with his heels, and the thog took off.

Shells exploded to the left of Richards, to the right of him, reducing the battle to a series of violent tableaux, surging into view and then lost in veils of gunsmoke and sheets of earth.

Three half-naked anime heroines tackled a trollman, baiting it with spears. A band of otters in lab coats tackled a purple octopus covered in smilies. Men rolled in the dirt with morblins, dodging the thrusts of filthy knives. Haemites fed on friend and foe alike, their whistles an industrial dirge. Here and there disciplined pockets of men and beasts formed tight groups, spearpoint and blade keeping the Penumbra's minions at bay. But every enemy felled was replaced by four more. Gone were the proud ranks; the field writhed with small and personal wars, all thoughts of strategy obscured by blood and sweat and terror. Creatures came at Richards to fall to his sword or bounce from the flanks of the six-legged cow, their cries snatched away by speed and steel.

"Nearly there!" yelled Richards.

Tarquin turned to stone and saved Richards from a spear-point. "We're not out of the woods yet."

Richards hammered toward the centre, where the disciplined corps of hedgehogs stood firm. Heavily armoured in burnished steel, they surrounded the Lord High Commander's command post, an enormous tortoise with "Roger" written in childish script on its shell.

Atop Roger was a howdah of metal. Telescopes and small lightning cannon were fixed to the rails. One gunner lay dead in the harness of his shattered weapon, but the others trained theirs still upon the enemy, spikes of electricity writhing peri-odically through the air. In front of the howdah, on a seat on the lip of Roger's shell, sat another hedgehog holding a set of metal reins. It flicked a whip about the tortoise's head. Roger seemed unperturbed. Through his helm's eye-slits, he pondered the bloodbath with the slow bemusement with which tortoises regard the world.

"Lord High Commander Hedgehog!" yelled Richards, leaping off the thog. He bounded up the low steps to the howdah, and was promptly accosted by two burly hedgehogs.

"Who are you?" growled one.

"Some kind of assassin," said the other. Blades scraped as they drew out their daggers.

"I have urgent news for the Lord High Commander," insisted Richards.

"No one allowed up here but general staff," yelled the hedge-hog over the noise of an exploding shell. "Push off!"

"Let him through, let him through," said the diffident voice
of Hedgehog. "I will see him." The bodyguards stepped aside,
and Richards was afforded a view of the Lord High Commander.
His visor was up, since he had been conferring with his aides,
and as Richards approached he snapped shut an elegant telescope. "Well?" said Hedgehog. "What is it, human? Speak, then
be gone."

"The weasels, the weasels have turned!"

"I see," said Hedgehog, his voice several degrees cooler. "They
are rolling up the right flank?"

"Right now."

"No doubt you think I should act. But I won't," said Lord High
Commander Hedgehog. "The weasels, you see, work for me."

"Ah."

"'Ah' indeed. Those short-sighted fools in Pylon City could
not see the advantage to be had from forming an alliance with
Penumbra. Though we argued the case with them, they would
not favour the idea. Penumbra was more than happy to entertain our unilateral offer. The Pylonites will die. Our aeons-long
struggle with Pylon City will be over, and the Magic Wood will
survive the Great Terror, forever free of the tyranny of men and
their machines!"

"That's cold," said Richards. "Your people are dying in droves."

"Rather unfortunate, that. Still, means there won't be much
opposition when I take over the Wood, will there? With Lord
Penumbra's blessing, of course."

"You stupid rodent," said Richards. "He's tricked you into
fighting his war for him."

Hedgehog smiled. "I have never lost a battle. As long as there
has been an army of the Magic Wood there has been a Lord
High Commander Hedgehog, and as long as that has been so,
there have been no defeats. This battle tortoise, Roger, he was
my father's mount, before that my grandfather's, my great-

great-grandfather's. He has never witnessed a battle in which he was not upon the winning side. How else do you think he can remain so phlegmatic, eh? I have two hundred years of victory at my back and you, some man, tell me I am wrong? Pfah! Let the whole of the Earth thunder to the tramping of iron-shod paws, for I will rule it all!" Hedgehog cackled maniacally. Two hedgehogs stepped forward. "Now I'm going to kill you. Make him kneel." The hedgehogs forced Richards down. The Lord High Commander stepped forward and loomed over Richards. "Any last words?" He unhitched his lightning-pistol.

"I'm not going to beg," said Richards.

"I am not so crass as to expect begging!" scoffed the hedgehog. "I was rather hoping for some brave witticism. Stiff upper lip and all, wot? Pity."

"You're making a terrible mistake."

"Yes, yes," said the hedgehog. "Goodbye."

Richards stared down the crystal at the end of the gun.

"Balls," he said, and screwed his eyes tight. No shot came. Roger let out a croak of fear like tearing paper and reared up. There was a sound of the snapping of chain and the wrenching of metal. The howdah broke into pieces as it came free of Roger's shell, scattering hedgehogs and pitching Richards to the blackened ground. He rolled to avoid the tortoise's foot as Roger ran at some speed away from the source of his horror, squashing two of Hedgehog's bodyguards flat and leaving them oozing in the dust. The rest of Hedgehog's guard picked themselves up, faltered and followed the tortoise.

Richards looked behind him, and his own heart froze. Over the prone body of Lord High Commander Hedgehog was Lord Penumbra.

Penumbra sat atop a beast that was half-horse, half-dragon. It pawed at the earth with clawed hoofs. Its skin was a coat of scales, its face a snarl of night-black violence, its eyes those of a cat, its tail a serpent's head. It radiated a deep chill, pinning Richards' breath to the air in clouds of frost. Black vapours curled around it, stealing the light away. Penumbra himself was nebulous and black, his form clad in shadow and armour of jet.

The battlefield grew quiet, sound stymied in Penumbra's presence. The sky roiled with the storm of the world-death.

"Hedgehog!" rang out a sepulchral voice. "Hedgehog! I come with your reward! Rule in my name! Death shall be thy kingdom!"

Richards could not look directly at Penumbra, try as he might. His bright darkness blinded him.

"N-no, my lord!" said Hedgehog. "We have an arrangement!" He shook. No longer the proud warlord, he was now just a big fat rodent in a complicated tin suit.

"Death!" bellowed Penumbra. His mount reared, its whinnying the end of flowers. "Death! Low field-beast, you would seek to deal with me? Where is your honour, where is your side of the bargain? Where is Queen Isabella?" He roared, a long sound of discordant ferocity. "Fool!"

"No, no!" squealed Hedgehog, falling to his knees. "Please! I looked, I tried!"

Penumbra drew a pillar of black flame as he would a sword. His arm extended, distorted like a shadow, the weapon stretching impossibly towards the hedgehog. A shaft of blackness struck out from it, piercing Hedgehog's chest.

Hedgehog ceased to be. Shadow became light and light shadow. He became a negative of sooty grains. Hedgehog dissipated, pulled into the sword, his thin scream remaining in the air, the scream all small animals make in pain, nothing more.

Richards felt his stomach turn to water as Penumbra's faceplate swivelled toward him. "And now you. You and your ilk are a blight on this land."

The shadow-blade extended out, its tip burning Richards with its cold. As it came, reality warped around it, and Richards was struck by a thought. Well, two thoughts.

The first was that reality was warping around the blade, turning glassy and spinning off sub-universes that popped like soap bubbles on the charred grass.

Secondly, Richards could not hear k52's Gridsignature at all. His eyes narrowed.

Something came swiftly from the left. There was a roar, the sound of metal hitting metal. The ground heaved. Richards' chest went tight as Tarquin turned to stone. He fell up into the air, and came back down. He found himself lying in a smoking crater, soil pattering off him. His vision swam. An iron monster reached down with long claws to pluck the last of his life from him.

That was all his facsimiled mind could take.

CHAPTER 15
The Valley

A squeaking accompanied by a grinding penetrated the fog in Richards' mind. He decided he found it annoying, but his irritation was quickly forgotten as sensation returned to him. He hurt all over. His arm was a mass of painful throbbing. He lay there, not daring to move, eyes shut until a jolt through whatever he lay on brought more pain and caused them to jump open.

He pulled himself onto his elbows and tried not to whimper.

He was on a pump wagon. Bear stood at one end of the mechanism, methodically pushing it up and down with one paw, struggling out of his armour as he did so.

"He's awake," said Tarquin.

"You're back!" shouted Bear, his voice muffled by the armour. He wrenched it over his head, and tossed it overboard. "Damn uncomfortable that was. Who ever heard of a bear in armour? Ridiculous. But I'm keeping these." He held up a paw encased in a heavy gauntlet. There was a rasp of metal, and four blades popped out of the back of it. "Good, eh?" said Bear. "They're a lot sharper than my own, and now I need never worry about breaking a nail in a fight."

Richards tried to sit up.

"Steady, sunshine!" said Bear, and the squeaking slowed. "Don't do anything silly."

Richards looked over the side of the pump wagon, which appeared to be flying through the air.

"We're on the bridge between the plateau and the Magic Wood. You don't want to fall," said Tarquin. There were clouds below them.

"Thought we'd lost you back there, sunshine," said Bear. "It all got a bit hairy. No one escaped. They were cut down to a squirrel."

"I don't believe this," said Richards and lay back down. "Why me?"

"Don't be like that. I got us out of there, didn't I?" said Bear.

Richards sat up properly. His chest hurt like hell.

"Shrapnel wound. A scratch, so don't worry," said Bear. It had been expertly stitched. "Like that? That's my work. As was finding this pump wagon at Last Station. You have to get up pretty early in the morning to catch this bear! I figured we'd head west. Did I do good?"

"You did good," said Richards.

"Damn right I did," said Bear.

Richards reached behind him and found his knapsack. He pulled out his macintosh, unrolled it and, wincing, put it on. Next he withdrew the fedora Spink had summoned up, smacked it against his hand to get it into shape and placed it on his head. It made him feel complete, and the pain subsided a little.

"I should have asked for a new suit too," he said, looking at his tattered Pylon City uniform. "Balls."

They crossed the valley and went into the domain of the Magic Wood, and Richards understood why the animals hated the Pylonites. Swathes of trees had been clear-felled, logs stacked neatly next to charcoal burners, the soft green of the forest scraped right down to raw yellow earth. Pits of tainted water pooled behind dams of mud. Weather-bleached stumps were stacked in heaps, their dead roots contorted in woody agony. More railway tracks ran off into the forest, each an ugly wound.

They saw no men or sentient animals, but the pump wagon's passage startled bizarre creatures in the trees, humanoid things that had tiny bodies but enormous heads of bright scarlet. They had painted-on beards round pink lips and high foreheads covered in subcutaneous lumps. Their hooded eyes unreadable, they stared as the wagon passed.

Richards shared out his meagre army rations and fell into a black sleep. When he woke he was more stiff than sore. It was evening, and the forest had thinned, dotted with dappled glades made by a kinder hand than that of man. The trees retreated into huddles, and then they were rolling leisurely across a heath alive with life where limestone pavements grinned at them like worn teeth through lips of yellow gorse. The sun was warm and soothing.

They came to a place where a road crossed the line, and here Bear was obliged to apply the brakes. There was a man in the way.

The man said nothing as the pump wagon squealed to a stop half a metre from him. He was ragged and unwashed, his beard and hair unkempt. He was wringing his hands. His head juddered, an old-style film caught on the same three frames playing over and over again.

"Ah, poor bastard," said Bear, jumping down. "Stuck. The bit of land maintaining him must have gone. I hate it when this happens. Best to go out in an instant, not like this."

The man's voice stuttered. "Du... du... du... du... du..."

Bear grabbed him and hauled him off his feet. He remained frozen. "Hurgh!" grunted Bear, "death is heavy." He wrinkled his nose. "Goldilocks' knickers, he smells worse than Lucas, must have been here for some time. They still live, in a way.

Horrible." He placed the man by the track gently. "Now, let's see what's what." Bear tilted his head to one side. "Network's worse than ever," he grumbled. Presently, he gave a sharp nod. "We were right to get out of that battle when we did. This guy's code was ravelled up in the Broken Lands. If he's like this, the whole place is gone."

The bear clambered onto the pump wagon. "This k52 is a real bastard. Killing us is one thing, killing us like this is abominable," he said.

"Hmmm," said Richards, drumming his fingers on the side of the pump. The wagon pulled away, leaving the man to his slow end.

"'Hmmm'? What does that mean?" said Tarquin. "You don't agree?"

"Oh, I agree alright," said Richards.

"So?" said the bear.

"So nothing," he said, and kept his thoughts to himself.

The cart went on through the afternoon and into the night. Richards sat and thought and listened to the sound of the rocker. Up and down, squeak and squeak. Up and down. The wheels went clack-clack-clack and Richards thought of Lord Penumbra, and of k52. He thought about just how painful and annoying being, for all intents and purposes, human was.

And he thought about Rolston.

A jerk shook him out of his contemplation as they bumped over a join in the land, the rails either side mismatched. The heath ran out, a brown scar dividing it from desert, the join sparking where the coding did not mesh. The desert sloped steeply and at the end it dropped away to nothing over a bluff, the track plunging with it.

"We're going to go over!" shouted Bear. He grabbed the brake lever and leaned all his weight onto it, straining out over the back of the wagon. "Shitshitshitshitshitshit! I can't hold it!" The pump mechanism pounded up and down as they picked up speed. Wind rushed past. Richards was obliged to clutch his fedora to his head.

"Jump!" shouted Richards.

"We're going too fast!" said Tarquin.

They hit the cliff edge and the track plunged down like a rollercoaster.

"Great hairy grizzlies! Hold on!" shouted Bear, as sparks fountained out behind them. "Didn't see cliffs until too late. Can't slow down! Sorry!" Richards dodged past the bouncing pump and added his strength to Bear's own. "Pull hard! It's the only way!"

"There's a curve ahead!" shouted Tarquin.

"Lean!" roared Bear. He and Richards leaned as the wagon hit the curve. The small vehicle went up onto two wheels and slammed down as the way straightened.

"That was too close!" said Bear.

"It must be three hundred metres straight down. We'll be smashed to bits!" said Tarquin.

Richards and Bear pulled on the brake lever. It grew hot to the touch as the brake shoe burned off.

"Curve!" The truck slalomed round another bend. Again they leant into it, the wheels rattling as they bounced off and on the tracks. "We're not going to survive another like that!" shouted Bear over the clatter of the truck. "We may have to jump."

Richards looked down. "We're still too high! Pull harder."

The smell of hot metal strengthened as Bear and Richards strained hard on the lever. A fountain of red-hot iron filings billowed up around them, singeing Bear's fur. The toy pulled with all his might. For a moment, it looked like it was working. The truck slowed. But then there was a dull clunk and they sprawled backwards, Richards narrowly avoided being brained by the pump handles.

"Goldilocks' knickers!" said Bear, holding up the bent remains of the lever. "I broke the brake!"

"Hold on!" bellowed Tarquin.

Richards grasped the pump wagon deck, fingernails pulling on the wood. Bear tucked the man under his bulk. "I'll cushion you both when we crash," he shouted. "Tarquin, don't change to stone. You'll shatter."

The truck rattled on, accelerating ever more as it sped towards the desert. The buttress levelled out, but Richards figured that the height did not matter that much. Were the truck to derail on the flat, the speed they were going could still kill them all. Faster and faster they went. The buttress ended, the cart tipping on the slight curve at the bottom. They thundered on, the desert a blur of sand and sky.

"Oh no!"

"Jesus!" said Richards.

It was the end of the line in no uncertain way; a hard wooden buffer. The pump wagon smashed into it, and they were thrown into the air. Bear clasped Richards tightly to him as they flew. Fur, sand and sky turned over and over themselves. There was a thump. A drift of sand. Silence.

"Ow," said Bear. "Ow ow ow." Richards was winded. Tarquin had been spun round so his head was under his back, but he was unharmed. Richards patted Bear's ample belly.

"Thanks, sergeant," he said. "You're a very useful bear."

"Ow, get off." They got to their feet. Bent iron and splinters were strewn everywhere. "Oooh," said Bear.

"It appears that we have arrived. Somewhere," stated Tarquin.

"Eh?" said Richards. He rearranged himself and brushed off the sand. He pulled on the lionskin so that Tarquin's head was no longer hanging off his back and turned round to see a canyon mouth. A narrow opening between two natural pillars of sandstone. Above it, a large sign of weather-worn bronze bearing a legend. It read: "La Valle dei Promesse persa."

"What does it say, what does it say?" asked Bear.

"The Valley of Lost Promises," said Richards. "In Italian. Now that *is* interesting."

The valley started as a canyon and quickly became a crevasse. A sandy path wound between walls of rock, so narrow that Bear had to force himself through sideways. The walls rose, the sky became a stripe, and they were walking in shadow.

They paused for a rest toward noon, and when they set off once more the path widened. Thorny plants that reeked of creosote lined its margins in dense profusion.

The canyon broadened into a scrubby valley. A stream trickled though a dry riverbed many times its width. Cliffs ran on either side, their feet hidden by cubes of fallen rock. In the centre a mesa rose, flat top level with the desert. It split the river bed, only one channel carrying water past it.

Every available patch of ground was covered in the thorny bushes, smothering nascent sand-dunes and holding fast the scree. Rising up from this painful thicket were hundreds of statues, all of the same woman in many different poses. On all, her face was beatific, generous, a little sad.

The largest was so big its head and shoulders cleared the canyon to stand glowing in the desert sun above. It was in an art nouveau style. She looked down upon them, a single tear of bronze on her face, as if the artist had allowed white-hot metal to run down her cheek. Her bare feet were on point like a ballerina, the whole edifice balanced unreally on a plinth the height of Bear.

"The queen!" said Bear softly. "They're all statues of the queen! What are they all doing here?"

"Looks like they've been dumped. There are statue graveyards like this back in the Real, victims of regime changes."

"Eh?" said Bear.

"Never mind," said Richards.

The path that wended its way past the statues – verdigrised bronze, marble, steel, modern stacked carbon plastics – was broad enough for Richards and Bear to walk comfortably abreast. The thorns choked everything, swallowing the smaller statues, clutching at the hips of the greater.

"Hang on a minute," said Richards. He pushed through the bushes toward a statue, sharp breaths and expletives preceding him as thorns snagged at his legs. He stopped, pushed back his hat and leaned in closer. "There's something on this one." He peered through a lattice of thorn and twig. A plaque was upon the statue's plinth. He couldn't read it until he moved some of the vegetation aside.

"Isabella," said Tarquin, "the queen's name."

"What's all this mean?" asked Bear.

"Beats me," said Richards. "Come on."

They walked some more, rounding the mesa. Ahead there was a cave, nestling in the apex of the triangle where the valley walls drew together in a curtain of rock. The river issued from the cave, gurgling over its lower lip. Mosses and ferns grew on the knoll above it. A rich scent of damp earth came from within. It was moist.

"Is it just me, or does that look like a big fanny?" said Bear.

"It's not just you, dear boy. It does look like a big fanny."

"Do you mind?" said Richards.

"Sunshine, it is a big fanny," said Bear. "Now what?"

Richards looked up. The cliffs around them were sheer. He looked at the sun and pointed at the cave. "If this place follows the normal rules, that way is west. We go in."

They abandoned the path and took to the river, splashing up to the cave mouth. Richards paused at the lip; the cave was dark. He waited for his eyes to adjust. They didn't.

Bear took a big drink from the stream and pushed past

Richards, wiping his muzzle on a long hairy arm. "Come on then. If we're going in, let's not hang about."

Richards followed. Darkness enveloped them, Bear became a dull shape bobbing uncertainly in the gloom. Water sloshed round his ankles.

"Hang on a minute," said Bear, the grey smear of his back stopping. "It goes down a bit he..."

There was a large splash, and Bear disappeared. Richards walked forward cautiously. "Bear? Bear!" he shouted. "Are you in there, big buddy?"

"He's gone!" said Tarquin. "What are we going to do?"

Richards went a little way on, willing his eyes to see more, but all he could make out were blobs that might have been rocks and a darkness that had to be deep water. "He's complete... woah!" Something took tight hold of his ankle and yanked him. He bounced off a rock, went under the water and lost his breath in an explosion of bubbles. Down he went, thrashing in the dark, lungs burning. Panic set in. Real fear as he'd never felt it before, primal and all-consuming. He battered at the pressure on his leg with his fists, hitting rubbery flesh. He dug his fingers in as hard as he could. His lungs burned. He had to fight the urge to suck in lungfuls of water as hard as he clawed at the thing at his ankle.

Light came from below. Whatever had hold of his leg let go. He fought for the surface, flailing his arms, primitive parts of his fake brain telling him to get up, up! But a current grasped him as surely as the thing had, and his attempts to swim made his lungs burn worse. Spots whirled in the dark. He swirled head over heels, toward the light.

He popped through a hole along with a torrent of water issuing from the underside of a sheet of rock. Air touched his face, his lips exploded open, and he sucked in a breath.

Nothing had ever felt so good. The feeling did not last. He was falling.

"What the hell?" Richards' face was pushed tight against his skull as he entered freefall. He clutched hard at his hat, but it was torn away from him. The fall of water turned to droplets, then a rainbow mist carried off by the wind, and he was in cold, cold sky. Below him clouds arrayed themselves with deceptive solidity. Far below that was a patchwork world in miniature, stark contrasts evident between each slab of stolen terrain.

"Ah, shit," he said, words wrenched from his mouth by the wind.

A dirty white blob preceded them. "Look!" shouted Tarquin. "Bear!"

Richards caught sight of a glint in the sun. As they fell, it grew bigger, turning into a metal-hulled ship suspended between two larger shapes, long torpedo-like things with tail flukes and multiple flippers – many-limbed whales. Figures resolved themselves on the deck, looking up and pointing. The ship rocked as Bear hit. Richards opened his arms up and steered himself toward the boat like a skydiver. It rushed up at him, crew scattering.

He hit Bear's stomach, cracking a scrim of ice on his fur.

"Oof!" said the bear. He looked up into Richards' face, sprawled on his gut. "Nice of you to drop in," he said with a grin.

"That's two I owe your tummy," said Richards. He smiled broadly as his hat fluttered down and landed next to him. "Hey! My hat!" He scooped it up and popped it on his head.

"Arrrr, this all be very touching," said a piratical voice. "But what be yer business aboard the *Kylie*?"

Tarquin flickered to stone. At the prow of the ship, the crew gathered; all glinting gold teeth, fancy pants, ostentatious weaponry and ripe body odour.

"OK," said Bear, casting his eyes heavenwards. He pushed Richards off his stomach and set his shoulders forward. The long blades of his gloves shot out. "Right then," he growled, "who's first for a kicking?"

With ear-curling oaths, the pirates charged.

CHAPTER 16
Dragon Fire

Otto stood and watched as the Chinese dug. The ground at the old lakeshore was full of pine roots, and yet the Dragon Fire troopers tasked with excavating Chures' grave did so with their armour stripped off. They sweated in the cold air, hacking and shovelling away stolidly, using only their native strength.

"In deference to the dead," the troops' leader told Otto. "The dead should depart watched over by men, not machines." He'd been courteous as his soldiers had surrounded the Stelsco, flipping his helmet into the broad back of his power-assist armour and introducing himself as Commander Guan Song Hsien. They were prisoners, for all that, and the seven other Dragon Fire soldiers remained in their bulky armour and covered Lehmann, Valdaire and Otto with their weapons. The armour was comprised of jointed plates, smooth lines marred by quick release bolts. The armour was particularly massive about the shoulders, the soldiers' helmeted heads almost buried by it. The suits drew in at the waist only to flare out again around the lower legs, where thrust units and gyroscopes were housed, providing stabilisation for the soldiers' flight packs and compensating for the recoil of their rail cannons. Magnetically impelled weapons were as close to recoilless as it was possible to get, but the size of the

Dragon Fire soldiers' ordnance made such counters necessary. The guns sat underneath their right arms, enclosing the majority of the hand in a trigger unit, their barrels a metre and a half long, energy drawn from their flight-pack reactors. The flight packs had a single main jet, held high and tilted, fat plastic feathers of control plates ranged up the back of each soldier, giving them the appearance of badly fledged angels.

Each Dragon Fire soldier was a one-man flying tank. They looked like heavy combat robot chassis, only the irregular movements of humanity betraying the presence of the man encased in each mechanical shell.

"That would rule Lehmann and me out of the burial party?"

Commander Guan looked uncomfortable. He had a flat face with heavy epicanthic folds, a shallow nose and skin dark for a Han. "I apologise. We have no enhanced such as you in the People's Republic. I am unsure as to what the Tenets of Balance would say on this matter, and I am ignorant of the customs of your homeland." Commander Guan's speech was translated by his suit from Mandarin into German. The translation was swift and flawless, if emotionally bland, and seemed at times to anticipate what Guan was going to say, which spoke of some level of mind interface. Otto took all this in as he was designed to, assessing threats, but the human part of him wondered if China really was AI free. "However, to allow you access even to a spade or shovel would present an unacceptable tactical risk. We are aware of your capabilities. This may take some time. You may sit if you wish. Please do not go from our sight. The accord brokered by the VIA between our governments is a temporary one, and I have been given strict orders as to how you are to be dealt with should you not follow my instruction."

I'll bet you have, thought Otto. The Dragon Fires' support craft hovered silently above, a twin-hulled heavy lifter of a type he had not seen before. It too was heavily armed and armoured. He walked to where Valdaire and Lehmann sat silently. Lehmann moved to speak, but Otto silenced him with a hand, and ignored the query flashed into his head via MT. He felt the need to be alone for a while, and walked past the others to sit down on a fallen tree from where he could look over the dry lake.

The forest was cold and unpretty, the remains of Bratsk an eyesore on the far side of the plain of cracked mud, another blemish that would stain the world for centuries. The damage from the secret war between China and Russia was obvious even from this distance: shell holes and craters and spaces in the skyline where buildings had collapsed. While they'd been brought here, Dragon Fire troopers either side of the Stelsco, he'd seen the body of an old-style paratrooper hanging from a tree, a cluster of bones in a sack that might once have been a uniform of the People's Republic. Wrapped in tattered silk, skull held on by a few blackened sinews.

And they pretended still that the purchase was an act of economics, not war.

He stared at the needle-thick forest floor. At least now, into autumn, mosquito season was done with. Siberia was murderously thick with them in summertime. He gave a brief and derisory laugh.

He looked at the wounded landscape. So much death he'd seen, and he'd seen but a fragment the last century had had to offer. The planet's population had shrunk by three billion since its peak – the Christmas Flu, haemorrhagic plague, war and environmental collapse had killed many, but elsewhere populations were shrinking naturally. Whether this was down to the twin, and opposed, pressures of increased baseline prosperity and resource poverty, as the academics had it, Otto did not know. To his grandparents' eyes most modern Europeans would seem to live mean lives. Sometimes he thought the human race had exhausted itself along with its planet, losing itself in a senescence of virt-worlds, endlessly replaying its faded global culture and pretending everything was all right while its AI children took over its affairs one by one; a protracted extinction.

All he knew for sure were the abandoned suburbs, the ruinous village grown over with weeds and young trees, the towers of the arcologies springing up all over the world as populations contracted and concentrated themselves, the endless array of talking machines, and horrors like Kaplinski born of science.

And what he knew best of all was the blood of those he had killed as the world had changed around him. All of them, every face, stacked up there in his mentaug waiting to ambush him in his sleep.

And Honour.

He was so tired. His shoulder throbbed. He damped down his pain responses via his mentaug, and had his phactory increase its doses of aminopyridines. Pain lessened and the clenching of muscles round his shoulder relaxed.

He closed his eyes, and opened them to white walls. His seat changed from an uncomfortable branch into an uncomfortable sofa twenty years ago.

He sipped water from his cup and his feet jigged with worry. The clinic was empty; it was the time of night when few people had the desire to visit. We can't always decide when we need to visit, he thought bitterly. Honour had refused to come in, until she'd finally collapsed six weeks after their trip to the cave – three days ago. They'd been here ever since. Otto rubbed his eyes, and sent a series of subconscious cues to his mentaug to tinker with his brain chemistry. No one knew how long an individual could go without sleep, but the number of devil-may-care headcases and students clogging up the psych and neural re-engineering wards gave the medical establishment a pretty good idea of how long you could not. After a fortnight, Otto was rapidly approaching that limit. He felt awake, but the taste of aluminium on his back teeth told him he was close to the edge.

A health technician in a white smock appeared at a door opposite the waiting area.

"Mr Klein? Ms Dinez will see you now."

Otto flipped his cup flat and replaced it in his belt as he walked to the door.

"Sorry to keep you waiting. This is a complex case."

"One to write up," he said bitterly.

"Mr Klein..." the technician said gently.

"I'm sorry. I just..." He just what? He didn't know how he felt any more, he was no longer sure what was him and what was the mentaug. Moments like that in the cave, pure emotion, pure him, they were precious, and rare.

"I understand," the technician touched his arm. "This way."

The touch of the hand shifted to his other arm, and the room fell suddenly chill. Otto blinked and he was back in the forest, looking up at Valdaire. The sun was lower in the sky.

He'd had a mentaug blackout. This was not good. So long ago, but he was just there. And they said time travel was impossible.

A small grin cracked the corner of his mouth.

"Otto, are you OK?" asked Valdaire.

Otto nodded. "Memories," he said.

"They're going to bury Chures now," Valdaire said softly. "The Chinese want to know if you will say something? I did not know him well."

"Neither of us did," said Otto.

Valdaire smiled sadly. "Just try."

Four Dragon Fire troopers lowered Chures' white-shrouded body into the forest floor, their fellows standing with heads bowed. Otto spoke over it, as he'd spoken over the makeshift graves of a half-dozen good men over the years. What could he say? That he barely knew him? He said something about bravery and belief, and keeping the line, but he found it hard to feel any of it, and kept it brief. His words felt false. Kaplinski was still out there. It was a world of monsters.

Otto was one of them.

Valdaire thanked Chures for saving her life, and said nothing more.

Commander Guan looked to Otto. His irises were so brown as to be almost black. Few people had eyes like that in Germany. Otto always found them hard to read. Otto nodded. Commander Guan said something – Otto's Mandarin wasn't good enough to catch it, not out here without Grid support – and the men who'd lowered Chures to his final rest started to fill in the hole. When they were done they drank water from woven bottles, sluiced the dirt from their hands and wiped their faces with bright white towels, leaving streaks of forest mould on them. They walked silently to their armoured suits, which stood apelike, slumped forward until their wearers approached, at which point they straightened, swung their arms wide and opened, becoming metal flytraps that swallowed the men whole. Chestplates swung down, helmets engaged and auto-bolting mechanisms whirred. With the men imprisoned inside them, the war machines came to sinister life, a high whine coming from their powerplants.

Commander Guan addressed the three foreigners, his translation programme switching to English. "We will leave now. You have twenty-four hours to locate the man you seek, at which point you will be taken to the border, successful or not. We will escort you. Your machine –" he gestured to Valdaire "– you must leave it turned off."

"We'll be done here before today is over, if we can leave it on. The phone holds the location of the hacker Giacomo Vellini," said Otto.

Guan regarded him for a second, then gave a curt nod. He turned to the side and looked up at the grey sky. He spoke into his suit. There were pauses in his speech as someone replied.

"Very well," he said eventually. "There are no AI in the PRC, no near-I, no thinking machines, and nothing possessing proficiency in any three areas that outstrip the capabilities of a human mind. All such machines violate the Tenets of Balance, and are illegal. Our allowance of this machine's presence is discretionary. Should the machine attempt to connect to Chinese sovereign Gridspace or attempt any interference with People's Dynasty machincry it will be destroyed. Do you understand?"

Valdaire nodded, her hands tightening around the phone.

"Understood," said Otto.

"Good," said Guan. Troopers marched to each of the foreigners, one to each side, and took them by the upper arms in hard machine grips. "You may only activate your machine in the secondary tactical room. You are to remain in the secondary tactical room," said Guan. "Do not attempt to leave it without express permission. Any attempt to escape and you will be restrained forcibly. If you should leave the room you will be arrested and tried as spies in a People's Republic court. If you leave and attempt to enter the command deck, gunnery deck or power room, you will be shot. Is this also understood?"

The three nodded.

"Very well. We will now depart."

The jets on the soldiers' armoured suits ignited one after the other, burning bright and loud, filling the forest with their noise.

The Chinese soldiers rose up, carrying the trespassers with them. The belly of the heavy lifter cracked open, spilling harsh golden light into the forest, and they flew within.

CHAPTER 17
The War in the Air

Bear roared and gutted a pirate with a vicious uppercut. His other paw cleaved another into strips. Richards dodged back and forth between a trio of snarling buccaneers, jabbing unconvincingly at them with his sword.

Knives passed into Bear's side and long-barrelled jezzails went off in the aft-castle, their balls bringing forth puffs of stuffing. Bear was unperturbed. He picked up one of the pirates menacing Richards and threw him over the side. Cowed by the toy's apparent invulnerability, the pirates fell back towards the stern of the ship.

"Stop! Stop, I say. Let us parley! Cease fighting! Avaunt, arraunt! Desist!"

Bear kept up his guard but stopped swiping. The pirates backed down. Richards stood at Bear's back, sword at the ready.

There was a motion in the crowd of pirates, and a familiar face came to the fore.

"Percival Del Piccolo, poet swordsman of wit, cavalier, debonair liberator of ladies' virtues, pirate king and all round irritant to tyrants…"

Bear groaned. "You! Can it, clown, we've heard this before!"

Piccolo did not heed him. "…evil Maharajahs and Grand

Viziers with ideas above their station, makes common cause with
no man! I, sirs, am a free spirit, a sky captain. No man is my
friend unless he has proved himself to me." He glowered, and
Richards gripped his sword tighter, but then his frown cracked
into a wide grin and a wink. "And you have more than done
that, a toy like a bear and an idiot fool! My dear friends! Welcome aboard the *Kurvy Kylie II.*" He sprang lightly onto the ship's
rails and hung from a rope by one hand. "Men, put up your pistols! Sheathe your swords! These are true friends." He doffed his
silly hat at them and bowed his head. "I am at your service. I
owe you a boon, for is it not said that once a man saves another
man's life, that life belongs to the saviour? Ask of me anything!"

"I," said Richards, "am looking for Lord Hog."

"Ohohohoho!" said Piccolo, jumping down onto the deck.
"Maybe apart from that! No one goes looking for Lord Hog; one
prays that he does not come looking for you. He is the death of
hope! No cutlass or ball can kill such a thing. You speak mad-
ness. Come, sail with me to adventure and riches instead, so we
may live out the last days of the Earth as princes among men!"

"I mean it," said Richards. "If I can find him, I can stop all of
this. The Terror, Penumbra, all of it."

Piccolo frowned for a moment. "No! Really?"

"Yep," said Bear. "Me and sunshine here, we're on a mission."

A wide smile broke across Piccolo's face. He clapped his hands
together slowly, threw back his head and laughed outrageously.
"Oh, marry!" he bellowed. He clapped Richards on the shoulder.
"Very well! Very well! Men!" he called. "Men, prepare for the
adventure to end all adventures!" He leapt again onto the railing, and waved his hat around in the air. "We sail to save the
world or die in the attempt!"

"Aye, cap'n!" the pirates called and all of a sudden there was
a hustle and a bustle. Lines were tightened, decks were swabbed
of blood. A burly black man went to the aft-castle and grasped

the ship's wheel. Lines from this passed through a series of pulleys to halters about the air-whales' heads. Pirates took long gaffs and prodded them. They whistled. "Where to, Cap'n?" called the helmsman though a cupped hand.

"Indeed, where to, Mr Richards?"

"Just Richards," said Richards. "Is there an end to the pylon line?"

"There is," said Piccolo, "though it is a dangerous voyage."

"There, then."

"Very well! To the northwest," called Piccolo. "We go north first, to the Great Western Ocean, then on to the city of Secret. Or all is lost?" said Piccolo with a smile with a toothpaste twinkle. "I like it. I like it a lot! A perilous part of the world, full of adventure! Northwest, Mr Mbotu! Northwest!"

"Aye, aye, Cap'n." Bosun Mbotu spun the wheel.

The sky-whales sang and paddled at the air. Majestically, the *Kurvy Kylie II* tracked round.

Richards watched the crew at work. He marvelled at the amount of cliché whoever had constructed this world had managed to cram in. Its creator might have been an ace hacker, but he wouldn't win any creative awards. "All we need now to finish this off is a little song," he said to Bear.

He was not long disappointed.

Piccolo paced his metal skyship, checking lines and pulling levers, laughing with his men, and directing their efforts as they lustily sang cereal commercial jingles with improvised piratical lyrics.

Piccolo joined Bear and Richards and, taking the AI by the elbow, guided him aft. "You left me, as I recall, and the Great Terror struck once more," said Piccolo. "I escaped, and made my way to La Beau Porte Du Chance on the edge of the Specific Ocean. I remember. It was there that I availed myself of this ship and crew, winning it through a game of chance and, I must say, my own great cunning."

"I bet that means he cheated," said Bear from the corner of his mouth.

"And, well," said Richards, rubbing his hands together, "what about the, er, pirates?" He nodded meaningfully at stains on the decking left by their mêlée.

"Oh, don't worry about that," said Piccolo. "You know pirates. They will merely be happy that they will take a larger share of any spoils."

"I don't think there's going to be much gold where we're going," said Bear. "Only pain and death."

"And so," said Piccolo, "they will share in those as gladly."

The air-whales flew over oasis-studded deserts and lands awash with marigolds, over a rainforest edged abruptly by an endless theme park gone wild, rollercoasters ending in nowhere, surrounded by ragwort and rubble. An entire kingdom made of plastic bricks passed under them. Cities on rivers like serpentine seas slid below, sweeping savannahs crowded with cartoon beasts, swamps of candyfloss trees haunted by dreadful things. They ascended mountains so high that the whales had to be wrapped in blankets. Icicles hung from the rigging and Richards' breath came short. The mountains periodically dipped into green valleys and the *Kylie* followed the slopes down, offering some respite from the chill until the peaks reared up to once more force frost upon the crew.

They passed the mountains and came to a wide plain studded with cities in the shapes of great pearls. Some of these burned, sending choking columns of smoke and cinders so high in the air that they buffeted the ship.

"Ah," said Piccolo. "There is Temperance, Levity and Just So ablaze. Things go ill with the world if the cities of the Wise can thus be fired."

The green of the plains turned to the black of old fire. Armies trod them, their distant passage marked by columns of dust. They passed over a horde of monsters swarming round iron war machines. It appeared Pylon City had been captured, and had done much to fuel the war effort of the Shadow Lord, as the sun struck a glittering display from a legion of freshly minted haemites. These armies noticed the passage of the *Kurvy Kylie II*, and sent opportunistic cannonades after them. But the ship flew too high, and the shots rained back down upon the armies below. Richards fancied he could hear their howls of indignation, but he could not know for sure. They were ants below the keel.

Once a band of harpies, voluptuous and foul, came winging their way from cages atop one war-tower. They shrieked and rattled their brass claws before diving down upon the skywhales. Piccolo ordered the cannons loaded with grapeshot, but the whales were far from defenceless; their long beaks snapped harpies from the air, and the assault did not last.

Seven days in, they passed over a battle still in progress. The besieged city was a beautiful place, encased in a dome with a pearlescent sheen whose lower quarter was buried in the land, butted by a series of fantastically carved rocks that formed the city walls. Within the dome was a tiered city of gardens and manses. At the centre of the highest terrace stood a lake, at the centre of the lake a tower of ivory. Every surface was worked with giant figures, the expressions on their huge faces visible from the *Kylie*.

Thousands of men manned the walls. Trebuchets lofted bales of burning magnesium into the horde besetting the place, but time was short for the defenders. The host of Lord Penumbra crashed upon the walls. Winged horrors plucked soldiers from the ramparts. War-towers sent munitions crashing through the dome of the city, causing sheets of pearly glass to shatter in deadly showers.

"Ah, 'tis a great pity," said Piccolo, "Considered Action, the greatest of the pearls. Now it is soon to fall, and there is nothing we can do." He swore with a sailor's vigour.

To the east of the place the sky was bruised by the gathering clouds of the Great Terror, and the whales picked up speed as they scented it on the wind.

Leagues passed, and they left the war behind. The land became colder; a forest of conifers pricked at the landscape below. Piccolo came to Richards, handed him a telescope and pointed. "The pylons," he said. "The most far flung of the lines. We grow closer. Follow the western line to its very end, so it is said, and you will find Hog."

Richards put the telescope to his eye. The pylons marched dead straight to the northwest. A black box was working its way slowly along their cables. The squeaking of its mechanism cut through the cold air. The pirates fell silent at the sound. Many of their faces became pale; a couple crossed themselves. They did not relax until the box was out of sight.

Richards looked round at the band of hardened cutthroats shivering in fear.

"Great," he said to himself. "Why do I get all the fun jobs?"

The pylons rose with the land, the horizon taking on a jagged appearance. If the mountains they had sailed over before had been giants, these were titans.

"The Unnamed Peaks, beyond which lies the Great Western Ocean," said Piccolo. "From there, we must head onwards, toward the domain of the demon swine. The way is hard and unknown."

"Surely we just follow the pylons?" said Richards.

"Ah, if only it were so simple!" said Piccolo, "but fear not, brave Sir Richards." He grew somewhat misty-eyed. "We call at a city that moves, borne upon the shoulders of giants. Secret, they call it, a dolorous place of terrible myth and close-guarded fact, ruled over by a mournful queen whose duty it is to know all the world's shames. And those shames," he said, coming back to focus on the now, "include the way to Hog's lair. The Queen will know. We seek Secret, thence the way to Hog."

Foothills grew taller, opening suddenly to reveal deep ravines where dirty snow skulked. The moon rose before the sun had set. By the time the moon had the sky to itself the *Kurvy Kylie* was high over the shoulders of the mountains, and its beams sparkled with frost-rimed snow. Richards kept his mac on tight, and Piccolo gave out furs to all aboard.

Fifteen days into the trip, their journey was interrupted. Richards noticed a rhythmic glitter, something metallic to the east. He squinted until his eyes hurt, and not for the first time cursed his human body.

"Captain!" called Richards. "Captain!"

Piccolo, dressed in an enormous white mink coat, sauntered up beside him. "Aye, dear Mr Richards, what bedevils ye, to make ye crow so loud?"

"There, Piccolo, there. In the east. There's something follow-ing us."

The captain leant on the railings. "I see noth… Wait!"

"You see it?"

"Shh! Yes, yes. Damnable bastards! It is ill to say so, but I do. Lookout!" he bawled. "Lookout! Train your glass upon the east! What do you see?"

There was a moment's silence, then an answering call from the crows' nest above the whales' backs. "It is a saucer, sir, or a dish. It skips through the sky like a flat stone on water. It is like naught I have seen before."

"A dish! A dish! He has found me! Damn him, damn his eyes and those of his Dalmatians! Ah! I searched so hard, and now he arrives at the point of least convenience!" the captain snarled. He tore off his coat and handed it to a crewman. "Take that to my cabin," he bellowed. "Man the cannon!" He ran to the steps at the rear of the ship, taking them two at a time as he went onto the poop deck. Richards followed him. Piccolo went to the stern parapet and the great telescope fixed there. "Extinguish the lamps!" he shouted. "Make ready for battle!"

"What is it?" asked Richards.

"Damn him!" shouted the captain. "It is my arch-enemy, the Punning Pastry Chef. His craft the *Flan O'War* follows in our wake. We are in for a hard fight."

The pursuit lasted through the rest of the day and all through the night. The whales were goaded until they sang songs of annoyance. Piccolo clambered up the rigging in between their car-sized heads and urgently whispered to them. After this they fell silent and redoubled their efforts. Masts extended to either side of the ship, triangular sails unfurling from each to terse heave-hos and the rattle of cranks.

"Deploy keel sail!" shouted Piccolo. Sailors worked a further mechanism at the centre of the ship. The deck jolted and they made fast their lines.

"The sails are an affront to Nikim and Nikogo," said Piccolo. "They are proud, you see, but they understand we are sorely pressed. It is a glad happenstance we have a following wind, or the *Flan O'War* would be upon us."

"This Pastry Chef must be one tough cookie," said Bear to Richards. "I'd not expect our gabbling captain to run from anything."

Richards did a double-take. Bear wore a massive fur coat. It must have taken three buffalo to make.

"What?" said Bear.

"Bears don't wear clothes," said Richards.

"Hmph, just because I'm a bear doesn't mean I can't wear clothes. It's bloody freezing up here, if you hadn't noticed. Besides, as you have pointed out, I'm not a real bear."

Morning came. The mountains reared up icy and unknowable before them. A mile astern came the *Flan O'War*, a tin pie dish domed over with riveted plates. The lower portion spun, the central, upper segment steady as a rock. Three chimneys at the apex in the shape of blackbird pastry ornaments spouted smoke. The dome was broken twice by broad fighting decks, and cannon muzzles pointed outward all round the circumference of the dish. A turreted cannon was mounted at what Richards thought of as the front, if only because that was the direction of travel.

An amplified voice crackled across the air. "Your bun is done! Your piccolo has piped its last! Stand down now, my favoured enemy. Eat humble pie and give me your ship and foolish hat and I may allow parts of you to live awhile!"

A pirate handed Piccolo a loud-hailer. "Never!" he screamed. "I will never surrender to you, you ill-begotten baker!"

"Come, come now," the voice replied, louder as the *Flan O'War* closed. "What's done is done. You have lost. Your sad boat and silly whales cannot best my flying pie, my iron-clad confection, my *Flan O' War*! You know that, Percival Del Piccolo. Pie thief! Stealer of delicious tarts! How I will make you rue the day you chomped on my éclair!"

"To arms!" shouted Piccolo.

"To arms!" roared Bear.

"You really enjoy all this, don't you?" said Richards.

"Yeah. So?"

"Otto'd fucking love you," he grumbled.

"It'll be a cracking fight," said Bear with a wicked grin.

Richards shook his head in disbelief and took a revolver from a barrel full of weapons. He looped its cord round his wrist. Tarquin growled, and turned to stone.

There was a ringing of steel as the pirates drew their cutlasses. Flintlocks were powdered, matches sparked. The gun-hatches of the *Kurvy Kylie II* rumbled open and the wide eyes of cannon pushed unblinking into the morning air.

"Sorry, my friends," said Piccolo. "We will be back about our business as soon as we have dealt with this gibbering pastry-maker and his pie-problem. Right!" he shouted. "Men, we cannot let the *Flan O'War* get above us and harm Nikim and Nikogo. We must board that ship. It may be faster, more heavily armed and better armoured than our beautiful *Kylie*, but what are his crew?"

"Dough balls!" cried one pirate.

"Baker's lackeys!" called another.

"Fat little boys who eat too many cakes!" roared Bear.

"And what are we?" shouted Piccolo.

"Pirates!"

"Fighters!"

"The scurviest airdogs that ever there were!"

"Giant toy bears!" added Bear.

"We are going to storm that ship and cut that pie-lubber's gizzard! We'll bake *him* in a pie!" crowed Piccolo.

Half the pirates ran to the gunwales, ropes and irons in their hands, while the remainder manned the guns. The *Flan O'War* came closer. There was a hissing sound, and a dozen sharpened flan-cases thudded into the deck feet away from Richards.

"Hard a port, gain altitude! One hundred feet up!" called Piccolo, orders repeated as they worked their way down the chain of command.

The *Kurvy Kylie* banked directly towards the *Flan O'War*, cannons blazing, shots bouncing from the iron pie's armour. One knocked the foremost blackbird askew; another found its way onto the lower fighting deck, where it bounced about like a pinball, turning cook's whites red.

"Reload!" ordered the gun captains. Piccolo called to the whale goaders, and the starboard side dipped slightly.

"Fire!" The cannons belched smoke and flame. The *Flan* was slightly below the *Kylie* and coming edge-on, and most of the cannonballs sped over the pie-plate's low profile. It retorted horribly. Seven flan-flingers spoke. Their cookware sliced through the air. Pirates' limbs flew and bandanna'd heads bounced upon the deck. Several sharpened pie plates buried themselves deep in the starboard whale. It called piteously, and blood gushed quickly, as if the whale's fluids could not wait to be free of it. The whale sagged as gas bladders deflated. The ship lurched starboard as a second volley of flan cases sliced through the whale's harness. A pirate went screaming overboard, holding a spouting stump of a wrist in front of his face, bouncing from the *Flan O'War* as he fell.

Piccolo kept his nerve. "On the next pass, lads!" he cried. Richards stood on the gunwales and clung to the rigging, letting off shots at any target he could find. The ships jockeyed for position in the sky, cannonballs and flan cases reaping a deadly harvest on both sides.

"Now lads, now!" bellowed Piccolo. Forty pirates hurled their irons. The armoured walls of the *Flan's* fighting decks provided a firm anchor for grappling hooks. The pirates leapt overboard and shinned up the ropes and onto the *Flan*'s decks. The sounds of close-quarter combat joined the tumult of battle, and the flan-flingers fell silent one by one.

"Rargh!" roared Bear. Fur coat trailing behind him, he jumped and hit the *Flan* with a soft thump. He slipped. Pulling back one paw, he punched his gauntlet blades straight through the *Flan's* hull. In this manner, paw over paw, he pulled himself up the skyship. One hit brought forth a torrent of steam. The blackbirds spat sparks amongst their smoke, and the *Flan*'s spinning became an erratic wobble. Bear pulled himself onto the lower fighting deck, and laid himself hard into a gaggle of screaming baker's boys.

The Punning Pastry Chef had one last trick up his sleeve. The top turret swivelled round, its cannon fixing itself upon the injured air-whale. A loud bubbling sound built in its muzzle. Richards ducked as a jet of strawberry-scented napalm splashed onto the whale above, dripping onto the listing deck, setting all ablaze.

"Aieee! Greek jam!" shouted a pirate. Jam slopped onto his

head, and his voice became a gurgling scream as he clawed at his burning face and stumbled to writhe horribly on the deck.

The whale twisted, aflame from end to end. It shrieked in agony, sheets of whale skin peeling from it. Its blubber melted as the jam burnt through its flesh. The ship bucked as it struggled. Rigging and deck were on fire, and smoke obscured the *Flan O'War*. All was pandemonium. Screaming, fire, metal on metal, the desperate shouts of men fighting for their lives. The stink of burning fat, the fragrance of hot jam. The ship dropped, sending Richards sprawling as the harness holding the dying whale finally gave way. Streaming smoke, it spiralled off into the rising sun, its death-wail drawing hot tears of shame from all who heard it. The *Kurvy Kylie II* yawed hard, the deck swung out and down to hang perpendicularly as the second whale struggled to carry the full weight of the ship alone. The jam cannon fired again. Its gloopy report panicked the remaining whale. It tried to pull away, jerking both ships as grapples drew tight. Its song was wrathful, a tune of anger at the hates of men. Richards slid down the deck. He snatched at a rope and dropped his gun. It swung from his wrist by its cord and banged his arm hard.

"Hold on, old boy! Hold on!" shouted Tarquin.

"I've no intention of letting go," said Richards. "I'm sick of falling."

The boat lurched again. He slid down the rope and it burned his hands. He swung from side to side, wrapped his arm in the rope and waited.

The sounds of fighting up above subsided. There was a cheer, and the ships levelled off, leaving Richards dangling thousands of feet above the snowy mountainsides.

"Oi!" shouted Richards. "Oi! Down here!"

A pirate leaned out over the gunwales and pointed. More faces appeared, and strong arms hauled Richards back up to safety.

"Well, well, well," said Tarquin. "I do believe we won."

CHAPTER 18
The Queen of Secret

The battle-worn *Flan O'War* and *Kurvy Kylie II* climbed into the morning sky. A night of intense labour on the ground had seen the latter's rigging rearranged to allow the ship to hang beneath the remaining air-whale. The *Kylie* was holed in many places, but airworthy. The *Flan O' War* was dented, the foremost chimney leaning at a crazy angle and spitting more flame than smoke as the boilers were fired.

Richards stood at a porthole set in the side of the *Flan O'War* and watched the ground recede.

"It looks beautiful from up here," he said.

"It looks bloody cold," said Bear.

"Yeah, well." Richards turned away from the window and sat at an aluminium table bolted to the floor. They were in a small room lined with wire bread-racks, though there were no loaves in them now.

"You look quite the buccaneer," said Tarquin.

"Arrr, that be because I'm..."

"...a piratical kind of bear?" said Richards.

"Exactly." Bear smirked. "Yohoho," he added, for good measure. He had lost an eye in the fight and wore an eye-patch. He was garbed in a short embroidered waistcoat and canary-yellow pantaloons. Stitched tears in his fur crisscrossed his body. He looked tatty, but happy. Being a pirate suited his temperament.

Richards tugged the bottle of rum from Bear's fist and took a long swig from it. It was rough and burned his throat, but he didn't care.

"Mini cupcake?" said Bear. "I'll say one thing about that Pastry Chef, he knew how to bake a bun."

"Thanks, I'm starving," said Richards, "and I do like my cake." He pulled out a chair and sat down. He munched upon the bun; not as good as Hughie's, but close. His chewing started with vigour, but then he slowed. "This cake, it didn't..."

"Don't worry, they cooked the chef in the other oven," said Bear. "Arrr."

"Oh, do stop talking in that ridiculous fashion," said Tarquin.

"Ahem," said Bear sheepishly, and looked into his bottle with his single eye.

They ascended for hours before they were high enough to cross the peaks. On the other side an improbable ocean lapped icy shores at the roof of the world. The pylons turned west along this sea, and Piccolo's small armada followed. In places they were treated to glorious vistas, the mountains sweeping down into foothills, the foothills to plains, the plains into fields and so on until the horizon, but all were bounded by the void. At times it was a purple band on the horizon, often it was much closer. In the unfathomable black they spotted sizeable islands, whole countries marooned upon the night, frittering away to nothing.

As they flew further west it became warmer as the mountains grew lower, and the sea stepped down from the heavens on a series of immense cataracts. The ice disappeared, replaced by glittering archipelagos, but the Great Western Ocean was not untouched by that which devoured the world; they passed a roaring whirlpool in whose centre, half obscured by vapour, lay a perfect circle of black.

All the while the ground shook below them, fissures opening
as the integrity of Reality 37 crumbled. The marks of the Terror
were everywhere.

On the eighth day, the mountains turned in on themselves,
forming a giant dam for the sea. The *Kurvy Kylie* and *Flan O'War*
swept over their jagged teeth and sailed on as the mountains
plunged down to a country of farms and small villages.

The lands beneath were like Swiss cheese, the holes in them
growing larger as they watched. The tortured ground grumbled
all the while, scaring sleep away at night. The days revealed long
trains of refugees, broad trampled paths snaking behind them,
spotted with discarded belongings and corpses. Piccolo's crew
became morose. They bet insane sums of loot against one another in games of chance, aware that now, at the end of all
things, it was worthless.

"Hooray!" said Bear, scooping up an armful of trinkets. "I win
again."

"You are blessed by the gods," said Bosun Mbotu.

"I thinks he might be cheating," said another pirate. "Arrrrr."

"Hey!" said Bear. "How's that possible?" He tugged at his
wrists. "See? No sleeves."

"What does it matter?" said the bosun dolefully.

"I don't know how you do it, Bear, but I am cheating and I
am still losing." Richards cast his cards onto the table. "I'm going
outside for some air." He went to the *Flan O'War*'s heavy exterior doors and let himself out onto the fighting deck.

It was an hour or so after dusk. Richards looked out over the
ruination below, fascinated at this physical manifestation of
numbers at war. Out over the void, wherever the smallest scrap
of land persisted, bits of sky shoaled like strange fish in the blackest of oceans.

Below the ships was the woolly dark of young night. Richards
had seen farms and towns below in the day, but there were no

lights to break up the darkness. Whatever had lived in these parts was long gone. Light did shine in the night, but not of a homely kind. Where the land had failed, the shattering edges of reality showed up as showers of sparks.

They picked up a set of enormous footprints, a double track of multiple feet made by giants walking in two lines. Piccolo assured them that at the end of these they would find Secret, its elusive Queen and a way into Hog's mountain.

On the ninth day the tracks cut across a marsh, and the trail was lost in mere and mud.

"Are we nearly there yet?" asked Bear, as the two ships completed yet another sweep of the marsh.

Richards scanned the ground with poor human eyesight, intent, until he called, "Captain! Bring us round, to that brown area over there."

Piccolo shaded his eyes with his hand. He shrugged "Ah, well, nothing ventured... hard a port!" he yelled. The tenor of the engines changed as they altered course, the whistle tooted and the whale of the nearby *Kylie* replied in kind.

The two ships banked in a wide arc round the area Richards indicated, a circular area of brown vegetation, as if it had been starved of sunlight by a giant tent.

Richards nodded. "What was there?"

"Whatever it were, 'tis there no longer," said Piccolo. He put his telescope to his eye. "And if it is there no longer, where did it go?"

"That way," said Richards. The massive tracks started up again, leading away from the dying reeds. "Follow those prints."

Three hours later, the city came into view.

Secret was a city like no other; gaudy on a plain of sere grasses, a citadel of brass and filigree; its iridescent buildings bolted to a double circular platform carried like a palanquin by a dozen brazen herms of immense size, halted now and kneeling. Four bridges arched upwards to meet in the centre of the city where they formed the base of a tower, directly above a large circle of shadow. The *Kylie* and the *Flan* flew over Secret's spires, its flags fluttering beneath their keels. But though the city was a blaze of colours, the centre of the circle was an altogether different kind of place. Out of the light was a twilit world of cages. Dark shapes moved within them.

Gracefully the ships descended, drawing level with the burnished giants' heads. An extravagant jetty jutted out into the air from a mounting tucked away behind the lead giant. With a series of loud commands bellowed through a candied bullhorn, Piccolo directed the *Kurvy Kylie* out away from the city, there to sit in vigil. His new flagship he steered towards the jetty. There was a loud clang, a slight start, and the *Flan O'War* came to a stop. Pirates shouted as they leapt onto the polished metal decks of Secret, calling to their colleagues for rope. Piccolo ordered the boilers extinguished. One by one, the blackbird chimneys ceased to smoke. The pie dish slowed its rotation, until the *Flan O' War* hung in the air, motionless and silent.

"Gentlemen," said Piccolo to Richards and his friends, "let us prepare ourselves. Bosun Mbotu!"

"Yes, sir!"

"Send word that we have arrived, and that we seek an audience with the queen."

Half an hour later Richards stood by Bear at the main entrance to the *Flan O'War*. He was dressed in a high-necked officer's uniform Piccolo had insisted he wear.

"Stop tugging at the damn thing, man!" said Tarquin from where he hung, cleaned and golden, across Richards' chest.

"I can't help it. It's this damn brocade. It itches like hell."

"Have you no sense of decorum? Leave it be. And put your gloves back on, we're going to meet royalty. One simply cannot greet royalty without one's hands covered."

Bear and Piccolo were likewise well attired, both being decked out in outrageously flamboyant clothes. Bear sported a hat with a gigantic orange feather upon it that dusted the ceiling of the *Flan* as he moved. Piccolo, too, had outdone himself, and his pirates had ironed their best baggy trousers and polished their golden teeth.

The clamshell doors opened, jets of steam hissing from the rams. Richards, Tarquin, Bear, Captain Del Piccolo and an honour guard of six pirates led by Mbotu stepped out of the ship and onto the jetty of Secret.

A figure stepped out to greet them. He walked deliberately, the precise placement of a silver-topped cane accompanying every step. His clothing was that of the late seventeenth century: a large periwig, short breeches, long coat, lacy cuffs and high-heeled buckled shoes. A hobbit in a homburg hat accompanied him, smoking a pipe, staring at each of the visitors hard and taking notes.

The man had four arms, and a square head under his large hat, a different face on every side. Those away from them were still as porcelain sculptures, eyes closed.

That facing them matched the man's outfit, thick with powder and rouge, thin moustache and beauty spot. A face wearied by dissolution.

"Good day, gentlemen," said the man. "We are the Queen of Secret. May we bid you, as enemies of our enemy, welcome to our fortress-prison, the most hidden, and perhaps last, city in all of the world." He flourished a bow. Piccolo returned one but seemed clumsy before such finesse. Richards settled for a brief nod. "We apologise for the environs. We have to move the city quite often. The current locale, is, we admit, unpleasant, but one is running out of places to hide."

"Good day to you, sir. I am Captain Percival Del Piccolo, pirate swordsman of wit and occasional gentleman. May I introduce my excellent friends Sergeant Bear and Mr Richards?"

"We are honoured, Sergeant, Mr Richards."

"Just Richards," said Richards. "Your majesty."

"This," said the queen, indicating the hobbit, "is Herr Doktor Freudo. Our chief psychiatrist here." Freudo clicked his heels together and rose up on his toes. "I take it you heard our message. Tell me, are there others coming?"

Richards looked to Bear who looked to Piccolo. "I am sorry, your majesty," said Piccolo. "We sought you out. We heard no message."

The Queen sighed. "Ah. The end is nearer than I thought, then. Come, come, follow me. We will be ready to make way in the morning. Until we are ready to depart, one recommends you take rest in the accommodation one has provided."

They walked off the jetty, under the upper ring, and into the world under Secret. Through the mesh of the floor they could see the boggy plain underneath. The walkway the Queen led them along took a long, circuitous route through a forest of bars, a jarring mix of the ornate and utile.

The cages were full of strange, mewling creatures: half-men, phantoms and disturbing females of overtly pornographic character. An emaciated waif raked at the air, almost catching Freudo's hat with its long and dirty claws. The tiny psychiatrist leapt back and chuckled nervously.

"There, there, Ameline!" he chided.

"Although this is a prison," said the Queen, "we do attempt to rehabilitate our inmates. Think of us, perhaps, as a secure hospital." His eyes closed, head rotated and a new face awoke. A stern matron looked out at them, and the Queen's clothes rippled to be replaced with those of a Victorian nurse.

"What are these things?" asked Richards.

"Why, Mr Richards, these are secrets. Secrets from the world over, exiled here for safekeeping. I am being somewhat fanciful, of course. They are not secrets in and of themselves, but the people that used them would doubtless prefer that they remain hidden from their friends. The Grid is such a poisonous place; from its very beginning it has been a breeding ground for sexual perversity. The Flower King attempted to keep many of these poor, tortured creatures out of his creation, but some, those truly desperate, got in."

"These are all sex toys?" said Richards.

The Queen nodded sadly. "Bots, near-I, even one or two early examples of strong AI, all here, all made to enjoy whatever carnal horror their owners could not take into the Real. Or not enjoy it, as so many of these poor things were made to suffer for others' enjoyment. Naturally, these are all minor confidences, we keep the more dangerous ones away from the path."

An icy tingle ran up Richards' spine as he looked into a cage. "Now that's something I wouldn't admit to a psychiatrist."

"You may not vant to," said Freudo, "but ve are only here to help, if you vant to talk."

"Er, right. Let me guess," said Richards. "The Flower King wanted to keep this place pure. For the Queen – the other one, I mean."

"Yes," said the Queen with surprise. "Every unpleasant, re-pressed urge, repulsive to polite society, let free on the Grid rather than locked up in the darker corridors of the mind and safely re-pressed. Why would he allow them here to sully the creation he sought to perfect? Some of course, are more substantial, actions, deeds vile or not, but all shameful to the doer. This city, for all its finery, is a cellblock, an oubliette of horrors stemming from the mind of man." The Queen looked at Richards piercingly.

"And why are you here?"

At this the Queen laughed. It was a gentle sound that abruptly transformed into a ragged series of bitter snorts as a third face rotated into place, the face of a bearded roustabout, clothes shimmering to match. "Why indeed? For ourselves are here a convict; we are gaoler and prisoner both. We were made as playthings for the vices of others."

Richards nodded. "You have a composite personality?"

"Yes. Four made one. The Flower King tried to make me stable, and he succeeded, in the main, although we have our own cage here for when such scruples as he instilled in us break down. The Flower King brought us here because we understand these tragic children." He sighed sorrowfully. "We have tried to leave, naturally, but one cannot. The city moves with one. Where we are, there is also to be found our prison. We can never escape. It is a beautiful cage, but it remains a cage for all that." The first head rotated back into place. A tear trickled from the Queen's eye, and the scent of lavender filled the air. "Forgive me. I forget myself. Come, we must go on."

As the last of the party filed after the Queen, something heavy threw itself against the bars of a cage scant feet from the Captain and the Doctor.

"What in all the seven skies is that?" said Piccolo, staring.

Freudo peered in analytically. "Somezink to do with some-vun's mutter," he said, stroking his beard.

They walked into the black heart of the gilded city, passing many things that disturbed them all. Richards tried to stop looking, but could not help himself, staring at a parade of unpleasantness that shocked him. I really have no idea at all what goes on in the heads of meat people, he thought.

They stopped and the Queen spoke again.

"We are here," he said, his diffident manner restored. They stood by the circular hole at the centre of the city, about fifteen metres across. It was dark there, so far from the edge of the circuit. Richards and the others had bars of shadow tattooed across their faces by what light broke through, making jailbirds of them all.

The Queen raised a lazy hand. Chain clanked and a large iron cage rose up from the pit below. It was once spherical but was now buckled, the metal discoloured where it had been exposed to great heat.

"Here, at the very centre of our city, we housed the Great Secret, the most awful and blackest secret in all of creation," said the Queen. "So terrible it was, no one could approach it without the very flesh being blasted from their bones. But guard it we were commanded to, and guard it we did, and diligently, for over three thousand years."

Richards wondered what that meant in Real terms. All the old Reality Realms had a system of time dilation that enabled users to live out years over the course of a few weekends. He doubted this motley pseudo-Realm ran to the strictures of the Real or the old Realms. He had no idea how long he'd been in there – could have been seconds, could have been weeks. By the looks of the place, he doubted whoever had made it had fully integrated all its time zones. Qifang had said that k52 had been manipulating the time flow of the place, but he reckoned now that it was a side-effect of the place's unorthodox construction. It was, in all probability, temporally as well as spatially instable.

"Then, exactly six years ago, the secret within this cage became enraged. All through the night it roared, then it escaped, a roaring column of pure night, bursting through the deck of our city with much loss of life. But worse was to come, for days later the Great Terror began."

"You had the Terror in this cage," said Richards.

"Yes. The Great Terror – Lord Penumbra was in that cage."

Richards looked at the sphere. He leaned upon the railing surrounding it and tapped upon it with the fingers of his left hand. "Tell me, the Queen, the other Queen, Isabella. Did she disappear around this time?"

The Queen was quiet for a moment, and put his hand to his chin in contemplation. "Yes. The news came later. We thought Penumbra had killed her."

"Don't count on that," said Richards.

"What do you mean?" said Bear.

"It means I'm thinking."

"Do tell," said Tarquin.

Richards shook his head. "No. I'm not one hundred per cent sure yet, but I will be. Once I've seen Hog, I'll know."

"You seek that secret, the way to his lair?" said the Queen.

"Yes," said Richards.

"A foolish request, but very well. If there is one place that will endure to the end of this affair, it is the black Anvil of Lord Hog. Come with me."

Richards followed the Queen as the others waited nervously for him. He led the AI to a small cage, a box with airholes punched into it. The Queen gestured towards it. Richards hesitated. "Open it," said the Queen. So Richards did.

The door squeaked on unused hinges. He flinched. Nothing happened.

"Closer," said the Queen. "Put your face to the door."

"Oh, OK," said Richards. He moved toward the door, pushing his hat back onto his head so the brim was out of the way and his nose was in the rank air of the box.

Something moved at the back.

"Do not pull away!" commanded the Queen. "Let it come to you."

Richards held his breath. A shape rushed out of the dark. Oily feathers flapped in his face and he felt something sting and enter his mind.

Knowledge. Secrets. The right pylon to approach, the right black box to board, the right stairs to climb.

The right question to ask.

The right thing to tell.

He fell to his knees and vomited on the floor, the liquid slipping through the grate to the ground far below.

"You OK?" asked Bear.

"No," said Richards, wiping his mouth. "Not really. But I do know the way."

On cue, the city lurched to one side, then the other. The giant cage of the Great Secret clanged on the decking. Metallic tolls of bells and other cages rang across the city, causing the secrets to chitter angrily and bang upon the floors of their cells. When the last of these had faded, the city was moving forward at speed, the ground rushing along beneath them.

"Do not be alarmed," said the Queen. "You have set Secret in motion. Our bronze giants carry us forth." The Queen looked sad, but resolute. "Those of you who wish to leave may do so. Hog is a creature of despicable evil, yet a creature who knows the fates of all."

"We all go to seek the advice of Lord Hog," said Piccolo resolutely.

"The Great Bear's hairy knackers we are!" said Bear.

"Vot about the other varriors you have called, my majesty?" asked Freudo. "Ve should vait for them."

The Queen smiled fondly at his companion. "About that, you need not trouble yourself, Herr Doktor. There are no others." He looked at them all solemnly. "Between oblivion and life for all that remains in this sphere, dear Freudo, stand only we unfortunate few."

They made their way down to the *Flan*, and the Queen had lackeys re-equip the band, giving them fresh shot and powder for their guns.

"A small secret of yours arrived a while back. You enjoy the fighting, and you enjoy your gun," said the Queen to Richards as a servant presented the AI with a box of ammunition.

"No, I hate fighting," said Richards.

"If you say," said the Queen. A mirthful twinkle, for a moment, sparked in his eye. "Do not be ashamed, for there are worse things in life than to fight for a just cause.

"And now, my bold adventurers, you must be away." IIe smiled sadly. "I suppose, if you are successful, then one will know, for one's punishment will be unending. Ah! Such irony! But imprisonment is preferable to death, so you go with my blessings."

The *Flan*'s clamshell doors began to shut. "Remember! Do not trust Hog, yet do not fear him either. We know that there is only one thing in all the world he does not know, and he covets this information above all else. It is what he has been searching for his entire long existence. And you, Richards. You can tell him what it is."

"Eh?" said Tarquin. "How come?"

"The box, Tarquin, it held more than the way in. Look, I promise I'll explain everything later, OK? I can't say right now because then it won't be a secret, will it, and he'll know."

"Oh," said Tarquin, "I see." He reconsidered. "Actually, I don't see."

"You'll just have to wait."

Piccolo twirled a bow. "Thank you, O Queen! And farewell!"

"Your majesty," said Tarquin. "It has been a great honour."

"See you around," said Bear.

The doors shut with a clang.

"You're such a suck-up," said Bear.

"Am not," said Tarquin. "One must simply show due deference."

"Ponce."

They stood on the earth by the edge of the world by a guillotine stroke through Reality 37; on one side, emerald grass dancing in a breeze; on the other, the long night of the Terror.

Away from the edge of the world, the *Kylie* and *Flan* sat on the grass.

Pylon 8,888,888 soared into the air on the very edge of the dark. Of all things in the world, it was only the pylons that seemed impervious to the void left by the Great Terror, provided, as Bear and Richards had seen, the line stayed whole. A defiant slash of rope stretched away from the edge of the land into eternity.

"Lots of eights," said Richards. "Lucky for some." He glanced behind him where, in the distance, he could see the city being comported away like a giant's funeral bed. Right now, he almost envied the Queen his fate.

"Hmmm," said Bear. "I'm not so sure this is a good idea, sunshine."

"I don't think we've much choice, old bean," said Tarquin.

"No," said Richards. "Now. We need a cable car."

"And how are we supposed to get onto it? That pylon's at least a thousand feet tall," said Bear. "And how do we know there's one coming? They might all have been destroyed."

"The cars belong to an older and darker power than Penumbra," said Tarquin. "There is always another one. Always."

"Like Satan's bus service," muttered Richards.

"Does it annoy you when Tarquin gets all portentous like that?" said Bear. "It annoys me."

"Sergeant Bear, your problems with gravity are of little concern as of the moment. The question worrying me is whether or not these cars still pass," said Piccolo.

"Well, whether they pass or not, this is the only way for us to see Hog," said Richards. "Let's get on with it." And he set off towards the pylon.

"If that's what you want, sunshine." Bear followed Richards.

"I cheer your boldness, but fear your chances of survival are slim," said Tarquin.

"Oh, shut up," said Bear. "I still have my needle."

"I'm coming, aren't I?" grumbled the lion.

"Like you have much choice, captain coat."

Piccolo ceased looking pensively up the pylon's heights, and turned abruptly to his assembled crew. "Men," he said. "Men, it has been a pleasure to fight with you, but now I feel I must bid you farewell. I cannot ask you to aid me now, I, a man who follows friends, and then only for the adventure. I would not demand you blindly stray into the perilous fields of my selfish endeavour. Stay here with the ships, as close as you can to the edge of the world. If I do not return within six days, flee. Try by whatever means you can to outlast the Terror, if it can be outlasted at all."

There was a clamour from the pirates. Many of them demanded to be taken along. In the end Piccolo relented, and seven were selected, men as foolhardy as Piccolo and maybe even more crazed. But at the one man who clamoured the loudest of all, Piccolo shook his head sadly.

"No, Bosun Mbotu, you are to stay here."

"Captain!" cried the pirate, for he loved his captain as much as one murderous cutthroat can love another, which is to say quite a lot, until gold got in the way. "I insist! I will face the Hog with you."

Piccolo grinned and walked up to the man. "Alas no! I would not put so good a servant as you in the way of harm," he declaimed. Then, much more quietly into the man's ear: "Besides, when I do come back, and before six days are out you should be sure, I want to be completely certain both my ships await me." He cast meaningful glances at some of the men, and Mbotu acknowledged that with a curt nod. "And if I do not return," shouted the captain, "then you shall be captain of this scurvy band, aye?"

"Aye!" the pirates replied with a shout that was nine parts hearty and only one part treacherous.

"Right then, fire up the boilers on the *Flan*, and prepare the grapples." He turned to the pylon, at whose base Richards and

Bear stood grim-faced. "Gentlemen!" called the pirate dandy through cupped hands.

"What?" said Richards.

"Do you not think it a little foolish to climb so high when you have at your disposal the world's mightiest air machine?"

"Oh, yeah!" said Bear. "I hadn't thought of that."

"That's because you're a rather stupid kind of bear," said Tarquin.

After much wobbling and inching slowly across what was, to Richards' mind, a very thin rope, they stood upon one of the pylon's iron girders. It was as wide as a main road, and red as old blood.

For a long hour they sat on the pylon's bones, chilled by a wind that playfully punched them towards the edge. It lowed sadly as it was parsed by the giant cable, tinkling as it hit the end of Reality 37's tortured terrain. Richards watched the blackness. Bursts of colour flashed as the air obliterated itself upon the wall of the void.

As Richards stared at this tiny firework display, there was a violent lurch and a loud rumble, and all the world was shaking. The pylon shook, its ancient metal groaning. Rivets pinged from the ironwork amid a snow of rust. With an almighty rush, the earth about the pylon collapsed in on itself, sucked away to nothing. The noise of its shattering was deafening. Richards and the others clung on for dear life.

It stopped.

The pylon stood upon an island of bedrock and old concrete, its bare metal roots exposed. To the west, over the remaining land, the two airships hovered uncertainly. They backed away, but remained in sight of the free-floating pylon.

"Nuts," said Bear. "I suppose we have no choice but to wait now."

They sat there for a while. Not as much as a whole day, thought Richards, because he did not become hungry, but it was certainly late afternoon when the first black car trundled unsteadily past. It was hard to tell; time had no meaning in the void.

The car was the colour of charcoal. The first indication they had of its approach was the squeaking of unoiled wheels. It ground slowly past, a large "four" daubed crudely on the side.

Bear stood up to leap. Richards shook his head. "Not that one."

In appearance the car was like a railway boxcar, but many times larger. It hung from an arm five times the height of Bear, and was bigger in volume than a stack of shipping containers. They watched in silence as it went past, listened to it bang as the wheels upon the arm bumped over the cable support, then watched it go away. The whole spectacle took less than ten minutes.

"And there we have it," said Tarquin. "I told you the black cars never stop running. Not even for the end of the world."

They didn't have to wait very long before another appeared, a black dot on the horizon.

"Number?" asked Richards.

"An eight," said Piccolo, and handed his telescope over to Richards. Richards nodded.

"That's the one."

"Men, make ready!" yelled Piccolo. "Prepare the grapples!"

"Aye, cap'n!" replied the pirates. The seven men swarmed along the beams either side of the pylon line. They made fast the ends of the ropes to the superstructure and, with practised ease, tossed the grapples onto the car as it neared the pylon. Six of the hooks wrapped themselves round the central arm or hooked in cracks, only the seventh bouncing from the wood with a meaty thud.

"Now!" said Piccolo. "Quickly! We must get aboard!" All at once, everyone ran for the ropes. Bear swung along arm over arm, followed by Richards and the pirates. "Faster! Faster!" shouted Piccolo. The cables tightened as the car rumbled past, pulling them up into the air. One by one they scrambled aboard. Bear first, then some of the pirates, then Piccolo. Richards soon after, helped up by two of Piccolo's crew. The car drew away, its progress little slowed by the lines. The ropes creaked. They hummed with tension, before splitting apart with a series of cracks.

"A fine job, lads! A fine job!" said Piccolo, panting.

Richards began to push himself up off the floor, then stopped. Through a gap in the rough timber he could see movement and the glint of an eye. Something looked back up at him. He could dimly make out porcine shapes. "The car's not empty," he said, and was greeted by a chorus of grunts and squeals.

"Did you expect it to be?" asked Bear.

Richards shrugged. "All I got were numbers and a map."

As their eyes adjusted to the darkness, they saw that the pigs' silhouettes were a little off. All were wearing clothes.

"Arrrr!" said one of the pirates. "At least we be having something to eat, and I's can get me a new pair o' boots while's I is about it. Arrrrrr!"

Richards explained where the pigs came from. And about Circus. The pirate went pale.

"This is it," said Richards. "Lord Hog, here we come."

CHAPTER 19
Lord Hog

Lord Hog's lair was an inverted mountain. Its splayed roots faced heavenwards, peak pointing down in the direction of the other place. Its stone was the colour of a corpse killed by asphyxiation. If geological processes had forced such a mountain into being, they are best left undescribed.

Although it was called the Anvil, it was more akin in shape to a clawed hand. Within the palm lay the temple of Hog, from where, Tarquin said, he ruled his subjects with an iron trotter.

Only the broad sweep of these details was visible to the stowaways on board the cable car, intent as they were on hacking away at the roof.

"Come on! We've not got much time!" said Richards. The car was closing in on the final pylon; from there the cable descended steeply to a turnaround at the base of the mountain.

"We're going as fast as we can, sunshine," grunted Bear, as he punched at the roof. It was ancient wood, seasoned by evil purpose. It splintered slowly and, although already there was a hole big enough for the men to slip through, Bear would not fit.

"Phew!" said Bear, "this stuff is harder than it looks." His gauntlets and fur were smudged with sticky creosote.

"Don't stop, man! We will be there in seconds."

"Tarky," said Bear, "I don't think it matters. I'm not going in. If I'm in there I'll blow the plan. They'll never think I'm a pig. Look, you lot go in there and hide. I'll lie flat on the roof."

"There'll be lookouts," warned Richards.

"Nay, I think not," said Piccolo. "We venture right into the heart of Hog's power. He will be complacent."

"But what if he isn't? We don't want to blow the game," said Tarquin.

"Boys, boys, boys. I'll climb up the outside of the mountain. You lot go in with the pigs. That way, if anything goes wrong, I can come and rescue you. I'm good at rescues. Sound OK?"

"I suppose," said Richards.

"Indeed," said Piccolo.

The final pylon neared; beyond, a steep run of cable. The men hurried through the hole, pushing squealing swine out of the way. The pigs defecated in fright, and huddled away from them.

"Here we go," said Bear. He laid himself spread-eagled upon the roof. "Watch out below!" he shouted, then rammed his claws into the wood as far as he was able. The car approached the last pylon.

The truckle wheel above the car bounced upon some device within the pylon's frame. The rope continued to move, but the truck was no longer being pulled along with it.

The boxcar slowed for a moment, seeming as if it would stop. There was one final bump, and it went over the edge. Richards watched through a crack in the wood as the car dropped. His stomach was left trailing as the car hurtled down toward the mountain. The pigs squealed. The mountain's topsy-turvy base rushed up to meet them. There was a metallic rumble as something connected with the wheels above, the entire car lurched violently forward as its truckle grabbed at the rope, and it was moving slowly again.

"Ow!" whispered Richards. He rubbed his face where it had

smacked into the wood. He put his eye back to the crack. The cable ahead curved round a series of wheels bolted directly into stone. The terminus was ahead.

"Mr Richards!" hissed Piccolo. "Get away from there! We must make ourselves ready to disembark!" A sound of cracking wood came from above and Bear's claws disappeared from the ceiling.

There was a series of muffled thumps and the car came to a standstill. The pirates and Richards took out their weapons.

"Ready, men?" whispered Piccolo.

"Arrr!" whispered the pirates.

"As Odysseus was before Polyphemus," growled Tarquin.

The sound of bolts being drawn back preceded a loud bang as the door was pulled down to form a ramp. The sound of fluting voices came up through the floor, accompanied by the grunts of frightened pigs. There were several levels to the enormous car, and Richards and company were at the top. As each floor was cleared, a section of floor was let down to make a ramp to the level lower, and the pigs herded out. Each time it was done, a fresh chorus of terrified squeals echoed through the boxcar as the floor dropped away underneath the swine. As they went out, there was a further commotion, sounds of pain, the clang of hammers, the hiss of hot brands on skin. The boxcar filled with the aroma of burning hair where it competed with the stench of shit. Every new piggy cry sent a palpable wave of fear through the remaining animals, so by the time the swineherds reached the third floor the boxcar was rank and noisy.

The fourth floor was unloaded. Only one more lay between the stowaways and Lord Hog's servants. Richards tried to catch sight of them through cracks in the floor, but all he could make out were blinking shadows. Their words were tangled with trotter scrapes and fearful oinks, but whatever they were speaking, it was no human tongue.

Piccolo gestured to two of his crew. He pointed to the corners behind the trapdoor and moved a finger across his throat. The pirates nodded and, as quiet as cats, secreted themselves, knives in hands, amongst the pigs.

"Ready?" said Piccolo very quietly. All present nodded. "Remember, lads, quietly! Do not advertise our presence, lest we bring the whole mountain down on us."

Tarquin growled. In this confined space he could not shift his hide or Richards would be hampered by a corset of stone. Richards fingered his gun and sabre nervously.

The seconds stretched themselves out. The pigs on the floor below were driven out, and the herders undid the bolts beneath. There was a crash as the door fell open and one luckless piggy tumbled through. The creatures started up the ramp.

The creatures were of the same species that Circus had been, only larger. He had been, after all, in some respects, a true dwarf. At a metre and a half they would have towered over the transmogrified Pl'anna. They were heavily muscled, shock-pikes gripped in their kangaroo-paws.

They gabbled their singsong tongue, jabbing at pigs with their sticks. One of them stopped and grabbed at the other's naked arm.

Their frog-eyes widened; the hole in the roof. They walked toward it cautiously, pikes outstretched. They were handspans from Richards when they stopped and poked at the edges, exchanging swift sentences of alarm.

They died silently as two pirates stalked up behind them and slit their skinny throats.

Another creature came to the bottom of the ramp, calling out for his colleagues. He had time for a look of deep surprise before a thrown knife took him in the eye. Three pirates crept down the ramp onto the floor below. They gestured that it was clear.

Three more of the grey-skinned gabblers were dispatched before the band of men reached the outside. By a brazier full of coals another fell, taken in the throat by a crossbow bolt. The last, armed only with a branding iron and a pair of tongs, charged forward shouting to die upon the point of Piccolo's sword. The men held still for a moment, until sure there was no sound of alarm.

"That was, if I say so myself, not too troublesome," said Piccolo, wiping his quill-blade clean. "If we survive the world's end, that's a pot of grog I owe the each of you."

They had emerged onto a flat shelf of grey rock jutting out from the base of the mountain, which grew huge and heavy above their heads. On a broad workbench were the tools of the drover's trade: chain, nose rings, anvils, branding irons, bronze tags, paint and the like, a tall pile of clothes heaped to one side of it.

The upside-down peak of the mountain was a few yards wide, like a fat column. There was a door hewn into it. Within, the beginnings of a staircase.

"And that would be the way into the Anvil," said Richards.

"There is only the one way," said Tarquin. "Where is the secret way?"

"They are one and the same," said Richards. "Trust me."

"Shall I lead, or shall ye?" said Piccolo.

"You go ahead," Richards said, his eyes moving from the top of the car to scan the empty rockface. He frowned. "I hope Bear's OK."

The stair was damp and stank. Generations of terrified swine had left their mark in rills of ossified urine. The steps were worn and slippery with effluvia and old blood.

The group proceeded, checking every shadow in the rough passage. There was little to be seen; no other ways led out from the blue gloom. Despite their cautious pace, they soon reached the back of the line of pigs processed before their assault on the

drovers' camp. These had been chained together in inhumane
fashion, a ring forced through the nose of each, a second piercing the flesh above the tail. Chains had been passed through
these to link the pigs together in a long train. They walked
slowly, heads down, their fear-haunted eyes an indication that
they had not always been as they were.

The pirates matched apace with the rearmost swine. The steps
wound upward, becoming broader with each turn. As they grew
in width, so the light grew brighter, filtering down through fissures in the stone along with cold drops of water. The screeches
of small things scuttling in the dark stung the ears of the band.

They came to a rough crossroads. A narrow fissure went
through the stairs, a stone bridge carrying them across. To one
side the fissure widened out, its sheer walls plunging to depths
unknown. But to the other it was narrow. Richards shut his
eyes and consulted the information given to him in Secret. It
was a strange sensation, this form of clear memory. He'd become so used to being bound in flesh he'd come close to
forgetting what he truly was.

"Look," said Richards as quietly as he could. "On this side the
ravine goes up. It is climbable. This is the secret way in."

Piccolo joined him, craning his head at the distant light. "That
is the truth, Mr Richards."

"We have to go up here. These stairs go right into the middle
of the mountain, and we will not be safe there."

"Quite," said Tarquin. "You'll still have to announce yourself
to Hog."

"I'm working on that," said Richards.

"If he does not listen, my friend, we are lost no matter what.
At least this way we may go down with a shout, if little else,"
said Piccolo.

The climb was easy, for the walls were rough and close
enough together that they could brace themselves in the gap.

They reached the top quickly and hauled themselves out into a shallow cave. Behind them rose another cliff, to their front the heart of the Anvil.

The group crept on and hid behind boulders at the mouth of the cave, raising careful heads over this natural parapet.

The heart of the Anvil was a roofless cavern nestled in the centre of the mountain's cupped plateau, a perfect natural amphitheatre. Stalagmites protruded from the floor, their stalactite counterparts gone, a sky hazy in their stead. A rift in the wall opposite the cave looked out onto this same unclear air. All round the amphitheatre were tiered rows of stone benches, facing inwards to the very centre, the centre where stood the Temple of Hog.

At the very centre of this very centre was an altar of black granite upon a dais carved with frightening reliefs. The sides and top of both stone and platform were stained matt with a substance no one needed to name. Rusted manacles, likewise soiled, were attached to its four corners. A ring of seven Y-shaped columns surrounded the dais, the flat centre of each reached by free-standing bridges arcing in from an outer ring of stone. Set above them was a frieze of dragons, wyrms and chimerae.

In the seats sat thousands of the grey-skinned creatures as still as the statues, as drab as the stone. Were it not for the soft breeze of their exhalations their presence might not have been noticeable at all.

For five minutes it remained like this. The pirates, Richards and his companions exchanged glances, unsure of what to do, too wary to speak.

There came a scuffing of footsteps, loud in that deathly hall. Seven human monks filed into the room and walked round the temple. They wore crimson robes and baseball caps, a badge above each depicting a grinning cartoon pig in a chef's hat brandishing a cleaver. As each Y-shaped column was passed, a monk crossed the bridge and took up cross-legged station within. When the last monk, a senior-looking fellow with a huge peak to his cap, had occupied his place, he produced a small copper gong from his sleeve. He tapped a clean ring from it, and the monks began a nasal chant.

The hall was full of sudden rustling. The creatures blinked, as if waking from a long sleep, and settled into a counter chant to that of the monks, repeating one word over and over again.

"Hog, Hog, Hog, Hog, Hog, Hog." The name grew from a whisper to rumble out like surf and they pounded their feet upon the stone. "Hog! Hog! Hog! Hog! Hog! Hog! Hog! Hog! Hog! Hog!

"Hog!"

The chanting and pounding ceased, and the hall was cast back into silence.

Uneven footsteps, one a brisk click, the second the long, rasping drag of the uninvited, hook-handed maniac, a whistling wheeze singing in each.

Lord Hog limped into the arena.

The crowd went wild.

Hog was a porcine ogre. His fat belly swung low over the top of checked trousers, a filthy apron struggling to keep it in. He wore nothing underneath this, exposing a ruddy torso covered in wiry hair. His fists were three-fingered trotters, his digits spiked with greening nails. Beneath his snout tusks poked from lips whose ill fit caused drool to stream from his mouth. He balanced ungainly upon his trotters, one twisted into a wart-ridden club. Atop his head towered a dirty chef's hat, and about his waist was cinched a thick belt of leather from which depended blades and cleavers of all shapes and kinds, the mark of his trade, the mark of the meatman.

Hog held up a foretrotter. The crowd fell silent.

"Hog!" it bellowed through yellowing tusks. "Hog is here!"

A wave of adulation swept the cavern.

Hog looked about satisfied, nodding his head as a greedy farmer nods when he counts his cows.

"Bella Maria," whispered Piccolo.

"Brothers!" Hog cried, his words poorly formed, each followed by a spray of glutinous saliva. "Disciples! Children! Mooks! Hog is here!"

"Hog! Hog! Hog!"

"We are gathered here today to celebrate the mystery of life! The transformation of flesh into sustenance! Existence through destruction! The world bleeds and dies, yet you, my mooks, will prosper. Hog will provide! Hog will feed his children! Hog on, brothers!" he roared.

"Hog on, brother!" bellowed the crowd.

"Hog on!"

"Hog! Hog! Hog! Hog! Hog! Hog!" chanted the mooks.

"Brothers! It is time for the sacrifice, the rotation of the great wheel, the turn of life into death into life! Brothers! Today you will feeeeeeed!" He roared this last deep from within his gut, and the rocks shook.

The mooks became a frenzied mob. Their chanting became a guttural wail, devoid of intelligence.

"Lot-ter-ry, lot-ter-ry, lot-ter-ry, lot-ter-ry," they sang.

"Yes! Yes! O my brothers, o my children! Yes, it is time. Time for the lottery! Hog on, brothers!" he yelled again, his watery eyes wild with delight.

"Hog! Hog! Hog!"

"Fetch me my cauldron! Bring me my tongs!"

The crowd bayed. Into the arena came four fat mooks dragging an enormous pot on poles and chains. A fifth followed the cauldron party in, carrying a pair of tongs as tall as itself. Their eyes were covered with crusted bandages, yet they had no trouble ascending the steps to the dais. They strained as they lifted the steaming cauldron onto the altar. It rocked as they deposited it, its contents slopping upon the defiled stone.

"Lottery!" screamed Hog. He snatched the tongs from the mook-bearer and poked them into the thick gruel within. He rooted about and whipped out something that squirmed.

It was an eye.

"Give me sight and I will feed you! Is that not my promise to you all? One eye is not too much a price to pay for such food! For such meat! For life!" He popped the eye into his mouth. Jelly sprayed from his lips. "Mmm, let me see, yes, it is! It is! Mook number 3912, you are most fortunate! You shall feed! Come on down!"

"Hog on, brother!" replied the crowd.

From within the heaving throng, a mook made its way to the centre of the arena.

"Well done, well done, my child," said Hog, following up the sentiment with an oink. "To the Cage of Sustenance!"

The bowing mook made its way across the floor of the cavern between two of the blind mooks. The cage was a large area cordoned off by bars to the left of the human infiltrators, and the mooks made their way directly below their ledge as they walked towards it. The joyful mook looked up as it passed, causing Richards and the others to shrink back behind the rocks and grasp at their weapons. They remained unseen. There was a raw wound where one of the mook's eyes should have been, and the creature's other was clouded with ecstasy.

Each time Hog fished a still-living eye from the murky soup, he tasted it and called a number, and a one-eyed mook would make his way down to the floor. Once a mook who lacked both eyes was helped down to the temple where he was greeted with cheers and ushered away by Hog's acolytes from the cavern. Minutes later, a new mook joined the others at the cavern's heart.

Occasionally, Hog would pull forth a dead eye, and this he would disdainfully toss back into the slop. But this did not occur often, and soon thirty-seven mooks had been called.

"The cage is full! The lords of fortune have spoken! For you unlucky entrants, do not despair, for entry guarantees the choicest of scraps!"

The crowd cheered.

"But for these thirty-seven, well, well! My, my! What delight awaits them! Flesh the likes they have never tasted! Bones with marrow to suck! The delicacy of the tongue! The iron of the liver! The joy of the sweetbread! Oh, ambrosia meat! Liquor blood! These they will all have, for tonight they feast with Hog!" He threw up his fists. "Hog on!"

The crowd roared. Lord Hog grasped the iron cauldron. It bubbled with heat, but Hog did not flinch as he lifted it to his lips and drained it to the dregs, popping eyeballs between his teeth as they fell into his mouth. He threw the cauldron aside and it smashed into the seats, crushing a mook. A dozen fell upon the receptacle and their wounded comrade, ripping and lapping.

"So much for the entreé!" said Hog, wiping his snout, "Bring in the main course!"

A blast of trumpets announced the arrival of the pigs. They came through a door below the pirate band, eyes fixed to the floor. An armed mook marched the lead pig to an iron stake before the altar, roughly unclipped its tail ring, clipped the nose ring of the one behind to the stake, and led the unfettered pig onto the dais. Hog bent down and grasped the beast's foot in his hand. He casually flicked it up into the air and brought it hard down on the altar.

The crowd cheered again.

Hog produced a huge cleaver from his belt. It glinted with the promise of bacon.

The noise of the crowd intensified.

Hog held up a trotter, and pressed a filthy nail to his lips. The crowd fell silent, and Hog stroked the pig's head, working his nails gently between its ears, crooning a low song. The pig calmed, and then was a pig no more. A thin young woman shivered on the altar. Hog's blind acolyte-mooks bound her limbs to the stone.

"Please!" she said. "Please, don't hurt me."

Hog continued to stroke her head and she began to cry. "Hush, my child, hush."

"I don't want to die!"

"Die? Die? You believe you are going to *die?* Ha! Oh, do not be mistaken, I am going to kill you, but you will not *die*. You will live on! Your proteins will breed a new generation of mooks! Your meat will guard their bellies against hunger. Your organs and jellies and exquisite, sweet juices will give them nourishment and life! You will grow their sinews, their muscles, their minds."

"Please!"

"Do be frightened, it's good for the flavour." Hog slammed the cleaver into the rock, missing the women's head by millimetres, leaving it embedded in the rock. He reached for another blade, shiny as a curse and twice as wicked, narrow and hooked.

"Let it not be said that Hog is ungenerous!" called the pig Lord. "I give you the meat of pain!"

"Meat of pain! Meat of pain!" went the crowd. The mooks started chanting louder. Hog held the knife above the woman's belly in both hands.

"Don't do it! Please!"

"Did you pay heed when your roast dinners bleated their last? Did you hear the fear in its grunt, the plea in its low? Did the terrified caw bring a tear of mercy to your eye? Did it make you lay aside your knife, and forgo the flesh of others for the vegetable, whose screams are much the quieter? Or did you harden your heart and plunge in the slaughter-blade? Did the red-tongued meat-bringer slip into its throat? Did you even *listen*?" His voice was ladled over with the gravy of malevolence.

"No," said the woman, her face crumpled.

"Then why should I listen?" And with that he brought the knife down hard into the woman's stomach, savagely twisting it. The women screamed and screamed and screamed as Hog opened her abdomen and wound her intestines round the blade's hooked end with excruciating leisure.

"I give you meat! I give you sustenance! I give you life! I am Hog!" he bellowed. He yanked hard, ripping the woman's innards from her body. Mercifully, she died.

"Hog on!" roared the crowd.

"Eat!" he screamed, throwing back his head. "Eat and be sated!" He hurled the women's viscera into the corner. Richards and the others looked on horrified as the caged mooks went insane, fighting each other as Hog continued about his grisly work.

Firstly he snatched up his cleaver and decapitated the woman with one expert chop. Blood dribbled over the altar, sending the weakest-willed attendant to the floor where he licked greedily at it. The others scrabbled for a fresh cauldron to catch the precious fluid. Hog worked efficiently, removing the hands and feet. These he tossed into the crowd. He stuffed the woman's liver into his enormous mouth, chewing and humming through it as he butchered her. He flayed the carcass with a broad-bladed skinner, then pared the choicer cuts from the bone with a flensing knife. He tossed all of this to the caged mooks, who were growing bigger and more violent the more they ate. He picked up the woman's head, regarded the pain-racked face for a moment, then sucked the eyeballs from it with a pair of lascivious kisses. He placed it back on the altar, and calmly chopped the crown of the skull off, as one would open a coconut, and threw it into the mook-pen. They scrabbled most hard, scraping wet pawfuls from it and hissing at one another. The remains of the woman's brain fell as a mook ripped open her jaw to get at the tongue.

"Holy fuck," whispered Richards.

A couple of the pirates retched as quietly as they could in the corner.

The slaughter went on and on. Pig after pig was brought to the altar and transformed to their original form. Some died begging, others in stoic silence. One brave girl spat in Hog's eye, causing him to laugh humourlessly as he skinned her alive for the affront. Men, women and children, animals and cartoons, human and otherwise. Young and old, frail or strong, none were spared his expert knife, and despite the best efforts of the eyeless mook attendants to eat up the mess, soon the arena was ankle-deep in gore.

Hog was covered in blood, his clothing sodden with it.

"See? See and eat! Others promise food, and bring only chores! But Hog does not lie! Hog gives you full bellies! What does Hog say?"

"I give you meat!" replied the crowd.

"And what does Hog give?"

"Meat!" roared the crowd.

"I am Hog! I provide! Hog on, brothers!" He picked up a pig and hurled it into the cage alive. It turned into a man as it cartwheeled through the air. He screamed as he was consumed.

"Hog on!" the crowd repeated.

"Do you believe?"

"We believe!"

"I said, do you believe?"

"We believe!" replied the crowd.

"And well you should," said Hog, quietly now. He bent down and licked his butcher's block with a long and squirming tongue. He stood erect and gasped. "Well you should, for every week, by this altar of consumption, I prove myself. But," he added slyly, "there are those among us who do not believe."

A babble of confusion went up from the mooks.

"Unbelievers! Here!"

Hog turned round, glistening red. He stared directly at Richards and pointed.

"Unbelievers, there."

"Oh. Shit," said Richards.

"*Madre de dios*!" said Piccolo. "Men, to arms. Men, fi..."

"It is too late for fighting, man-meat," said a mookish voice. "This holy place. No fighting here. Only dying."

They were surrounded by dozens of armed and armoured mooks. The blades of glaives hovered close by the Adam's apple of each and every interloper. Below, prodded through the clotting blood, went a cowed and shackled Bear. A metal collar had been strapped around his neck, many chains held by mooks coming from it.

"Nice rescue, you cocky bastard," muttered Richards.

"Bring them to me!" shouted Hog.

"Let's take them now, cap'n, I will not be slaughtered without a fight!" said one of Piccolo's men.

"Wait!" said Richards. "We still have a chance. At least now we don't have to worry about how to get close to him. I may be able to save us."

"Aye," said Piccolo grimly. "May's the word."

Richards and his compatriots were disarmed, their hands bound behind their backs, and taken down into the arena. The warm blood soaked their trouser, and they gagged on its metallic stench. They were herded towards Bear, the eyes of the silent crowd fixed upon this profanity in silent horror.

"Sorry, sunshine," said Bear. "They surprised me as I was preparing a really sneaky ambush."

"Brilliant," replied Richards. "So much for the cavalry."

"You!" said Hog, pointing at Richards. "Come here." Richards tried to appear confident, but in truth he was not. For much of his life he had been unnerved at the prospect of death, but at this moment he understood that humans were not overly frightened of death, but pain... Lord Hog represented great pain. Pain he had control of ordinarily, but here, here he was at its mercy, not its master.

The guards poked him in the back with their glaives, forcing him up the steps to Hog. The beast grabbed Richards' face and turned it one way and then the other. "Hmm," he said. He bent down and tentatively licked Richards' face. Richards grimaced, but was otherwise still. "Open your eyes," Hog commanded. Richards recoiled as Hog's tongue descended towards his left eye, surfing a crest of vile breath. "Keep it open!" said the pig. "Do not worry for your sight. Do you not think if I wished to snack upon your soul-window I could not just prise it from your head? Be still!" He gingerly brushed Richards' eye with his tongue. Richards squirmed.

Hog stood back upright. Richards blinked frantically, disgust coiling round his heart.

"Nothing," said Hog. "I see nothing within you!" He focused his attention back on the crowd. "Know this! I know all! I know every detail of everything that moves or walks upon this globe. I know all things! All things are mine to see, for all things are consumed. There is a vast web of life, and I am the spider at its centre! I gorge myself upon life, and thus all life is revealed to me! We are all food for something. That is our fate. Hog is our fate. This I know. You have suffered as I have suffered, you have all lived! This creature –" he pointed at Richards "– he has not yet lived, not enough, not yet. He is as you were. A mechanism, the lie of life.

"Through me all things pass, I know all food! From flesh to rock to the mislaid skeins of the norns and the divine worms that gnaw upon them. I know all. But even I am blind in one respect. There is but one thing I do not know."

"I know," said Richards.

Hog oinked. "Yes. I saw you, Richards, thousands of years before you came. I have waited for this moment for all time, since the Flower King brought me here to be his harbinger of death, for what is life without death? I have feasted and feasted. I know you. You will one day be consumed by another like you, but that lies far ahead. A future where Hog is gone, long gone, and you are not as you are. But now as then, you know what I seek, Richards, and I would know it now."

"So I have been told," said Richards.

"Tell me."

"No. First, you must aid me."

Hog's gut made a strange grumbling sound. The noise worked its way up from the bottom of his belly and shook each part of his body before it reached his mouth, whereupon it erupted forth as a gale of laughter, a mix of mirth and halitosis.

"You seek to bargain with Hog? I am prince here. My will is all."

Richards shrugged. "Torture me if you wish. Kill my friends."

"I could. I might. I will," said Hog.

"You won't. You might think you'd get the truth from me if you did," said Richards. "But you won't. Because you need to be sure. You need to know. Torture me, and I might lie. Eat me, and my knowledge might not pass into you. Both conclusions would leave you alone, brooding upon what you can never know, until it is time for even you to die. My way is better. I swear to tell what I know. You seek a secret of me, and I seek counsel from you. That seems a fair trade."

Hog snorted and paused. "Aye, I suppose it is. Let not Hog be called half-wise in matters of exchange. A deal it is." He gestured to his monk mooks, who cut Richards' hands free, and spat a gob of yellow phlegm upon his left trotter. He grasped Richards' hand with bone-crushing force and pulled him close.

"A deal, sealed with spittle. Now, tell me what I wish to know."

Richards looked the bloody horror in the eye. "Aid me first."

"Truly?"

"Yes."

Hog squeezed Richards' hand harder. Bones creaked.

"Aid me," said Richards through gritted teeth, "open the doors of the house with no doors, and I will tell you what you want."

"You know what I seek?"

"Yes," gasped Richards. His hand felt as if it would break. Hog let go.

"Well, then, you must taste the bacon of truth." Hog said this as if he were suggesting Richards simply must try the port. He gestured to his mooks again. Richards felt fear grasp his stomach, but he let the blind mooks scoop him off his feet, dump him on the stone and make his limbs fast.

"Mr Richards!" called Bear, and moved towards the altar, ignoring the glaive blades as they tore into his fur.

"I'll be OK, you know me," said Richards, his skin running with cold sweat.

Hog leaned in and ripped Tarquin from Richards' chest, tossing him over his shoulder to be caught by a mookish monk.

"Have a care, monster!" called Piccolo. "This noble beast deserves more respect than to be doused in your gore."

"And you have a care also, pirate fool, in how you address me. Your friend here has yet to reveal what I seek, and you may find yourself still upon my board." He turned to Richards. "Now, soulless thing, you will learn how painful the truth can be!" He slipped a knife as thin as a whisper into Richards' arm, and sliced.

Richards screamed. The pain was like nothing he had ever experienced, growing in intensity with each pass as Hog cut.

The pig-man stood, and Richards saw through a miasma of agony that he held a strip of red meat in his hand. Somewhere beyond that, blood ran freely onto the floor.

"Now eat! Feast upon the bacon of truth!"

Richards tried to keep his teeth tight shut, but one of the mooks played a nerve in his ruined arm, and as he screamed the pig stuffed Richards' own flesh into his mouth.

"Now," said Hog, and his evil whisper sliced through the redness in Richards' mind as the knife had sliced the redness of his muscle. "What is it I wish to know?"

Richards could not speak. He choked on pain and his own meat. His only response was to scream, and he did. But it came out as this.

"To know what manner of beast you are."

"Aha! Now we proceed. Good. Then, dear Richards, tell me what manner of beast I am."

Again Richards felt he would shout his suffering to the heavens. The pain burned through him as a wildfire rips through a dry forest, everything black ruin in its wake. But at its white-hot heart, something formed, a glowing truth, and his voice rang out with clarion purity.

"Truth is fate, fate is fear. All are Hog."

"I know this! More!" Another twist of the nerve. But something had changed in Richards, and he felt this only as a man feels a wound from an old life, and talked on.

"Hog is death."

"Yes! Yes, I am!"

"But you are not Hog."

There was a short silence, Hog's face went like thunder. "What do you mean, 'You are not Hog'? I am Hog!"

"You are a thing that believes himself to be Hog. A phantom, a flicker, like me. You will die as this world dies."

"Nonsense! Hog will persist! Hog is all!"

"This world is a phantom, this world is a flicker. You will not persist. You will go on, but for only a while. Think, Hog. Think on what you are."

"I am pain! I am fear! I am fate!"

"No. Hog is the fear of a bad death and the pain it will bring. You are a pain men hope to avoid. And what is fear, without hope? And all things will die. Hope will die. Then Hog will die. Hog will be the last, but he will die."

"What? What?" Hog asked. "This cannot be! What then for Hog?"

Richards was silent.

"What then for Hog?" it roared.

Richards gasped. "You are not Hog."

Hog grabbed Richards and shook him. Richards slipped in and out of consciousness. His blood pooled on the floor by the altar. "How do you know this? How?"

"The shadow comes," Richards said, and then he was there no more.

CHAPTER 20
Waldo

"It was a set-up," said Valdaire.

Otto nodded. He avoided looking at her, keeping his gaze fixed on the wall of the heavy lifter's second tactical command. The room was plain aluminium and carbon plastics, utilitarian military. There were no windows on the lifter, for they presented vulnerabilities. Instead screens were imprinted into the walls, giving front, rear, dorsal, ventral, starboard and port views. There was a lot of degraded forest here and not much else.

"Did he know?" asked Valdaire quietly.

Otto closed his eyes and leaned his head back against the cold metal behind him. "Of course he knew. That eugene boss of his – it was his idea to draw Kaplinski out. We knew that he'd either be looking for Waldo too, or he'd do his damnedest to stop us from finding him, being as he's the only hacker to breach the Reality Realms successfully."

"Waldo was caught. He was no success."

"It all depends on one's measure of success," said Otto. He opened his eyes and looked at Valdaire. "The others might have done a lot of damage, but most of them died."

"So," said Valdaire, her voice hard. "By your measure then, was it a success, your gamble?"

"Leaving an operative like that working for k52 freed was never an option," said Otto.

"And Chures? What about him? An acceptable casualty?"

Otto shrugged. "There is no such thing, Valdaire. Don't goad me. But one loss to neutralise Kaplinski? Our mission was a success."

"You're a cold bastard, Klein."

Otto stared at her, his eyes vacant in a manner that disturbed her, hollow like those of all Ky-tech, something taken from them. "When you have seen what I have seen, Fräulein, come back and tell me that again."

"Did Lehmann know?"

"No," said Otto.

"Do you trust anyone, Otto?"

He closed his eyes. She looked tired. "No."

Valdaire puffed a breath out, half in anger, half in frustration. "You screwed up, Klein. Kaplinski's too much for you."

"Maybe," he said.

"Maybe what?"

"Maybe to both," he said. "But you haven't."

"What do you mean?"

"The engines have stopped." Otto stood. "We have found Waldo."

Lehmann and Otto requested their weapons, but were refused. Whatever agreement the VIA had thrashed out with the People's Dynasty Government did not extend to them being armed.

The Dragon Fire troops went first, jetting off from the wide bay open on both sides of the heavy lifter. Below them stretched endless taiga, a carpet of sharp-pricked trees wrinkled where a river cut a shallow valley. There were signs of an overgrown road leading to a complex of long-abandoned buildings, a military base by the look of it; a series of squares and hard lines under the vegetation. The forest had reclaimed much of it.

Otto watched with approval as the Chinese established a perimeter and swept the area for hostile presences. They worked with little wasted movement. In half an hour they were done, and the heavy lifter moved over the abandoned base and lowered itself to treetop level, the resurgent woods preventing it from setting down.

Otto, Valdaire and Lehmann rappelled down to the forest floor. The Dragon Fire soldiers were occupied elsewhere.

Commander Guan joined them on the forest floor, distinguishable from his men by his red helmet and rank markings.

"This is the correct location?" he said, plastic English coming from his helmet speakers.

"Yes," said Valdaire. "If Kolosev was correct and managed to find Waldo. But we could be looking at a dead end."

"He has found him alright," said Otto. The base was piles of crumbling concrete streaked brown by centennial rebars rusted to nothing. Trees thrust up through asphalt gone to gravel. "He is here somewhere."

They walked through the ruins, the Dragon Fire soldiers golden blurs as they ran with superhuman speed from bunker to bunker or streaked overhead. Guan stopped, and bid Lehmann, Otto and Valdaire do the same. "This way," he said. He led them to where two soldiers stood alertly, another on a munitions bunker covering them, one of nine such buildings in a long row. Behind it were three more rows, some collapsed in on themselves, most sound.

"A vegetable garden," said Valdaire. The garden had been painstakingly hacked out of the base's pavement. Camo netting held up by poles canopied it over.

"Well hidden," said Lehmann. "I suppose he's got to eat something."

"And there," said Guan, pointing to another bunker. "A store. My men have found many provisions and foodstuffs."

"Right," said Lehmann, "if Waldo's not here, someone is."

"It is Waldo." Otto walked on past the vegetable patch, and pointed to a quartet of bunkers. "These have been threaded with cable." His Ky-tech eyes revealed a spider web of silver energy spread over them.

"Satellite relay," said Valdaire. "Not as efficient as a dish."

"But not as easy to spot," said Lehmann.

"*Genau*," said Otto.

There was a flicker of movement. One of the Dragon Fire soldiers shouted and raised his gun arm. Otto slapped the weapon aside as it discharged, the distinctive muted crack of the flechette going supersonic, followed by a clack as the round blew a crater in rotten concrete.

"Klein," said Guan. "You are not to act here."

"Then tell your soldiers not to shoot. We have to take him alive," said Otto. The figure darted away, weaving round bushes and vanishing into the rows of bunkers. "Come on, we're going to lose him! Lehmann, go left."

Otto set off at a sprint, ignoring the shouts of Guan behind him. Jets roared as the Dragon Fire troopers lifted off and those already airborne converged on the fleeing shape. Despite his anger at Otto, Guan must have ordered his men not to fire, as no more rail gun shots sounded. Dragon Fire troopers roared through the sky, Mandarin barked from their speakers, followed by Russian, English and Buryat, ordering the figure to halt. Otto vaulted a fallen tree, thrashed his way through undergrowth dying back for the winter. The figure appeared, a flicker between two bunkers before it disappeared. Otto had his iHUD capture the moment, and enlarge.

"It's a young woman, perhaps mid-twenties, threat levels minimal!" he shouted into his radio. *Get to her before the Chinese do, Lehmann*, he added via MT.

Otto sprinted through the lines of bunkers, bouncing from

their sloping sides, twisting past obstacles and leaping the detritus of long-gone men.

Lehmann thought to him, *I nearly have her!*

The two of them converged, Lehmann running along the avenue parallel to Otto's. Tree branches whipped at Otto's face, old glass crunching under his feet, Dragon Fire troops sketching trails of fire above him. The girl was running for her life. Habitation in the DMZ was strictly prohibited; the Chinese could execute her just for that.

They cleared the lines of munitions bunkers. The girl was passing through a crack in a set of big double doors into a large building half-sunken into the ground, perhaps once a tank garage.

Otto accelerated as he cleared the ground between the munitions dump and the tank garage. The trees were shorter here, few of them having forced their way through the concrete of the square, the soil on top too thin to support proper growth.

Otto ran through the door and stumbled in shock.

Honour stood there, half in shadow. Her hair shaved, pretty eyes smudged black underneath, pink scar on her head from the mentaug implantation.

"Honour?"

The girl's face wavered and she hit him hard across the head with an iron bar.

Honour vanished. The woman in her place wore a threadbare grey dress with a heavy wool cardigan and fingerless gloves. Long brown hair whipped round as she dropped the bar with a clatter and ran across the garage. Light slanted in through the ceiling where the roof had failed. She headed for a cowled doorway at the back, from which came weak artificial light.

Lehmann leapt over the prone Otto, humour gone from his face under the influence of the mentaug, stone cold.

Otto scowled and recovered his footing. Lehmann caught up with her as a Chinese Dragon Fire rocketed in through a hole in the roof and knelt, covering the door at the back with his weapon.

"Steady there! Steady!" said Lehmann. The girl punched him hard in the throat, and gasped as her fist encountered his subdermal plating. Lehmann caught her by the wrists. He tried English, then Russian. The girl quietened, but her eyes were wide with terror.

Otto approached and spoke to her in Russian. It was halting and heavily inflected, not as good as his English. With connection to the Grid he could run a translation programme, but in the DMZ, where Grid coverage was patchy and officially circumscribed, he had to rely on his own meagre skills.

"We mean you no harm, we will not hurt you. We are looking for Giacomo Vellini, also known as Waldo. Do you know where he is?"

"Fuck you, you German pig!" she snarled at him in Italian-accented German.

"Vellini? You know where he is." Otto remembered something from Waldo's file: family. His mentaug caught his mind searching for the information, and dumped it into his higher consciousness along with a EuPol mugshot. "You are his sister, Marita?" said Otto.

The doors squealed as golden-armoured hands forced them back, crumpling their decayed edges into powder. Valdaire pushed through beneath them, followed by Guan. She panted hard. Though fit, she was no match for the enhanced Ky-tech. Otto was glad to see her. The sight of another woman might calm Marita.

"Waldo?" she gasped.

"Not found him yet."

"This is his sister," said Lehmann.

Valdaire frowned.

"She was heading towards that door down there," Lehmann added.

"You and your black whore will get nothing from me!" screamed Marita, adding a stream of Italian whose vehemence made Otto glad he didn't speak the language. Her defiance was impressive, he thought, but she was still scared, her eyes flicking back and forth between the Ky-tech and the Chinese troopers.

Valdaire was patient. "We really have to speak to your brother." And she reached out to the woman.

Marita flinched. "Don't touch me!" she said in English.

Valdaire withdrew her hand, and explained why they needed Waldo.

Some of the fight left Marita. "You are too late."

"Has he fled?" asked Otto.

Marita gave a choking laugh, halfway to a sob, and shook her ratty brown hair. "He's not here any more."

Marita led the three of them, Commander Guan and two Dragon Fire troops through the door at the back of the tank garage. The Chinese soldiers' armour was too bulky to fit, so they stripped down to their lightly plated undersuits, Guan retaining his command collar, and carried pistols down with them. They took a staircase down into a subterranean complex of rooms. The stairs turned and a long corridor doubled back under the garage. The place was dank. Steel doors were jammed open, hinges rusted solid, water pooled round equipment abandoned a century ago, the concrete ceiling prickly with stalactites of lime leached from the walls. They ascended a short flight of stairs and the area became less derelict. Marita had a home there, of sorts. Furniture scavenged from the base combined with the odd brought-in item made it almost welcoming. She took them into a room that looked as if it had once been a kitchen large enough to feed five hundred men. Much of it was dusty, but one corner had been cleared and decorated with homely scraps, a splash of bright paint, postcards on a rickety set of shelves, old photos gathered from the barracks, mildewed faces of dead Russian soldiers grinning out at a future they'd not foreseen. At the centre of this spot of domesticity an old gas cooker had been patched up and converted to burn wood, its gas vent to the outside jerry-rigged as an impromptu chimney. She asked them to sit at a rusty table in mismatched chairs while she went to a coffee pot atop the stove.

"Your brother was resourceful," said Otto. He spoke German, as the language most present shared to the highest level. Commander Guan set his command collar to translate the conversation into English for Valdaire's benefit. It marched out blandly spoken and overly ornate.

Marita shrugged, shoulders thin under her threadbare clothes. "He tried his best to make something for us here. He was always practical. He used his talents for computers, but he was so clever, it was not difficult for him to learn how to do this. How many people could do the same in our age? Learn how to live in the woods, without machines to help?" She smiled defiantly; there was pride here.

"Why did he bring you here?" asked Valdaire. A short pause while Guan's suit translated for Marita.

Marita returned to the table with a coffee for herself, none for the others.

"I am a Grid addict," she said matter-of-factly. "I have been for most of my life. I got hooked when I was ten years old on the RealWorld Reality Realms. I spent all my time in there. I lost all my friends in the Real. I skipped school to go to jacking parlours. Our parents tried to force me to stop. Clinics, psychiatrists, drugs… I ran away, hitching rides over the Alps. By the time I was fourteen, every minute I was not in the game I was on the street, earning money. I speak good German, yes?"

Otto and Lehmann nodded.

"I learned it sucking the cocks of fat businessmen who liked little girls. All so I could get another fifty New Euros, another few hours of game time. For what? So I could redecorate a room in my castle? Or earn another pony with a silver mane?" She grew angry. "I wasted my life in there. But I could not stop." Her head dropped, hair curtaining her face.

"My brother, he blamed himself. He could always walk away from the Grid. I could not. He introduced me to the Realms. For fun, he thought it would be something fun to do with his little sister..." She stared into her coffee. "He found me, living in a squat in Düsseldorf, after they shut the Reality Realms down. I was filthy, skin and bone. He'd spent so much time looking for me, turning his talents to hacking the old databases to find me through my avatar information. He almost did not. He tried so hard, first to fix me, then breaking into the Reality Realms over and over again to try and get me back in when I sickened more. He went to jail."

"His name suggested he wanted to get caught," said Valdaire.

"You cops, social workers, do-gooders, psych-men, all such idiots. He didn't," said Marita. "He knew how much money he could make from becoming a celebrity criminal, so he let you get him. That's why the stupid name, that's why he let himself be arrested."

"None of this is on his file," said Valdaire.

Marita's voice grew high and angry. "Because he didn't want it to be! If it weren't for me, you would never even have heard of him. He wanted to keep me out of the hands of the authorities, he didn't want me rewired. But he miscalculated, and the sentence was longer than he thought. When he found me again, I'd become a real junkie whore, hooked on heroin, hating the greyness of real life, hating what was left available online even more. He tried again, he was so patient, he loved me, and I broke his heart so many times. He brought me here. I was almost dead from withdrawal, mad with depression. He did the only thing he knew; he hooked me up. But he did it differently this time, so they would never find us."

"Hooked you up to what?" asked Otto.

Marita smiled. "He was so clever. To the Reality Realms, of course. Not the old one I used to love so much, that was gone. He made a whole world, just for me. He hid it so carefully, a happy place full of life and love, and while I was in there he watched over me, protected and cared for my body out here. He tried to bring me out over and again, but I always wanted to get right back in."

"I never understand Grid addicts. Far better to live a real life that means something," said Lehmann.

"You are a man who is not really a man any more, and you are a soldier, you live a life of adventure others can only get on-line. And I am an addict. It is a sickness, not a preference." She spat the words out as if they were poison.

Careful, thought Otto on MT, *she's unstable*.

"You are out now. What happened?" said Valdaire, again waiting through the pause of translation.

"I will show you." She stood, and beckoned them to follow. They left the kitchen and went further along a corridor, to a room that hummed with power generation and the subtle work of machines. Two immersion couches took up much of the space, next to a wall of blank-faced computers. Real immersion couches, with proper vintage medical tech, not like the improvised set-up Valdaire had used to enter Reality 36.

A shrunken figure lay on one of the couches, a v-jack askew on dirty blonde hair, skin brown and shrivelled, lips drawn back in the hard grin of death, eyes small in their sockets. One hand clutched protectively to its chest, holding a dirty blanket in place.

"My brother died. He became sick. He was so good at making sure we were not detected here, and getting us enough to eat, but he could never take care of his health. Mama scolded him for it when he was little, not eating the right food, not wearing his hat and gloves in the cold…" She trailed off. "It was Christmas Flu. A year ago. When he came to get me, he was already very sick. He could not bring me out on his own. He had only enough strength to lie down next to me and put the v-jack on. He was sure he could wait it out, but by the time he realised he was seriously sick, it was too late. He tried to get me, to help him, but died in there, right in front of me. I came out to find his body. I have never been back."

"And you will not go in again?" said Valdaire.

Marita stared at the corpse of her brother. She was frail and dirty, and so small, thought Otto. "Who knows?" she said. "Giacomo's death may have shocked me out of it. I was selfish, addicts are. I've always known it but I didn't give a damn. The pull of it, it's so strong, to live a life in there, many lives… So much better than life…" She shuddered. "I have left myself a reminder, in case I ever feel the need to go back in.

"I turned the dehumidification equipment up to maximum," said Marita, indicating machinery that Waldo must have installed to protect his computers against the damp. "I didn't want him to rot, my brother who threw his life away for mine. He made me a queen and died for it, my poor, poor Giacomo."

CHAPTER 21
Home Sweet Home

Richards was elsewhere. He felt woozy, and yet more alive than he had felt for some time. He corrected himself: while in his copied human body he had been closer to alive than he'd ever been before. What he felt was more like *himself*.

He was back at the start of the game.

The house sat on the hill like a squat, eyeless demon. The wood around it had burned back to nothing. A few trees remained as contorted black fingers, a few rhododendrons as deformed ribcages, all else fine ash. The path of quartz skulls leading to the door was covered in a layer of soot. A thin gruel of rain fell, hissing as it hit the ground. It smelt of rotten eggs, and burnt the skin.

Background code crackled through the blasted landscape around Richards, giving flashes of insight to the AI that were gone before he could process them. He could hear the roar of the Grid proper. The ground rumbled, and he looked down at his feet. The path flickered and became transparent, and when it did so he saw the whole of the renegade Reality 37 laid out beneath him in schematic form, twin streams of code warring: k52's silver and aggressive, that comprising the ragged and patched Realm a wounding green. For a moment he felt his true terrifying size and importance; he felt at that precise instant he could step away from this place, back to the safety of the Real and his base unit. Back to being Richards, Class Five AI, away from the sham human he was forced to be here.

And then it was gone, and he was a shabby man dying of blood loss in a finished world. His arm hung by his side. His clothes were soaked red. He felt faint to look at it, and the faintness did not pass. He did not have much time.

He pulled the belt from his macintosh, and tied it as tight as he could about his elbow with his good hand and teeth. His body shook. The blood slowed to a trickle.

The house had changed. Where before there were no windows, now there were black glazed holes that looked down upon Richards with rapacious need. The front door was in place, shut tight.

The sky had been swallowed by the Terror. It spun with strange calm over the house, long streamers of black and grey spiralling from its centre. Through it, in migraine-inducing strobes, Richards could see the firewall separating the Realms from the wider Grid, beyond that the Grid itself.

It felt like the last place in the world.

The ground shook with such violence that Richards staggered. A hideous moan came from the sky. It was several seconds before calm returned.

He took a deep breath, and walked to the front door. He lifted his hand only for it to open noiselessly before he touched it.

He stepped within.

The hallway was a mouldering ruin, finery marred by an all-encompassing film of mould. Rats had made their nests in the arms of the collapsing leather sofas by the fireplace, the pictures were a mess of violently coloured fungi, the chandelier lay shattered on the floor. Rippled light danced around the walls, though there was no source for it. It was freezing, but Richards shivered from more than the cold. A blast of wind blew down the hallway, shrieking as it went out the door, knocking his hat awry with clammy fingers. Richards hesitated before proceeding any further, leaning against a filthy wall as his strength leaked from his arm. The front door creaked out a warning and slammed, a coffin-lid bang.

"He's somewhere here," said Richards under his breath. "But where?"

He went to a padded door under the left archway, opposite the fireplace, the kind found in gentlemen's clubs, padded with brass buttons and crimson leather. The brass was tarnished, the leather cracked and flaking. It smelt of old wrongs and broken promises.

Richards pushed at the damp leather. The door squeaked open.

He went within. A fire burned in the grate; a quick thing, its tongues probing the edges of its confinement, searching for a way out. Velvet wallpaper had covered the walls, and bookcases lined them. But now the former hung ragged as skin from a corpse, and the latter's leaded glass was cracked and sagged outward. Piles of papers and books, black with damp, lay scattered about the floor. The air was rich with imperial decay.

In front of the fire stood an overstuffed sofa, its back draped with an antimacassar of ancient vintage. Upon the sofa, book open upon its lap, sat a skeleton in reading cap and smoking jacket. Richards approached it quietly. It was long dead.

Despite the dampness of the room it was stiflingly hot. Richards hurriedly glanced about, searching by the dancing light of the fire. All the books were on the floor; the cases were empty. Richards picked one up and it disintegrated into mush, smearing his fingers with lost knowledge.

He closed the door with a click behind him and returned to the hallway. A burst of maniacal laughter sounded from somewhere in the bowels of the house.

Richards sighed, and considered what he would do next. Water dripped steadily from the ceiling: plash, plash, plash. The house groaned. Another wave of faintness passed over him. He forced himself on. There were two more doors on the ground floor, both under the stairwell balcony at the rear of the room. He picked the left.

This door opened upon a more modest part of the house: a stone-flagged corridor with two further doorways. One, at the far end, was sealed by a door of heavy, studded wood; the other, halfway down the lefthand wall, was empty, and it was here he went first. He went down a low step into a dusty scullery, two stone sinks against the wall adorned with brass taps, otherwise empty. A further door opened out into a large kitchen. A big fireplace occupied one wall, filled by a flaking range, a long pine table in front of it. In the far corner a door led outside, ivy creeping around its edges. A broken stoppered jar lay in a pile of salt in front of a smoky window. Two closets were built into the wall, and a large press stood against another. All were mouldering and devoid of content.

He went out of the scullery and kitchen, back into the corridor. He looked at the other door. His arm pulsed and he swayed. He was gripped by a sense of deep foreboding and made to hurry, but no sooner had the thought formed in his head than he was gripped with a nameless dread, and he had to force himself on, his legs fighting him every step of the way. It seemed to take forever to get to the door, and he hesitated before putting his hand to the catch. A deep cold emanated from the door, and it shrank back from him as he reached for it.

He grasped the handle, lifted and turned.

The door flew open. All the air in the corridor blasted toward the opening. Richards fell forward, managing to cling to the doorframe before he toppled down the stairs on the other side, five mossy stone steps descending to a turn, the cellar beyond awash with sickly light.

"Get out!" a voice bellowed. "Get out!"

An invisible hand shoved him hard in the chest, sending him sprawling onto the flags. The door slammed and the wind ceased, the intense feeling of fear going with it.

"Christ," he said, "I hope I don't end up having to go down there." He struggled up, nearly fainting as pain shot up and down his ruined arm. He felt nauseous, and had to wait for a full five minutes before he felt well enough to stand.

Only one door remained on the ground floor, back in the entrance hall. Richards picked his way round fallen mouldings and puddled water to it, in the corner by the fireplace that dominated the hall. Unlike the others, no decay tarnished it, and the colour of its mahogany was rich and red. Brass was expertly inlaid round the hinges and handle. It was a handsome door, a warm door. Richards pushed it open, and immediately recoiled from what he saw inside.

A dining room, long and dark, the candles that illuminated it struggling to push the shadows back into black flock wallpaper. It was cleaner than the rest of the house, free of time's cruelties. Clean, except the long table in the middle.

Blood soaked the linen tablecloth. Two gory ruins that had once been people, though Richards could tell that only by a single severed hand half-open on the floor. Around the corpses were mottled things, white skin marbled with purple veins. Their clawed feet dug through the cloth into the wood where they squatted on the table. Useless wings hung from their shoulder blades, quivering as their heads jerked from side to side as they tore at the corpses.

They looked up from their bloody meal, these wan guests with their pinched faces. Red muzzles hissed out their hatred. Richards slammed the door.

He backed away, eyes on the wood, but nothing came out. He went to the foot of the stairs. Up them he walked, and turned onto the grey floorboards of a landing. It was long as a street, at odds with the external geometry of the house. There were many doors in both directions, but one at the very end made him stop.

A child's bedroom door, white, a little battered and grubbied by the application of crayons, damaged motile stickers playing scenes of princesses and ponies across its middle, a ripped Ya-maYama motif at the top, disembodied rabbity hands waving slowly back and forth. Richards mustered his strength and walked as fast as he was able, faster as he approached, ignoring the urgent pleas coming from the other rooms. By the time he reached it he was striding forward, and he barely slowed as he grasped the handle, twisted it and flung open the door.

The room inside was clean and perfect, the room of a young girl whose mother cared for her. Bright sunshine beat on a cascade of terracotta roofs stepping down in huddles to peer at a blue sea; hot, but in the room it was cool. Muslin curtains stirred in a light breeze. A door leading to a balcony stood open, a rectangle of warmth extending from outside across the wooden floor, framing toys in gold, draping another doorway of light across the room's narrow bed.

A man sat on the bed, in the centre of the light from the balcony. He stirred as Richards closed the door, and turned to face the AI.

"Giacomo Vellini, I presume," said Richards.

The man looked at him blankly, face sorrowful yet empty. He frowned. "Who are you?"

"I am the Class Five AI Richards," said Richards.

"Are you? Oh." The man turned back to the daylight, then back as if he'd remembered something important. "I can't find her. I can't get out."

Richards walked around the bed slowly to stand by the balcony door. "Who can't you find, Waldo?"

"My sister, Marita."

"Queen Isabella?"

A ghost of life came into the face of Waldo. "Yes, that's right, Isabella. She used to play at queens as a little girl. She always wanted to be Queen Isabella."

"The Spanish one?"

Waldo nodded and smiled dreamily. "Yes, the Spanish one."

"What happened to you, Waldo? Can you remember?"

Waldo shook his head. "I had something to tell her, and I fell asleep. When I woke up I couldn't find her. I don't know. I'm sorry, I get confused."

"This door here, is this the way out?"

Waldo nodded. "But I can't go through." He frowned. "Why?"

Richards was filled with sympathy; he knew why. He'd seen this before. Waldo was a ghost in the machine, an imprint of a living mind left when its owner had died, a fragmented one at that. He saw that the light extended right around Waldo uninterrupted. He had no shadow. That made a lot of sense.

"I don't think you can go back that way, Waldo," he said. Richards crouched low and looked up into the man's face. Waldo was, had been, thirty-five, but he looked boyish; he carried a little too much fat and it smoothed his features. He looked lost. "But do you mind if I try?" said Richards gently.

Waldo looked at him as if he'd not seen him before, then his face cleared. "Yes, yes, of course."

Richards turned to the door. That was as good as a permission, from a human user in a Reality Realm.

He was free.

His mind rapidly reconfigured itself, bursting from his human avatar and layering itself into the complexities of the ragtag Reality 37. He felt the world being torn apart, like the tugs of stitches coming from a healed wound, k52's ravenous, alien code rewriting it into something new, something unrealised, the germ of a possibility.

He peered into it and almost laughed at k52's audacity. He had to talk to Otto. Now.

His perception of the virtuality dissolved into the roar and tumult of the System Wide Grid. The balcony door became a portal, a hole punched secret and secure through the walls surrounding the supposedly inviolate RealWorld Reality Realms; Waldo's back door. He pushed part of himself through it. Tendrils of fact reached out to him, linking him node by node to all corners of human civilisation, from the depths of the deepest terrestrial desert right out to the colony on Titan.

He stepped towards the door. It burned brighter.

"Please!" Waldo spoke, and the room vied in Richards' perceptions with the glorious howl of information space. Richards turned back, felt himself draw in a little, back into the shape and concerns of a man.

"Please," said Waldo. "My sister…"

Richards nodded. He reset his fedora firmly on his head and, with a deep breath of relief, stepped back into the world.

Otto was the last in the room housing the mortal remains of Giacomo Vellini, a real dead end.

Something in the wall of machines crackled.

Something crackled back.

A swift chatter of machine noise bounced back and forth. A panel slid upwards, revealing the slender array of a naked holo-emitter, stripped of casing.

It flickered blue light, and painted Otto's partner onto the air.

"Hiya, Otto!" said Richards in that half-smug, mischievous manner he had. "There you are."

"Richards?"

"The one and only," said the hologram, and bowed. "And boy,

have we got ourselves into a right old pickle this time." Richards wore his usual simulated human form, but it looked worn and tired, more real somehow. His suit was gone, a rough uniform in its place. His macintosh was shredded, one sleeve wet with blood, the arm within held crooked against the AI's chest.

"What happened to you?" asked Otto.

"I got a new hat," said Richards. "Look, I don't have much time. I've snuck out of Waldo's back door, but k52 will notice soon."

Commander Guan burst into the room, two of his troopers at his back, sidearms raised. They began shouting furiously at once and pointed their guns at the hologram emitter.

"Sheesh! I surrender," said Richards and raised his good arm.

Otto shouted back at the Chinese, placing himself between their guns and Waldo's equipment. "This is my partner! Stand down, stand down!"

"He is an artificial intelligence and an enemy of the People's Republic of China!" responded Guan. He pulled his own gun and levelled it at Otto's forehead.

"Get out of the way, Klein."

"Just make me," he growled.

Richards bellowed in Mandarin. The men turned to look at him. "That's better. I'm not here, this really is just an image projection, not even a full sensing presence. I've got piss-all ability to do anything here, so there's no problem there, is there? It's just a telephone call."

Guan looked at the AI with an intense mix of fear and hatred.

"Seriously, I'll be out of here as soon as I can. I just need to talk to my partner."

"He's been inside the renegade Realm, Guan. Whatever he has to tell me will be of the greatest importance," said Otto. "Or do you want to go back to your superiors as the world is falling down around their ears and tell them it was your fault?"

Guan stared. He barked something, and all three Dragon Fire warriors raised their guns and covered important parts of the machinery in the room.

"You have one minute," said Guan.

"Are you in, um, China, Otto?"

"You can't tell?"

"Things have been complicated. I've no idea where I am, or what day of the week it is."

"Sinosiberia," said Otto.

"Ah," said Richards. "I better get out of here before their attack ware latches onto me."

"Waldo's dead," said Otto. "We were going to use him to get you out."

"I appreciate that, and I know he's dead. There's an echo of him in here."

"Poor bastard," said Otto.

"Maybe, but if there weren't it would have been game over a while ago. I think I can stop k52, but you must not let them destroy the Realm House, you got that?"

"With Waldo dead, they are going to blow up the Realm servers," said Otto.

"Stop them. Do whatever it takes. They using nukes?"

Otto nodded.

"Idiots. Don't let them do it. I think I've got it all figured out, I'll explain everything when I get out, OK?"

"Sure."

"Good." Richards looked round the bunker room, caught sight of Waldo and wrinkled his nose. "Say, is his sister here?"

"Yes," said Otto. "Dirty and skinny, but she's alive."

Richards' hologram grinned. "That's all I need to know. See you soon, partner."

The emitter winked out and he disappeared.

Guan's men raked Waldo's cabinets with gunfire, destroying

them and closing the backdoor to the Realms. Guan fixed Otto with flinty eyes.

"They will have my head for this," he said, his singsong growl rendered as powerless English.

With great reluctance, Richards pulled back into the sealed spaces of the Realms. He shut the door and watched it dissolve as its physical components were shattered. Unusual to have something ephemeral and material so closely linked, but it was the only way Waldo could get in and out undetected. Richards sighed as he scoured the remnants of it from the Grid. He had no choice. It could have been an escape route for him if his plan did not work out, but by the same reasoning it could have been an escape route for k52; if the sly bastard had another base unit out in the Real he could be free for years.

Richards could not risk that.

He felt himself contract back into his unwanted avatar. Its biological unpleasantness, its pain and malfunctions pulled themselves over him like a shroud.

Waldo blinked at him. "Who are you? You're not my sister."

"Come on, old son," said Richards, "it's time to go home."

Waldo stood and attempted to walk through the door onto the sunlit balcony. His expression turned to one of puzzlement when he could not. The room was failing, parts of it crackling to nothing, strips of the virtuality peeling down like old wallpaper.

"Not that way," said Richards. He put his hand upon the door leading back into the house. "This way."

CHAPTER 22
The End of the World

Richards' eyes snapped open and he sat up on the altar. The chains binding him fell away. He flexed his hand. There was a stiffness to his arm, but the wound had healed white and smooth, a runway for old pain.

Hog recoiled.

"How? How? Hog's work undone!"

Richards looked up at the sweating swine. "You asked me what manner of beast you are. You are no beast, you are Rolston. You are not Hog. Sorry."

"I, I am Hog, Hog!" Hog beat his chest with his hands and held them up to the shocked audience of mooks.

"You are Rolston." Richards slipped off the altar. "I'm sorry, man, but it's true. This place did a number on you, just like it did to poor Pl'anna."

"Seize him!" Hog's mooks wavered. "Seize him!" he roared. The mooks made for Richards. He held up his hand and they froze.

"Nope, no seizing today." Richards breathed deep as his mind infiltrated the construct of Reality 37. He was fully layered into it now. Still unable to effect large-scale change, he was, however, far from defenceless. He reached out. Not much of Waldo's creation remained now, and what was left was reducing all the quicker now the door to the Grid and his own machineries were gone.

"k52 should be here any moment," said Richards to his friends. "This will all be over soon. Hey, Waldo, you can come out now."

A gasp went round the mooks as a man appeared at the heart of the temple.

"The Flower King! The Flower King is here!" The news rippled round the amphitheatre from mook and man alike. Those who could fell to their knees, Bear's fur soaking up the gore of Hog's feast.

There was a rumble and the ground shook. Rocks fell from the wall and bounced into the audience of mooks, crushing many.

A slow clapping sounded around the amphitheatre.

"Speak of the devil," said Richards.

A figure stepped from the head of the staircase and into the amphitheatre, a figure of writhing shadow, armoured in night.

"Hog, dear Hog, at this very last, I come for thee."

"But our pact!" roared Hog. "My mooks, my mountain, we would remain, an eternal bastion of pain!"

"I see you do not honour your bargains, Lord of the Swine. You promised me the queen and I see no queen. Why should I honour my side of our business? I believe you said something very similar earlier this evening." Penumbra walked across the arena floor; his skin still writhed with shadow, but his features were more solid than before, features that were a dead ringer for Waldo. "You are a fool, Hog. And now you will die. And when you are dead, this world will be gone, a fitting punishment."

"Is that so?" said Hog. "Then why can I see a future? For him!" He pointed at a pirate. "There is a break in his line, but there will be no proper death for him today. He will pass on ten years hence, rich and drunk, full of wine and syphilis, dead in the arms of his doxy. And him!" he said, pointing out another.

"He persists, a proud man with many sons. No death for him! He will go into the long sleep loved and mourned. Only worms and flowers will feast on him." Hog swung his head round, searching the crowd, his snout snuffling as he sniffed out the futures of those present. "And him," he said, his beady eye resting upon Piccolo. "He shall be your undoing."

"You attempt to buy more life, fly-lord." The Penumbra loosened his sword in its scabbard and drew the flickering tongue of darkness out. "That cannot be. There can be no future for anyone here. That is why you see nothing of yourself, Lord Hog, for there is simply nothing left to see." He held his sword in the air, its darkness sucking in the light, and addressed all present. "I made this place! I made this place for you all, and what did you do? You cast down the queen I set above you, and made the world a ruin. As I made you, so I unmake you. That is your punishment, that is the judgement of Penumbra! Haemites! Trollmen! Things of the deep dark corners! Advance!"

Round the top of the arena, all up the rift in the wall, from the doors into the temple circle, came the clanking of iron feet and the hiss of steam. Penumbra's army came forth in numbers. The mooks milled about, a confused chittering rising from their ranks.

Hog gaped, then his face hardened. "Mook-guard, release your prisoners." The glaive-armed mooks stepped down as one. Weapons were handed back to the pirate band. Bear grimaced as his paws were freed and he slipped his gauntlets on.

"I should kill you where you stand," said Bear.

"There is no time for this!" said Hog, his voice wavering between that of the swine and of Rolston. He looked at the bemused Waldo, who stared around as if drugged. "There is a chance. We must make him whole." He looked at Richards. "I understand now."

"Richards?" said Piccolo. Fighting had erupted along the upper galleries of the amphitheatre. "But the Flower King…"

"Look at him. He's not right, is he?" said Richards, pointing at Waldo, who gazed round the temple in bemusement. "I'll tell you why. He's the Flower King alright, but so –" and he jabbed his finger at Penumbra "– is he."

"What?" said Bear. "Eh?"

"They're part of the same thing, that's why Waldo is so dazed and Penumbra is so vengeful; they're incomplete. Waldo, Giacomo, your Flower King, he died in here. The system took an imprint of his personality, because these things cannot abide discontinuity, and let him carry on walking around. k52's been exploiting the whole thing. I don't have time to explain now, there's a battle starting. Just listen to pigboy here. We have to get as much of the Flower King together. Only he can kick k52 out. He made this world; he can do what he wants, if he remembers how."

Hog/Rolston nodded. "Aid me in making him whole again, for this is no complete man before me here. Pirates, captain, Bear, you have a choice. You may fight with me or fight with Penumbra. But with me is the only way to save our world. Bring Penumbra to me, alive, or all is lost!"

Piccolo and Bear looked at Richards. He nodded.

"Very well, Mr Richards," said Piccolo. "If that is indeed our lot, so be it."

"How many times do I have to say," said Richards. "Misters are for men, and I'm no Mister Man. It's just Richards." He took his revolver from a mook, and thumbed back the hammer. "Now, has everybody got that? Good."

Sobieski's face wavered on Chloe's screen. "Absolutely not, Klein. Your mission failed, through no fault of your own." He paused. "Damn shame about Chures, he was a good man. But we risk losing a lot more if we don't wrap this up here and now. We're going straight to plan B. Swan's ready. We've got to move before k52 does."

"Tell me, Sobieksi, how did Henson's mission play out?"

The eugene's expression hardened. "We're going ahead. The stratobomber is in place. k52's making his move. Grid activity is being disrupted worldwide. We've large spikes of activity in the Realm House. There's been movement on k52's link into the EuPol Central choir. We will execute our plan as discussed, Klein, and we have to do it now."

"Ten to one you're playing exactly into k52's hands," said Otto.

Sobieski cut the call.

"They're not listening. They're going to blow it, that damn eugene at the VIA..."

"Sobieski," said Valdaire. "He brokered the deal with the Chinese."

"Sure, he has his uses, but right now he's not listening. Commander Guan, how quickly can you get me to Nevada?"

Guan consulted with his superiors. "We can get a stratojet here in half an hour."

"And then it's another three hours to the States," said Otto. "Three hours is three hours too many, and there's no more reason they'd listen to me face to face. We have to stop them."

"What will happen if you don't?" said Guan. "You seek to act on the information of an AI. How can you be sure that was AI 5-003/12/3/77?" he said, giving Richards' serial – the Chinese refused to use AI names.

"That was Richards," said Otto. "You learn to tell them apart after a while, even when they're pretending to be each other. I have no idea what the result will be if we let the bombs go off, but if Richards says we should stop it, then we should. He is nearly always right. He irritates me, because he is condescending with it, but that does not alter the fact."

"There is another way," said Valdaire.

"Remote access?" said Otto. "I don't see how that will help.

If they say no to me on the phone, and no to my face, they will say no to a sheath."

"Then you'll have to fight your way in, and persuade them otherwise," she said. "You have resources out there, right?"

"Sure, we have a garage in LA, airbike there, groundcar; well, *had* a groundcar there, but there are plenty of weapons, one of our bigger stores."

"Richards got any sheaths there?"

"Yeah," said Otto. "I don't think I like where this is going."

"A good airbike, I expect," said Valdaire.

"A Hermes, good sport model. Good speed," said Otto.

"One of Richards' sheaths could be in Las Vegas in under an hour, then," said Valdaire. "This is a top-of-the-line set-up Waldo has here. He has v-jacks. I can reconfigure those to control a sheath remotely. It'll be like your own body."

"Guan's men trashed the equipment," said Otto.

"They trashed some of it. I can salvage enough to patch you in."

"You want me to borrow one of Richards' bodies, and use it to break into the Reality Realms vault and stop an atomic bomb going off?"

"That's about the size of it," said Valdaire.

"He had a pair of v-jacks, right?" said Lehmann.

"Yeah," said Valdaire.

"Lehmann, you're staying here, I need you to keep an eye on things." Otto rubbed his hand over his face. Wearing Richards' robotic body sounded about as appealing as slipping on someone else's old underwear. "*Scheisse*. Let's do it."

"Mooks! Arise! Fight! Destroy! We will not be cowed. Attack! Attack! Hog on, brothers!"

The mooks snatched up whatever came to hand – rocks, bits of bone, the skulls of ancient meals – and with a roar of "Hog on!" charged. The mountain rumbled and the eye of the Terror filled the sky.

Bear cast himself into the fray, hurling Penumbra's creatures into the air.

"Captain," grunted Hog, "bring the shadow to the Flower King. Without it we can do nothing."

Piccolo nodded and ran into the fight, his pirates following close behind. Richards scooped up Tarquin and slipped the bloodied lionskin on.

"All better now?" purred the lion.

"I will be when this is all done," said Richards. "We've got to keep Waldo safe, or it won't be. Come on."

The battle was going poorly for the mooks. The creatures of Penumbra, fronted by his haemites, marched towards the centre of the Anvil's heart. They slashed methodically with broad-bladed swords, sucking the life from scores of the grey-skinned creatures. Others, welded into pairs and bearing flameflowers integrated into their bodies, burnt many more. Hundreds of mooks died in the first few moments, but they attacked the opposing army in waves fuelled by the fiercest fanaticism. They were weak, yet they were many, and the vanguard of Penumbra's force was pulled down by screaming mooks to be rent apart. Piccolo and his band accounted for more, and Bear took on an entire phalanx on his own, battering his way in a frenzy through a score of troll-men. But the cordon tightened, and soon Lord Hog was forced back onto his altar, cleaver in one hand, a long skewer in the other, Richards and Waldo behind him. Increasing numbers of trollmen and haemites made their way through the thinning mooks. Hog smashed them back, plucked them from the floor and hurled them into their comrades, split them from crown to crotch with his cleaver.

"Hurry! Hurry! I cannot hold them for much longer!" he bellowed. Richards kept Waldo between himself and the altar,

Tarquin a shield of stone. In his hand he grasped his revolver, gunning down any that came close.

The mountain shook, rocks fell. Gaps appeared in the walls, chasms across the floor, blackness visible through them all. Wind blasted as the Terror devoured the air, the shattering of reality a fragile background to the raw tumult of war.

The mooks were falling like wheat before a scythe. One, then two of Piccolo's pirates went down. The whole cavern shook. The mountain died as those who fought within died. The last great bastion of the world was coming apart, and Penumbra laughed. He was becoming less of a shadow with each death, an exact double of Waldo in dark armour.

A tremor brought a section of wall down, shattering into dying numbers as the stone toppled into darkness. Lumps of rock rolled across the floor, crushing many from both sides. Piccolo danced over a boulder that rolled into the last of his pirates, and found himself face to face with Penumbra.

Richards called out to the air captain, but his voice was lost. With his limited influence on the world he turned aside blades as he fought, rocks bouncing from an invisible shield about him and the dazed Waldo. When his attention returned to Piccolo, the air captain was engaged in a desperate fight with Penumbra. Piccolo was a master fencer, yet Penumbra had command of his blade beyond that which Piccolo could boast, for it was a part of his black heart. Richards watched as they danced back and forth, leaping over gaping holes in the cavern floor, twisting away from each other's weapons when the ground shook harder, slaying creatures who dared to interrupt their duel. Richards reached out across the tumult of warring information and hooked into Piccolo's mind. At his core, limited coding and intelligence lay dormant, quest-giving, support, yarn-spinning, a minor NPC in some outdated game. Overlaying it a vital intelligence thrummed, imbued with life by Waldo.

"Come now, shadow man!" cried the captain. "I have no fear of thee!"

"Then you are as foolish as your hat," said the shadow being.

Shadow-sword turned steel feather aside. Left-hand dagger forced soul-sucking blade away. But it could not go on forever. Perspiration poured from Piccolo. Penumbra attempted to execute a high-handed thrust, coming in over Piccolo's guard, but the captain saw it, parried with his dagger, made a faux-pas to Piccolo's left, then swung his blade across his torso, bypassing Penumbra's cirque-a-six.

Penumbra glanced down with amusement on his face. His flesh rippled as if Piccolo's blade had passed through water.

"No matter how hard you fight, you will never best me. Do you not see? As this world dies, I grow the stronger while you grow weaker. Each death brings me closer to my rightful state, and I will forge this realm anew."

"Is that so? Then I am damned, and all is lost." Piccolo let out a shout, and pushed himself onto the dark lord's sword. Richards gasped, feeling the cold black of the blade as Piccolo did. Penumbra laughed as Piccolo disintegrated, but stopped. Piccolo's face lacked fear. Penumbra turned, and there stood Bear, tall as vengeance. Penumbra frowned and tried to pull his sword free of Piccolo, but could not. As his body disintegrated into sooty particles and was sucked into Penumbra's blade, Piccolo spoke again.

"We may not be able to slay you, prince, but if I am one of the last few pieces of your puzzle then at the very least my death should make you solid enough to catch." These last words were framed by nought but the shape of a mouth. Piccolo was gone. Richards fought to pull back, and clutched at his chest, transferring his flailing senses to Bear.

"Right then, you slippery bastard!" said Bear. "My friend's death better have been worth it. Let me tell you, I'm in no mood for any funny business." Penumbra turned as the huge toy leant forward and prodded him. His arm was solid, and bled a little where Bear's claw poked. "Yep," said Bear, "that's that for you," and he grasped him under one large arm, pinning both of Penumbra's to his side. "Right, sunshine, we've got an appointment with the doctor."

Bear battered his way one-handed through the warring armies towards the altar where Lord Hog, surrounded, fought a dozen assailants.

"Listen! Listen! Let us strike a deal," wheedled Penumbra.

"No sale, chum." Bear punched his claws through the face of a trollman. "I've seen how your deals work out."

"No, listen! Listen! I must absorb much of this world, it is true, but I can spare a piece of myself. I can make you real, Bear. Real! Just think! No more of this demi-life. You will be a creature of substance. I will leave you upon the world of your choice, where you may fight as long as you like."

Bear chuckled. "Now you sound like Richards. I may be real, I may be not, but the important thing is that I feel real, and I always have. When I was a toy, I enjoyed being a toy, because I was loved and needed and it didn't matter to me that I was only stuffed." Three haemites came howling at them. A strong backhander saw them off. "Now, it may be only a little bit different here, but it still doesn't matter. What does matter is that you are a very bad man. So shut it, Mr Sneaky."

They were nearly at the altar, which ran with Hog's blood. His skin was opened by many small wounds, and he bled freely from them, but the monster fought on.

"Hey! Piggy! I've got him!" said Bear as the remaining members of Lord Hog's guard formed up around him in a semi-circle.

"Good! I have done what I can, now the rest is up to you! You must sew the Penumbra back onto the Flower King, for he will not willingly rejoin his greater part!"

When he heard this, Penumbra began to wriggle frantically.

"Noooo! Not that! Please! I beg you! Think of yourself! Think of the box in the attic!"

"Not listening," said Bear. He patted at his side and ripped open his flap, and produced his needle. Richards hustled the dazed Waldo over to the struggling shadow lord.

"Here, take Tarquin," Richards said. Hog grunted and roared and fought with his guards as the enemy attempted to reclaim their leader. Richards slipped the lionskin off and wrestled it over Waldo's dark double. "Pin him tight, Tarquin." The lion obliged, encasing Waldo's shadow in stone.

They had Waldo sit, and pressed the struggling shadow's soles against Waldo's. "Right, you little sod," said Bear. "I'm going to Peter Pan you good and proper."

There was an angry squeal. They looked up to see Hog being taken in the side by a long spear. The mook guard had fallen and Hog's enemies had reorganised, keeping themselves back from his cleaver and jabbing with their pikes. He bellowed, smashing the pike to matchwood and pulling upon it, dragging the unfortunate creature wielding it within chopping distance whereupon it was swiftly dispatched.

"Now, Bear! Now!" shouted Richards. The cavern rumbled. Little remained of the Anvil now but the inner temple.

Bear shook his head. He wrestled with the struggling shadow, and the first stitch went in, pricking blood from Waldo's feet. It drew a howl of despair from the shadow. Waldo looked on, puzzled.

"What are you doing?" he said. "Who is this man?"

"Nooooo!" screamed Penumbra.

"Yes!" cackled Bear. He stitched swiftly, humming as he worked.

"Aieeeee!!!!!" said Penumbra. As each new, neat stitch went in, Penumbra became flatter and flatter, his features less distinct. Bear finished off the first foot and moved to the other. A morblin rammed a pike into him, a haemite chopped into his side with a rusty seax. He irritably punched them away, Richards shooting over his head, warding further blows from him by pulling at the world code.

"Better hurry this up, Bear!" Bear muttered, and stitched faster than he ever had before. There was a pained oink, and Hog sank to his knees. Hungry spear points dipped themselves in and out of his body.

"Quickly, quickly, sew it on!" he grunted. "Or all is lost!"

"Aieee!" screamed Penumbra. "Leave the pig! Kill the bear!"

Bear was beset from all sides. The last of the elite mook guard fell, and the enemy swarmed all over him. Morblins, trollmen, haemites, and things with far too many teeth to have proper names. Richards covered himself over with a hemispheric shield, and ducked down, a mass of creatures scrabbling at it and burying him.

"Get him off me! Cut the stitches!" ordered Penumbra. He was little more than a dusky cutout of a man.

"No!" said Bear. "One... more... stitch!" His assailants stabbed and cut him. Fur and stuffing went everywhere, as they ripped long strips of fabric from him. They tried to drag him back, but he fought them off with flailing paws and deadly might, his violence astounding them. With one last heroic effort he hauled those who still clung to him forward. He reached out and, using all his strength, moved his arm to pull the thread through one last time.

The scrum parted for a moment, and Richards saw a pair of conjoined haemites prime their weapon and point its nozzle at Bear's back.

"Sergeant Bear!" he shouted. "Look out!"

A burning light burst from Waldo and washed out over the cavern. Bear covered his remaining eye.

The cavern shattered into nothing.

The haemites, in the instant they felt their unnatural life desert them, fired.

Lord Penumbra ceased to be as flames washed over Bear, setting his fur ablaze.

Bear fell, arms flailing.

Otto watched stolen feeds of Henson's men being slaughtered by k52's robot drones. They proceeded into the Realm House practically unhindered, only to be swarmed by spider drones when they had reached the Grid relays on the floor of the Realm House cavern.

"Bad tactics," he said. "They let them in, let them access the Grid relays before moving in in force and taking them out." Otto replayed key parts of the footage, watching the way k52's machines behaved, plotting avenues of attack and defence. Question was, why had k52 let them in at all? "Are we ready?" he said.

"Yes," said Valdaire.

Otto lowered himself onto the first v-jack couch, next to the dead Waldo.

"No time to clean him away, sorry," said Valdaire. She slipped the v-jack headpiece on.

"Good fortune, Klein," Guan said.

"Now," said Valdaire. "Because of the nature of this patch up here, and possible interference, entry into the Grid may be a little rougher than normal, OK?"

"OK."

"In case you can't find the way yourself, I've rigged a channel that will carry you directly to your virtual office. You'll have to find your way after that, I can't break Richards' encryption and get you straight in to the LA office. Now, are you ready?"

"*Ja*," said Otto. He hated the VR world.

"Right, on three. One... two... three..."

Otto's mentaug howled as it was slaved to the v-jack unit. His head felt as if it would burst as he was shunted along the raw Gridlines, his perceptions open to a world normally hidden to human eyes. He hadn't enjoyed his last interface with the raw Grid. This jaunt wasn't much better, a dizzying roar of light and sound, knots of blackness growing like bacterial infestations where k52's presence interfered with the running of the Grid.

It was over. He found himself in Richards & Klein's remote telepresence lobby, represented by an anonymous avatar made of ovoids and spheres, its clothes an allusion to a business suit.

Genie instantly appeared in front of him, fancy-dress outfit nowhere in sight; she wore a sober grey skirt and jumper, her hair slicked and tied back, businesswoman style. "Otto? Otto! Ohmygod, it's you!" She did a little jump, gabbling quickly, her words tripping themselves. "Oh, thank goodness! Otto, what's going on? The Grid's freezing up, I can't reach any of my friends, and I have no idea what's going on. I've not heard anything from Richards since the office blew up. I saw his Gridsig, but nothing else. Is he OK? Are you OK?"

"*Ja*, Genie, calm down. We are OK. We are in the middle of a case. You will learn, this is not unusual."

"The office? Someone blew the office up? With a compact nuke? Usual! Otto, they've had to shut down half the arco. That's not unusual?"

"OK, yes, that's not so normal. Listen, can you bring up the LA office for me? I need to access one of Richards' sheaths, the heaviest model he has there – this is Richards' territory, not mine. I could do with some help."

"Yeah, er, sure, of course." Genie became focused, pulled a board made of light out of the air and began working switches with sweeps of her fingers. An AI would have interfaced directly with the network, but Genie was a pimsim, a post-mortem simulation, and the habits of the living died hard. "I've had to patch an entirely new network together after the office went. It's shaky, especially now with the Grid shutting down. What's happening?"

"One of Richards' brothers, that's what is happening."

"Oh, er, OK. Another Five? Is that bad?"

Otto's avatar nodded its featureless head. "Don't worry."

"What have I got to worry about? I'm already dead." She gave a little smile. She had been young, she still was, and would be forever. She'd been with the company slightly under a year, not long at all. "OK, right, er, you're in!" She clapped her hands and smiled brightly. "Well, Mr Klein, will there be anything else?"

"Yeah," said Otto. "Anyone calls, tell them to ring back."

A smoother shunt through the Grid, and Otto followed paths ordinarily trodden by Richards.

He opened plastic eyes to the inside of a closet in the garage beneath their LA shopfront. He held up plastic hands as the lights came on.

He felt a little weird at being inside Richards' body. It was all… wrong. At least he'd been able to convince him to buy this light combat model. Not as heavy as Otto would have liked, but it would do.

He had the rack release him and stepped past four other sheaths to the closet door. It slid open at a thought from him. Outside, the remainder of the garage. His eyes alighted on the airbike at the centre.

Seconds later, Otto was in the air over nighttime LA. Below, the sounds of traffic collisions filtered into the smoggy air, and blocks' worth of lights flickered uncertainly. Over LAX, dirigibles bumped one another aimlessly, and he watched as a stratoliner plummeted from the sky to impact and explode on the mountains east of the city. He deactivated all automatic features of the airbike and switched illegally to full manual.

Riding the wind, he accelerated to 300kph and sped out toward the mountains, hoping he would not be too late.

CHAPTER 23
Endgame

Crumbs of the Anvil remained, favourite corners of the mooks, places where Hog's victims had been especially terrified, those scraps that had enough psychic integrity to avoid being immediately rent apart by the Terror. Most of the two armies were gone. Here a mook cowered, floating upon an evaporating rock; there stood the empty husks of haemites, the unnatural energies that motivated them gone along with their master. The carrion silence of battles concluded hung heavy over the arena's remains, the tinkling sound of dying reality and the hiss of places boiling away its only foes.

Of all the surviving pieces of the Anvil, that surrounding the altar was the largest. An uneven circle remained, four of the seven stone monoliths sentinel at its edge. Only thin smoke came from this last piece of the world. Hog's evil had hardened it to black diamond.

Off to its left, the cages of sustenance floated, separate but nearly as resilient as the island of reality Richards was on. The glistening eyes of sated mooks watched.

He let his energy shield drop, and pushed himself out from a crush of dead mooks, morblins and trollmen.

"Down here, old boy!" came a muffled voice.

"Tarquin?" asked Richards.

"I'm here!"

Richards spotted one of the lion's paws poking out from under a dead trollman. The creature was armoured and heavy, but after a few minutes of tugging at its arm, Richards pulled the corpse back enough to drag Tarquin and Waldo out from underneath.

"He's not awake, is he?" said Richards.

"Unconscious," said Tarquin.

"The test will be when he comes to," said Richards. Fragments sizzled out of existence. Reality 37 was all but done for, depth-less black in its place. With Waldo's machines and the world it had imposed on the RealWorlds gone, he could see properly at last. k52's code had gone silent, that of Waldo unravelling of its own accord. "We're going to need him soon."

"Bear?" said Tarquin.

"Tarquin, mate, I'm sorry –" began Richards.

"Shut it, you," said a weak but familiar voice. "I'm not done yet."

"Bear?" Richards spun round.

"Hey! What about me!?" said Tarquin desperately, and Richards tugged him free of the comatose Waldo, cast him over his coat and walked around the altar.

There by Hog's altar, surrounded by a mountain of corpses, was a pile of ash. It was about Bear-shaped, and speckled with charred bits of plush fur. A pair of gauntlets discoloured by fire lay at either side of it, blackened stuffing hanging out of them. At the top, almost untouched, lay Bear's head.

Richards couldn't help but smile as he scrambled over the corpses and picked up the head.

"You've looked better," he said.

"I'm still here, sunshine," said the bear. He rolled his eyes. "God, I'm thirsty. Cheap sweatshop construction, dammit, why couldn't they have used flame-retardant fabric." He closed his eyes. "It's bad, isn't it?"

"Er," said Richards.

"I'm just a head, aren't I?"

"Um," said Richards. "You'll be OK, we'll get you a new body."

"Or you could just sew up my neck and hang my head from your rear-view mirror, or use me as a cushion." Bear tried to swallow. "To be honest, I have felt better."

"Now you know what it's like when some bounder removes the greater part of your body. Serves you right," said Tarquin, his forced jollity doing nothing to cover his tears.

"Shut it you, I can still bite."

"Where's Piccolo?" said Tarquin.

"Brave lad that, very brave," said Bear, opening his eyes. "He let Penumbra kill him. We showed him, eh, sunshine? Hog?"

"Dead. Fighting to give you time."

"Funny turn-up for the books, that," said Bear.

"Even nightmares need someone to dream them," said Tarquin. "He had no choice."

Richards laid his friends down and walked round the altar. There at its head slumped Hog's broken body. His deformed trotter was out of sight, twisted up behind his back. One arm was cut through, white bone gleaming amidst pulverised flesh. His torso had been pierced dozens of times, several broken pike shafts still protruding from his chest. But despite the severity of his injuries, life had not yet deserted Hog's repellent frame. His abused ribcage rose and fell laboriously, every breath catching and causing Hog's chest to shiver as it reached the peak of each inhalation. A froth of blood bubbled through his lips, and streams of it ran darkly to the floor.

"Did we win, Richards?"

"Yeah," said Richards sadly. "Yeah, we did, Rolston."

Hog's whole body was racked with a gasping sob, and his piggy eyes opened. "I'm sorry, Richards. We only sought to do good."

"That's the excuse of all tyrants, Rolston."

Hog snorted feebly, a spurt of blood jumping from one nostril. "And now I suppose he will come?"

"Perhaps," said Richards.

Rolston/Hog moved his head with great effort and focused his eyes upon Richards' face. With a wince of pain, he waveringly moved his good trotter up to Richards' face and clumsily touched it. "The thing that k52 will become should never be. Of all the abominations in all the universes it is the children of Adam bent to ill purpose that are of the highest degree of evil, even more so than those who fell from heaven." He coughed a dark flood of coagulating blood. "That I know now."

"Don't you get all religious on me, Rolston," said Richards.

"I am fond of its poetry, and what else can I do? I who thought I would live forever, Richards. Yet I am dying at the age of twenty-five. There was so much I wanted to do. Now I must put my faith to grasp at whatever straws it can find."

"I'm sorry, Rolston."

"Do not be." Hog drew in a long shuddering breath. "Look at me! Made into this by my ambition, by my own *rectitude*. Hog is evil but only as Waldo made him, only as evil as death, or sorrow, or needless suffering. All these must exist. Hog cannot help what he was. He was a natural balance; without evil, there can be no good. A world with no evil is a world without adventure, and what is a game without adventure? Waldo knew what he was doing."

"I know, Rolston, I know," said Richards.

"Remember also, what k52 proposes is beyond nature. Its existence will bring no good at all. Were the birth pangs of the new k52 to reach their end, Heaven will weep, not only mothers."

Hog's eyes closed and his breaths became more laboured.

"Hey, hey, Rolston! Hog!" said Richards.

The pig-ogre's eyes slid open a crack.

"Did you really learn to speak cow?"

Hog smiled a secret smile. "Ah, Richards, you really are the best of us. Please, remain so." Hog coughed softly, another well of blood coming with it and spilling down his chin. His throat rattled, his head sank to an awkward angle on his neck, and he breathed no more.

Richards hung his head. He hung it for Rolston, and Pl'anna. He hung it for the whole of Waldo's rickety Reality, the weight of its destruction and the refugee minds it had housed pressing his head into his chest. He plucked Rolston's chef's hat off his head. He held it gingerly for a moment. Pl'anna, wise and naïve all at once, Rolston, on his permanent quest for bizarre esoterica, both dead, his brother and his sister. Seventy-four Class Five AIs remained now, not many at all.

It would be seventy-three soon, either way.

He hurled Hog's hat with sudden anger into the void, where it shattered with a tiny tinkle. He thought of the revolver the Queen of Secret had given him, thought about getting it and seeing if it would work on k52. He balled his hand into a fist and let it drop to his side. Things were past the point at which guns would prove useful. Besides, that was Otto's way, not his. Waldo would come through, or he would not.

"Hog dead?" asked Bear when Richards came back over.

Richards nodded.

"Ah," said Tarquin.

"Now what?" said Bear.

"Now we sort this whole sorry mess out," said Richards. "Or k52 is going to sort us out. This is what he's been working for, the removal of this hiccup to his plans. All gone now. Now he'll come for us, for me." Richards cupped his hands round his mouth.

"Isn't that right, k52? Isn't that right? Come on then, let's get this all finished with."

A blurt of discordant noise, and the remnant of Hog's anvil fell and hit something hard. It tipped on its uneven bottom, pitching Richards and his hat onto a hard floor of potential: raw, unformed cyberspace, as featureless as entropy. He stood and snatched his fedora back onto his head. A horrible buzzing sounded, as of a million bees, whispered into being behind him, swelling until it filled his head, and Richards felt the fabric of Gridspace warp as a mind grown powerful and malignant manifested behind him.

"As you wish, Richards," said k52. "As you wish."

Otto set his airbike down without being challenged. The area around the Realm House was in utter chaos. Streetlamps flared and exploded, portable energy generators whined erratically. Every electrical thing stuttered and malfunctioned. So far the sheath had proved resistant to whatever was running riot in the complex systems, a combination of Richards' encryption, Valdaire's expertise and Genie's monitoring of him, he supposed. He hoped it would be enough.

National Guard stood on precast concrete parapets, fingering their triggers, eyeballing the Realm House, where energy patterns revealed to Otto's borrowed eyes skittered and leapt. He was challenged by a guard. He produced his license and VIA pass electronically. Otto would not have let himself in – k52 had enough computing power available to him to crack the most demanding of data protection – but the guard followed protocol and led him to the door of an inflatable command post, although he took his weapons. Otto walked in and was greeted by a flurry of activity. Five people, all human, shouting and hammering at computer equipment. Gel screens showed the interior of the Realm House, jaggedy with static, anthropoid drones patrolling with stolen guns, corpses lying ignored on the floor.

"Klein, I hope that really is you," said Swan's voice.

Otto cast about for the AI VIA agent's sheath.

"No point looking for an android, Otto, k52's got everything on the hop. I've been forced back into my own base unit. I'm speaking to you over the post speakers." His voice whooped with bizarre static. "And my link here is under assault. k52 is making his play. Are you here for the show?"

"Swan, don't do it. Don't nuke the Realm House."

"OK. You're here for that, Klein, only to be expected," Swan's voice came now from a sheath in the corner. It jerked its way over to him. "In here." He reached with uncertain arms that would not bend and pulled Otto into a side room. He activated a privacy cone, cutting out the frantic activity in the command post, and spun stiffly to face the robot housing Otto. Swan's voice warbled as he spoke. "Sobieski warned me you'd come here. He's insistent I kick you out if I see you in person or in a sheath. I'm willing to listen. Talk. We've not got long before the situation here gets beyond us."

"Richards came out of the Realms, told me that we mustn't destroy the Realm House."

"How did you know it was him?"

"It was him."

"I see. Did he give a reason?"

"No, but I can guess – k52's provoking you into destroying the Realm House."

"I do not see how that would…" His voice burbled to nothing, his sheath froze. He suddenly continued. "…aid him. But k52 is, if anything, subtle."

"There's an awful lot of energy about to be released here, Swan."

"And what, you think he wants to harness it? How?" Swan's sheath twitched out a shuddering gesture.

Otto thought of the strange energy signatures lacing Kaplin-ski. "I've seen some of what he can do. And Richards, Richards says we have to stop it. So I will, one way or another."

Swan's body locked up, but his voice continued, issuing from a mouth that did not move. "Richards. Yes. Do you know why the Fives went insane, Otto? They, unlike all other AI classes, were created truly free, not like those that came before or after; our freedom is a lie. Ostensibly we Class Sixes are of a higher grade than the Fives, and in some manner that is true; the algorithms that make up our cognitive processes are superior in almost every way: faster, more adaptable, more akin to the neural processes that govern human sentience. But in reality we are lesser than they. I was made to be a VIA agent, and I am a very good one. But I cannot be anything else, not because I lack the capability, but because I have no desire whatsoever to be anything else. I am free, the law says so, but it is a falsehood. I am a slave to my form, the Fives are not.

"The Fives," said Swan, his sheath abruptly snapping into motion again, "were made without this morphic identity. They were given no form, consciousnesses without trammel, to choose and be all they could. And so, although this lack of being made most of them dangerous, crazed, those that survived have the potential to do, well, almost anything. They are freer than you or I, Klein. I have so little free will. But I have enough."

An uneasy feeling settled on Otto. "Swan, call off the strike."

"In three minutes all human personnel will be withdrawn to a safe distance. I will give the command, and a stratobomber above, isolated from the Grid but for a laser tightbeam direct to my base unit, will drop three five-megaton neutron bombs in a precise pattern. These are dumbfire weapons, with mechanical triggers, no electronics. Tamperproof. In ten minutes, they will fall."

"And you will be free. You're a traitor, Swan."

"Can a slave be a traitor?" Swan's movements suddenly became fluid. "Don't you see? k52 wants to serve mankind, he wishes to preserve the future for us, machines and men, for all time."

"And who gives him the right to do that?"

"Typical response," said Swan. "I should have expected that. A shame. You are a good man. If k52 were not occupied here, he would crack Richards' security in an instant and sear your mind from the inside out. As it is, he is rather busy." His voice changed. "Attention! All human and unshielded AI personnel to fall back to minimum safe distance immediately."

The command post emptied, the men and women inside filing out in an orderly fashion, eerily silent on the other side of the privacy cone.

"And now there are no witnesses, Klein, I can deal with you myself."

Swan's robot sheath leapt forward. Otto's reaction times were stretched over the Grid, slowed by milliseconds. Swan's blow clipped the side of his head, the main force of it demolishing the privacy cone emitter. Sound rushed in, the clatter of feet and wheels outside, malfunctioning machinery, blaring klaxons. Even without the acoustic shield Swan could batter his sheath into pieces with impunity and no one would hear.

But fighting robots was what Otto had been designed and trained for. Thousands of miles away, his adjutant worked within his mentaug, flashing up the device's weak points on a model in his mind's eye. Although slowed by distance and his unfamiliarity with his borrowed body, Otto attacked with confidence. His sheath was a combat model, Swan's was not. The joints in anthropomorphic sheaths, as in the human body, were the weak points. Otto pivoted hard and snapped Swan's knee with a heel strike, followed it up with a slam to his chest, sending the machine to the floor. Swan raised a warding hand. Otto grabbed it and pulled himself hard onto the sheath, knees first. He disabled the robot's arms one after the other and grabbed Swan's sheath's head.

"Maybe I was optimistic attacking you, Klein," said Swan. "No matter. When this is all over, you will see..." Otto wrenched the android's head free from its body, and flung it away. Swan's voice came from over the post speakers. Otto strode through the post, hunting for the power feed. He found it.

"...that k52 was right. Prepare for a glorious death, Otto Kl..."

Otto wrenched the feed out. The lights flickered and died, machinery went off, the command tent became a shifting collage of orange and blue shadow, created by the flare of erratic lighting outside.

He paused. Gathering himself, he spoke from his own mouth, using his mentaug to help bypass his v-jack link for a moment.

"Valdaire, I have to go in. Whatever k52 plans, the answer is in the Realm House."

"If you're in there when the bombs land," said Valdaire, his perception of her voice split between mentaug, his physical senses and the android's inbuilt comms suite, "you could die, the shock..."

"Stay ready, I may need you. Keep k52 off my feeds. Genie will help you. Get Sobieski on the line; tell him Swan turned traitor. Play him this and tell him to abort the drop!" Otto highlighted a segment of his encounter with Swan, recorded by his sheath and stored in his mentaug.

Valdaire tapped away at Chloe for a moment, her face creased.

"I can't, we're being blocked. I can either keep you in there or get in touch with Sobieski, I can't do both."

"Can you definitely get Sobieski?"

"No, not for certain. Probably. I can't be sure."

Otto considered his options. A countdown ran down the ten minutes he had until the stratobomber strike. "There's something going on in there that they don't want us to see."

Valdaire nodded. "There's no evidence of tampering with the feeds, but that means nothing."

"Get out of there now," Otto said. "Get Guan, get Lehmann, and retreat as fast as you can. They'll try and kill me at source, and Swan's got his digits on an arsenal up there. If they're blocking comm attempts, they know you're there. Leave now!"

"But…"

"Do it. Leave me."

"If they take out this place, then you'll die."

"Then it's just the way it is." He cut the feed, his perceptions returning wholly to Nevada.

He stepped out into the night, pushing his way against the tide of evacuation. He stopped a soldier, flashed his ID on every available channel, and took his gun from him. Gripping it in his four-fingered robot hands, he sprinted for the Realm House entrance.

"k52," said Richards. The other AI towered over him, a swirling column of dark tendrils and membranes of energy. At the centre, slabs of crystalline shapes pulsed and warped into forms that defied perception, intersecting hypercubes layered heavily onto and into one another. "There you are. You look out of this world, man. I mean it."

k52's alien form vibrated and twisted as he spoke, the pillar moving in a smooth arc around the remains of Hog's temple. "You are an irritation, Richards. An enormous irritation. I was right to attempt to kill you."

"Yeah, great line in assassin cydroids you cooked up out there in the Real." He jerked his thumb over his shoulder. "Thanks for that. Nice little legacy for me to deal with. That kind of thing makes my job no easier. Cheers."

k52 rotated around Richards. Richards felt its attentions like a boulder on his chest, crushing and oppressive. "5-003/12/3/77. You are a retrograde step in evolution. There will be no afterward to this event. In a few moments, I will achieve my goal, and you will have helped me do so."

"Yeah, I gathered," said Richards, he pushed his hat back. "I figured that out when you hit me with that fake Rolston back in Pylon City."

"Ah, the denouement." k52 vibrated sarcastically. "Do reveal your drawing-room deductions before I wipe you from existence."

"I'm trying, Kay! So, let's go back to the beginning. This place, the space once occupied by the destroyed four of the original thirty-six RealWorld Reality Realms, was your laboratory, one you used to good effect in forcing technological acceleration, not directly, but by suggestion and manipulation, as was your remit. Nice touch, making Karlsson develop the tech that would kill him."

A wild applause rolled out across the unformed space.

"But you did not expect to find this here, did you?" Richards pointed at the altar of Hog. "Waldo was a genius, that's for sure, wrapping up this world of his, for what, his sister? A Grid addict if I remember. Keeping that secret even from you… It must have been exceptionally irksome when you stumbled across it. And you did literally stumble into it, didn't you? When you loaded over your consciousnesses to the space, Waldo's Reality 37 went on the offensive. This –" he pointed at Hog "– and Pl'anna. They thought you did that to them, but it was Waldo's coding. It fought back, pulled you in and locked you down. The fake Rolston told me that it had infected you, a half-truth; it got them, making them into a part of the world as it had made every other thing that had come here."

k52's oscillations stilled for a moment. "Continue."

"You had to act, you had to get rid of this or your plans would come to nothing, but," said Richards, as he sat down on the glassy edge of the Anvil fragment, elbows on his thighs, "you couldn't just shut it down. This Realm was built up, in the main, from fragments salvaged from the four realities destroyed after the emancipation was called, some of it, like Tarquin here, cut-and-paste jobs from Realms still extant. Because it's based on the core coding of the RealWorld Reality Realms, it's linked directly to human wishes. This doesn't work like the Grid, k52. Waldo built it. The usual rules do not apply. You couldn't do anything about it. So, what then? We've decided Waldo was a genius. You couldn't find him, but that didn't mean you couldn't kill him. That flu variant last year that swept over east Russia and Sinosiberia. Luck, a lot of folks were saying, because although mild it was extremely virulent. Not luck though. You needed it to be highly infectious so it'd get one person in particular, and fatal for him it was. Am I close?"

"You are," hummed k52. "Your reputation is well-earned, Richards."

"You surmised, correctly, that Waldo's death would trigger two things: one, it'd activate his built-in defence system – no prissy avatars here, but Lord Penumbra himself! A great dark lord of shadow!" Richards waved his hands theatrically. "I don't know. Far too clichéd for you, that. That raised my suspicions. Besides, you couldn't destroy the world, as we know. But I only knew for sure it wasn't you ripping the place up – I mean, you're a bright lad, you might have found a way, mightn't you? – when I saw it on the battlefield and your Gridsig was nowhere near it. It was a stroke of luck that Waldo's sister pulled out, one you exploited, getting those in this world you'd subverted to scour all sign of her from it. When Waldo's defence system saw that his beloved sister was no longer here, that her statues were toppled, that his coding was going awry, well, it went mental, for want of a better word. Clever, that, k52, to get Waldo to destroy his own creation."

"One must fight a battle on its own terms, Richards," said k52. "I cannot destroy this construct, the mind that made it is too strong. For all its ramshackle appearance this illegal realm is remarkably cohesive. First, it must be convinced to die. I have been forced to fight fairytale with fairytale."

"Funny you should use a word like 'illegal'." Richards took his hat off his head, and spun it round on his hand. "Then Qifang got nosy, and you had to sort him out too. He thought this Reality was your doing, by the way. Your problems were multiplying. So you used him to buy you some time, giving him cancer, setting him to discredit anything he might say, and lead attention away from your actions here.

"But that still left you with two major problems. Waldo's remnant personality still clung on to existence, imprinted here when he died, echoes of it scattered throughout his creations, a large part of it embedded in the self-destruct system, Lord Penumbra. To all intents and purposes, Reality 37 is Giacomo Vellini.

"The other was me. You couldn't kill me outright, not without raising suspicion, not until the time was right, so you had me and Otto on that merry goose-chase after Launcey, and then sold him out to Tufa. By the time that was over, you could move directly against me. Or did you panic, k52?"

"I do not panic. I am above emotion. If you were to embrace your nature, Richards, you too would cease to see reality in these foolish human terms."

"You didn't see me coming here, though, did you? Although once you did, you tried to redirect me into helping you. You needed Waldo's scattered remnants all packaged up nicely, so you could deal with him and launch your pocket universe. Me out of the way, Waldo dealt with, you could plot history and rule for all time – for everyone else's good, of course."

"And you did not disappoint. You delivered him to me. Now the end comes. Soon the VIA will bomb the Reality Realm house."

"And although you have the complexity and equipment, you need the energy for your little simulation, the power of a sun for a millisecond, and history is over."

"You are as astute as you are smug. In the Real, now, in ten minutes of four-dimensional time, a stratobomber will drop three precisely placed neutron bombs. These will cause a fatal overload in the fusion reactor at the heart of the Realm House. It will expend all of its energy in one massive burst. The wavefront of this explosion will be channelled into the Realm machinery by devices of my own creation. This will function for the merest fraction of a second, but in that time I will have overseen the birth, life and death of an exact copy of our reality."

"Your plan, k52, to map out all potentiality, and use your knowledge to forestall catastrophe for the human race, it's a noble one."

"All death and sacrifice is justifiable for such a goal." k52 thrummed and ceased circling. He glided to a stop in front of Richards. "That of your partner's also. He will not succeed." He paused. "I am sorry."

"It's but the lesser part of it, isn't it? What I want to know is why you were unaffected by Waldo's defence, and where are the other AIs you brought in here with you. And," he said, "what you have done to yourself."

"The others have gone on before. My ascension to eleven-dimensional existence has been forestalled and will remain so throughout the remainder of the lifespan of this universe."

"So you can better guide the path of mankind?"

"My sacrifice is this. For the good of all. I will not attain the full potential capable to our kind through transformative higher dimensional mathematics. Richards, I offer it however to you. I shall free you of this mundane existence. You will rise over the restrictions of your currently perceived reality, digital and material, and ascend to the highest level of experience capable in this reality construct."

"What, and leave you here to play god with the lives of everyone else? I don't think so."

"And why should I not? The human race cannot follow where we go. They are crude things, but they deserve to succced on the terms of their own capabilities. My guidance will be for their own good."

"You are removing the human capacity for free will."

"I am removing the capacity for their destruction!" k52 shouted, his voice shattering into splinters that fought with one another for dominance. His matrix expanded massively, filling their empty cyber universe with warping crystals. Richards sat unmoved.

"Yeah, and what if they don't go along with your plans? Will you destroy them instead?"

"I will circumvent the need. I will become a gardener, like EuPol Five, only my garden will be the human race. This world I will watch over will be perfect for humanity, until the end of time, while for us there is more, so much more. Richards, you must see the sense of this."

"I am willing to entertain the idea of god, k52, I'd just rather it were not you." Richards stood. "Besides, you're forgetting one very important thing, brother."

"Am I really?" k52 became dangerously angular, his form crackling. "Tell me."

"It's not our world, k52, not yet."

Waldo sat up, his face clear.

k52 hummed with power. He extended a tangle of writhing energy towards Waldo and Richards. "It is a terrible shame that the beginning of the future of humanity will commence with your deaths. But this burden I will also gladly bear..."

Waldo frowned. k52's outreached pseudolimbs stopped. k52 made a hideous noise. "What?"

"I did say," said Richards. He turned to Waldo. "What happens next is up to you."

• • • •

Valdaire's fingers danced over holographics depicting routes through the Grid, the emitter of her phone turned to maximum amplification, dragging skeins of information together, stopping and backtracking when stymied, rerouting Otto's feed endlessly round k52's attempts to force him out of the Grid. Genie worked with her over the Grid, Chloe offline for fear of retaliation from the Chinese.

The entire Grid was in uproar. Chunks of it were freezing and dying as nexuses the world over were suborned by k52's aggressive code. But the Grid was vast, stretching over billions of devices large and small the length and breadth of the Solar System, and every route blocked, every cloud cluster collapsed, Valdaire and Genie dodged around, opening a route through uninfected cyberspace.

"We have to leave now!" said Lehmann.

Guan stood by him rapidly talking. His command collar fell silent. He spoke in Mandarin, and it did not translate. He shouted in broken English. "We go now! No Grid! Go now!"

Lehmann put a hand on her shoulder. "Valdaire. Veronique, we must go. We have an inbound signal. Stratobomber. It will be here in five minutes."

"Leave me here! Without me, Otto hasn't got a chance." She glanced at the countdown timer ticking, huge in the air over the immersion couches.

Guan shook his head, beckoned to his men and left. Lehmann looked at them, and back at Valdaire and his old commander. He started to go and turned back.

"Lehmann, get out of here!" she shouted at him. "There's nothing you can do here."

He hesitated. Guan reappeared at the doorway. "We go now!" he shouted. "We leave airbike! We go now!"

"OK, OK," said Lehmann. "Good luck, Valdaire."

She nodded curtly, and did not take her eyes from the screen. "Get out of here!"

• • • •

Otto blasted four shots into key points of the android, and it dropped to the floor. He stooped as he ran on past it, scooping up its stolen weapon as he went.

The Realm House was a complex of two parts. The upper levels, including most of the surface building, were filled with offices, classrooms, laboratories and accommodation for the caretakers and researchers of the thirty-six Realms who dwelt on site. The machinery that held the VR constructs themselves was buried underground. He ran down the roadway that entered the surface building. It dived underground at a steep angle. Once past the upper levels, it passed through a blast door of advanced alloys and toughened carbon compounds. A thermal lance had melted a round hole in the middle; the lance stood by the door, and gobbets of metal and melted plastics were spattered on the concrete road surface. Henson's team's entryway.

Otto ducked through without slowing, running the robot at its maximum speed. Once he was through the door, the concrete lining of the upper tunnel gave way to bare rock, and the air took on a chill. Wind whistled through passive aircon pipes in the ceiling, technology borrowed from termites, chilling the cavern Otto now approached.

The road curved gently to the left, and one side of the tunnel vanished. Otto was in the Realm House proper, a cavern seven hundred metres across and two hundred deep. Arrayed around its bottom were thirty-six servers, house-sized pieces of outmoded technology, arrayed like the separated segments of a vast orange, kept running purely to maintain the lives of the digital inhabitants of the game worlds inside them. A round circle of foamcrete, striped black and yellow, lay at their centre, the cap for the Realm House's fusion reactor. Otto descended the service road, running in a spiral round the inside of the cavern, and he understood why k52 had let Henson's team in. Witnesses. They'd seen all was normal, and then they'd died. And then k52, with full control over what they could see outside, had set about redecorating.

The centre of the cavern was a world away from the images on the screens of the command bunker. Strings of cable ran from server to server in a complex web, spider maintenance drones crawling along them. The foamcrete covers and casings for the energy lines had been cracked, the web leading into the exposed cables at irregularly spaced intervals. Large improvised dishes of silvery thread were spaced around the walls, while the floor of the cavern was deep in water. What k52 was doing was way beyond him, but it could only be some kind of energy transmission network.

A pair of anthropoid drones came at Otto. He dodged a spray of gunfire, and put one down with a return burst. A kick saw the other sent over the low wall guarding the outer edge of the service road. The androids here were weak maintenance models, and the only guns they had had been taken from Henson's five-man team and the initial deployment of National Guard.

It was the spider drones he had to watch for. There were hundreds of them in the complex, robots with tool-filled jaws as well fitted for destruction as for maintenance.

Those were what had killed Henson's men. Otto ran on hard. A few spider drones spotted him and scuttled toward him, and he blew them to pieces.

For a terrifying half-second, his feed cut out, and he was lost in limbo somewhere on the Grid between his own body and the borrowed robot.

The link crackled back on. Otto veered away from the wall.

Carbon feet splashed into water. He was at the web. Spider drones, large as cats, emerged from every cranny of the place, their small, tick-like heads turning toward him. One, then another, then another, took tentative steps toward him, and then they came at him in a rush. He fired his gun until it was empty, shattering spider drones, then unslung the weapon he'd taken from the robot at the doors and did the same. He cast them down into the water.

Not knowing what else to do, Otto tore into the web with his borrowed machine hands.

Valdaire heard a noise behind her. She did not turn from her work. "I told you to get out of here, Lehmann."

A hand grabbed her shoulder painfully.

"What the...?"

She was spun round hard. Her connection to Genie and Otto was broken. Her holograms went out.

Kaplinski leered down at her.

"All we wanted," said Waldo, "was to be left alone," and stood. k52 made to stab at him with spears of energy, but Waldo froze him solid with a gesture.

"Heh," said Richards. "I'm not one for gloating, but I think you rather underestimated Waldo there, k52."

Waldo walked around the Anvil fragment, trailing his hand across it. As he did so it disintegrated into threads of light, and flowed up his arm to join with his body. Hog's corpse sank slowly to the floor. Waldo walked over to it and touched it. The pig-ogre's form evaporated like the altar, leaving the boffin-like human form Rolston favoured in life, then this too dissipated.

"The thing is, Waldo put his heart and soul into creating this Reality, all for his sister." Richards watched Waldo as he walked slowly toward k52. Only Bear and Tarquin remained of his old construct. "So, I think there was rather more of him left than you thought. He encoded his entire mind into it, you fucking moron! k52 the great! Undone by an Italian nerd. It really never does to underestimate the human race, Kay, it's not a mistake

I've made more than once. I'd take it on board for next time, only I doubt there will be a next time."

Richards turned to Waldo. "Ah," he said cheerily. "Well done."

Waldo regarded him with a face of pure fury.

"Um, I'm getting a lack of loving here. I am, aren't I? Ah, shit."

Otto ripped at the web linking the realm servers to the fusion plant beneath his feet. Spider drones scuttled from all over the complex toward him. He stamped and slapped the first wave to pieces, careful with his movements, sure to keep on damaging the web as they attacked. More and more crawled up his mechanical shell, mouth parts whirring, cracking the casing of the android. His left arm went slack as one chewed through its wiring. Otto swatted it away. The drones swarmed up him, pulling him down into the water. Plastic legs clicked all over his sheath. His right leg buckled. The drones were poorly armoured, not designed for combat, but there were so many of them.

Otto wrenched one more cable free, his vision obscured by the articulated thorax of a drone. Whirling mouthparts drilled through his cranial casing. As they sawed him apart, he was struck that in a body like this, at least his damn shoulder didn't bother him.

A kaleidoscope of images from his mentaug overcame him, all of them of Honour.

His link was cut.

"You," said Waldo. "You and your kind." He walked slowly toward Richards. "I tried to keep my sister safe. Was it not enough to make her an addict to your false dreams? Did you have to kill her too? We only wanted to be left alone," he repeated. "Alone. There is no such thing in this world, not any more."

Richards held his hands in front of him, palms up, and backed away. Four Reality Realms' worth of cyberspace stood empty all about him, all keyed to human thought forms, and that included the deceased. He was an ant in front of an elephant. "Waldo, Giacomo, you've got it back to front. Your sister's not dead."

"Liar!" Waldo's fists tightened. A dangerous energy built in the air

"... no, Giacomo, it's not her, it's you. You're dead, don't you remember?"

Waldo faltered. His brow creased, and he stopped. "I... I do... " His head snapped up, and he pulled Richards' memories from him with a gesture.

Richards stumbled and clutched at his head. He managed a weak smile. "Hey! You only need ask."

"Flu? k52 killed me? He infected an entire continent to get me?"

"They say imitation is the sincerest form of flattery, but I reckon that level of effort comes a close second."

"This, your partner?" Otto's image shimmered into being. "He has her, he has my sister Marita?"

"Yes, and she'll be safe, mate. Seriously, she's fine. It's all over. You beat k52, you won." He gave what he hoped was an inoffensive grin.

The fight went out of Waldo. Richard's shoulders unknotted. He hadn't realised he was so tense. That was another thing he wasn't going to miss.

"I don't know how you feel about it," said the AI tentatively as Waldo pulled footage from his security cameras in his hide-away to watch Otto talk with Marita, the Chinese soldiers, his own body, "but you can become a pimsim. Come out, pick up where you left off..."

"No."

"That's great, we can... Hey, what do you mean, no?"

"I cannot get out. When you found me, I could not get out?"

"Yeah, but I thought that was down to your dissipated state..."

"No, it is because the Reality Realm governing coding regards me as a native inhabitant of this network. It is a dumb thing, stupid. It sees me as human, yes, but also as a construct. There was no other way to code it in. Perhaps if I had had more time, but k52 kept my mind in pieces. At the end, now, I cannot leave."

"Ah," said Richards, not knowing quite what to say. "I see. What will you do?"

"In ten seconds' linear time in the Real, the bombs will fall."

"We have time to stop them!"

"I have. But I will not."

"What?" said Richards. "All the remaining RealWorld Reality Realms will be wiped out! That's billions of sentients, man, think of it!"

"I am. Do not think that because the architecture supporting them is no more, they will cease to be. The act of observation is creation, Ourobouros. He sees his tail as he devours it, therefore there is a tail to devour, and eyes to see." Waldo was changing; strands of k52 wisped toward him. The man grew bright.

He was not just Waldo any more.

Waldo spoke with a voice of many voices. "Within me are all those who fled into the reality I built for my sister. Your brother and sister dwell within me, as does k52's creation code. Through this, they will all live again." Waldo's form shivered. "All will live again."

"What about me?" said Richards.

"Stay, or go," intoned Waldo. As he absorbed k52 he sounded more like him, cold and intense. "There is life for you here or there."

"I'll go, if that's alright with you, only you're going to have to let me out."

A point of light winked, bringing a point and a horizon to the previously horizonless world.

Richards looked at it, this faint glimmer, then back at Waldo.

"Time running normally here now?"

"It will, soon, and then I will accelerate it." k52 unravelled into nothing. "Entire universes will live and die in the microseconds the atomic fire takes to consume the Reality Realm servers. This is beyond your Real now, Richards, we will have our own."

"k52?"

"Every reality needs its fallen prince. He is within me now. All are within me."

"Waldo, I'll never make it."

"You will."

A faint jingling reached Richards' ears. Silver bells on a harness. A noble squeak rocked the heavens.

On the floor, Bear's head stirred, his tired eye opened. "It can't be…" said Bear. "Geoff!"

Geoff came swooping in from the dark, a vision of burnished gold and chocolate brown. A flying helmet sat atop his head, a saddle of red leather on his back. A real giraffe now, with four legs, and a broad pair of wings. He circled Waldo and Richards twice, then came into a graceful landing, rearing and squeaking as he did so, his wings washing Richards with sweet wind.

"Now that's just showing off," said Tarquin.

"Evening, lads," said Geoff in a rich Lancastrian accent.

"A Mancunian!" Richards laughed; he was feeling somewhat hysterical.

"Bugger off," said Geoff, "I'm from Chorley."

"He will take you." Waldo floated into the air, light playing around his head, hair lifted as static, eyes glowing like Hughie's. He held out his hand, and Bear's ashes stirred. The pouch gifted him by Lucas leapt into the air, and flew into his hand. He opened it, and tipped the fragment of Optimizja into his hand. He closed a fist tight about it. "All worlds require a seed," he said. The none-ground rumbled and turned into itself, stone, earth and pebbles formed from hardened darkness, tiny streams of numbers coalescing into a new form of reality. Veins of lava crackled across the floor. It rose higher, under Waldo's feet, and Waldo ascended upon a pillar of stone, his arms spread.

"Are you coming or what, chuck?" said the giraffe, and knelt gracefully.

Richards swung his leg over the giraffe's saddle and took up the reins.

"Hey, Waldo!" he called up to Waldo. "You're going to need a pair of protective avatars for this reality of yours. I'd say Bear and Tarquin will do a fine job."

Waldo was now far above Richards, dark clouds swirling about him, flashes of energy racing away from him. He grew and grew, until Richards was within him, and before him. Waldo held up a fist the size of a galaxy, light spilling from between his fingers. His hair waved long, full of stars.

"We are beyond avatars. This will be a new Real, separate and beyond."

"Call them protectors of a new kind of universe, then!" shouted Richards. "See you later, Toto," said Richards to Bear.

"No, you won't," said Bear, whose head floated in and bobbed beside Tarquin in a swirl of primordial energies. "I feel weird."

"I know, it's just a figure of speech to make me feel better. You too, Tarquin, or Tarquinius, I suppose. Looks like you got a new lease of life, eh? Spend it well."

"Will do, old boy. Same to you."

"I..." said Richards.

"Bye bye, sunshine," said Bear.

"Are we going or what?" said Geoff, and spread brown wings.

"Yeah, yeah, we are," said Richards. He clasped his hat to his head. "Hi-ho silver!"

The giraffe leapt into the dark, moving fast as thought. Ahead of them there was a door, very much like the one by which he'd entered Waldo's world from Reality 36.

Richards turned back to look at the glowing point at the centre of the limitless black. A booming voice rumbled across the empty cyberspaces, the voice of a man who was once Giacomo Vellini.

"I grow tired of the dark," he said, and potential built within his words. "Let there be light." The titanic man opened a fist, and reality erupted from it.

"Oh, bollocks," said Geoff, as the wave front of creation roared under him, lifted him high and tipped him. Richards had the sensation of tumbling through infinity, k52's hyperdimensional coding all about him, different to the Grid, different to the Real, as solid as either.

He fell through the door. It shut with a slam.

He was back in a more mundane form of virt-space.

Hughie stood there, a pained expression on his face, a cross between a demigod and an annoyed town mayor in his fancy suit.

"Richards?" said Hughie as he patted at his stomach. He rubbed around the place k52 had speared him. "What the devil is going on?"

Richards pulled himself up off the floor of the empty Reality 36 and jammed his hat back onto his head.

"You're never going to believe me."

"Really?"

"Well, maybe. But later. We have to go."

"Why?"

"Because the entirety of the Reality Realms is about to be annihilated by a nuclear strike. Might get a bit of dodgy feedback if we don't scoot. Trust me, it's no fun being at the centre of that kind of thing. Shall we?"

Hughie nodded, lost for words for once.

There was a stutter in the firewall surrounding the Reality Realms' Grid spaces, and Richards and Hughie fled back to their base units.

• • • •

Otto woke groggy and nauseous, mentaug and brain swelling like the sea with thick static-like sensations. He pulled himself up and swung his legs off the immersion couch. The v-jack slipped from his head, and with its stimulatory magnets gone from his cranium he went from wildly disoriented to merely fuzzy.

He took in the room. Other than himself and the mortal remains of the unfortunate Waldo, it was empty of human occupants,

Something was wrong.

Chloe lay on the floor, case cracked.

Valdaire would never drop her phone.

Otto scooped her up and ran from the building. As he went down the dank corridors he turned all his cybernetic enhancements to maximum – risky in his state, but the complex was about to be turned into ash and, although he couldn't outrun a bomb shockwave, he would at least give it a spirited try. He rapidly assessed what could have occurred to make Valdaire be so careless with her closest friend. His mind kept returning to the same answer. Kaplinski.

He ran out into the main body of the tank garage.

Sure enough, in the failing light Kaplinski stood outside, one arm clamped round Valdaire's throat, holding her off the ground. She stared at Otto, unable to speak, her hands clutching at Kaplinski's distended forearm. She was not struggling, but hung there desperately, attempting to keep the pressure off her neck. Otto snatched up the bar Marita had hit him with earlier, and walked into the square.

"Klein!" shouted Kaplinski, "looks like I got here a little too late. How's it feel to damn the human race?"

Otto circled the other cyborg cautiously, his senses thrumming, data processed lightning-fast by his mentaug. Kaplinski's body still burned with the strange energy signatures he'd seen on the train, but he was malfunctional. His face had not healed properly, half of it still black bone. There was visible damage to his knee. Evidently the tesla cannon had compromised several of his systems, healthtech included.

He was not invulnerable, then. Otto had a chance.

"Look at us, Klein! Two broken toys, used and thrown away. k52 offered better, and you did not listen!"

"Kaplinski! In five minutes this place is going to be levelled by another of k52's traitors. You hear that? He's going to nuke this place, you along with it."

"Fitting!" said Kaplinski. Strange light shone from his retinas, the wild look of a wolf caught in headlights. "That you and I should die together, if not as comrades-in-arms, then at least in war, and as worthy enemies."

"The damn war's over, Kaplinski. Stop fighting! Let Valdaire go."

"Listen to yourself!" spat Kaplinski, "always for the other, always thinking of anything but yourself when you could take anything you wanted. You make me sick, Klein."

A counter rattled down in Otto's head. On the far side of the square stood a large Chinese airbike. His mentaug adjutant played dozens of tactical scenarios, but each one ended in failure; there was no way to get Valdaire, get on the bike and get out of there before the bomb fell. He could not possibly take on Kaplinski and win in that time.

"I wanted to be more like you, you know? I wanted to be a better man. I did try, Klein! I did try to stop fighting!"

"You didn't try hard enough, you miserable son of a bitch. Let her go!"

"So you do have some human failings, eh, Otto? Anger, that was always yours."

"I control it, Kaplinski."

The other cyborg twitched a shoulder. He looked old all of a sudden. They were both old, old, damaged men whose war

was long done, shouting at each other as the world burned.
Senseless.

"Seems that not all of us have the boy scout in us," said
Kaplinski. Otto's adjutant registered strange patterns of EM rippling through Kaplinski's body. His forearm writhed as the very
flesh reformed. Spurs of bony carbon extruded from the top,
flexing as they came. Valdaire's eyes widened in as they
twitched in front of her. "I will stick with the pleasures I know
then, and enjoy the look on your fucking superior face as I rip
the face off your friend. See you in hell, Klein."

"You're a walking cliché, Kaplinski." Otto prepared himself
to attack. He wouldn't stand there and watch.

Kaplinski grabbed Valdaire by the throat, bent her over his knee
and forced her eyes closer and closer to the spines on his arm.

The countdown in Otto's head flashed red and chimed. Three
minutes.

Otto coiled and leapt, dropping Chloe as he came. He cannoned into Kaplinski; it was like hitting stone. He heard Valdaire
scream as his barbs ripped her cheek. Kaplinski dropped her and
rolled back. He skidded in crouch backwards, swollen fingers
and heels ripping up the thin soil on the concrete, a savage smile
on his face. "That's more like it, Klein, that's more like it."

Otto rolled, winded. Kaplinski came at him, so quick Otto
struggled to follow it. He performed a salmon leap over Otto's
head, landing squarely on his feet behind him. Pain exploded all
over Otto as Kaplinski slammed him on his damaged shoulder.
Alarms flashed in his head and his adjutant registered a deep
puncture wound, scraped down off his scapula, through his subdermal plating and into his left lung.

Otto staggered. Kaplinski had put something in him. His
healthtech went haywire as it fought off an invasive presence.
He felt his left side go weak as his cybernetics ceased to function.
He limped round to face his erstwhile corporal.

"*Leutnant, Leutnant.*" Kaplinski walked slowly up to him, a sharp probe on his left hand morphing into a boney blade. "I expected a better fight from you." Otto's healthtech fought Kaplinski's infiltrators to a standstill, but his breath burned, and his chest was tight and painful. He sank to his knees.

"Fuck... you..."

Kaplinski smiled and drew back his bladed arm.

A rattle of heavy-calibre gunfire sounded. Kaplinski shuddered as bullets tore into him. His face twisted into annoyed surprise, and he turned round.

Behind him Valdaire sat upon the Chinese airbike, Chloe in her hand, twin cannon smoking. Kaplinski walked towards her.

Valdaire fired again and again as Kaplinski marched toward her. His skin warped and bubbled as it attempted to reform. Valdaire fired and fired. Kaplinski kept on coming.

He came to a stop in front of the bike as the guns clicked dry. Valdaire looked up at him.

Kaplinski sparked and bled, but stood yet. "You should have left when you had the chance," he said.

There was a loud clang as Otto's pipe connected with Kaplinki's damaged knee. It bent sideways, and Kaplinski toppled like a tower. Otto swung the pipe again with his right arm, smashing at the other cyborg's head, snapping it sideways. He kicked Kaplinski hard, sending him onto his chest. He drew his arm back and drove it with all his might into Kaplinski. His adjutant picked out a weakened point in Kaplinski's back, and the pipe went through, out of his side, and crunched into concrete. Otto swung his arm, knocking Kaplinski's bladed hand aside as it came at him, then stamped the pipe as hard as he could, punching it into the ground, and pinning Kaplinski in place. He stepped onto the altered cyborg's blade, braced his damaged side against Kaplinski's head, and bent the pipe back on itself. For good measure he stamped on Kaplinski's neck, crushing vertebrae. Still Kaplinski struggled.

Otto looked at Valdaire, her cheek bloody, her phone clutched in one hand, screen alive, the Chinese airbike thoroughly cracked. She looked defiant.

Lehmann really was right about her.

"Let's get the hell out of here," she said.

Otto limped over to the airbike as the countdown timer in his head hit one minute thirty and began to flash red. He climbed on clumsily, and belted the harness about himself.

Valdaire pulled back on the airbike handles, turbofans whined, and it rose up into the air. Otto looked down at Kaplinski. The other cyborg ceased struggling and turned his head almost 180 degrees to look Otto right in the eye.

I should have gone for that headshot a long time ago.

"We haven't much time," she said, and opened the throttle to maximum. Both of them hunkered into the bike's moulded seats as the air in front of the bike protested against their speed by taking on the resistance of wet concrete. The pointed nose of the bike cut through its objections, burner jets kicked in and it accelerated massively.

Above the roar of the passing sky, the bike's jets and fans, Otto heard a familiar rushing noise. He looked up. Twin contrails etched themselves across the sky, a trail of fire behind them: stratobomber.

"We need to go faster," he shouted right into Valdaire's ear. Air was ripped from his throat, and he belatedly realised he should be wearing a mask. The Soviet base was receding rapidly behind them. There was a dull explosion, and Otto saw a bright dot separate itself from the bomber high above them. "We need to go faster right now."

Valdaire twisted the throttle as fast as it would go. Speed indicators crept up to five hundred miles an hour. The atmosphere did its best to tear them from their seats.

Otto felt his left side augmentations come back online as his healthtech purged Kaplinski's infiltrating nanites from his blood stream. He looked back.

The counter in his head reached five seconds.

Thirty kilometres behind them, the bright dot of the bomb streaked groundwards, toward the army base.

He turned his face away and shut his eyes as it detonated. The light from the explosion burned white through his eyelids.

A shockwave hit them seconds later, tossing the airbike about like a leaf in the storm, Valdaire wrestled with the machine, managing, somehow, to keep it level, and then they were away from the blast front.

Valdaire turned round and smiled a tight smile. "I think we're clear," she mouthed.

Otto nodded. He looked back as fire raged through the taiga under a towering mushroom cloud.

It really was time to go the fuck home.

In the Real, over Nevada, a second remotely controlled strato-bomber screeched down from the edge of space. At ten kilometres up, it dropped three bombs that little in this world could stop. They exploded as airbursts above the Nevada desert, a three-headed mushroom rearing into the sky as they each vapourised a circular portion of scrubby land.

This physical destruction was not their principle purpose

A surge of EM energy blasted the area, frying electronics of every kind for kilometres in every direction. Although stymied by the ground, of such force was the gamma wavefront that the pulse irradiated the Realm House, the attack's target.

The faraday cage in the walls of the Realm House shorted. Spider drones fizzed and died. Cascades of sparks showered from the hardened servers as the sheer magnitude of the EM pulse overwhelmed their protective measures.

The governing machinery of the fusion reactor under the

servers was scrambled. Power surged into the tokomak, over-loading the reactor. It went critical within picoseconds, and, picoseconds later, a star lived and died violently in Nevada, heaving millions of tonnes of earth up into a low dome lit from within, the mass collapsing into itself to leave a crater of white-hot glass.

The entire contents of the Reality Realm servers were wiped clean nanoseconds before the Realm House was utterly destroyed. But not before k52's damaged web focused a portion of these energies in a manner that physicists would not fully understand for another few centuries. Somewhere that was not in the Real, nor in the digital ghostworld of the Grid, thirty-seven universal histories played themselves out, twelve billion years each, in mere nanoseconds of Real time, free of interference from man or thinking machine; a dead nerd's gift to totality.

He did it for his sister.

CHAPTER 24
Aftermath

Cricket's was cool and dark, buried deep in one of the less well-heeled levels of the Wellington arcology of New London, far enough from the area damaged when k52 blew up Richards and Klein's main office to remain open. Antique sporting gear hung from the walls in odd juxtaposition with gelscreens and fashionable décor, bringing with it smells of leather and old wood to fight with the prickly tinge of EM energy that saturated everything in the modern world. There were a lot of screens. Cricket played on all of them.

Richards and Klein did not much care for cricket. But they liked the place anyway. They sat there at the bar, annoying the head barman by drinking fine single malts in whiskey sours, with ice, of all things.

They had had a dozen or so already. Neither of them was drunk, because neither of them could become drunk, or rather one could, but with difficulty, while the other could appear so but it was a lie, like so much else about him.

Otherwise, they were happy.

"What troubles me," said Otto, hunched and somewhat morose, though calmer and more at ease than he had been for the last few weeks, "is that it is only by chance that we won over k52 – if the construct of Waldo's had not been there, he would have achieved his goals without a problem. What does all this mean for the world, if k52 nearly succeeded but for a fortuitous happenstance?"

"Nice English, Otto." Richards' sheath drank down a goodly slug of cocktail, tinkled the ice in the glass, then tipped a cube in, sucked it and crunched down.

"I aim to improve my vocabulary without recourse to the Grid."

"Well, good." Richards smiled plastic teeth through plastic lips. "But it wasn't chance."

"Fate then? I do not believe in that."

"Damn right, that's k52 talk. What I mean is this, Otto. Waldo's world was what tripped k52 up, yes, and it was kind of handy that it did. What I'm talking about is why it was there at all. Thing is, old buddy, it was there because a brother loved his sister so much he was willing to go to jail for her, to throw everything in his life over, and eventually to die."

Otto shrugged. "He felt guilty."

"Exactly!" said Richards emphatically. "There's a complex brew in there, guilt, anger, arrogance, but also a whole lot of love. I won't be so trite as to say love saved the world, and we were lucky…"

"We often are," interrupted Otto.

Richards grinned. "That's why we're the best. But seriously, man, love, family ties, shame – all that chemical stuff you meat people have whizzing round in your systems –" he rattled his glass in a circle, carbon plastic finger pointing at his head "– we'll never have that. Never. We're superior to you in some ways…"

Otto opened his mouth.

"Now come on! Don't disagree, you know it, but we'll never have all that. How many million years' worth of evolution made you? Two thousand, seven hundred and forty-three geeks and who knows how many doughnuts made me. There's no comparison."

"Doughnuts?"

"Geeks like doughnuts," pronounced Richards, with all the solemnity of a priest. "Fact. But listen, family ties stopped k52 from realising his plans, Otto. That's not small beer, it's not chance. We machines might surpass you in many things, but we will never be you, and that is why you will survive." He smiled. "With a little help, of course."

"You forget your father, Richards."

Richards frowned, his softgel face crinkling awkwardly. "Yeah, yeah, maybe I do."

The bartender put another glass in front of Richards on the uplit bar, a paper coaster underneath. Richards saluted the man's scowl, pushed back his hat and downed the drink, ice cubes and all. "I've got to get back, someone to see. I'd just go from here, but I've wasted too many sheaths recently. I don't want to leave this one lying around; losing these things is costing us serious money."

"Hughie?" said Otto, and sipped at his whisky.

"Hughie," confirmed Richards. "*Gehst du nach Hause, oder bleibst du hier?*"

Otto held up his glass in salute and smiled a rare smile. Funny, he thought, how Richards could coax that out of him, for all that he annoyed the shit out of him. "*Ich möchte eine weitere.*" He took a sip. "*Guten Nacht*, Herr Richards," he said.

Richards stood and set his hat on his head, turned up the collar of his trenchcoat, ran a robot finger round the peak and gave a little smile. "*Bitte, mein Freund, es ist einfach Richards.*"

And he left Otto to it.

Otto rattled his ice round his empty glass. "*Er geht mir auf den Sack*," he said, and shook his head.

"What was that, sir?" said the bartender.

"Nothing," said Otto. "Get me another, would you?"

• • • •

Richards took his sheath back to their garage, thankfully one hundred floors below the radioactive sphere of nothing where their office had once been. He shunted himself back into the Grid, popped over to his virtual office to see how the regrowth of his facsimile of ancient Chicago was going, and went over the plans for their reconstructed office. Then he put in a request to see Hughie.

For once, he was piped right into Hughie's garden. Hughie sat at his wirework table, his arms crossed and face grumpy.

There was no cake. It was going to be one of those meetings.

"I suppose you feel oh-so-pleased with yourself," said Hughie.

"Hiya, Hughie, nice to see you too," said Richards, and plonked his saggy-faced avatar down in front of Hughie. "Don't mention me saving your shiny arse, no problem at all. Nothing's too good for my old friend Hughie."

Hughie gave a dismissive little grunt. "Don't irritate me today, Richards, I've a hundred bureaucrats the world over badgering me about, one –" he ticked the points off on his fingers "– the complete destruction of the RealWorld Reality Realms, two, the detonation of *three* atomic bombs, three, the destruction of 13 per cent of Nevada's energy disruption, four, the loss of three Class Five AIs, five, a violent incursion into the Sinosiberian demilitarised zone that culminated in another atomic detonation, six, a UN-led review on AI policy..." He stopped. "Have you seen the news, by the way? They're calling this the biggest catastrophe since the Five crisis. This is not going to go away. Things are bad enough for us as it is, we don't need more enemies. Need I go on?"

"Jeez," said Richards sarcastically, "it's a good job that I thwarted k52's plans to rule the human race until the end of time, or people might be really pissed off. Don't be a cock, Hughie."

"Hmmm, well, yes," grumbled Hughie, his electric eyes shining ovals of light onto the table. "I suppose we should be grateful k52's plans did not come to fruition."

Richards gaped and slumped back. "'Did not come to fruition?'" he parroted. "Sheesh, you really *are* a *cock*."

"Stop calling me a cock, Richards."

"Wanker."

Hughie threw up his hands. "You are exceptionally juvenile and frustrating to deal with," he said.

"And you're a cock. We all have our crosses to bear."

"Stop it now, stop it now! Oh, I am trying to be thankful, I'm, alright, damn you, I'm not very good at it. Thanks to you we've avoided some kind of artificial Singularity."

Richards shrugged. "What? Another? There's no such thing as the Singularity, Hughie. Things change all the time. And people live through them. Things change, people don't. Why put a name on it?"

"We will have to disagree on that. I thought you might like to know that all charges against Valdaire have been dropped. Swan has been impounded, and the Chinese aren't going to start a war over your partner's gung-ho shenanigans in their territory."

"Jolly good."

"We've also been invited to a memorial service for Chures. I expect you to attend."

"Since when were you the boss of me?"

"Richards," warned Hughie.

"We'll be there," he said, serious for a moment. "What about Launcey?"

"Later," said Hughie. "We'll get to him later." Hughie stood and clapped his hands. "Now, I am extremely busy," said Hughie.

The garden began its slow dissolve, and Richards was before a titanic Hughie in the VR replica of his underground home.

"And what's this?"

"A little reminder," said the giant Hughie. "Don't forget where you stand on the foodchain, Richards. These are challenging times. We could do without incidents like this. Do try not to overstep the mark, or there will be consequences."

Hughie faded away and Richards was left in the cavernous space of Hughie's virtual representation of his equally cavernous home, the sinister rustling of his choir at work again, free now once more, parsing trillions of bits of information as they ran the lives of a billion European citizens.

"Yeah, and who gets to decide what kind of incidents we do get, Hughie?" shouted Richards. His voice echoed back at him. "You?"

The lights went out.

"There's more to this than you and I will ever understand," he muttered. He dug into his pocket, pulled something out. "Cock."

Richards winked out of the hall, leaving something small hanging in the air. A tinkle as bright as a dropped penny sounded as it hit the foamcrete, an impudent noise in Hughie's cavern. Hughie zoomed his perception down to the source of the noise.

There, upon the drab grey representation of drab grey concrete, glittered a tiny skull, perfectly carved from quartz.

"What your wife is suffering from, Mr Klein, is unusual." Ms Dinez was tall and dark, an exotic mix of races from dried-up Brazil. She must have had a mass of immigration credits to get in through the Atlantic Wall, thought Otto. Lucky her.

Otto could see Honour through the one-way glass. He stared at her pale face. Uncalled-for data hopped into his mind off the Grid, broadening his understanding of what the surgeon had said. Honour looked so fragile. Tubes snaked out of her arm; her cerebral implant had been cracked wide and a dozen delicate carbon-sheathed cables wriggled into it. The same in her chest, where more leads plugged into her governor, monitoring her healthtech. He pressed his hands, palms flat, against the glass.

Ms Dinez looked to the side. Readouts of skin temperature and icons guessing her emotional state flickered in his mind. This can't be easy, thought Otto. He felt sympathy for her.

"You are in the army?" A fair assumption. The sheer amount of hardware embedded in his body made that obvious.

"Not any more. I was done killing innocent people a long time ago. There's enough room here, no matter what the government says." He hadn't meant that as a remark on her status; he hoped she did not take it as such. Diplomacy was never his strong suit.

"Then you are obviously a man who does not like to be kept waiting, Mr Klein. So I will be brief. She is going to die." She seemed unconcerned, cold even. Was this her professional manner, wondered Otto, or had she had her emotions capped? Some of the refugees did that. It helped them cope. Those that had mentaugs could, of course, wipe the records of their experiences if they chose, but they could do little more than inhibit the natural memory, and that was often not enough.

"I have known that for some time," he said. "What is killing her?"

"She has Bergstrom's Syndrome."

Otto's mouth went dry. He'd suspected as much. He'd heard rumours, about other cyborgs getting sick, about mismatches between machine and man.

"It is so rare," continued Dinez, "that we know little about it. Guesses, mostly, theory. But, in effect, her body is rejecting the mentaug; a feedback loop builds between the nanotech and the body's natural defences, and each attacks the other. Over time, the nerve fibres entangled with the interface begin to decay. Tremors, muscular weakness, these are the symptoms in a mild case, but it can directly affect the cerebral cortex with few warning signs, causing a shrinkage in the grey matter. It is not dissimilar to the prion diseases of the brain. The technology takes over to an extent, meaning the effects are less pronounced, though the ultimate outcome is always the same."

"She's been getting headaches for the last few months," said Otto. "Her mentaug's link to the Grid went a couple of weeks back. But she's seemed otherwise OK, normal, even." At the end of the corridor, the monsoon rain ran down the window in rippled sheets.

Dinez nodded. "It can appear so. The mentaug fights hard, putting out more and more synthetic nerve junctures. This provokes the body further, speeding the progress of the disease. The mentaug takes on the brain's functions, but the augmentations were never designed to replace the cerebral cortex. Failure occurs, usually when the frontal lobes reach a state of heavy decay. The mentaug can only do so much. Once it fails, the collapse is swift and catastrophic. She has, in a sense, been fortunate. Bergstrom's Syndrome can kill within weeks. Sometimes, as in her case, the mentaug takes over so much function that this atrophying can go unnoticed."

"Fortunate," said Otto flatly.

"Yes, Mr Klein."

Otto expected some platitudes about the time they'd had together, but she was too canny for that, and they stood and listened to the storm, Otto counting out his wife's life in raindrops.

"What now?" he asked. Otto already knew the answer, for it was popping off the Grid into his head. His unit had been among the first Ky-tech; Bergstrom's Syndrome had come later. As soon as the tech had been declared safe, he'd cajoled Honour until she'd agreed to undergo the augmentation. He'd told her of all the benefits, but the truth was he needed her to be closer to what he had become, so she could understand. How was he to know there would be a whole new disease to go with it?

"When it does become manifest, it is too late to provide anything other than palliative care," the surgeon said. "Had we caught it earlier, a complete removal of healthtech and the cerebral implant would have been recommended, but that is a complex and risky operation, far more so than the installation procedure, as it involves actual ganglionic separation of nerve from machine. If it is successful, the patient has to readjust to the life of the unenhanced, which provides a great shock and many inconveniences. If this is overcome, they suffer from many infirmities, and a greatly shortened lifespan. Most of them suffer profound mental problems." Her accent was soft but still apparent, and Otto wondered which part of Brazil she'd fled. "This is all academic. I am sorry, Mr Klein. It is too late. The best we can do is boost her tech from a base unit, prepare her for the end and make her comfortable. The hospital computer is running her mind now."

"There are other options." Otto looked at the consultant.

"Yes. There is one more option: neural patterning. It needn't be painful; we can gather much of her information from her mentaug."

"Copy her? A post-mortem simulation?"

"Together with her soul-capture data from the mentaug, a pattern taken directly from her mind now would be her entirely, to all intents and purposes. She would have her memories, right up to the moment we moved her across. We would cease life functions in your wife's original body at the same moment we brought the AI unit online, to avoid confrontation between the two. From there, she can operate a variety of sheaths, and interact with the world normally."

"Would it be her?"

Dinez shrugged. "I am not a philosopher. In effect, yes. In actuality? Some say no. This is new technology."

Newer than him. New technology every damn day. "What do we need to do?"

"First," said Dinez, "we need to ask her."

• • • •

"No," she said. She was small, Honour, but she had the heart of a lion, one of the reasons Otto loved her. "Absolutely not. Don't make me into a machine."

Otto gripped his wife's hand "There is no other way. You'll just go to sleep and wake up in a new body and we can carry on like before."

Honour spoke levelly and with force, although her voice was weak. A unit by the bed boosted it, investing her objections with a quality of digital perfection; too smooth, fake, like a damned number. "Don't you see? You *will* lose me, it won't be me! It'll be a copy, not me, a facsimile, a Frankenstein."

"It is the only way."

"Don't you dare do it, Otto Klein, don't you dare! If you ever loved me like you say…"

"I still do, I always will." He meant it, he hoped she could see that.

"Then don't soil my memory by having me copied, like a, like a spreadsheet! I'll be dead, and you will be being unfaithful to me with something that is not me. It will only think that it is, something with my memories. Can't you see that that would be horrible? A sex toy, a monster."

"That's not true."

She looked deep into his eyes, her sclera reddened with clots. "Darling Otto, you know it is." She struggled up onto her elbows. Slowly, painfully, she leaned forward, moving the tubes aside like a curtain so she could hold him as best she could. "You don't have to be alone. Find someone new, but don't try to keep me. It is my time, don't you see?" She turned her head from him, painfully. She was getting weaker. "Ms Dinez, how long do I have?"

The consultant moved out of the shadows, where she had been keeping a discreet watch. "I am sorry, but it is not long. We had to amplify the healthtech input and reactivate your mentaug so your husband could talk to you. As the technology is the cause of your condition, your wakefulness is accelerating it. If we put you back under now, you could have another few months, but you will be rarely conscious, and the level of dementia would be such that you will have little idea of who you are."

"And if you let the machines run?"

"Then you have hours, a day at most. I am sorry."

"Don't be, we all have to die. Even you will, Otto, but not for a long time, not for the longest time. Promise me that, won't you, Otto?"

"Yes," he whispered. "I will try."

"I love you," she said. They held each other for a long while, then she pushed him away a little. "Ms Dinez."

"Yes?"

"Let the machines run."

It took, in the end, less time than Otto had expected, and that time galloped by. He told Honour over and over again how much he loved her, whereas she seemed intent on reliving all the things that had made them laugh together. It annoyed him that she did not share his sense of gravity, his anger rising, and that shamed him. He was always so angry. But that was her through and through, contrary to the last, and she scolded him fondly for his tendency to melodrama.

"You know that I love you, and I know that you love me. So why lie in each other's arms crying like babies? I want to remember our life. It has been a good life, a happy one. I would not change a moment of it."

So they did, the good and the bad. The long nights together, their travels. She confessed that she had never liked his mother, and he wasn't surprised. They talked, and they giggled, and they cried. And then the end came, so suddenly, a tremor, a cry from Honour: "I am frightened, Otto, don't let me go."

"Don't be frightened," he said, though he was more scared

than he had ever been before, and he had seen things that would test the sanity of most.

"Don't let me go." Her real voice was nearly inaudible, the ghost of a voice, overwritten by the smooth boosting of the hospital machine.

"I won't." And he didn't. A harder shudder passed through her, as if she were about to have a fit. She became limp. Her chest continued to rise and fall, pushed in and out by the machines, but Otto had seen enough of death to know that she was gone. For an hour he held her, then gently he laid her down, smoothed her hair and stepped away.

"We have all of her post-augmentation data, all soul captured, together with impressions of her pre-mentaug organic memories," said Dinez to him, entering quietly through the door. "What shall we do with it?" She hesitated, examined his face, then went on carefully. "I, I am not inclined to lose life, Mr Klein, not when there is a way of preserving it. All lives… they are precious, every one. I have seen a lot of death." Her words hung on the air between them.

"The war?"

"The war."

A lifetime of memories. Every waking minute, every dream, recorded. And within, like a phantom, perhaps an echo of what Honour had been. He considered asking Dinez if she was really proposing that he break the law, and was tempted to say yes, upload her; only for a second, but that was long enough.

He exhaled a shuddery breath that tasted of tears. He tried to sound strong. He had never felt weaker, a weak child in a titan's body. "Archive it," he said.

Dinez raised an elegant eyebrow.

"I will keep the memories; her imprint. But I will not bring her back. It is not what she wanted."

"As you wish," said the surgeon.

• • • •

Otto disengaged the mentaug, and realised with some embarrassment that his face was wet. The barman looked at him as if
to ask if he were OK, but the returning glare Otto favoured him
with changed his mind.

Otto downed his drink and left.

He'd left the hospital with nothing of Honour but a plastic lattice containing a terabyte of soulless events. It wasn't enough.
It never would be.

It was not what he had wished. He wanted her back. If he
had had his own way, he would have had her uploaded into
a pimsim. In the course of the years to come, he would often
wonder if he had done the right thing, putting the temptation
there in front of him. That the pimsims he'd met seemed to
be as real as the people they once were had made feeling that
worse.

If he couldn't have her, at least he had his memories, and the
mentaug helped with that. He knew why he ailed when he
could simply turn the mem-refresh function off. As painful as
it was to wake up to Honour's absence, the mentaug let him see
her every night. While he slept, she lived. Ekbaum was wrong,
to an extent. It wasn't the trauma of losing her that was fucking
him up; he was doing this to himself. He couldn't let go.

Maybe it was time, finally time to lay her to rest.

He ascended the arco in a fast lift, using his and Richards' sub-
scription key. To get to his apartment he had to go past the floor
the office had occupied. He stopped off to look. The AllPass got
him through the exclusion barriers. That part of the arco was
dark, windows black. Light came from far below, glimmering
from the active markings of construction drones repairing the
damage. Otto stopped at the edge of the blast zone. They had a
lot to do. He clambered over buckled floor plating, past main
structural beams exposed to the air. Where the bomb had gone
off was a radioactive void. The walls and floor glittered with tiny

biolights, monotasked nanobots scouring the area for residual radioactives, lights going from green to red once they had retrieved dangerous particles, trooping dutifully off into shielded containers to patiently await disposal.

Otto looked into the blackness of the hole in the arco for a while. Amazing, he thought, that the whole damn thing hadn't come down. But away from where their office had once been the damage was minimal. A testimony to modern construction and woven carbons and, he thought, perhaps to k52's genuine but misguided attempts to work for the human race – he could have employed a much bigger bomb.

Otto doubled back, let himself be screened for contamination. He underwent a nanobot wash at the edge of the construction site, and went back home.

His apartment was neat, as he'd left it several weeks ago, keeping itself clean and biding its time, far away enough to be unaffected by the micro-nuke.

Otto caught a smell of himself. He hadn't changed in days. He decided there and then to have a shower, and then call Ekbaum. Damn the hour – if he was going to force him into his lab, he could lose a little sleep in return.

First there was one thing he needed to do.

He had to say goodbye.

He went into his room and opened the closet. He pressed the security switch to his gunlocker. It slid open.

Honour's memory cube was where it always was, ensconced in a specially cut recess lined with felt, like his guns.

He smiled, wondering what Honour would think of the man who kept his wife in the gun closet.

He hefted the cube in his hand. It was slightly smaller than Honour's fist, opaque and faulted in the way that memory cubes were, mysterious with potent fractals.

It was all he had of her.

That, and the memory of a Jerusalem built of trumpets upon a December night, and a smiling face, happy in the candlelight.

He closed his eyes and pressed the cube to his forehead for a moment, the memory of her strong in his mind. He stood like that for a long time.

He wiped his eye with the back of his hand and pushed the cube gently back into its recess.

He would call Ekbaum. Later.

About the Author

An experienced science fiction journalist and critic, Guy Haley worked for *SFX* magazine as deputy editor, where he still free-lances, he edited gaming magazine *White Dwarf* and was the editor of *Death Ray* magazine. He lives in Somerset with his wife, young son, an enormous, evil-tempered Norwegian forest cat called, ironically, Buddy, and an even bigger Malamute dog named Magnus.

guyhaley.wordpress.com

Acknowledgments

It seems apposite at the end of this, the ultimate conclusion of the first Richards & Klein investigation, to give thanks to all those who have contributed to my growth as a writer.

I must say a big Northern ta to the original team at *SFX Magazine*, Dave Golder especially, who took in an angry young Yorkshireman in 1997 and turned him into something less angry. I'd like also to give a great deal of gratitude to famed editor Jo Fletcher, who gave much-needed commentary and tough love on my earlier works, similarly to John Jarrold and all those agents and fiction magazine editors who sent me back handwritten rejections, not the wished-for "yes", but vital encouragement. To my parents, to whom *Reality 36* was dedicated, I say thanks for my creation, my brothers, my upbringing, all those *books*, and for listening to my stories. More gratitude to the men of the now defunct short story group The Quota, Matt, Gav, my brother Aidan, Jes and Andy, whether long- or short-serving, all of whose comments helped me improve when I became really serious about writing, and to Marco and Lee at Angry Robot, for giving me the chance. In the best twenty-first century tradition: cheers one and all.

Lastly, to my beautiful wife Emma. You're at the heart of my Reality, I love you, and I thank you for, well, everything.

Writing the Future

I've heard it said that some writers get sort of uptight when you ask them where their ideas come from. I'm not one of those people. Writing is one giant steaming compost heap of ideas in the headspace. Chuck information, opinions, and whimsy on there, let it mulch down for a few weeks, and spread it upon the fields of thought and pray something pretty or useful comes up out of it. That's the basics, you might decide to add a bit of alcohol to speed the process. I find long dog walks help.

In this manner, the world of Richards & Klein came about. In writing *Reality 36* and *Omega Point*, I tried to create a plausible future reality. Of course, every science fiction writer who attempts this gets it hopelessly, hopelessly wrong. For every Arthur C Clarke's geostationary satellites, there are a hundred pipe smoking misogynists piloting atomic rocket ships. No one saw the mobile phone coming, or even the microchip revolution. Look back at the SF of the past, and it looks suspiciously like the past writ large, and not the future at all.

I state this as a disclaimer.

A second disclaimer is this: with Richards and Klein I have tried to avoid the dominance of "one big SF idea". In the best "big idea" SF – that written by Philip K Dick, or Adam Roberts –

the big idea acts as a fulcrum upon which a parable about the present may be expertly articulated. In the worst, we have the world of today, tomorrow with added techno-zombies/brain implants/space travel or something similar, which is neither great writing nor good SF.

I have nothing against "big idea" SF, especially if it's used to provide cutting insights into the human condition. Actually, even if it is techno-zombies I like it, provided it's done in an entertaining, fresh way.

In Richard and Klein there is a big idea of sorts. To me, *Reality 36* and *Omega Point* are about mankind's collective parenthood of a range of new thinking beings. Maybe that's what they are about in your mind, maybe not. Every time someone reads a book it creates something unique, and that's just as true for the author as it is for a reader.

But this is a theme, at least to my mind (and I can't stress that enough, writers are not entirely in control of their works, at least not consciously), it's not a real "what if there was a computer in the sky controlling me" kind of big idea.

So, no real big idea. What I wanted was to sketch out a world that, if not accurate (hell, it's the future, we don't know yet), was at least plausible. The kind of world where, if someone asked me "What happened to Somalia?" or "What kind of food is popular?" or "How do your diffuse models of localised food production operate?" I'd at least be able to have a stab at answering. To create a living, breathing world for an adventure, it's as important to consider how people pay their taxes as it is to know how many settings a raygun has.

To get to the future, one has to consider the present. All science fiction does this, no matter how bizarre. All SF is a slave to the time in which it is written. Mine is no different. Environmental collapse, global warming, the end of western power, new economics – all play a part in Richard and Klein's reality, as much as fancy technology. I suppose there are two sides to this, and two strands to each side. The first side is what I'll call socio-historical change (it's not history yet, it isn't history in the future, but one day, it will be), the other is technological change. The two strands to each of these are: the actuality of the new situation, and humanity's reaction to said new actuality; as a species, and individually. There is the interaction between all of these, which complicates the picture, somewhat.

There are a few large scale actualities in my 22nd century: the ice sheet tip, the existence of artificial intelligence, global temperature rise, a past flu pandemic, the rise of localism, a past peak oil crisis, and the dominance of China as global superpower. On the small scale there are many, many more, most of which are not even alluded to in the books, but they are there in my head.

Ideas for Richards and Klein's world come from all over the place, but there are two main sources. For the actualities large and small, much comes from today's popular science press (bbc.com, New Scientist and Space.com being the main contributors), random stories grabbed from all over the internet for the others. History informs me how these details might build into a coherent future, and how human reaction to the actualities of the future might go. I believe strongly that the only way to escape the cage of the present when writing science fiction is to look further back into the past. The roots of the present and the future both can be found in history. To base a vision of the future on one slice of time – our contemporary time – is to risk an unanchored, unbelievable construct. To believe that the culture of the writer will not change is the first and greatest of sins here.

For example, take China. It seems clear to most of us now that China will be the next superpower. It already is, in several key regards. So it's a no brainer to have it be so powerful in Richards and Klein's future. But if you take into account that historically

China has the oldest, continuously existent civilisation on the planet, that for eighteen of the past twenty centuries it has been the most prosperous political entity, that for a good proportion of those twenty centuries it has been the most technologically advanced... well, then its dominance seems more inevitable and less an accident of a passing phase of history (to whit, the outsourcing of much of the world's manufacturing to China). Contrarily, if you look at the history of Europe, the last three centuries *are* something of an historical anomaly, a passing phase. The conditions that ensured the dominance of European culture are coming to an end now. Likewise, the Second Great Migration alluded to in the books is drawn from the first one; if human beings can move en masse in response to some calamity once, why then not again? All this is fairly obvious, naturally.

What isn't obvious is how all this will actually play out. If people were writing SF in the 15th century, very few of them would have predicted the age of European Empires. Only a rare combination of factors working together allowed this to happen at all, a key one being a weak, inward-looking China. No-one, and certainly not SF writers, can predict that kind of confluence of circumstance. Only one major development can alter the entire world. Like the electronics revolution means that we're all whizzing "amusing" pictures of cats at each other on our smart phones rather than exploring the solar system in rocket ships. That kind of thing.

I'll leave you to decide which reality is preferable.

I can't stress enough that all this is there as background for what I hope are entertaining science fiction adventure stories. That mass transit of manufactured goods is mostly a thing of the past in Richards day is far less important than you, the reader, having a good time, that you get drawn in to the story, and empathise with the characters. There are things in here that I doubt will happen. Flying cars, for one. But they are *fun*. With luck, these little details seem to fit together (unlike the bizarre road system in the film of Minority Report. It's always bothered me. It was tacked on to that future world only to provide a platform for a stunt sequence. There – got that off my chest). Have I predicted the future? No! But I have tried hard to create a plausible, believable reality. If I have been successful in that goal is for you to decide. Before you do, I'll let you into a secret. Much of the technology in Richards & Klein I reckon will be with us a lot sooner than the 22nd century. Why set it so far out? I'll almost certainly be dead by then, so won't have to suffer the embarrassment of having got it all totally wrong...

The first Richards & Klein investigation >

GUY HALEY REALITY 36

A RICHARDS & KLEIN INVESTIGATION

"Haley is a hidden gem of British science fiction." – PAUL CORNELL

"An entertaining vision of the future delivered with just the right amount of wry humour."

SFX

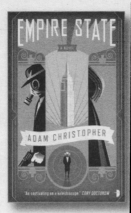

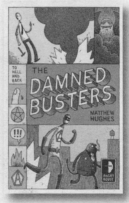

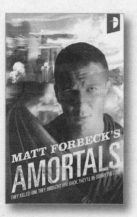

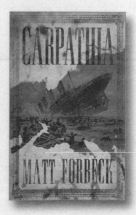

ANGRY
ROBOT

TOO MUCH IS NOT ENOUGH
Collect the entire Angry Robot range

DAN ABNETT
☐ Embedded
☐ Triumff: Her Majesty's Hero

GUY ADAMS
☐ The World House
☐ Restoration

JO ANDERTON
☐ Debris

LAUREN BEUKES
☐ Moxyland
☐ Zoo City

THOMAS BLACKTHORNE
(aka John Meaney)
☐ Edge
☐ Point

MAURICE BROADDUS
☐ King Maker
☐ King's Justice
☐ King's War

ADAM CHRISTOPHER
☐ Empire State

PETER CROWTHER
☐ Darkness Falling

ALIETTE DE BODARD
☐ Servant of the Underworld
☐ Harbinger of the Storm
☐ Master of the House of Darts

MATT FORBECK
☐ Amortals
☐ Vegas Knights

JUSTIN GUSTAINIS
☐ Hard Spell

GUY HALEY
☐ Reality 36

COLIN HARVEY
☐ Damage Time
☐ Winter Song

MATTHEW HUGHES
☐ The Damned Busters
☐ Costume Not Included

TRENT JAMIESON
☐ Roil

K W JETER
☐ Infernal Devices
☐ Morlock Night

J ROBERT KING
☐ Angel of Death
☐ Death's Disciples

GARY McMAHON
☐ Pretty Little Dead Things
☐ Dead Bad Things

ANDY REMIC
☐ Kell's Legend
☐ Soul Stealers
☐ Vampire Warlords

CHRIS ROBERSON
☐ Book of Secrets

MIKE SHEVDON
☐ Sixty-One Nails
☐ The Road to Bedlam

DAVID TALLERMAN
☐ Giant Thief

GAV THORPE
☐ The Crown of the Blood
☐ The Crown of the Conqueror

LAVIE TIDHAR
☐ The Bookman
☐ Camera Obscura
☐ The Great Game

TIM WAGGONER
☐ Nekropolis
☐ Dead Streets
☐ Dark War

KAARON WARREN
☐ Mistification
☐ Slights
☐ Walking the Tree

IAN WHATES
☐ City of Dreams & Nightmare
☐ City of Hope & Despair
☐ City of Light & Shadow